CLAIMED BY AN ALIEN WARRIOR

A Novel

TIFFANY ROBERTS

Blurb

An otherworldly warrior desperate to escape Earth. A curvy human female who's his only hope—and his deepest desire.

After losing her job, apartment, and boyfriend in one afternoon, Zoey doesn't think things can get any worse. Then an uninvited passenger—green, four-armed, and sexy as sin— proves her wrong by dragging her into his frantic escape. Helping Rendash is the right thing to do, but it means becoming a fugitive and risking the only things she has left—her life, and her heart.

Weakened by years of captivity and torture, Rendash, an elite aligarii warrior, seizes his only opportunity for freedom. Alone in an alien wasteland, he seeks the aid of a human, one of the very species that imprisoned him. But he finds himself inexplicably drawn to Zoey, and his need to protect her soon wars with his mission to return to his homeworld.

With a shadowy government agency pursuing them, Zoey and Rendash must race across the country before he is recaptured, and she is thrown in a dark cell as a traitor to her kind. But their greatest obstacle may be the most unlikely—their insatiable attraction to one another.

Copyright © 2018 by Tiffany Freund and Robert Freund Jr.

All Rights Reserved. No part of this publication may be used or reproduced, distributed, or transmitted in any form by any means, including scanning, photocopying, uploading, and distribution of this book via any other electronic means without the permission of the author and is illegal, except in the case of brief quotations embodied in critical reviews and certain other noncommercial uses permitted by copyright law. For permission requests, contact the publishers at the address below.

Tiffany Roberts

authortiffanyroberts@gmail.com

This book is a work of fiction. Names, characters, places, and incidents are products of the author's imagination or are used fictitiously and are not to be construed as real. Any resemblance to actual events, locales, organizations, or people, living or dead, is entirely coincidental.

Cover Character Illustration by Vic Grey

Cover and Typography by Naomi Lucas

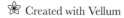 Created with Vellum

To all of you, our readers.

Chapter One

What am I going to do now?

That question echoed in Zoey's head as she drove home with her final paycheck and a handful of tip money stuffed in her purse.

Now, she wished she could take back all her complaints — about the filthy, greasy kitchen, the rude customers always trying to scam free food, her touchy-feely coworker, and her drunk of a boss — just for the security of having her job back. But it was too late.

What was done was done.

Waiting tables and cooking at Bud's Diner was shitty, backbreaking work, but it paid the bills, even if only barely, and it had been the best she could get.

"Place not good enough for you?" Bud had said. His breath had only smelled faintly of whiskey. He'd scrawled out a check and slapped it on the dirty counter. "Don't bother coming back. You're fired."

I should have just kept my mouth shut and worked.

How would Joshua react when she got home and told him?

He'd been fired from his construction job a month after they rented their apartment together. It'd been a devastating blow to their income, and he'd been unable to find any replacement work in the five months since. He was trying. While she was out working, he was going through classifieds and hiring websites, and making phone calls.

Things would get better soon. Zoey had to believe that. They just needed to hold out…

They were approaching the one-year anniversary of their first date. Though things had been tight financially, they got along well and rarely argued. Maybe they weren't as intimate as she'd have liked, but things were good between them. Sex wasn't vital to a healthy relationship... Right?

Zoey parked at the curb in front of her building. It was early afternoon, still a couple hours before most people got off work, so — for once — she had a decent parking space.

Squeezing the steering wheel, she stared up at the chipped, faded red paint of their door up on the second floor, which only made the pine wreath she'd hung on it look withered and sad.

A rush of anxiety filled her. She didn't want to go up there. Didn't want to explain her failure to Josh. Her only solace was the knowledge that their bills were paid through the end of the month. One of them would find work in that time.

"He'll understand," she mumbled.

Turning off the car engine, Zoey leaned back against her seat, closed her eyes, and searched for inner calm. For strength.

"One day at a time," she said, hearing her father's voice in her mind as she spoke the words.

The past is gone, and tomorrow will come. Live for today, Zoey, he'd tell her.

A mingling of sadness and hope swept through her; she always felt that way when she thought of her dad. *One day at a time* had been their saying. Whenever things got tough, whenever she'd felt overwhelmed with life, they'd chant those words together again and again.

There was no sense in worrying about a future you couldn't control when the present was slipping by.

Those words had seen her through many rough patches over the years.

Zoey lifted her head, opened her eyes, and looked up at her apartment door.

"Just one day at a time..." She exhaled. "Let's get this over with."

She got out of the car, slamming the door behind her, and paused briefly at the mailbox to pick up their mail as she walked along the path to the stairs. She flipped through the small pile of letters and frowned when she discovered an envelope from their landlord. Tearing it open, she unfolded the paper and stopped dead in her tracks.

For a moment, her chest was too tight to breathe, and her surroundings blurred to leave only the cold, black text on the crisp white paper in focus.

FINAL NOTICE: You are in default in payment of rent. You must either pay the overdue amount of $2100.00 or vacate the leased property within three (3) days of receiving this notice. If you fail to comply, eviction proceedings will begin immediately...

.   .   .

"This can't be right," Zoey whispered, rereading the letter twice more.

She hurried to the staircase, rushed up the concrete-slab steps, and jogged to her door. Sweat dampened her hair and trickled down her neck, back, and between her breasts.

Josh paid them! This is a mistake. It has to be.

Her hand shook as she fished her keys out of her purse, and it took several tries to insert the right one into the lock. Before she turned the key, she forced herself to take a few slow lungfuls of air.

"We'll work it out. There was a mistake. We'll fix this," Zoey whispered, barely hearing herself over the hum of the air conditioner in the front window.

She pushed open the door and stepped through, closing it gently behind her. The cool air was a blessing against her flushed skin. Normally, she'd be freezing — it was December. Who used air conditioners in December? But Joshua insisted on running the damned thing if the temperature outside was above sixty degrees. Today happened to be closer to seventy.

It was a wonder she'd been able to keep up on the power bill.

The living room TV was on the pause screen of some video game, the volume cranked up to blare orchestral music that seemed entirely too dramatic for a menu with options like *RESUME GAME, SAVE,* and *EXIT.* An open pizza box on their thrift store coffee table held two uneaten slices of pepperoni pizza and three empty beer cans.

Zoey frowned; random pizza and beer was outside the budget. They'd barely been able to afford the little Christmas tree in the corner with its single string of multi-colored lights. Did he have a friend over who'd paid for the food?

"Josh?" she called after switching the AC off.

A quick glance in the kitchen confirmed he wasn't in there.

She set her purse and the mail — except for the notice about the rent — on their little kitchen table and walked to the bathroom. The door was open, lights off.

Where is he?

If he was out job hunting, why leave the TV on and leftover food in the living room?

That was when she heard the sounds from beyond the closed bedroom door — muffled, high-pitched cries and low grunts.

Hurt and shame wrapped their cold fingers around Zoey's heart.

There was nothing wrong with masturbation, and she knew men were visual creatures. She couldn't hold that against Josh. But she couldn't help feeling inferior when she compared herself to the women in the porn he often watched. They were beautiful and thin while Zoey...wasn't. She'd always been on the plump side, with a larger backside and thighs, heavier breasts, and a little extra around her middle.

She'd struggled with her weight and self-image for most of her life, ever since her father died. It hurt to know that Josh preferred those women. He'd never said it out loud, but he'd never really tried to hide the fact, either.

The last time they'd been intimate was more than two weeks ago; they'd done a little heavy petting before Josh asked for a blowjob. She'd felt so...detached from the act, as though she were just going through the motions. He'd been watching porn while she sucked him off.

After he'd gone to sleep that night, Zoey had crept into the bathroom and cried. The whole experience had been so demeaning and hurtful. And it was her fault.

Why hadn't she tried harder to be attractive for him? To exercise, to pick a piece of fruit instead of a candy bar she shouldn't have spent money on, anyway? If she cared about him, wasn't it worth the effort to make him happy?

At heart, she knew that train of thought wasn't right, but that didn't help her derail it.

Zoey hadn't found the courage to tell him how she'd felt that night — how she'd felt during most of the rare nights when they actually did something in their bed other than sleep. She'd been so starved for intimacy when it happened that she gobbled up whatever attention he offered, like a dog waiting under the table for scraps.

She clenched her fists and wrestled back more tears, clawing for that calm she'd found a few moments before.

Under the current circumstances, whatever Josh was doing right now was an insignificant issue.

Turning the knob, she pushed open the door and stepped in.

The breath fled her lungs like she'd been punched in the sternum.

The stuffy air was pungent with the smell of sex. Joshua stood directly ahead, completely naked, his ass cheeks flexing as he thrust into the woman he was holding up against the wall. Her long legs were crossed at their ankles behind his back, her arms were draped around his shoulders, and her head was tilted back. The woman's cries of pleasure sounded from her parted red lips, loud and clear now that they weren't muffled by the door.

Anger sparked in Zoey's belly. "What. The. Fuck!"

"Shit!" Joshua yelled, turning toward Zoey. He grunted suddenly, his face contorting in that way she knew so well as his muscles spasmed; his orgasm face. He stepped back from the wall, and the woman fell to the floor with a curse.

Josh grasped his cock in one hand as though it pained him. Jets of semen sprayed from its tip to splatter the woman's chest.

"Shit, Zoey!"

Guess he got his fucking money shot.

"Ugh." The woman grabbed Josh's rumpled t-shirt from the floor and wiped off her spunk-splattered breasts. "Seriously?"

"Who the hell is she?" Zoey demanded, pointing at the woman.

"What's going on, Josh?" the woman asked, tossing his shirt aside and standing up. She seemed unconcerned with her nudity as she gathered her discarded clothes. She was tall and slender, with subtle muscle tone under her tanned skin. Everything Zoey wasn't. "You said you were single."

Zoey glared at Josh. "He *what?*"

He lifted his hands in a placating gesture, but when he realized it left his dripping erection exposed, he dropped them to his crotch. "Now calm down, Zo."

"Calm down? You're telling me to calm down when I come home to find my *unemployed boyfriend* having sex with another woman while I was at work?"

"Why are you home so early, anyway?" Joshua asked, turning away from her as he hurriedly pulled on his boxers and a pair of shorts.

"Because I lost my damn job!" she shouted. "But I'm not going to let you turn this around on *me!*"

"I'm out of here," the woman said, sweeping past Zoey. She carried her wadded clothing over her abdomen, making no effort to cover her nakedness.

"Bridgit, wait—" Josh moved to follow, but Zoey blocked him.

"Don't you dare," she growled before slapping the letter against his chest. "I want you to explain this."

Scowling, Joshua took the paper and held it out in front of him, lips moving silently as he read. "I didn't pay it," he finally said, tossing the letter onto the bed.

"What?" Zoey's heart stopped.

Josh shrugged. "I didn't pay it."

"Why not?" she demanded. "When I handed you that money, I said it was to pay the rent! You *knew* that. Why the hell wouldn't you take care of it?"

"I used it for a new console and some games, and took a few buddies out for lunch and drinks."

"That was our *rent*, Josh!"

The apartment door opened and closed as *Bridgit* left.

Josh's eyes flicked in that direction, and he hardened his features. "And I'm tired of sitting cooped up in this place with nothing to do!" he yelled. "I'm bored as fuck. I want to have fun."

"I can't believe I'm hearing his. You're thirty years old and you spent our rent money on video games and booze?" Zoey turned away from him. Her eyes burned with tears of anger, frustration, and hurt. She latched onto that anger and frustration and swung back toward him. "You cheated on me!"

Remorse flittered across his features; for an instant, he looked like a child who'd been caught sneaking cookies without his mother's permission. "You weren't supposed to know."

"And that makes it right?" Zoey shook her head. "How long? How long have you been going behind my back?" She pressed her lips together to keep them from trembling.

Joshua averted his gaze and sighed. "Since the beginning."

Zoey stared at him. The tightness in her chest made it hard to breathe, but her heart wasn't breaking. For that to happen, she would have had to love him. It surprised her to realize she didn't. She *cared* for Josh, but her feelings had never quite strengthened to the point of love.

Regardless, what he'd done still hurt like hell.

"Why?" she asked, unable to produce more than a rough whisper.

"I love you, Zo. I know it doesn't seem like it, but I do. I'm just…not attracted to you." His eyes roamed over her body as he stepped closer to her. "I tried. Believe me, I tried, Zo, but what you have doesn't turn me on. Maybe if you'd have put in some effort to lose a little weight. I just can't—"

"Get out," Zoey said. She didn't want to hear any more. *Couldn't* hear any more.

"Zo, don't be like that. Where am I gonna go? We can still be room—"

"Get out!" she screamed. Tears streamed down her cheeks. "Get out! I never want to see you again."

God, she'd never felt so used, so worthless, so…disgusting. She didn't want to let his words affect her, but they did. They tore her up inside and left her feeling ugly.

"We'll figure it out," Josh said, stepping closer and raising his hands to touch her. "You're hurt, I und—"

Zoey flinched away. "Don't touch me!" Knowing that those hands were covered in both his and Bridgit's filth made her sick to the stomach. "And if I have to tell you one more fucking time to get out…" she gritted through her teeth, staring into his eyes.

His face visibly paled, and his tongue slid over his lips

nervously. "I'll come back when you've calmed down. I can't deal with this right now."

He grabbed a shirt off the dresser and walked past her. She didn't try to stop him this time.

His car keys jingled as he tugged them off the hook beside the door. "I'll text you later," he said.

When the door closed behind him, Zoey's legs gave out and she crumpled to the floor. She covered her face with her hands and cried.

She couldn't even lie in her own bed; the rumpled blanket and sheets likely meant he'd had sex in it with that woman. How many times had Zoey slept beside him without knowing he'd had another woman in her place while she'd been gone? Everything about their home, about their relationship, was tainted. It had all been a lie.

What stung most was how hard she'd lied to herself.

"I can't stay here." She straightened and wiped her eyes, laughing without humor when she saw the rent notice on the bed. "We were going to get kicked out anyway." A fresh torrent of tears spilled from her eyes. "What am I going to do? All alone, no job, no home…"

I have nothing left.

Placing a hand on the bed, she pulled herself to her feet. She managed a semblance of numbness as she retrieved her purse and walked to the couch, plopping down and settling her bag on her lap.

She glanced down at the pizza box. The empty cans remained, but the leftover pizza was gone. That rekindled her anger; he'd cheated on her, used her, spent her money on meaningless shit, and after everything, he couldn't even leave her a couple slices of goddamned pizza?

Zoey dug her phone out of her purse, scrolling through her short list of contacts and selecting the only person she could talk to about *anything*. It rang three times before Melissa picked up.

"Zoey! I haven't heard from you in ages! How are you?"

"Josh cheated on me, Mel. Used me for money and cheated on me," Zoey replied, suddenly fighting back more waterworks.

"Oh, my God. Sweetie, are you okay? Well, of course you're not *okay*, but are you okay?" Melissa's voice had softened, brimming with love and concern. "Do you need me to come visit? I think I can get my baseball bat through security if it's in a checked bag."

"No. I'm... I don't know, Mel. I'm so lost right now. My landlord is kicking me out because Josh blew the rent money, and I got fired today, and I came home to..."

"Don't even think of that piece of shit. He's not worth it. *So* not worth it." Melissa sighed. "I know you don't want to come back to Iowa, but...you can come stay with me, if you want. You know I'd love to have you as a roomie again. It'd be like old times."

Zoey wiped tears from her face with the heel of her palm. "Mel, I—"

"What's there for you in California? I know you wanted to get away, to start a new life, but what's there for you, really? You can go *anywhere*, Zoey, and all I'm saying is I'd love it if you came back here."

She looked around the apartment. In the months she'd lived here, she'd accumulated items to make it feel homier — a few pictures, a couple plants, some strange-but-appealing wall décor, and two or three pieces of old furniture, most of it obtained at secondhand stores. She'd taken pride in what she'd accomplished here. Though her job had sucked, she'd busted her ass working double shifts to have a decent place to live and make sure her bills were paid. She'd planned to eventually build a life out here. With Josh.

But that, apparently, wasn't meant to be. This was just a place. It wasn't *home*, and never had been.

She'd forgotten what it felt like to have a home, by now.

"Come stay with me," Melissa urged.

"Okay," Zoey replied.

"Wait, what? *Really?*"

"Really."

"Yay! We can spend Christmas together!" Melissa yelled so loudly that Zoey had to pull the phone away from her ear. "Do you need help with a flight?"

"You don't have to do that, Mel. I think I'll drive. I don't want to sell my car, and it'll be easier to fit my things in it." What did she really have to bring, other than clothes? Nothing else here had any meaning for her. "It'll also give me time to… to think."

"Take all the time you need, Zoey. And if you need me for anything — *anything* — just call. Day or night."

"I will. Thank you, Mel."

"Hugs! Of course. I know things suck right now and you're in a bad place, but I'm happy! I can't wait to see you."

Zoey smiled despite everything. She knew what Melissa meant. "I can't wait to see you, too."

"Get some rest, okay? I'll talk to some people to see if anyone's hiring around here. And don't let that douche bag back in."

After they exchanged goodbyes, Zoey pressed the end button and slipped her phone into her purse. She looked around the apartment, at her eclectic decorations, at the massive TV Josh *had* to get when they first moved in, the video games laying on the shelves below it, at the few pictures of her and Josh that she'd put up.

She couldn't stomach another night here. He'd be back, and Zoey refused to be here when he showed up. There was plenty of daylight left, and she wasn't going to get any closer to Des Moines by sitting on the couch. She could stop at the bank to deposit her check on the way out of town.

Returning to the bedroom, she pulled her suitcases down from the shelf in the closet and filled them with clothing, shoes, toiletries, and the small, timeworn photo album that held all the pictures she had of her dad. She hummed to herself, refusing to recall the scene she'd walked in on not long before.

She had her check, her tip money, and a few hundred bucks she'd stashed in her underwear drawer, knowing deep down inside that Josh would never think to look in there for anything. She could do this. This was easy.

Despite her self-reassurances, she cried as she packed. Everything important fit in two suitcases, supplemented by some toiletries and a box of romance novels she couldn't bear to part with.

"One day at a time, right dad?" She brushed the backs of her hands over eyes. "Someday I'll find someone who will see me for *me*."

Chapter Two

Rendash's existence had become an endless cycle of darkness and light following no discernable pattern — there was no star, whether familiar or foreign, to illuminate the days, no reflective moons to set the night aglow. If this planet had day and night, he hadn't the faintest guess as to when either was occurring. Time had lost all meaning to him long ago — it had become a fluid, malleable force that evaded definition or measurement. He knew only that his captors seemed to hold no schedule.

They arrived at random and switched on near-blinding lights before speaking with him in their clumsy, overly-complicated language, trying to hide themselves in the glow. But he knew their faces — especially Charles Stantz, their leader, who was always present whether he participated or not. Sometimes, they experimented on Rendash, taking samples of his blood or tearing off his scales. On other occasions, they inflicted pain with little apparent reason, beating him with blunt weapons or slicing his scales with sharp instruments.

When they finished, they would inject him with chemicals he

could not identify before turning off the lights, plunging him into total darkness again. They usually left food, which he'd locate by smell and touch and ate only out of necessity.

Today was the first time the humans had taken him out of his small holding cell in a long while. They'd forced him into a large, metal chair, restrained his arms and legs with heavy shackles that were bolted directly to the chair, preventing him from moving his limbs, and pulled a dark hood over his head. He'd felt numerous turns and inclines as they'd wheeled him through their facility. The shuffling boots of the human soldiers spoke of a great distance being traveled.

Finally, they'd brought him in here — they called it a *mobile containment unit*. They'd secured his chair to the floor and sealed the entry, leaving him alone in the dark once again. The entire contraption moved afterward. Given the rumblings and jolts that shook the walls, Rendash could only assume he was in some sort of primitive transport.

Though the mobile containment unit was just as dark as his cell, and the steady hum of the unseen ventilation system was similar to the one he'd known in the facility, the tremors, clangs, and slams of the transport bouncing over an irregular surface were new, offering him a bit of hope when paired with the other key difference.

They'd neglected to inject him with the chemicals today.

For the first time since the humans had taken him, he could feel his nyros; healing his wounds after the crash had demanded so much of its energy that he'd been unable to call upon it when the human soldiers arrived and subdued him. Whether they'd known it or not — and he was hesitant to give them credit enough to presume they knew what they were doing — their injections had kept his connection to his nyros suppressed.

Another jolt; the transport bounced, and Rendash's restrains bit into his scales. He clenched all four of his fists and squeezed his eyes shut. The mobile containment unit had been moving for quite a long while, though he couldn't be sure how long or of how far they'd traveled. Stantz had mentioned something to his fellows about another facility with better *equipment*.

This was the first opportunity Rendash had been presented. It was like to be the only one.

I cannot allow my Umen'rak to be forgotten casualties on this unknown planet.

Rendash inhaled deeply; the air inside the transport was warmer and drier than that in the facility and possessed a hint of freshness that suggested open skies and wind.

Drawing in another steadying breath, he focused on his nyros.

It crackled to life at his mental command, flowing through his blood with new warmth, lending much-needed strength to his muscles. But it fizzled as it coursed along his limbs; he increased his concentration, and the resulting heat was disproportionately small. He feared it wouldn't be enough.

With this nyros, I give myself into the service of the aligarii, my people.

He'd taken the oath a lifetime ago. He recalled the words now to draw upon the pride he'd felt on that long-ago day, to taste the power that had blazed through him.

With this nyros, the strength of my people, I become the Blade of the Aligarii, to be wielded with honor and integrity in the defense of my people and all others in need of aid.

The flame sparked deep in his chest, but it was weak. His connection had been broken for too long. His strength had waned too much.

The humans had captured the rest of his surviving

Umen'rak — the warriors he'd fought beside since his youth, his brothers and sisters in arms, who he'd been bound to by millennia of tradition and connected nyros — and dragged them into underground cells along with Rendash. Those few who'd survived the crash and the emergency ejection were gone now. And Rendash's imprisonment prevented him from completing his Nes'rak, his final mission, and returning to his home world to commend the unerring honor of his brethren through to their ends.

As though all that weren't enough, the humans had nearly taken his nyros from him.

Though humans were a relatively primitive species, and he was dishonored by being their captive, it would be foolish to underestimate them. Succumbing to his rage and bitterness would only ensure that his escape would end in failure — that he'd never return to his people and report the outcome of his Nes'rak, that he'd never add the names of the dead to the annals of the valiant slain.

He would never end his duty and close the circle.

Humans are not the enemy of the aligarii, he told himself. *I must not forget the korvaxx, who are the true threat. The creatures on this planet have no understanding of what it is they have done.*

No…Stantz understands. He knows exactly what he's done and holds no remorse for it.

Growling to himself, he cast aside the outward distractions — and his own negative thoughts — and focused on the lessons of his youth.

Control. Detachment. Instinct. Selflessness. Honor.

All things in service of the Nes'rak. My life for the aligarii.

He'd been trained since his earliest youth to be a warrior. He was Aekhora, one of the chosen warriors, whether his companions lived or not. He was Rendash.

He clenched his jaw as the fire inside was stoked, spreading heat to his extremities. If this was his sole opportunity, he would seize it, and he would put *everything* into the attempt.

Control.

Rendash's nyros poured strength into his arms, and his muscles bulged. Nostrils flaring, he exerted force against his arm restraints. The metal shackles groaned and dug into his skin. He pushed his nyros harder, fanning the internal flame and forcing more power from it. Pain coursed through him, biting down into his bones and threatening to steal his breath.

Detachment.

With a growl, he shoved his pain aside and pumped more energy into the effort, straining his body and mind beyond their current limits. A metallic pop signaled one of the fasteners finally giving. The sound repeated several more times as the remaining bolts broke free. His arms darted up over his head with the sudden release of pressure, jolting his entire body.

His upper and lower arm on each side were bound together by the heavy cuffs, which had detached from the chair but not opened, effectively leaving him with two functional arms rather than four. In that respect, at least, he was currently on equal footing with the humans.

The transport shook with a sudden loss of speed, stuttering violently and forcing him back into his rear-facing chair. Rendash tugged the black cloth off his head. The chamber was filled with impenetrable darkness. His nyros could be used to alter his vision, but it wouldn't be worth the expenditure of energy.

He allowed himself a moment's rest, relaxing his muscles

and his nyros. Fully recovered, he would have been able to massively increase the strength of his muscles through his nyros with little more than a thought, but he'd fallen far.

Rendash raised his left arms and clenched his jaw in concentration as the transport came to a full stop. A vrahsk — flickering and sputtering like it had during his first inexperienced attempts to form it, so many years before — extended from the back of one hand. The wide, curved energy blade cast a soft purple glow over Rendash and his surroundings, revealing smooth, bare metal walls.

He ignored the pain in his stiff muscles as he bent forward and set the vrahsk to his leg restraints. Metal sizzled as the blade sliced through it. The shackles fell to the floor of the transport with heavy clangs, and Rendash stretched his legs gratefully.

A light flashed on overhead, pure white and blinding in its intensity. Slitting his eyes, he lifted his right arms to shield his face. Machinery rumbled; they were opening the door.

Awareness pulsed through his mind — the command module of his ship. It was very distant, but the tracking beacon was operational. That meant there was a chance the module itself, which could operate as a ship on its own, was functional.

There was a chance it could get him home.

Rendash's eyes adjusted quickly to the light, but he didn't lower his hands. He peered through the gap between his right forearms to see four humans in dark attire gathered at the opening. They directed their blaster-like weapons at Rendash.

"Sedate the specimen and get it restrained!" Stantz commanded, voice muffled by his mask.

Instinct.

Rendash released his conscious thought, devoting his mind

to controlling his nyros. He projected a shield in front of himself and filled his legs with additional strength.

For my Umen'rak.

He leapt forward.

Startled, the humans shouted and fired their weapons. The solid projectiles disintegrated against Rendash's shield. Each impact jolted him, threatened to bring down the barrier, and added to the heat building inside him.

He landed in the middle of their front line, knocking two humans to the ground. As he rose, he plunged his vrahsk into the chest of the third human, simultaneously swinging his right arms to hammer his shackle into the face of the fourth. Warm blood splattered on Rendash's scales as both men fell.

Large, black human vehicles — filled with more of their ill-equipped soldiers — were lined up behind the mobile containment unit. Rendash shifted his shield to intercept the other soldiers' gunfire; many of them shot at him from the cover of vehicle doors. To either side, a vast landscape stretched away from the hard road; it was dust, hills, and mountains as far as he could see, lit only by ambient light from the night sky.

"Do not fire on my specimen with live ammunition!" Stantz shouted over the roaring weapons.

Rendash met Stantz's eyes. The human was beside the nearest black vehicle, face grim and gray eyes gleaming behind the clear plate of his mask.

Those eyes had always been steady, *hungry*, regardless of what the man behind them was doing — droning through infuriatingly circular lines of questioning; watching as large, uniformed humans beat Rendash with fists and clubs; slicing Rendash's scales with sharp instruments and prodding at his flesh, unconcerned about the pain he was inflicting. Stantz's gaze hadn't wavered for an instant when he confessed to having *overexerted* the other aligarii survivors. They were only projects to him, things to be dissected and studied — to Stantz, Rendash was only *Specimen Ten.*

In all his life, Rendash had never hated another being as he did Charles Stantz. Their time together — four years, though that human reckoning of time meant little to Rendash — had been a torturous, hellish dance. Stantz had pushed ceaselessly to break Rendash, to discover his secrets, but the aligarii warrior had given *nothing.*

Now I show what I truly am. Rendash, Aekhora, Blade of the Aligarii. Your doom.

He could get to Stantz and kill the man before the other humans overwhelmed him and the exertion of maintaining his nyros became too much. He could avenge his own suffering, could avenge those of his Umen'rak who perished in human captivity. It would mean death, but it would be a good death, a death in combat. The sort of end any true warrior would appreciate.

But then his people might never learn of the korvaxx's plots, would never know to immortalize the memories of his fallen Umen'rak in the fashion they deserved. His pride, his bitterness, his shame — all was meaningless compared to his mission.

All things in service of the Nes'rak.

Selflessness. Honor.

Two more humans charged Rendash, the long rods in their hands crackling with electricity. They attacked in unison, swinging and thrusting their weapons with one goal — to strike a blow anywhere on Rendash's body. He knew the muscle-locking pain of such devices well enough, by now. He couldn't withstand the jolt of one in his current state.

Rendash backed up, swaying and dodging the blows, the shackles on his wrists heavier with each passing moment. He caught one baton with the edge of his vrahsk, shearing the rod in half. The other soldier lunged and thrust his weapon. Rendash dodged the attack, clamped both right hands on the human's extended arm, and brought his blade down on the man's elbow.

As the screaming soldier grasped the smoking stump of his severed arm, Rendash sliced his vrahsk across the other man's gut.

The two humans he'd knocked down in his initial charge had regained their feet; one collapsed after Rendash landed a bone-crunching kick on his chest while the other fell back to join his advancing comrades, their blasters at the ready.

Rendash counted fifteen soldiers making a slow, methodical approach. His shield couldn't handle much more.

His *body* couldn't handle much more.

There was no time to assess his strained nyros. Forcing a surge of strength into his legs, Rendash leapt off the hard, black stone road. Wind whipped past him. The air was chilled; normally, his nyros would regulate his internal temperature to counteract that of his surroundings, but now it was only the fires of overexertion that protected him from the cold.

Humans shouted behind him, and Stantz barked orders. Engines roared to life as Rendash landed, crashing into the dried-out dirt and sand and sending up a cloud of dust. The beams of light projected by the black vehicles swung toward him. The humans were leaving the road in pursuit.

Rendash leapt again. Projectiles cracked through the air around him, but he could spare no more focus on maintaining his shield. Everything went into his aching muscles. He would follow the call of the command module's beacon once he'd outrun Stantz's soldiers.

He jumped again, and again, nearly crashing to the ground in a heap with each landing. Only honor, duty, and desperation kept him upright, driving him forward. The far-off mountains, which looked like piles of smooth, folded cloth, served as his immediate goal. The clumsy human ground vehicles weren't likely to be capable of traversing such terrain.

As the lights behind him faded into the distance, he found more energy — somehow — to enable a cloaking field, rendering him all but invisible to anything but the most advanced detection systems.

His control of his nyros flickered, and he narrowed his focus, eliminating all concerns beyond reaching the mountains. The heat in his body was approaching a dangerous level, and the mental strain threatened to tear his mind asunder. But he could not stop.

An alien landscape sped by below while alien stars, twinkling in their multitudes, watched from above, all indifferent to his plight.

When he reached the foothills, he paused long enough to form a vrahsk on each side to slice the shackles from his wrists before scrambling higher, leaping and hauling himself into the mountains with arms and legs alike. As he finally reached the crest of the nearest peak, he poured another surge of strength into his limbs and launched himself high into the air.

For an instant, a sense of freedom settled over Rendash — the universe was open to him, the possibilities infinite, endless, and exciting. Though he'd enjoyed the rush of battle, had taken pride in serving the aligarii with honor and skill, he *craved* change. Craved the rest he'd fought so long and hard to earn. He'd known only conflict throughout his life.

Detachment.

As his upward momentum faded, a fleeting weightlessness settled in. He scanned the landscape stretched out before him — more sand and dirt as far as he could see, flat in many places, bunched into hills and mountains in others; all barren but for small, scruffy clumps of vegetation, all bathed in the silvery light of the stars and a pale-faced, lonely moon.

This was a wasteland of seemingly endless breadth. The command module lay somewhere beyond, outside his reach. As he was now, he wouldn't survive crossing these wastes.

Moving lights caught his attention. Made tiny with distance, they moved smoothly across the flat portion of land; he guessed they were more human ground vehicles creeping along another road. Their path led to more lights — brighter and unmoving. A structure of some sort.

Then natural law declared it was time to return to the ground. His stomach lurched as the dust rushed to meet him. He braced himself with his nyros as best he could.

He hit the ground hard, teeth clacking together, and tumbled down the slope, kicking up dust and battering his weary body along the way. He scrabbled for purchase with all four hands but managed only to alter the trajectory of his roll and set himself to flipping backwards. Each time his torso hit the ground, a little more air was forced out of his lungs.

Finally, he reached a more gradual slope, and he slid to a halt. Lying on his back, he stared up at the unfamiliar sky as he caught his breath and reviewed his new aches. Somehow, he'd avoided serious injury.

A cold breeze flowed over him, chilling his scales; though he was burning up inside, his outer layers were like ice. That was far more uncomfortable than the pain in his limbs.

When his ragged breathing finally subsided, he became aware of other sounds — the airy whooshing of ground vehicles speeding along the distant road, the soft whisper of wind over the sand, the rustling of vegetation, and something else. His scales prickled.

Rendash sat up and turned his head to listen. It was a whirring sound, almost like the rapid popping of human blasters, but this was constant and seemed to originate from somewhere high up. He lifted his gaze.

The sound gained strength gradually, drowning out Rendash's thumping heart, and soon pulsed through him. Suddenly, a black object roared over the mountain peak he'd just crossed.

The vehicle was long and dark, its tail end narrow. Huge blades rotated atop it — a primitive but effective means of flight. A bright light beamed from its underside to cast a broad circle of illumination on the ground. He longed for a blaster; he'd even accept a human weapon, so long as he didn't have to rely upon his nyros to fight.

Rendash pushed himself to his feet to face the new threat.

The aircraft passed directly overhead. Its vibrations jarred the loose dirt around Rendash, and its spinning blades battered him with violent, freezing wind. Two more of the vehicles flew over the crest, veering in opposite directions along the mountains as the first continued toward the distant road. The noise of the aircrafts quickly faded.

They cannot detect me while cloaked.

A small boon, and not much of a surprise, but how long could he maintain the cloaking field?

He turned toward the stationary lights. Until he recovered more of his strength, a human vehicle would be the only reliable means of covering considerable distances. They were rudimentary conveyances; surely, they'd be simple enough to operate.

Without wasting more time — or precious mental energy — he hurried down the slope and sprinted toward the distant structures. The faces of his Umen'rak flitted through his mind, affording him impossible reserves of strength as his limbs threatened to fail. He leapt over a strange pathway that was set atop a mound of small, dark rocks in a narrow valley. It consisted of two relatively thin metal rails that ran as far as he could see to the left and right, which were bridged by shorter, thicker beams along the way.

Despite his cloaking, he kept low and to the shadows as he approached the structures. The buildings were well-lit, and several immobile ground vehicles sat nearby, some beside posts bearing more lights.

Rendash froze and pressed himself flat to the ground as the sound of an aircraft suddenly grew. The aircraft passed directly overhead, drawing the attention of the few visible humans.

Another ground vehicle — dull gold with four doors, small compared to Stantz's black transports — arrived and stopped at the edge of the lights. When the door opened, a human female climbed out, but she turned and walked toward one of the buildings before Rendash caught even a glimpse of her features.

The whirring of the aircraft continued in the distance. This was potentially his only opportunity before his nyros failed.

He crawled forward, remaining in the shadows as he approached the gold vehicle. Its size became more apparent as he neared; he doubted he'd fit in the operator's position without tearing the seat out completely. He glanced toward the buildings. None of the humans were watching, but the other transports were too clustered together for him to access without being noticed.

Slowly and quietly, Rendash opened the rear door and climbed into the back seat, gently pulling the door shut behind him.

He couldn't guess where the woman was heading, but he couldn't continue on foot. He'd simply have to make her go in the direction he needed until he could travel alone.

Chapter Three

Zoey flushed the toilet and stood inside the stall until the roar of the water being sucked down the pipe was replaced with eerie silence. The newer rest stops were like that — too quiet. That put her more on edge than the old, echoing, rundown restrooms did; at least in the old ones you could usually hear cars driving past on the highway, reminding you that you weren't all alone.

She would have preferred not to stop at all, but sometimes a girl just had to pee.

She stepped out of the stall and walked to the sink. After washing her hands, she splashed cold water on her cheeks and stared at her reflection as she dried her hands and face. She looked tired. Not an *I went to work at six this morning and have been driving for half the day* kind of tired, but a bone-deep, emotionally-and-mentally destroyed kind.

Zoey braced her hands on the edge of the sink and leaned forward. She looked herself in the eyes. "What are you going to do, Zoey? How much longer can you hold on before you break?"

Unsurprisingly, she had no answer.

Her eyes brimmed with tears. "I thought I had it for a while there, dad. I really did. A job, a boyfriend, a home. Not a great job, or the best boyfriend, or the nicest place to live, but it was stable. And now it's all gone." She blinked, and the tears spilled down her cheeks. Laughing humorlessly, she straightened and wiped her cheeks. "And here I am talking to myself in a restroom in the middle of nowhere. God, can I sink any lower?"

The answer to that question — deceptively bright and tempting — came promptly after she left the restroom and saw the row of vending machines beneath a nearby shelter.

"Aw, come on!" She spread her hands to either side as she looked up at the sky. "This is *so* not what I need right now."

Frowning, she walked to the machines and looked over the variety of snacks and drinks they contained. She didn't need any of it. These indulgences were part of why everything had gone wrong with Josh. If she'd developed a backbone and tried a little harder to resist, to avoid giving in to her temptations, she could've been what he wanted. She could've been more attractive, more pleasing…

Bullshit. Why couldn't he just love me for me?

That deep, consuming hurt spread through her chest again.

"Fuck it." She opened her purse, pulled some cash out of her wallet, and fed it into the machine.

A minute or two later, she was walking toward her car with a pair of Snickers, a Twix, a Pepsi, and a bottle of water. She thrust aside her pang of guilt; she was going to damned well enjoy this stuff before she let herself feel remorse about it.

A helicopter flew over the nearby desert, shining a searchlight below it. It sent a chill down her spine; she'd either seen the same one pass twice since she got here, or it was a second helicopter. What were they searching for? An escaped convict, a fugitive serial killer? And here she was, alone, at a desert rest stop in the middle of the night with who-knew-what out there.

She glanced around her. There were a few other cars parked in the lot, but no other people in sight.

"Stupid, stupid," Zoey muttered, quickening her steps.

She reached her car — more aware than ever of the busted locks — and peered into the back seat to make sure it was empty before tugging open the driver's side door. She tossed her purse and her bounty onto the passenger seat and got in. Fishing her keys out of her purse, she jammed them into the ignition and started the car. It sputtered for a few seconds before finally turning over.

Her nerves eased when she pulled onto the onramp, leaving the rest stop behind. She clicked her seatbelt into place and checked her mirrors as she merged onto I-15. The helicopter continued its sweep of the desert behind her, and another was moving through the darkness up ahead.

Something wrapped around her neck from behind — a powerfully muscled arm.

Zoey screamed, releasing the wheel to claw at the arm around her throat, fingernails scraping a tough, scaly material. The arm tightened, cutting off her scream. The car veered toward the side of the road.

"Control your vehicle, human!" a gravelly, strangely accented voice commanded.

Keeping one hand on the arm, Zoey caught the wheel with the other. Her stomach flipped as she corrected the car's swerve, directing it fully onto the shoulder, and slammed on the brakes. Her seatbelt locked, digging into her chest as the sudden stop pushed her body forward.

Whoever was in the back grunted, and a great weight pressed against her seat from behind. The hold around her neck loosened briefly.

She threw the car into park and reached for her seatbelt buckle, but before she could do anything more, the man pulled her back. "Move this vehicle, now. In the direction you were going."

"P-Please don't hurt me," Zoey begged. She clutched desperately at his scaly sleeve.

The car's shocks groaned as the man shifted in the back seat. Zoey glanced at her rearview mirror and screamed again. She fought against his hold, rocking the car with her struggles, and he clamped a hand on her arm — and then, somehow, another on her thigh and one over her mouth, all without releasing his grip on her neck.

He's just wearing some kind of mask. It's a mask, and there's another man hidden back there, grabbing me at the same time.

"Cease your struggles, human!" he growled.

Zoey stilled, squeezing her eyes shut. She just had to breathe, and all of this would go away. She'd wake up from the nightmare and still be in Santa Barbara with a shift coming up at Bud's Shitty Diner.

But when she opened her eyes, the monster was still there.

She stared at his reflection in the mirror. The light from passing cars highlighted the fine scales on his lower face, keeping his upper face in shadow, and as he turned his head toward her fully, his eyes — all *four* of them — met hers. Two of his eyes were positioned as a human's would be, but there was another set at his temples, higher and to the sides. They glowed green, like cat eyes in the dark.

She panted against his large hand. He smelled like the desert — earthy, dry, primal.

The monster turned his head to look out the passenger-side window. Zoey followed his gaze to see a helicopter searchlight in the distance. Was *he* the one they were looking for?

"Move this vehicle," he repeated, swinging his unsettling gaze back to the mirror. "*Now.*"

Zoey whimpered. She slowly raised her free arm and tapped the back of the hand clamped over her mouth.

He growled but removed his hand.

"Are you going to hurt me?" she asked.

"If you do not move this vehicle, I will have no choice but to harm you."

"Okay. Okay," she whispered. "I n-need both arms."

For an instant, his hold on her strengthened. When he finally released her arm, she numbly moved it to the shifter and switched the car into drive, turning the wheel to pull back onto the interstate.

She slammed on the brakes again as another car sped by with its horn blaring, and narrowly avoided a collision.

"Control yourself," the monster said, loosening his hold on her. "Breathe, human. Operate this vehicle as you would if I were not here."

Right. As if I could forget a four-eyed, four-armed creature is my car.

Zoey did as he instructed and took several deep breaths. It helped a little — she was still terrified, but at least her hands weren't shaking anymore. She adjusted her grip on the steering wheel, checked for cars, and eased back onto the interstate.

She drove in silence, her gaze shifting ceaselessly between the road, the helicopters patrolling the desert, and the monster in her rearview mirror. His hand was heavy, solid, and warm on her thigh, even through her jeans. It was a brand, a reminder that he was still there. That he was *real*. She risked a glance down at it.

His skin was green, though its precise hue was impossible to determine in the poor light. He had only three fingers and a thumb, tipped with blunt black nails. He was also covered in scales, but that hardly seemed the strangest part, by now. Her eyes flicked up to the mirror.

He was covered in dust, and something dark was splattered on his face and shoulder.

Don't try to guess what that is, she warned herself.

"Who are you?" She could be proud, at least, that she'd kept her voice from trembling.

He didn't answer.

Perhaps if she kept talking, if he came to see her as a…a *person*, he wouldn't hurt her before she found a way to escape.

"My name is Zoey. Zoey Weston. I am — *was* — a waitress in—"

"I have no interest in conversation." The arm around her neck loosened, and she felt him shift his weight back. "Continue in this direction. Make no signal to the other humans."

"Are they looking for you?"

The muscles in his arm flexed. "Whether they are or not, you would do well to obey my commands."

"I-I was just asking."

"And I have had enough human questions to last me a lifetime."

Zoey took that as her cue to shut the hell up.

The silence promptly resumed. Her frightened grip on the steering wheel soon had her hands aching, but she couldn't loosen her hold. Zoey's entire body was tense, waiting for the inevitable deathblow. What did he plan to do to her? What did he want? Would he let her go, or would he kill her once she was no longer useful to him?

They eventually overtook the farthest helicopter, and, before long, the aircraft were nothing more than faint blinking lights in the rearview. Immense heat seemed to radiate from the monster, but his hold gradually eased. Finally, the arm around her neck slid away, leaving only the scalding pressure of his palm on her thigh.

The desert flew by outside. She passed slower cars, and faster drivers — some of them *dangerously* faster — sped past Zoey.

A sign ahead declared Las Vegas was ninety-five miles away.

"Where are we going?" she chanced to ask.

He lifted a hand and pointed ahead with one of his long fingers. "That way."

"What is that way?"

"A place free of these questions, if I am fortunate."

A rush of anger surged inside her, obliterating her fear. She was tired of being disrespected.

"I didn't ask to be kidnapped by some green monster," she snapped, "so you're just going to have to deal with my questions! I'm scared, I'm tired, and I'm…I'm…just tired." She clenched her jaw and pressed her trembling lips together. She inhaled deeply and stared at the road ahead.

Stupid, Zoey! Don't antagonize him!

"I've just had a really shitty day," she continued, unable to stop now that she'd started, "and this just made it even worse. If you want silence, well…you're just going to have to kill me—" *please don't* "—or throw me out of the car. I can't just sit here and wonder what you're going to do with me, or what's going to happen. If you're going to do something bad, get it over with already."

He was quiet for a time, and utterly still. She glanced in the rearview mirror again to find that he'd changed position, hiding most of his large body in the shadows of the back seat.

"I wish only to return to my home," he finally said, his tone softer. "Aid me, and I will keep you safe."

"Safe…from what?"

"Though they are also human, I do not believe the people hunting me will leave you in peace, should they learn you've seen me."

"The helicopters?"

"Helicopters?"

"The things flying in the sky."

The fingers on her thigh twitched. "Yes. That is but a small portion of them."

Zoey nodded.

Okay. We're getting somewhere.

She could do this. This she could deal with, even if it was threatening to get into *X-Files*, government conspiracy territory. Too bad she'd never been interested enough in any of that stuff to pay attention.

Zoey caught a glimpse of him watching her in the mirror — that was *definitely* blood on his face — and quickly forced her attention to the road. "Did they…hurt you?"

He released a long, slow breath, and withdrew his hand from her thigh. The exposed spot felt suddenly cold.

"There has been much pain, yes. Harder to bear was the shame of being unable to fight back. Of being unable to protect my *Umen'rak*," he said.

"Protect your what?"

"My *Umen'rak*," he repeated. "My…team, to put it simply."

"Where are you from? How did you get caught?"

"I am from someplace very far away from here. Far enough that it is likely beyond your understanding. As for my capture… They discovered me while I was in a weakened state, after crashing on this planet—"

"You're an alien?" Zoey asked, eyes wide. It made perfect sense, now that it had been spoken out loud.

Monsters aren't real, but aliens are. Yeah, that makes perfect sense, all right.

"I am an aligarii. *You* are the alien."

"Sorry to break it to you, but on this planet, *you* are the alien. Not me." She met his gaze briefly in the mirror; it was riveting and disturbing all at once. "You mentioned your omen…uhmeanr…your team. Are there…more of you here?"

"None living."

None living?

The tone of his voice spoke far beyond his terse response. There had been others, they had died, and he carried the weight of their loss with him. Zoey could relate to that sense of loss and isolation.

"I'm sorry," she said gently.

"Sorry for what?"

"For the loss of your people."

"We are aliens to you. Why should you be sorry for their deaths?"

"Because you're still a living being, and…and you clearly cared for those you've lost."

The passenger seat creaked as he grasped it with two hands — two *right* hands — and used it as an anchor to pull himself into a partial sitting position. He filled the back seat completely, making it look like it had been designed for children. How hadn't she noticed him when she came back to her car? She'd made a point of checking! Had she been so preoccupied with her emotions that she'd failed to notice the huge, green alien ducking behind her seat?

"That notion does not seem to be shared by many of the humans I've encountered," he said.

"I guess you've met our government." She frowned. "What will they do if they get you again?"

"Restrain me, lock me in a dark cell, and question me incessantly between their *experiments* until my eventual death."

"Experiments?" Of course they'd experiment on him. He was an *alien*. "What…what did they do?"

The glow of his eyes flashed in the mirror for a second. "More than you would care to know."

Even if she'd never watched the *X-Files* and wasn't familiar with conspiracy theories beyond the one about the Illuminati running *everything*, she'd seen enough movies to have an idea of what *might* have been done, and her imagination took it far enough from there to send a shudder through her. Had some of his people died during such experiments?

"Okay." She took in another deep breath, stretched her aching fingers, and shifted on her seat. This situation was beyond belief, and a small part of her still insisted it couldn't be real, but…she wanted to help him. Hell, what did she have to lose? Everything else had already fallen apart. "If you swear you won't hurt me…I'll help you."

"I told you I'll keep you safe if you do as I say."

"That's not really the same as promising you won't hurt me in the process. Safe could just mean…*alive* for as long as I'm useful to you. I need a promise."

Her seat tipped back slightly as he clamped a hand on it and drew himself forward. She couldn't help but lean away to keep some space between them. She wasn't exactly in a position to make demands, yet here she was, throwing one out there like she had all the bargaining power.

"On my honor as an a*ekhora* blessed by the *Halvari*," he said, his low, rumbling voice sending a strange thrill through her, "I will do you no harm, *and* I will keep you safe, so long as you do not betray me."

She had no idea what those alien words he'd used meant, but the solemnity in his words told her an *aekhora blessed by the Halvari* was something very serious and very important to him. Her tension diminished, and she eased back against her seat.

"Thank you," she said.

Zoey squinted against the brights of an oncoming car, shifting her gaze to the rearview mirror. The fleeting light teased her with a glimpse of the alien's sharp, angular features, and his reptilian pupils shrank to slits in the glare. His eyes were a vibrant green. Her favorite color.

"Are you willing to tell me your name, yet?" she asked.

He lowered himself onto his back, dipping into the darkness.

"Rendash," he replied after a long pause.

Chapter Four

Rendash shifted to lay in the shadows, bracing two hands on the floor. The sounds of air rushing around the vehicle, the thrumming engine, and the wheels humming over the road were constant indicators of movement, but looking at the night sky through the far window almost created the sense that they weren't moving at all. Those unfamiliar stars hung motionless; they stared at him, mocked him, twinkled with cosmic mirth.

Detachment.

Those old teachings could only go so far now. He'd won some room to rest, even if the inadequately sized seat forced him into an uncomfortable position with arms and legs folded up awkwardly, but how far could he truly hope to get?

He had no allies, no weapons apart from his own body, no idea of where he was, and only a vague direction in which to head. He and his Umen'rak had often operated on alien worlds without reliable intelligence, but there'd always been some enemy to face, some invader to repel.

Earn the trust of the locals if you have a common enemy.

That wouldn't work here. His only enemies here were human, and there was a chance, however small, that they were the *only* species on the planet. He couldn't fight them all. At the moment, he couldn't even handle a few. He needed human assistance to navigate their world, but why would any of them betray their own on behalf of a stranded aligarii warrior who'd already killed several of them?

And yet here was this human — this *Zoey*. She'd regained her composure quickly despite her apparent fear and had already gone so far as to demand assurance from him as though she had leverage in the situation.

But she does *have leverage. Even if she doesn't fully realize it, I'm at her mercy, not the other way around.*

She didn't conduct herself like any human he'd met — she was certainly nothing like the people who'd held him captive — and she possessed an internal strength that seemed rare in most intelligent species.

And her *scent!* It was alien and familiar at once, bearing a hint of the fragrant flowers that blossomed in the jungles of his youth. It was alluring, provocative, and had subtly dominated the air inside the vehicle since he'd moved close enough to smell its fullness.

He'd never been so intrigued by a female's scent, but he couldn't allow curiosity to dictate his actions.

There was only one question regarding Zoey that needed to be answered.

Can she be trusted?

He glanced up at her seat. Her body was blocked from his view, but tendrils of her brown hair — most of which was gathered in a messy knot atop her head — hung over the headrest, and her pale neck was visible between the thin metal supports.

Her skin had felt strange against his arm; smooth and soft, so delicate he thought it might tear if he ran his scales over it too harshly.

Rendash's fingers twitched; he longed to brush his fingertips over her bare flesh again, to learn its feel properly.

What was he thinking? She was a human female, a member of the species that had held him captive for four of their years, the species that was hunting him like an animal. She was his enemy. It didn't matter if there might've been sympathy in her voice when she'd offered her condolences for his lost Umen'rak. It didn't matter that she said she'd help him.

What obligation did she have to him? What did these creatures know of honor?

Honor...

Those questions were irrelevant; he would keep his word. If she did not betray him, he would keep her safe, even from her own kind.

"Rendash?"

Her voice broke through his thoughts, serving as a reminder of just how tired he was — normally, he'd never drift so deep into thought that he lost awareness of his surroundings. That was an easy way to get killed.

"What is it?" he asked.

"There's something up ahead."

Grasping her seat, he pulled himself up to look between the front chairs. There were more ground vehicles stopped ahead, their rear lights lit bright red. Zoey slowed her vehicle as they approached the congestion. Just beyond the line of transports, flashing lights bathed the surrounding wasteland in blue and red.

"What is this?" Rendash asked.

Zoey leaned forward. "Looks like a police checkpoint. I...I think they are searching the cars." She turned her face toward him. "What are we going to do? They'll see you."

Thanks to the light from the vehicle behind them, he was finally offered a true glimpse of her features. Long, dark lashes framed her blue-gray eyes; those eyes were her most striking feature, wide and clear, snaring him within their depths. She had gently curved lines of hair on her brow over her eyes and full, pink lips that were currently downturned.

She was as bizarre looking as any human he'd seen, and somehow infinitely more appealing. There was a softness to her appearance to which he was wholly unaccustomed, a softness that made him want to touch, a softness that did nothing to diminish her underlying vitality.

"I will remain low," he said. "Tell me when we near the view of the humans searching."

At that moment, his life was entirely in her hands. Her small, soft, human hands. He held no illusions as to his ability to fight or flee on his own without significant recovery time. His strength was spent. His connection to his nyros was still disrupted by the human concoctions lingering in his system.

If she chose to betray him now, Rendash would be doomed.

"Oh God, I'm such a terrible liar," she said in a rush. "They're going to catch us. It's not like I have tinted windows, Rendash. They're going to see you and then they're going to—"

"Quiet, human," he snapped.

She obeyed. He felt a moment's guilt for the wide-eyed, vulnerable, nervous expression that overcame her face.

Control. Detachment.

"They will not see me, and you do not need to worry over

44

it," he said, taking a gentler tone. "Be...*honest* without revealing anything. Do you understand what I mean?"

She breathed slowly in and out several times. "I'll try."

"Remember, Zoey, my life depends upon your honor."

"More like it depends on my acting. No pressure either way, right?" She groaned. "We're so screwed."

Based on his understanding of *screwed*, her statement was nonsensical, but he didn't waste time asking for clarification. Humans were often imprecise in their use of words. He couldn't be sure if it was a result of their language's complexity or part of that complexity.

He lay back, pressing as much of his body as he could into the narrow space between the rear and front seats — which turned out to be two arms, his left hip, and a thigh. The position was uncomfortable, but it would reduce the chances of the humans detecting any faint anomalies in the light while he was cloaked. Some creatures were more sensitive to such phenomena, and he wasn't sure where human eyesight ranked in that regard.

"Okay. We're getting close," Zoey said. "Just a few more minutes."

The flashing lights shed alternating blue and red glows across the ceiling of the vehicle. Rendash's field of view was limited to the ceiling, the back of Zoey's seat, and bits of dark sky visible through the rear windows. The situation was far from ideal, but he could do little about it now.

"Oh, shit. There's a cop walking this way." Zoey spoke rapidly, voice at a higher pitch. "He's got a flashlight and it looks like he's spot-checking the cars as he goes. There's no way he's not going to—"

"*Control*, Zoey. Control your emotions. Detach yourself from the moment. I am trusting you, and you must trust me."

"Control," she breathed. "I can do this. I can."

Drawing upon whatever concentration he could muster, Rendash created a cloaking field; it crackled and hummed around him as though it would fail at any moment. He clenched his jaw and willed it to hold. Immense heat flared inside him.

The vehicle eased forward and stopped again.

"Oh my God, he's going to see you," Zoey rasped.

Several moments later, there was a tap upon her window. It was followed by a soft hum, and the outside sounds grew louder — the sigh of ground transports passing on the opposite side of the road, voices from humans in other vehicles, the wind flowing over the wasteland, and the distant beat of *helicopters*.

"Do you have identification, ma'am?" asked a male human.

Rendash tensed; this was the moment in which everything would fall apart. He wouldn't to be taken again. He could only hope his nyros would be responsive enough to allow him a worthy final stand.

Zoey's heart raced. Her nerves were frayed, and she swore she was dripping gallons of sweat. Couldn't the cop see Rendash? Why hadn't he said anything about the giant, green alien filling the backseat of her little car?

She stared up at the cop with a wide, strained smile, probably showing way too many teeth. "Yeah. It's in my purse. Can I...can I get it?"

The cop nodded and turned his flashlight toward the backseat for a moment. Zoey froze, heart lodged in her throat.

Oh God, this is it. I'm done for. Rendash is done for.

Shouldn't she *want* them to find the alien? She could tell them she was forced into it against her will, that she was a hostage, that she'd been given no choice but to help him. She could tell them everything, and because she hadn't done anything wrong they'd let her carry on with her life. She'd resume her trip to Des Moines as though nothing had happened.

But what would become of Rendash?

She stopped her mind from going there fully; the half-imagined torture sessions she'd conjured up before still weighed heavily upon her.

How could I live with the guilt of knowing I willingly allowed him to be tortured or killed?

Zoey turned away from the cop to reach into her purse. Careful not to turn her head, she shifted her eyes to the side as far as they could go to glance at the back seat.

Her heart stopped.

I've lost my fucking mind.

Rendash was gone. Like, *gone*-gone. There wasn't a trace of the alien anywhere, except… There was a light coating of dust across the back seat, and the cushions sported large depressions as though something heavy was settled atop them. Had it always looked so broken-in?

"Quite a mess you have back there," the cop said.

Him calling attention to it allowed Zoey to turn her head toward the back without worry.

Yep, just seat depressions and dust. No Rendash.

Zoey swallowed, and let out an uneasy laugh. "Yeah. I was babysitting a coworker's dog this weekend, and well, you know how dogs are! They love to roll around in the dirt." She grabbed her wallet, flipped it open, and turned back to the cop, forcing her smile to remain in place.

A dog, Zoey? Think maybe he'll notice the total lack of fur?

"Here you go," she said cheerfully, handing him her wallet.

Frowning, the cop turned his attention back to her and took the wallet, shining his flashlight down onto it. She realized only then that he was wearing sunglasses. The lights weren't *that* bright, were they? Who wore sunglasses at night?

She forced her mind to abort that train of thought before the damned song popped into her head.

Control, Zoey. Not the time or place for eighties pop.

"Where are you heading tonight, Miss Weston?" he asked.

"I'm making my way to a friend's."

"And where would that be?"

"Iowa. Des Moines, Iowa."

"Quite a way to go," he said flatly, shifting the flashlight's beam to her face. Zoey squinted against the blinding glare. *Ass.* "Any passengers tonight, or are you making that trip all alone?"

He swept the light over the back seat again before moving it toward the passenger seat.

"Unless you can see my invisible friend," Zoey said with a nervous chuckle, "I'd say I'm traveling all by my lonesome."

He stared at her. At least she *assumed* he did, as his eyes were hidden. "Have you seen anything out of the ordinary tonight, Miss Weston?"

"Out of the ordinary? What would be considered out of the ordinary, these days?" she asked, speaking a little faster than necessary. They really were looking for Rendash! "Whole bunch of helicopters zipping around, making a bunch of noise and shining searchlights everywhere. Don't see that every day, right?" She grinned.

The officer's face was as unmoving and cold as stone. After

several uncomfortable seconds, he turned toward some of the other cops and signaled them. They began to direct traffic, albeit slowly, around Zoey's car.

"I'm going to need you to shut off the engine, remove the key, and step out of the car, ma'am," he said when he looked back at her.

The hair on the back of Zoey's neck stood on end as fear slithered down her spine. A chill raced through her body. "Um, what is all this about, anyway, Officer…?"

He took a long step back from the door and dropped a hand to the pistol on his hip. "Out of the vehicle. *Now.*"

"Okay! Okay! I'm getting out." She turned the key, pulled it from the ignition, and tossed it beside her purse. It was a struggle not to look at the back seat again; it'd be too obvious now. She opened the door and stepped out, keeping her hands up.

He waved his flashlight toward the hood of the car. "Move to the front of the vehicle and place both hands flat on the hood."

Zoey did as she was told, despite the fearful tremors in her limbs. What had she done wrong? What would they do to her?

Once she was in position, the officer leaned into the open door for a moment, reaching down to pop the trunk. She felt him glare at her from behind his sunglasses before he walked to the back of the car. It shook slightly as he shifted around the contents — two suitcases of clothes and toiletries, the little photo album, her box of romance novels, and her favorite blanket.

After a minute or so, the officer slammed the trunk closed and walked back to the front of the car. Zoey peered up at him but was careful not to lift her hands off the hood.

"I'm going to ask you one more time. Have you seen *anything* out of the ordinary tonight? Hitchhikers, cars stopped on the side of the road, anything? There is a very dangerous man at large, and your silence will make it that much harder for us to catch him."

"I haven't seen anything," Zoey replied, fingers curling on top of the hood.

"Your behavior suggests otherwise."

"What behavior?" she demanded. "I gave you my ID, answered your questions, and now you got me bent over my damn car like a criminal? I lost my fucking job today, got a notice that my landlord's about to evict me, and found out my boyfriend was cheating on me. Please excuse me if my *behavior* is unusual, but I say I'm holding it together pretty damn well, all things considered."

Zoey glared at the officer. Apparently, she'd straightened to stand with her fists clenched at her sides at some point during her blow up.

Whoops.

The cop's jaw muscles bulged, and his hand drifted toward his gun again. He hesitated, tilting his head slightly as though listening to something. "Negative. She's clear. Just got a nasty attitude." Another pause. "Copy."

Jerk.

"Back in your vehicle, Miss Weston," he finally said. "Move along."

Keeping her distance from Officer Asswipe, she got back into the car and slammed the door. She held a hand out the open window. "I need my wallet back. *Please.*"

Ignoring her extended hand, he tossed the wallet through the window to land in her lap. "Drive safe." Before she could hit him with a scathing — and foolhardy — remark, he turned and walked toward the next car.

Zoey stuffed her wallet into her purse, grabbed her keys, and buckled up. She started the car and glared at the cop's back as she rolled up her window. Throwing the shifter into drive, she promptly got the fuck out of there.

Once she'd passed the barricade and the police car lights were fading in the distance, Zoey was slapped in the face with the realization that they'd made it through. She released a shaky breath as relief flowed through her. "We did it."

She lifted a hand to adjust the rearview mirror, angling it to see into the back seat. Her eyes widened as a dark form materialized there. *Was* she crazy? She wasn't sure how to reconcile his appearing-disappearing act otherwise.

Rendash shifted to meet her gaze in the mirror. "You've kept your word thus far, human. I will keep mine."

Zoey frowned. "Told you I would."

A pang of guilt pierced her chest; for a single moment, she'd considered giving him up. Now that she was on the other side of the checkpoint, she was glad she hadn't, but she could only hope the decision wouldn't come back to bite her in the ass.

"What are the lights up ahead?" Rendash asked.

"A casino," she replied. "The first of many. Welcome to Nevada."

"I find myself more confused now than before I asked."

"Oh."

Despite his accent, he spoke English so well that she'd assumed he knew. Didn't aliens spy on humans? Didn't they abduct people in the middle of the night, stealing them away to flying saucers, to probe and prod and question? Aliens were supposed to be super smart.

Intelligence and knowledge are different things. This world is alien to him. Can't expect him to know all about the convoluted things humans do.

"Nevada is a state. We just crossed into it from California. There are fifty states in the United States. They're like...divisions of territory, I guess, and we might cross more of them depending on where you need me to take you. Um...where *do* you need me to take you, anyway?"

She felt his hand on her seat again, and he pulled himself into a hunched sitting position, placing his face between the two front seats.

"In the direction we are traveling," he replied. Just as she was about to get annoyed at his vagueness, he continued. "I know only that there is a great distance to cross. I have no knowledge of your world to provide you with even a general location to aim for, only the direction."

"All right. I...guess that's better than nothing."

"And what is a casino?" he asked.

"A casino is a place where people gamble."

"Gamble their lives?"

Zoey glanced at him. A chill ran through her. While his two center eyes looked ahead, the leftmost one stared at her. She forced her gaze to the road.

Creepy. As. Fuck.

"Might as well be their lives," she said. "But no. They gamble with money."

"Money. That is an abstract means of assigning value to goods and services, is it not?"

"You say that like it's a strange concept to you."

"My people do not have such a thing."

"Um, here, let me show you." Keeping one hand on the wheel, she blindly reached over and dug her wallet out of her purse. She glanced down a couple times as she withdrew a dollar bill and her debit card, holding them up for him. "This is money. There are lots of different paper ones, and some that are metal, and each has a certain value. The card is a...an electronic way of accessing the money we own that's stored in a bank — not that you're likely to have any idea of what that is, either."

He plucked the dollar from her hold. "This paper has value? What use can it be put to?"

She caught a glimpse of the confused look on his face in the mirror; his brow was furrowed, and his lips turned down in a deep frown.

"We use it to buy things," she said. "Food, clothes, our homes. Just about everything. If we don't have money, we'd be homeless and starving."

"So its only purpose is the procurement of other goods that actually have use? Does that not seem...foolish? Why not trade those goods directly?"

Zoey shrugged. "It's just the way that it is. We work and slave away the hours to earn it, and most of us barely make enough to get by."

"All aligarii serve their roles to ensure our society has all it needs," he said, his tone implying it was madness to do things any other way. "Even the other species who live among us want for nothing, so long as they do their part."

"I'm still wrapping my head around the fact that there's *one* kind of alien, so I definitely don't need to hear about any others right now." She glanced at a passing sign. Thirty miles to Vegas. "Your society sounds much nicer than ours."

"Perhaps. I have spent little time in true aligarii society."

"What do you mean?"

"I am *Aekhora*, born into the *Khorzar*. I have trained for war since my youth and have fought on many different worlds."

"Did you…" Her tongue slipped out to wet her suddenly dry lips. "Did you come *here* to start a war?"

He turned his head toward her, and reflected light made his eyes glow at the edge of her vision. Zoey tensed.

"Aligarii do not start wars. We finish them. We protect those unjustly attacked, protect worlds unable to defend themselves. My *Umen'rak* was simply passing through this system. We were unaware this planet bore any life."

"Okay," she sighed in relief. "No *end of all human life as we know it* anytime soon, then. Unless…you bring more of your kind back to take revenge for what was done to you."

Rendash released a heavy breath. "What was done to me would be my responsibility to avenge," he said. "I would not make your entire, primitive planet pay for a personal vendetta."

Zoey's muscles eased. "Thank you. Though I resent that remark about us being primitive."

"You drive wheeled vehicles over the ground. How could that not be considered primitive?"

"We're intelligent beings who have advanced quickly through the years. We are *not* primitive."

"By your own standards."

"And you're just rude," she shot back.

"Again, by your own standards."

Zoey cracked a smile and shook her head. "I give up."

"That you haven't given up yet is the only reason I am not locked in a dark room, Zoey." To her surprise, there seemed to be genuine gratitude in his voice.

Her smile faded as the weight of the situation settled atop her again. "Yeah, guess you're right."

What more would they have done to him if she'd given him over? Would they have shot him right in front of her eyes? The thought churned her stomach.

She swallowed back a sudden wave of bile and cleared her throat. "Are you thirsty? I have some water."

"Yes."

Zoey groped over the passenger seat until she found the water bottle and passed it to him. She watched in the rearview mirror as he twisted off the cap, leaned back, and drained the bottle in two gulps.

"We should probably grab some food and find a place to stop for the night. You can do that...disappearing act you did back there to hide."

"Stop? We must continue. As I told you, we have a long way to travel."

"I don't know about you, but this *primitive human* needs sleep. Even if I hadn't had a shitty day, I can't drive all through the night. I need to rest. So, if you're keeping me on as your personal chauffeur — that's someone who drives people around, by the way — then you go at my speed."

He was silent for a time. "Very well, human. Acquire lodging and sustenance for us."

"My name is Zoey."

She glanced in the mirror and caught a fleeting glimpse of his face; his mouth was quirked up at one corner.

"I know that, human," he said as he lay back on the seat.

Zoey rolled her eyes. She had a feeling this was going to be one interesting road trip.

Chapter Five

Before the SUV came to a complete stop, Charles Stantz threw open the passenger door. He stormed across the pavement after the driver slammed on the brakes, resisting the urge to adjust his tie; he refused, even with the current situation, to display so much as the smallest sign of weakness in front of his men.

An unexpected event had occurred, an *unfortunate* event, but it was being handled. There was no reason for the sour churning in his gut.

He climbed the metal-grating steps and entered the command trailer, closing the door quietly behind him. Before he rounded the corner, he fished a roll of antacids from his inside jacket pocket, peeled back the foil, and dumped four into his mouth. The packaging declared *Fruit Flavored!*, but they tasted like shit.

Once the antacids were chewed to a paste, Stantz swallowed and walked around the corner.

Banks of monitors of varying sizes lined both walls, and a

dozen technicians with headsets were at the controls. Currently, there were at least fifty camera feeds pulled up, including two for each patrolling chopper, more than ten from agents currently in the desert, numerous surveillance cameras from buildings in the search area, and first-person views from the agents operating the roadblock at the California-Nevada border.

The techs spoke in low, droning voices as they received and relayed information.

"Tell me we've got something," Stantz called as he moved down the narrow walkway to the center of the trailer.

"A few impact spots in the dirt, and his shackles, cut into pieces," Fairborough said, walking over to stand beside Stantz. His sleeves were rolled up and his headset was pulled back off one ear. "Trail's cold after he crossed the mountains."

Stantz growled. "How does a seven-foot-tall *green* alien vanish in a place with nowhere to hide?"

Fairborough didn't answer; the man was smart enough to know it had been a rhetorical question.

One of the screens caught Stantz's attention. He pointed at it. "What's Branson got there?"

The camera feed showed a curvy woman standing near the front of her car. She looked pissed, with her fists balled and her eyebrows angled down over the bridge of her nose.

Stantz grabbed a free headset and pulled it on. "Patch me through to field comms."

The closest tech nodded, and after a few quick clicks, audio crackled on in Stantz's headset.

"…pretty damn well, all things considered," the woman on the camera said.

The technician pulled up her info; Zoey Weston, age twenty-seven, most recently employed as a waitress in Santa Barbara, California. No criminal record.

"Agent Branson," Stantz said, "does that civilian have information on the Fox?"

The codename — Fox — was at once fitting and frustrating; Specimen Ten was cunning and dangerous, as four dead operatives now evidenced, but the naming scheme seemed ridiculously cliché and unimaginative. If the Organization wanted to move into the future, it would need to shed the trappings of the past.

Branson's camera angle tilted slightly.

"Negative. She's clear. Just got a nasty attitude."

"Then move her along. Our only concern is tracking down the Fox, understood?"

"Copy."

Stantz tugged the headset down around his neck and returned his attention to Fairborough. "I want all lines of communication monitored."

"Yes, sir. I've already got people back at base combing social media and cell phone traffic. Anyone so much as mentions something weird, we'll know about it."

Stantz's phone vibrated. He tugged it off his belt and glanced at the screen. "Shit," he muttered.

He yanked off the headset, tossed it down, and hurried outside, pressing *Accept* as he descended the steps. He lifted the phone to his ear.

"Director," he said, tongue suddenly like sandpaper.

"Charlie, tell me you have this under control."

"We're regaining control, sir."

"Not good enough, damnit! Do you understand the

resources we're pulling to fix this fuck-up? We don't need any elected officials asking questions, whether it's about your Fox or our sudden upswing in expenditures. Those bastards only care about saving money if they feel like they had no say in spending it, and they sure as hell don't have a say right now. I'd like to keep it that way."

"I'll bring this to a quick resolution, sir."

"The public *cannot* find out about this thing, Charlie. We have enough BS out there to muck up the water, but this one is too much. You do what you need to do to fix this. Even if that means putting your lost animal down."

Stantz clenched his jaw, grinding his teeth together. "Yes, sir."

When the call disconnected, he stuffed his phone back into its case and paced over the hard pack in front of the trailer.

He'd busted his ass for fifteen years to get to his current position, and his work with the group of aliens who'd crash-landed on Earth had yielded real results that government researchers and scientists would eventually put to good use. One day, he'd be recognized as the man who'd enabled America to move into a new age through his dedication. Few of the others were as willing to get their hands dirty. He'd been doing that dirty work with these aliens for four years.

Stantz wasn't about to let his life's work be swept aside because of some short-sighted bureaucrat. Specimen Ten was the last of its kind on Earth, and Stantz would have it back. Budgets and politicians were of no importance; this was about uplifting the human race, about bringing them to the next level of evolution. Anyone who couldn't see that was little more than an obstacle to be bypassed or destroyed.

He stalked into the command trailer and pulled on a headset.

"Call in some more hounds, gentlemen," he ordered. "We have a Fox to hunt. We're going to flush it out of this desert and throw it back in its cage."

Chapter Six

Zoey cringed as she stared at the old, rundown motel in front of her. The mattresses were likely soaked through with unidentifiable bodily fluids and crawling with bugs. But beggars couldn't be choosers, and Zoey didn't exactly have an overflowing bank account. This place would have to do.

"I need to go in and get a room," she said, picking up her purse from its place beside the fast food bag on the passenger seat. The smell of cheesy, greasy hamburgers permeated the air inside the car. There were so many other choices she could've made, but cheap and fast had proven to be the primary criteria in choosing; she was eager to get off the road, and a being as large as Rendash was likely to eat a lot.

She just wanted to get something solid in her stomach and get some sleep.

"I will await your return," Rendash said. He sounded exhausted. A few seconds later, he disappeared. Even though she already knew he could do that, it was a mind-breaking thing to watch.

Zoey shook off the lingering shock of it, opened her door, and stepped out. As she settled the strap of her purse over her shoulder, she leaned into the car. "I'll be back as fast as I can."

"On with it, human," he muttered.

"Zoey, *alien*." She closed the door before he could respond, feeling a bit of smug satisfaction for having cut him off, and walked toward the office.

The bright red neon sign in the window announced there was a *Vacancy*. Zoey pulled the door open and walked inside. The blended odors of smoke and must struck her immediately.

The lobby was a relic of the 1970s, with wood paneling on one of the walls, a low, puke-yellow couch, and a brown and orange pattern on the worn carpet. The battered counter was the same color as the cigarette-burned couch. A short hallway ran off the side of the room. The door behind the counter looked to be heavy-duty, possibly oak, but the *EMPLOYEES ONLY* sign didn't fully cover the hole punched in the paper-thin outer panel.

"Hello?" Zoey called.

She heard the muffled flush of a toilet. One of the doors in the hallway opened, and a woman stepped out. Zoey inwardly winced; coming out that quickly, the woman had likely skipped washing her hands.

The woman had long, blonde, bleach-fried hair with dark roots. The thick makeup on her face didn't quite hide the crow's feet around her eyes and the lines near her mouth, and her heavy black eyeliner was smudged in one corner. She was thin. Her crop-top displayed a tanned belly and a navel piercing, and the hint of a tattoo peeked up from the waistband of her low-riding jeans.

"What you need?" the woman asked as she moved to the

counter. She picked up a pack of cigarettes, shook one out, and stuck it between her bright red lips.

"I need a room," Zoey said.

"Course you do," the woman said from the corner of her mouth. She took a lighter from her pocket, flicked it on, and lit the cigarette before tossing the lighter carelessly onto the counter. Was smoking indoors even legal? The woman took a long drag and exhaled a cloud of smoke. "Fifty bucks for a single queen."

A single?

Oh, no, no, no.

"I need two beds."

"Sorry, honey." The woman took another drag, held the cigarette aside between two fingers — the butt was smeared with lipstick — and turned her head to release more smoke. "I only got two rooms left, and they both got one bed." Her eyes shifted past Zoey, looking toward the window. "You got someone waiting out there? Can book both rooms, if you really don't want to sleep together that badly. But this *is* Vegas, hun."

As tempting as that was, Zoey couldn't justify spending twice as much — otherwise she would've driven a little farther into Vegas and looked for a nicer place. "No, thank you. One room is fine."

The woman picked up an open ledger and plopped it on the counter in front of Zoey, pointing to a blank line with a red acrylic fingernail. "Print and sign here."

Zoey arched a brow. Apparently, the décor wasn't the only out-of-date part of this place. Didn't hotels do everything by computer these days? She glanced behind the counter; there was a single computer on a desk against the wall, a blocky thing with a glossy glass screen and a gaping slot for floppy disks. She hadn't seen one of those things since elementary school.

Unwilling to waste any more time, Zoey signed her name and paid for the room. The woman ran Zoey's debit card through on a tablet she produced from under the counter.

Guess when it comes to getting your money in their pockets as fast as possible, even places like this are willing to upgrade.

After sliding the book to its original place, the woman tossed a key onto the counter. "One-twelve. It's around the back," she said, gesturing vaguely toward the door.

Zoey snatched up the key and hurried out the door. As soon as she was outside, she sucked in a desperate lungful of fresh air.

Returning to the car, Zoey got in and started the engine.

The rear seat creaked as Rendash, still unseen, moved. "What is that stench clinging to you?"

"Cigarette smoke. Nasty stuff. I don't recommend it," she replied as she pulled out of their spot and drove to the rear of the motel.

"Your original scent is far more appealing."

"My—" Zoey looked in the rearview mirror, which was still angled to display the seemingly empty back seat. "You've been *smelling* me?"

"You emit a smell into the surrounding air. Are human senses so dull that you cannot detect such scents?"

"Of course not." Zoey blushed as she parked the car and removed the key from the ignition. "We're here."

She popped the trunk, snagged the fast food bag, and got out, slamming the door behind her.

The car rocked; Zoey assumed it was due to the movements of her invisible passenger. She opened the back door and continued to the trunk. After tossing her blanket over her shoulder, she set the suitcases on the ground and tugged up their handles. The box of novels was likely safe; a thief would have to be desperate to go through the struggle of hauling them down to a used bookstore to sell for a dollar of store credit a piece, if that.

She shut the trunk and — clutching the bag of burgers along with one of the suitcase handles — wheeled her belongings to the door of her room. She fumbled the key into the lock and turned it as Ren closed the car door. Opening the room door, she grabbed her stuff, stepped inside, and flipped on the lights.

She didn't notice anything skittering for cover in the sudden light; that was a good sign, even if it wasn't a definitive all clear. The lamplight was dull yellow, revealing a room that was a good match for the lobby — the same brown-and-orange carpet pattern, the same wood panel walls, and baby-poop-yellow bedding. Directly across from the foot of the bed sat a dresser with an old tube TV — complete with rabbit ears — on top.

"A blast from the past," she muttered, setting her things down on the floor and tossing the greasy bag of food and her blanket onto the bed.

The door closed behind her, calling her attention. She turned to see Rendash's form bleed into view. Zoey's eyes widened. The closest she could liken it to was dripping some dye into a glass of water and watching it diffuse to color all the water solidly, but that didn't do the image justice.

He was *tall* — like, duck-under-the-doorway tall. Seven feet if he was an inch. And *damn*, he was large. His shoulders were broad, and his arms — all four of them — were corded with muscle. He wasn't bulky like a body builder, but there was no doubt he was strong.

Where his scales weren't covered in dust, they were a deep, vibrant emerald that made her think of a dense jungle. The size, texture, and shade of his scales seemed to change at various points on his body. On his belly and the insides of his arms and legs, they were fine like snake skin and a bit paler. His shoulders and the outsides of his arms and legs had larger, darker scales, with raised ridges that would look at home on the back of an alligator.

His hair was a duller than his skin, forest green rather than emerald, and ran from the top of his head in thick, loc-like ropes that flowed down his back and brushed his shoulders. It bore subtle undertones of blue and yellow. The sides of his head were bare. His facial features were the embodiment of brutal sensuality and arrogance, almost elfin in nature — right down to his pointed ears. He had high cheekbones, a sharp, narrow jaw, and a wide nose. All four of his eyes were fixed on her, their color reminiscent of peridots.

Zoey's gaze traveled down his body. He was more or less humanoid in shape, but his musculature was different; everything was longer, leaner.

Of course it's different. He's a four-armed alien!

His lower arms were several inches below the upper pair, which created an overlapping set of pectorals, their lines blurred by his scales. His long torso tapered down toward a narrow waist. Despite the texture of his skin, all his muscles were well-defined — especially his *twelve*-pack of abs.

Better by the dozen, right?

She'd never seen so many muscles in her life. They were positively lickable.

Did I seriously just think that?

She hadn't merely thought about it, she'd *imagined* it, had pictured running her tongue over every ridge of muscle on his torso, lingering at his belly to offer individual attention to every ab. Her pussy clenched, and a sudden rush of arousal flooded her.

Her eyes dipped, and Zoey gasped, jaw agape. It was several seconds before she was able to overcome her shock and turn away from him.

"Oh, my God, you're naked! And you called *me* primitive!" She snatched up her blanket and blindly threw it at him. "Cover yourself!"

It wasn't like Rendash covering himself with her favorite blanket could erase the image from her mind — that would be scalded into her memory for the rest of her life. The size of his cock was breathtaking; she was frightened to guess what it was like at full attention. Though it had to be at least six or seven inches flaccid, it wasn't only a matter of length that had shocked her. It looked as thick as her wrist, and there were *ridges* along the top.

She could just imagine what those ridges would do inside her, all the spots they'd perfectly brush. She squeezed her thighs together as though it could ease the sudden throbbing of her sex.

Talk about ribbed for her pleasure...

Oh, my God, what is wrong *with me? He's an alien!*

She inhaled deeply. This was just her body telling her it'd been too long, that was all. A severe case of sexual frustration. Her body craved intimacy and sex and it didn't care who — or what — it came from.

"I do not understand why you are upset," he said.

Zoey wrung her fingers together. "I take it nudity isn't a problem in your society?"

"Why would it be a problem?"

"It's just that… No one—" She groaned. "Here, people don't just walk around naked. It's…indecent. Are you covered?"

"Which part do you prefer I cover, human?"

"Are you serious right now?"

"I am covered." His voice held a hint of mirth. "I hope you will forgive me. I wasn't satisfied with the clothing options when I fought my way out of the back of a transport and ran into the wasteland."

Zoey turned her head and chanced a peek at Rendash. He'd wrapped her blanket around his hips like a kilt; it looked startlingly natural on him.

"You just surprised a girl, is all." Her eyes helplessly roved over his body again before she forced them up to his face. She motioned toward the bathroom. "Do you need to, um…"

He blinked — his side eyes first, and then the front pair, just slightly out of sync. "You'll have to be more specific. What is back there?"

"A bathroom. Do you need to…pee or anything?" Zoey's cheeks felt like they were on fire.

"I believe I understand your meaning, human." His gaze swept over her, *slowly*, and she shivered under its intensity. He walked past her, pausing only to remove the blanket and toss it onto the bed.

"Ren!" she exclaimed, turning away, but not before catching a glimpse of a very firm, very fine ass.

"I will return. I'm sure you prefer I not soil the fabric."

"Yes, I prefer you don't. But you better cover yourself back up when you're done," she called, bending to pick up her purse from the floor and slipping its strap over her shoulder. "I'll go get us some drinks."

She walked to the door and opened it.

Rendash was suddenly behind her, catching her arm in his firm grip and slamming the door shut before she had a chance to step out. Zoey's heart leapt into her throat *again*; that feeling was becoming a little too familiar for her liking. He spun her to face him and placed his lower hands on her hips as he pressed her against the door.

"Where are you going?" he demanded.

Zoey tilted her head back to look up at him. His upper lip was drawn back to reveal an elongated pair of canines to either side of his mouth, like doubled-up vampire fangs. It wouldn't take a big leap in imagination to picture him using them to tear out someone's throat.

"I-I was just going to get some water from the vending machine. Drinks."

As he stared down at her, something in his face softened, and he eased his hold. "I cannot keep you safe if you are not nearby."

"The vending machine is near the office," Zoey said, her fear dwindling. He said he wanted to keep her safe; okay, sure. *Great.* But part of her suspected his reaction was because he didn't trust her not to run, and that he wouldn't hesitate to kill her if he believed she was going to betray him. "It's not far, and I won't be long. You can…do your business while I'm gone. Use the toilet and maybe…" Her attention shifted to the dried blood on his face and shoulder. "Maybe take a shower? We can eat when you're done."

"You will return soon?"

If she didn't know any better, she'd say there was the tiniest shred of desperation in his voice.

"Yes," she replied. "I'll be right back."

His thumbs moved in small, soothing circles over her hips, and he removed his hand from the door to cup her chin. The scales on his palm were rough, but not painfully so; they were just enough to elicit a thrill in her at every point of contact.

He lowered his face, and his nostrils flared as he inhaled. "Quickly then, little human."

Was she mad about him calling her *human* before? This time, his words ignited a fire deep inside her, his voice gently stoking the flame like a soft breath.

"Okay," she rasped.

He released her reluctantly and stepped back. She made the mistake of letting her gaze dip.

Oh, yeah. He took the blanket off, but never made it into the bathroom.

And he was hardening!

Eyes wide, Zoey spun to the door and fumbled for the handle. "Make sure you cover yourself before you come out," she said hurriedly, escaping the room the instant the door was open wide enough for her to fit through. Once she was out, she slammed it shut behind her.

Zoey hauled her purse strap back up and clutched the bag to her chest, taking a deep breath. Not in a million years could she have guessed how this day would go. Eighteen hours ago, she'd been getting ready for work, telling herself things were hard, but it would all work out while she brushed her teeth. That felt like a lifetime ago, now.

She walked along the building, rounding it to head for the vending machine. If nothing else, it felt good to be up and moving. She was so used to being on her feet for ten-plus hours a day, every day, that sitting in her little car for long stretches could shift from uncomfortable to painful rather quickly.

There was a loud thump from the inside of one of the

rooms as Zoey passed. She jumped and veered away as a man and woman began shouting at each other, their voices barely muffled by the wall.

How many times had she heard arguments like that in some of the foster homes she'd lived in, or from the surrounding apartments back in Santa Barbara?

"Right at home," she whispered.

When she arrived at the vending machine, Zoey opened her purse and reached in for her wallet. Her fingers brushed over the candy bars she'd stuffed inside before bumping against the slender case of her phone. She'd silenced it after loading her stuff in the car and hadn't checked it since. Closing her eyes, she took several fortifying breaths before taking the phone out. She held it in the palm of her hand for several seconds. There was nothing to be afraid of on the phone. It held nothing but words.

So why the dread in her gut?

Opening her eyes, she pressed the side button and looked down at her notifications. The screen was filled with texts and missed calls. Sighing, she unlocked the phone and went to the home screen. She had six missed calls and the little text icon showed twenty-six messages waiting for her in the corner. She pressed it.

Joshua was at the top of the conversations list, with twenty-five unread messages. Zoey bit her lip; she still felt something for him, even after what he'd done, and she hated that. His betrayal had stricken deep.

Will I ever be enough?

She checked the only other message first — a quick text from Mel telling her to be safe.

Knowing it was stupid, Zoey went back to the list of conversations and pressed on Josh's name.

. . .

im sorry zo. i was a jerk. plz dont b mad.

we can still b friends. i want 2 b.

zo, plz answer me. i didnt mean 2 hurt u.

Zoey scrolled through the messages. He begged her to forgive him, begged for another chance, told her they could remain roommates – even had the nerve to suggest a threesome. He didn't seem to know what he wanted, but Zoey had figured it out by now.

Joshua wanted the security of someone who would enable him to sit on his ass playing video games all day without getting mad when he brought other women over.

Her disgust was strong enough to make her nauseous. What made it worse was that she knew he cared, in his own, immature way. He'd never been cruel to her in their time together — well, apart from going behind her back with other women — but he'd never been attracted to her either, not in any way meaningful enough to count.

zo where r u? u at a friends? i know ur mad but b careful.

zo where r ur things? plz answer me!

. . .

The last message he'd sent had been two hours ago. He was likely sleeping by now.

If he's not banging some other chick.

Zoey switched back to Melissa's message and sent a reply.

Made it to Vegas. Call me in the morning. XOXO

Unmuting her phone, she dropped it back into her purse and took out her wallet.

She returned to the room a few minutes later with an armful of bottled water, slipping in and closing the door quietly behind her. The shower was running, which meant Rendash was still in there. Zoey tried not to imagine water streaming over his scales and between the ridges of his muscles.

She failed.

"Something is seriously wrong with me," she muttered. She dropped her purse on the table near the door, placed the bottles on the nightstand, and sat on the edge of the bed.

Grabbing the fast food bag, she laid the value-menu hamburgers — ten in total — atop the blanket. After a moment's consideration, she dug the candy bars out of her purse and added them to the food pile. She picked up a burger, unwrapped it, and ate, sipping water. When she'd finished, she reached for another one.

Her hand froze before she touched the wrapper as Josh's words echoed in her head.

I'm just…not attracted to you.

Maybe if you'd have put in some effort to lose a little weight.

She withdrew her extended hand, dropping it onto her lap. Her chest felt tight. It wasn't fair that he could just brush this all off like it was no big deal. It wasn't fair that *he* was the one who'd done wrong, but *she* was the one who got to feel shitty over it.

The shower turned off. Shortly after, the bathroom door opened, and Rendash stepped out amidst a cloud of steam.

She opened her mouth to tell him to cover up again, but she was distracted by the glistening droplets on his scales, which created little reflections as they rolled down his body. It was a welcome distraction, considering the place her mind had gone a few moments before.

"You have returned," he said. He stretched a towel between his lower hands and wrapped it around his waist as he walked toward her in long, slow strides. His muscles rippled with his movements, and once again, Zoey imagined running her tongue over them, catching each and every drop of water.

She cleared her throat — which was suddenly very dry— and forced her eyes away, pushing the food toward him. "Not the best food in the world, but it's food."

Stopping to lean over the bed, he plucked up a burger. He peeled back the wrapper and sniffed at the food within. Tentatively, he took the burger between two of his long fingers, brought it to his lips, and bit off a small piece.

Rendash chewed thoughtfully, took another nibble, and chewed more. Then he devoured the rest of the burger in two large bites.

"There's plenty more," Zoey said, grabbing one of the water bottles from the nightstand and handing it to him. "And water."

He accepted the bottle in his upper right hand and picked

up another burger in his upper left. In an impressive show of dexterity, he unwrapped the burger and opened the bottle simultaneously with his lower hands. He gestured at her vaguely as he sat on the bed. It dipped wildly under his weight.

"You must eat also, human."

"I ate already." Zoey pushed herself to her feet, walked to her suitcase, and kneeled to open it.

"Did you eat enough?" he asked around a mouthful that must've consisted of nearly an entire burger.

She glanced down at her body. "Yeah. Plenty." Frowning, she dug through her clothes and pulled out her pajamas and a pair of panties, folding the former over the latter. She closed the suitcase.

"I'm going to take a shower now." Zoey stepped past Rendash, careful not to touch him, and felt his eyes on her as she crossed the room.

Rendash watched Zoey, admiring the sensual swaying of her hips and backside as she walked until she slipped into the bathroom and closed the door behind her.

He'd encountered plenty of humans in his time on this planet — even if they were often in black uniforms and the lighting was usually poor — but Zoey was unlike anyone, human or aligarii, he'd ever seen. Aligarii females were built much like the males; lean, tough, and strong. There was nothing soft about them.

Everything about Zoey — at least outwardly — was soft and smooth. Where aligarii had angles and planes, she was all curves. There was something refreshing about that. Something appealing, something alluring. His brief contact with her before she'd left for the water had been a taste that only strengthened his curiosity. He wanted to touch her more, to hold her, to feel her softness against him.

He ate the rest of the *burgers*, unable to ignore his own ravenousness. They'd kept him underfed and weakened in the facility. He needed nourishment to recover his strength, to keep himself moving. The food was at once disgusting — dripping with grease and encased in what the humans called *bread*, an unappetizing creation to say the least — and ambrosial. The best he'd ever tasted, after surviving for so long on bland, unidentifiable food.

The shower turned on in the bathroom. He twisted to look at the door. Had she removed her garments before entering the water? It would make sense if she had, though he wasn't aware of the washing customs practiced by these strange beings. Thoughts of her bare body were too intriguing to entertain for long; human anatomy was unfamiliar to him, and his imagination would never conjure the correct images.

How simple would it be to slip into the bathroom and obtain a glimpse? The noise of the water was enough to mask the opening door, and she wouldn't be able to see through his cloaking field…

Honor.

Rendash didn't understand her preoccupation with covering herself and keeping him covered, but it wasn't a large leap in logic to guess she wouldn't appreciate him stealing a peek at her naked form. Even if she weren't helping him, he possessed more honor than that.

He finished the first bottle of water and picked up another, draining half of it in a single draught. Why was the air on this world so *dry*? His attention fell to food again; only the small items in smooth, glossy wrappers remained. The items she'd obtained while he snuck into her car.

He lifted one of the packages, gold with red human lettering. A pair of long, thin objects were inside. Curious, he tore the wrapper open, revealing a pair of narrow brown sticks. Though the food looked unappetizing, its smell was intriguing.

Pushing the end of one of the sticks past the wrapper, he lifted it to his mouth and took a bite. To his surprise, it was layered — the soft brown exterior hid some sort of chewy, gooey substance, which rested atop a crunchy center. Each layer combined with the others to create a taste like he'd never experienced. Sweetness burst across his tongue, overwhelming enough that his vision blurred for a fraction of an instant.

Before he was conscious of it, he'd devoured both sticks and had one of the other wrapped items in his hand. He stopped himself from opening it; she'd obtained them for herself, and even though she'd told him to eat, it was not right to finish *everything*. He returned the food to the bed as he ran his tongue over his teeth, sweeping away any lingering traces of sweetness.

Rendash realized only then that the water had been shut off in the bathroom. He gathered the discarded food wrappers and stuffed them into the empty bag for lack of anywhere else to put them before turning toward the bathroom, eagerly awaiting Zoey's emergence.

Why was he so attached to her already? It was a dangerous sort of bond to form, especially given his circumstances. She was helpful for now, but eventually he'd be on his own again, the only aligarii on a hostile planet.

Without an Umen'rak.

The reminder of their deaths stung. He'd carried the weight of their loss throughout his time on Earth, but that loss only became truly painful when he looked toward the future. When he thought about returning home, to Algar, where he would have no companions to share in the joy of his homecoming. Where the peace he'd earned would be diminished by the knowledge that all the rest had died. Rendash hadn't been better or more deserving than any of them, only luckier — though whether the nature of that luck was good or ill could be argued in either direction.

A strange sound came from the bathroom — a loud, high whine, like the blaring of some alien engine.

Rendash's senses shifted into high alert. Suddenly unaware of his aches, pains, and exhaustion, he leapt off the bed and skidded to a halt in front of the bathroom. He nearly tore the door off its hinges as he pulled it open.

Zoey screamed, stumbling back from the doorway to hit the wall behind her. Her eyes met his.

"What the hell, Ren?" she demanded over the loud whining sound.

His eyes darted to the object in her right hand. It looked like some sort of large-barreled blaster; an energy weapon being charged, perhaps?

He slowly extended a hand. "Give me the weapon, Zoey. It will only draw attention to us if you utilize it."

Her delicate brows lowered. "Give you the—" She looked from him to the gun in her hand. "You can't be serious. You think this is a weapon?" She directed it toward her head.

Rendash lunged forward to stop her, catching her arm before she pointed the barrel at her face and harmed herself.

In response — with her expression startlingly flat — she twisted her wrist and aimed the blaster at him. He tensed for impact; he wouldn't be able to form a shield in time.

He was struck by a blast of…warm air? His tension faded, free arms sagging in his ensuing confusion. "I…don't understand."

"It's a hairdryer." Zoey lifted a clump of her long, dark, wet hair — another oddity for him, as female aligarii did not grow crests like males. "I was drying my hair."

"I see." He released her wrist and straightened. "I'll leave you to continue, then."

As he was retreating through the doorway, his eyes flicked over her, and he paused.

Zoey was wearing only one of the cloths that had been hanging in the bathroom. She had it wrapped around her torso, and it revealed much of the pale flesh of her shapely thighs and calves. He followed her legs down to her dainty feet; she had five toes on each foot, and the nails at their ends were colored bright green.

She cleared her throat.

Rendash's gaze slowly trekked along her body as he looked up. She had set down the *hairdryer* and clamped one hand on the cloth over her chest, pinning it in place, while her other hand tugged down on the bottom as though to cover more of her legs.

"Is something wrong?" he asked.

"Oh, for the love of— Get out!"

Still confused — which was slightly better than acknowledging his embarrassment — Rendash backed out of the bathroom. Zoey slammed the door shut the instant he was clear of it. The noise of the hairdryer resumed immediately.

Lowering his hands to his sides, he walked back toward the bed. He was unused to these feelings — confusion, indecision, helplessness. And foolishness; how could he not feel foolish?

He'd walked on so many alien worlds, but he'd never felt so out of place as he did now.

Rendash had no Nes'rak here, no objectives to accomplish save to make his escape. And he had to accomplish that with no Umen'rak, no weapons but those provided by his unreliable nyros, and no understanding of where he was or where he needed to go. To further complicate the situation, everything on this planet — especially the humans — was so strange and contradictory.

Despite the far more advanced technology of his people, he was clueless about the devices and machines these humans possessed, had no idea what their true capabilities were as a species.

Just to add another complication, he was now attracted to a soft little human female.

Sitting on the edge of the bed, he stared blankly at the closed bathroom door. Perhaps it was a subconscious reaction. The notion that this was his final Nes'rak had been subtly laced through all his thoughts. He'd expected to complete the mission, return home, and retire. To take a mate and live in peace for the remainder of his days. When he'd first become an aekhora, retirement had seemed a silly notion. Why would he abandon the rush of battle, why forsake the pride of endangering himself for the protection of his people? But the notion had grown more appealing as time passed and the horrors of war mounted in his memory.

Still, a large part of him had considered the possibility of remaining an aekhora, as was also his right, of renewing his pledge and battling on with honor and courage until he met his inevitable end.

But then he'd crashed on Earth, and even with his nyros

disrupted, he'd felt his surviving Umen'rak. They had been bound by the same ritual, by the same nyros, and had thus shared a bond that few beings — including most aligarii — could ever understand. He'd felt as, one-by-one, their essences faded. As one-by-one they'd died, tearing his heart to pieces and leaving a growing void in its place.

He couldn't fool himself now. Perhaps it was against the teachings of selflessness, but he could not endure being bound to another Umen'rak, could not again bear the pain of feeling those connections breaking. He just wanted to live quietly.

His thoughts were disrupted by the opening bathroom door. He sat up straighter.

Zoey turned the light off and stepped out. She wore a blue top with sleeves that covered her arms and baggy leggings that matched, except for the white dots splattered all over them. Her long, dark hair was loose, flowing down her back and over her shoulders, so different from the coarse, thick crests of male aligarii. Though bathing seemed to have revitalized her — her skin had a more pronounced, if still faint, pink undertone now — her eyes displayed her weariness.

Rendash clenched his teeth. The fingers of his lower hands, which rested upon his knees, flexed involuntarily. At that moment, he wanted nothing more than to touch her skin, her hair, her lips, to lose himself in her softness and warmth. To forget about the troubles weighing upon him, if only for a short while.

It didn't matter that she was of another species; his body had gone so long without companionship, without release. He simply *wanted*.

A brighter flush spread across her cheeks as she met his gaze. She tucked loose strands of hair behind her little, rounded ear.

"Okay, so, um… I'm sorry, but there weren't any rooms with two beds," she said.

He tilted his head, focused more on the subtle change in her skin color than on her words; of what importance was the number of beds?

"Ren? Did you hear me?"

"Yes."

Amongst his people, it would be considered disrespectful to shorten an individual's name, but he took no insult in it. The familiarity with which she said *Ren* was a small comfort — and comfort had been a rare thing in his life.

"So…you're okay with sleeping on the floor, then?" she asked.

"Why would I need to sleep on the floor? This bed seems large enough."

"Okay then. If you want the bed, I'll take the floor." She moved past him and reached for the pillows.

Rendash placed a hand atop the pillows, preventing her from lifting them. "There is room enough on the bed, human. Causing yourself unnecessary discomfort will not benefit our journey."

Zoey frowned and tugged on the pillow. "I'm not sleeping in bed with you!"

"What is your objection?" he asked calmly. "I will be close enough to protect you, should an emergency arise, and it will allow us both the comfort of a decent place to sleep."

Not that the bed seemed particularly comfortable, but it was a massive improvement over the accommodations during his captivity.

She gave the pillow a final, fruitless tug and growled. Something about the sound sent it straight to his cock. He barely suppressed a groan. After seeing her reaction to his nudity, he had no doubt she would refuse to be anywhere near him if she knew how his body was responding to her.

"Fine." She stormed toward the door and switched off the lights.

The room was plunged into complete darkness for a few moments before Rendash's eyes adjusted to the faint light creeping through a tiny gap in the window coverings. He watched Zoey haltingly walk back toward the bed, arms extended in front of her. There was a thump, and she stumbled.

"Fuck!" Placing a hand on the end of the bed, she bent down and released a high-pitched whine.

Rendash pushed himself up and took a step toward her. "Are you all right, Zoey?"

"I'm fine," she gritted. "My suitcase decided to jump out in front of me."

"Is it a living organism, or some sort of artificial intelligence?"

"Of course not," she snapped. Keeping a hand on the bed, she limped around to the open side and tugged back the coverings. When she slipped onto the bed, she lay on her side at the very edge, wrapping the bedding tightly around her body.

Frowning, Rendash peeled back the blankets on his side of the bed and climbed on. The bed creaked and groaned beneath his weight. He froze, worried it would collapse beneath him. Slowly, he eased into a more comfortable position — *relatively* more comfortable, anyway, as whatever supports were inside the bed poked at him regardless of how he lay.

Perhaps the accommodations in the cell had been superior to these.

He eased onto his side, facing her, and inhaled deeply. There was an odd, musty smell to the bedding. It was made bearable only by Zoey's scent, which had strengthened after her shower. It lured him a little closer.

"You already have three-fourths of the bed. Stick to your side," she grumbled.

Rendash stilled again but couldn't help smiling to himself.

He lay for a long while, staring at her through the darkness, watching her little movements as she battled both for her own comfort and to maintain her precarious position at the edge of the bed. Eventually, her breathing slowed and deepened, and her body eased. He waited until he was certain she was asleep before he gently drew her away from the edge.

I am merely ensuring she doesn't fall off while she sleeps, he told himself, *fulfilling my word to keep her safe*.

But he couldn't deny the truth; that thinking was only a poor attempt to justify succumbing to an urge he could neither understand nor resist.

Zoey stirred, sighed, and settled again. He smirked. She possessed the spirit of a warrior, but she slept like the dead.

Rendash wrapped his arms around her and pulled her close. Her soft body molded against his, and her warmth seeped into him, triggering a surge of heat in his blood. He bit the inside of his lip against his body's reaction, against the rush of arousal and desire.

Instinct.

The urge to mate, the *need*, roared through him. He'd never experienced it with such intensity before.

He shifted his hips away from Zoey so his hardening cock wouldn't prod her.

There was something about this human that triggered

instincts far deeper and more powerful than those instilled in him during his training.

Aligarii women were powerful, as strong and capable as any male. They didn't need protection. But something about Zoey awoke Rendash's protective nature in a way he'd never experienced, in a way he'd subconsciously latched onto and could not easily dismiss.

Rendash held Zoey a little tighter, pressed his face into her hair, and closed his eyes.

He breathed in her fragrance. Its blend of familiarity and exoticism settled him; it reminded him of the home he'd left behind and inspired hazy mental images of the home he might one day have.

Chapter Seven

A high-pitched ringing woke Zoey with a jolt. Her body jerked as arms — *Ren's* arms — were yanked from beneath her. She opened her eyes to a flash of morning light, which was promptly snuffed out as the blankets were tossed over her head.

Zoey wrestled the covers and flung them aside to find a very naked Rendash prowling the room. The ringing continued.

"There is an alarm sounding," Rendash said. "We must leave immediately."

Trying hard not to look at Rendash — okay, so she *totally* peeked, and boy did he have huge morning wood! — Zoey swung her legs over the side of the bed and stood up.

The ancient digital clock on the nightstand read 8:23.

Ren stopped at the table near the door and leaned over it. Opening her purse, he reached inside and removed her phone, holding it between his finger and thumb like it was going to either bite his hand off or explode.

"It's vibrating," he said. "What is this device, Zoey?" There was a hardness in his voice she hadn't heard since he'd first made himself known, and it was mirrored in his eyes.

He looked as though he expected a betrayal.

Despite the menace radiating from him, Zoey approached and held her hand out, palm up. "It's my phone."

His eyes shifted from her face to her hand, finally settling on the phone, but he didn't hand it over. "What is a *phone*?"

The phone fell silent, and they both stared at the black screen. Within a few seconds, it started ringing again. It was probably Melissa; Zoey had told her to call in the morning, and Iowa was two hours ahead of Nevada.

When Rendash met her gaze, she thrust her hand forward, snatching the phone from his palm. She spun away from him and accepted the call.

"Melissa?" Zoey asked.

"Zoey! I've been trying to reach you since yesterday! Why haven't you texted me back? Where the hell are you?"

Her stomach lurched; it wasn't Melissa. It was Josh.

"Josh, it's none of your—"

"Are you communicating with someone?" Rendash asked from behind her.

"Who is that?" Josh asked, voice low with suspicion. "Are you with another guy, Zoey? Who the hell is he? He better not have touched you!"

"Yes, it's another guy," Zoey said, looking at Rendash. "We slept together."

"What the fuck, Zo?" Josh's voice blared through the speaker loudly enough that she had to move the phone from her ear. She couldn't deny feeling some petty satisfaction at his reaction.

Before she could respond, one of Rendash's hands shot

forward, and he plucked the phone from her grip with ease. His arm went up high. Her eyes widened.

"Ren, no!" Zoey thrust her arms out to stop him.

But it was too late. His arm snapped back down, and her phone hit the floor with such force that it shattered. As though that weren't enough, he slammed his heel atop it, breaking it, somehow, into at least a hundred *more* pieces.

Zoey stared at the wreckage, stunned. She'd worked her ass off to pay for that phone, and now it was broken beyond repair on this ugly, forty-year-old carpet.

"Why did you *do* that?" Zoey demanded. Anger flared in her gut as she looked up at Ren.

"If it can transmit and receive, it can be tracked." His tone made his displeasure clear, but Zoey didn't give a damn.

She stepped forward, pressed both of her palms to his abdomen, and shoved. Despite what she'd wanted to happen, *she* was the one who moved. She stumbled backward, nearly falling on her ass in the process. That Ren caught her effortlessly with one hand on her arm and kept her upright only further fueled her anger.

She slapped his chest. It stung her palm. "Do you have any idea how many hours I had to work to pay for that?"

"If your people have such devices for communication, it stands to reason that your authorities are capable of monitoring your communications," he said with infuriating calmness. "They will be searching for even the slightest hint of my whereabouts."

"I don't care! That was mine, and you destroyed it!" Zoey yanked on her arm, glaring at him, but his grip remained firm. For some reason, her vision blurred. "You had no right to do that."

"I am sorry, Zoey." He leaned down closer to her, and

slowly, gently, touched the pad of a finger to her cheek, wiping away a bit of moisture. "What is this?"

Zoey only realized she was crying when she looked at the wet spot on his finger. "They're called tears. They happen when people are really happy or sad, or very, very mad, which is what I am right now."

Yeah, let's go with very, very mad. That sounds a lot less pathetic, doesn't it?

"Though it may not be easily done, your *phone* can be replaced. My life cannot."

And now I just feel like a jerk.

She sniffled and looked away from him.

Gently clasping her chin, he guided her face back toward him. "You could have betrayed me. Could have left. But you did not. This is not easy for either of us, it is not convenient, but to keep both of us safe, we cannot leave such things to chance."

"I know, and you're right," she said, meeting his eyes. She wasn't sure which to focus on, so she picked the center pair.

At heart, she knew the phone wasn't the real reason for how she felt — a big part of it, absolutely, but not the primary motivation. It had been Joshua's voice that pushed her over. His lack of shame and guilt. The way he'd spoken like nothing had happened and then had the nerve to get mad at her for being with another guy. In his mind, Zoey was supposed to be grateful that he'd dated her *despite* her size. She was supposed to be the easily replaced one in their relationship, not him.

Zoey didn't doubt he was upset about her potentially spending money on another man, too. Even though she'd been the sole source of income for the last several months, Josh had a knack for viewing it as *his* money. He only called it *theirs* when she pressed him on the matter.

"You are also right," Ren said. "Even if the human method of toiling endlessly to meet basic life needs is foolish and cruel, I should respect your investment in that barbaric system."

The corners of Zoey's lips twitched. "It is pretty barbaric, isn't it?"

"Yes," he replied, and whatever smile he might've offered her faded with his next question. "Who was that male you were speaking to?"

"My boyfriend. Well...ex-boyfriend."

"You will have to explain. I was taught a great many words in your language, but that teaching did not extend to what many things are named."

"Um, a boyfriend — or girlfriend — is someone you're dating. A male friend, but someone you want to get closer to and have a relationship with. If you find the right one, you might end up marrying that person."

"You are speaking of mating?" he asked. "Of sex?"

Zoey's cheeks burned. "Well, yeah. That's usually part of being in a relationship."

"And your relationship with him ended?" His frown deepened. "Was it because he cheated in a game?"

Zoey's brows furrowed. "Cheated in a game? What are you talking about?"

"When you were stopped and questioned, you said your boyfriend was cheating on you."

Realization dawned on her; he'd heard her tell off Officer Asswipe. "Oh... No, it wasn't a game. He cheated on me. He slept... He had sex with other women."

Rendash's eyes darkened, and his muscles tensed. She was suddenly reminded of how close he was, of his hands on her, of his heat and scent.

"But you were mated," he said, as though that made the whole situation too ridiculous to have been real.

Zoey's eyes burned, but she shrugged nonchalantly. "It didn't mean anything to him."

"So he is a human without honor," Ren said, baring his fangs. "Is our current course going to bring us near him?"

Strangely, she wasn't frightened by his show of teeth. His anger wasn't directed at her — at least this time. "No. I left him. I'm driving away from him."

Rendash made a sound that was part grunt, part growl. "Unfortunate. I would have gladly spared some time to teach him the meaning of honor."

Zoey was somewhat grateful Rendash wouldn't be meeting Joshua. As hurt and angry as she felt, she didn't want to have Josh's blood on her hands, even if Rendash only meant to rough him up a little. "I don't think he has an honorable bone in his body. I would rather just forget about him."

"So…" He trailed his palm down her arm and covered her hand with his. Her skin tingled under his touch. "Being beyond his communication is a good thing then, isn't it?"

"Yes, but don't think you're off the hook for destroying my phone," Zoey said, shooting him a glare. "That was still *mine*. I could've just turned it off."

"We cannot risk it," he said, "just as we should not risk remaining here much longer. I sense we've a long way to travel, and we are far too close to where they must be searching."

Zoey looked down at his hand. It was so large compared to hers, the green of his scales accentuated against her pale skin. She dropped her gaze farther, and her eyes widened. She cleared her throat but couldn't look away from the massive erection between his legs.

"Yeah, well, it's probably best not go anywhere until we get you some clothes. Wait…" Her brow furrowed as she tilted her head back to look up into his eyes. "Were your arms around me this morning? Did you pull me closer last night?"

He grinned knowingly. "I cannot say for certain. I was asleep."

Despite everything, Zoey laughed. "Oh, my gosh, you cheeky bastard! What was all that about honor?"

"I was protecting you. You were so close to the edge of the bed, I didn't want you to fall and get hurt."

Zoey snorted and rolled her eyes, but something warm sparked in her chest. "Right. Protecting me from the big, bad, ugly floor." Smiling, she stepped back, and Rendash released her. "While you're battling the carpet, I'm going to get dressed. After that, I'll run out to find you some clothes."

He titled his head and narrowed his eyes. "What do you mean you're going to *run out?*"

She swept her arm across the room. "There are no clothes for you here. To get those, I need to go to a store and buy some."

"We do not need to delay for that. I will bring one of these cloths," he gestured to the crumpled towel on the floor beside the bed, "and cloak myself as necessary."

"Yeah, that's not going to work." She bent down over her suitcase and rummaged through her clothing. "I won't be long."

"I am not comfortable with this. You speak as though this is not like your trip to…to the drink machine, or whatever it was you visited last night."

"Because it's not." She stood and walked past him. Plucking the remote off the nightstand, she turned on the TV and offered him the control. "You'll be fine. No one knows you're here, and we have until eleven to check out of this room. I'll be back long before then. I promise."

She grabbed his wrist, raised his arm, and placed the remote on his palm. He stared down at it dully.

"Don't break that," Zoey said. "It just changes the channels on the TV."

Rendash looked up at her with a scowl. "And who will protect you, if I am not near?"

She arched a brow. "I take care of myself. I haven't had anyone protecting me for a long time."

His scowl shifted into an unhappy frown. "I will accept your word, human. You leave me little other choice."

Zoey smirked. "Doesn't feel so great, huh? And note that I didn't even strangle you or anything."

Chapter Eight

"This muck on my face feels disgusting," Ren grumbled from the back seat.

Zoey pressed her lips together to hold back her laughter. He'd been complaining incessantly since she applied the foundation to his face. It didn't look all that great, especially with it caking in the tiny gaps between his scales, but at least people in passing cars wouldn't see a big green alien if they happened to look his way. His hood and sunglasses helped obscure his appearance.

"It's not like I have tinted windows or anything, so it's kind of necessary." She glanced at him in the rearview mirror and finally lost her struggle, allowing a rogue chuckle to slip out.

"As I said, I could have just remained cloaked during the journey."

"How long can you keep that up?" she asked. "Because something tells me if you could maintain it, you would've kept it going during the entire car ride last night."

He muttered something in a strange language.

"What? What was that? I didn't quite hear you. Did you say you want me to turn around and go back to your friends with the helicopters?"

"No," Rendash snapped. "But nobody will be fooled by this *disguise*. It seems an unnecessary source of discomfort."

"No one will be staring at you long enough to notice that. You look human enough at a passing glance. Just…keep those extra eyes closed, and your extra arms out of sight."

"They are not *extra*."

"By your own standards." She grinned; she could *feel* his eyes burning into the back of her head.

"You are enjoying this?" he asked.

"No, not at all." She pressed her lips together tightly to keep from laughing.

"You told me yesterday that you are a terrible liar, and that was a true admission."

"Okay, so maybe I'm enjoying this just a teeny, tiny bit." Lifting her right hand, she brought her thumb and forefinger close, leaving only a miniscule gap between them. She looked at him in the mirror again and burst into laughter at his expression.

"Insufferable female," he said. "I should have waited for a different vehicle last night."

Zoey pressed her hand to her chest. "That cuts. It really does."

She really *shouldn't* have been enjoying it so much, but she was having more fun than she'd had in a long time. More than she'd ever had with Joshua.

Ren actually listened to her when she talked, and, apart from a few offhand comments, always took what she had to say into consideration. And the trust he'd placed in her thus far… It seemed wrong, given his situation, to *like* feeling needed, but she couldn't deny it. He needed her help, and that made her feel good. He wasn't just trying to mooch off her. Rendash genuinely needed her.

"You like me, admit it," Zoey said.

He grunted, and she felt his leg shift against the back of her seat. The only way he could fit in her car had been to sit with his back to the passenger-side door, legs stretched across the rest of the seat. He'd slouched to mask his true size a little.

"I do," he finally replied, perhaps a bit *too* seriously.

"I think that deserves a prize." She reached into the bag sitting on the passenger seat and pulled out a Twix bar, holding it up. "Don't think I didn't notice that empty wrapper in the motel."

His hand darted around the seat and snatched the candy bar from her grasp.

"It was moderately enjoyable," he said over the sound of crinkling foil.

Zoey returned her hand to the steering wheel. "Oh? Well, in that case, I won't buy anymore."

"You may continue to obtain them, human," he said through a mouthful of chocolate.

"What? *Human*, you say?"

"Are you of some other species? Have I been mistaken this whole time?"

"I suppose not, *alien*."

"I certainly look the part of an alien, after your *makeup*."

Zoey snickered.

"Thank you, Zoey." His words were punctuated by a crunching of cookie.

"You're welcome," she replied.

She drove on in silence, focusing on the busy interstate around her. They were making decent time, but she hoped traffic would thin out and they could move a little faster once they left Vegas behind.

"There are far too many vehicles nearby," Ren said after a while. "The likelihood of someone taking notice of me is great. Are there no other routes we can follow to avoid so many humans?"

"If *someone* hadn't smashed my phone, I'd have easy access to maps that could show us all kinds of routes. As it is, this one is the most direct. I'm *not* going to sit here with the road map I bought open on my lap, trying to puzzle out all the little lines around this city."

"But if I am seen—"

"That's what the disguise is for. I *know* it's not good, and I *know* you're not comfortable, but just relax and keep looking ahead. Most humans avoid eye contact with each other while they're driving, anyway. They have a lot of other stuff they're focused on, and unless you cut them off, they couldn't care less about you."

"Cut them off? Is combat a frequent occurrence when traveling on this planet?"

"No. It's if I were to swerve into another lane in front of someone without leaving much space between our cars."

"How do your people keep track of their words when so many of them have multiple meanings?"

"Our language is ever-changing," she replied, "but I guess it's easier to keep up with when it's all you know. Sort of. I'm still not sure what *on fleek* means."

Gaudy casinos rose over the interstate on either side. The

only other time she'd driven through Vegas had been at night, when she'd first gone to California, while everything was lit up and gorgeous. It seemed to lack a lot of that magic during the day, but it was still a struggle to keep her eyes from wandering.

After Las Vegas, they found themselves in the desert again; it stretched on in all directions, always seeming to lead to distant, blue-tinged mountains. The traffic thinned, but not enough to ease Zoey's nerves. She caught herself on numerous occasions watching for cliché black SUVs in her mirrors, expecting government agents in black suits and ties to leap out, toss a bag over Rendash's head, and wipe her memory with some high-tech gadget.

They took their first rest stop after an hour of driving. Zoey glanced out across the desert as she exited the restroom. There was a certain beauty to it, though she couldn't stand the heat or the blazing sun in such places during most of the year. The December temperatures made it bearable; today was cool and clear, the sort of weather she could appreciate.

To the south, a trio of aircrafts — made into tiny specks by the distance — sped through the sky. Her anxiety increased, constricting her chest.

People are flying around in helicopters all the time. It's nothing.

But what if they were the same ones that had been searching for Ren?

Zoey returned to the car, opened the door, and pulled out her road atlas. She flipped through the pages until she found their current position. Using the little scale ruler and her fingers, she measured the distance back to where she'd found Rendash, pausing to blow warm air into her chilled hands as she turned pages from Nevada to California.

She knew her estimate was inaccurate, but they were somewhere around one hundred and fifty miles from the rest stop where he'd entered her car. Would the search area really have inflated that much since last night? It seemed unlikely, but she couldn't dismiss the nagging fear that they somehow knew Ren was with her. Should she have told the cop she was heading somewhere else?

For the first time, she was glad Ren had destroyed her phone. There were stories on the internet all the time about the government and criminals alike hacking into phones, accessing data, and tracking them via GPS.

"I'm here," Rendash whispered from behind her, making her jump.

"Ugh! I'm never going to get used to that," Zoey whispered back. She stepped away from the car, checked for onlookers, and opened the back door. The brush of his invisible body as he passed her was equal parts eerie and exciting.

The car wobbled as it took his weight. Would her shocks hold up to carrying him for untold miles?

Why the hell am I worried about my shocks, of all things?

She tossed the map onto his lap, shut the door, and hurried to the driver's seat. She started the car and continued their journey.

They crossed into the northwestern corner of Arizona an hour later, where the terrain grew decidedly rockier, and forty more minutes took them over the Utah border.

They stopped twice more — once for gas and food, and once to stretch their legs and pee. Rendash didn't take any chances; he turned invisible before she entered the parking lots, and she slipped her purse into the back seat as an excuse to open the door and let him out without looking like a crazy person.

Each time they stopped, she expected him to return with the foundation scrubbed off his face, but he kept it on despite his complaints.

As they drove on through Utah, the mountainous terrain that had remained in the distance for most of their drive grew steadily closer to the road, much of it dusted with snow. The snow only deepened as they turned onto I-70 and moved up into the mountains. She'd turned the heater on to high as the day progressed. Too soon, the sky began to dim with the approach of evening.

"Is there snow where you're from?" Zoey asked.

"What is snow?"

Zoey swept a hand out to one side, indicating the land spread out around them. "All that white stuff. It falls from the sky in winter."

"Yes. But only in certain places. Much of my home world is too warm for it."

"It doesn't snow where I lived in California, either, but it did a lot in my hometown in the Midwest."

"I have been on a number of planets where it snowed heavily. It…" She saw him shake his head from the corner of her eye, and he said no more.

"It what, Ren?"

He sighed. "It serves as a stark contrast to freshly spilled blood."

"Oh." She was sorry she'd asked, but she couldn't leave it on that disturbing note. "I used to love it when I was little. My dad and I played in it for hours, throwing snowballs, building forts and snowmen. Our fingers and toes would be so cold by the time we went inside that we were sure they'd fall off. Afterwards, he'd make hot cocoa to warm us up." She smiled. "He always gave me extra marshmallows."

"You speak of him with great fondness in your voice."

"Yeah," she said softly.

"Is he who you are traveling to see?"

"No, I was going to stay with a friend." Her fingers tightened on the steering wheel, and her chest ached. It always did, when she thought about her dad. "My father...died when I was ten. He had cancer."

"That is some sort of disease?" Ren asked, voice uncharacteristically gentle.

"Yeah. We didn't catch it soon enough. By the time he was diagnosed, it was too late." Those last few months with her father had been at once the best and worst time of her life. If nothing else, they'd made what little time they had left together count. Now that she was older, she understood how difficult that must've been for him, the willpower he'd demonstrated in giving his daughter happy memories while he was dying.

Tears stung her eyes, but this time she didn't allow them to spill.

Ren was silent. She half-expected him to go off on how primitive humans were, on how his people likely had cured all the diseases that once afflicted them.

"I am sorry for your loss, Zoey," he said. For once, she was glad to have misjudged someone. "What of your mother?"

Zoey shrugged. "Never knew her. She walked out on us when I was two and never looked back. My dad took it hard, though. He loved her. I don't think he ever got over the pain of knowing she didn't care about either of us enough to stick around. But my dad was the best there ever was, and he made sure I knew I was loved." She glanced up at the rearview mirror.

Ren's face was unreadable in the deepening shadows, his eyes masked by his dark sunglasses. "What about your parents?"

"I was born into the *Khorzar*, which is the class of warriors in aligarii society. A soldier from birth. I knew my parents only as my earliest trainers and chose at a young age to be separated from them to continue my training. They were at the ceremony when I received my *nyros* and took great pride in my accomplishment. I have not seen them since."

"That's…kind of sad."

"What's sad about it?"

"It sounds like you never really had time with them. That you immediately went into this training program, or whatever, and that was it. I couldn't imagine not having my dad around as a kid. We did everything together, and if he were alive now, I'd be calling him every day to talk." She blinked back a fresh wave of tears. "I'd give *anything* just to hear his voice again."

"I had a strong bond with my *Umen'rak*. We spent every day together, whether in combat or not. They were my family. Their absence leaves a great emptiness inside me."

"I know I said it already, but I'm sorry, Ren. Blood doesn't always make a family. I'm sorry you lost yours."

A large sign up ahead caught Zoey's attention.

NO BULL

NO SERVICE FOR THE NEXT 110 MILES

SALINA-NEXT EXIT-ALL SERVICES

Zoey looked down at the dash. She had three-quarters of a tank of gas, a bag of beef jerky, chips, a few candy bars, and a small styrofoam cooler filled with bottled water and packaged sandwiches. It was only 5:42pm. They could make the stretch and book a motel in the next town.

"I'm curious about something," Zoey said as they drove past the Salina exit. "You keep saying *nuros*; what is that?"

"*Nyros*," he corrected before falling silent.

She glanced at his face in the mirror. His features seemed drawn in thought, though she couldn't be certain between the caked-on makeup, the sunglasses, and the deepening twilight.

"All of the aligarii receive a lesser form of it, called *uldros*," he finally said. "They are…machines, too small to see with the naked eye, that mend the body from within and prolong life. They allow us to heal quickly and battle disease without additional treatment. But *aekhora*, like me, receive the stronger form, *nyros*, when coming of age. Strong enough that the bonding kills many hopefuls despite spending their youth in training. Those who survive are honored to become *aekhora*, the greatest of our soldiers. Those who do not are honored for giving their lives in the attempt to serve the aligarii in a greater capacity."

"Wow. That sounds amazing and totally scary all at the same time. No wonder you call us primitive. You have tiny machines inside your body." An oncoming car in the far lane flashed its headlights as it passed. Zoey flipped hers on; it didn't seem like it should be so dark already, but she'd been caught up in conversation. "So…what does your *nyros* do? Other than heal you, I mean."

"I should not tell you any of this," he said softly. "I've already revealed too much."

"As curious as I am, I can respect that. Betrayal of your kind to a weak human—"

"It is not because I distrust you, Zoey. The more—"

"Ren, I get it. You don't have to tell me." She cleared her throat. "Besides…it might be for the best. What if one of those guys gets hold of me and tortures me for information? I don't like pain, and as much as I'd like to say I wouldn't break, I can't make that promise."

"That is the only reason I am hesitant, Zoey. The more you know of me, the more valuable you become to them."

"Yep. Totally not looking forward to torture."

Despite her genuine fear that such a scenario would come to pass, Ren's words had softened something inside her. He trusted her. Though he'd chosen her car at the rest area by chance, though he'd known her for less than twenty-four hours, he *trusted* her.

"I gave you my word, on my honor, to keep you safe." The tone of his voice — the dedication, the graveness — drew her eyes back to the mirror. He'd removed the sunglasses and opened his side-eyes to meet her gaze. "I will not fail in that."

Zoey smiled. "I know you won't."

They continued driving in silence, through snowy hills blanketed in shadow now that the sky had darkened to night. Under other circumstances or with different company she would've turned on the radio. Even while she and Joshua were good, their conversations usually died out within fifteen or twenty minutes. With Rendash, she felt no need to fill the silence. It was oddly comforting.

The more she thought about her relationship with Josh, the more she realized how blind she'd been. Sure, he'd often made her laugh, and he had shown her kindness while they were

together, but it was nothing more than she had with Melissa —
a friendship. Zoey could count on one hand the number of
times they'd had real sex during their relationship. All those
rare occasions had been in the dark with little foreplay — at
least on his end — and usually wound up with porn on at some
point.

She'd told herself repeatedly it wasn't about the sex. What
did sex matter when you had someone you could talk to,
someone you could depend on?

But Joshua wasn't dependable. Zoey had worked every day,
taking every extra shift available, and he'd taken her hard-
earned money and spent it on himself — and on other
women, too.

Had she been so desperate for love and companionship that
she'd allowed herself to be used for a year?

Pathetic as it felt, the answer was *yes*. She'd been lonely and
craved some stability in her life, a family...*something*.

Her decision to stay in California, to make it her new beginning, hadn't gone as she'd imagined. She'd worked small jobs,
earning barely enough to pay for her first apartment — a
cramped studio — and rarely had time to socialize. After she'd
been hired on at Bud's, she happened to wait on Joshua's table.
His easy smile and laidback manner had drawn her in, and he
must've seen something in her because they became friends and
things quickly progressed from there...

The warning lights on the dash suddenly lit up and the car
slowed. Zoey frowned and pressed her foot on the gas pedal, but
nothing happened.

Ren grasped the front seats and pulled himself forward.
"What is wrong?"

"I-I don't know." She attempted to turn the steering wheel,

but it barely moved, as though the power steering had failed. "Oh no, oh please, don't do this to me."

She battled the wheel to guide the coasting vehicle onto the shoulder, where it finally came to a stop. Shifting it into park, she shut it off and turned the key to start it again. A high-pitched, electric spinning noise — almost like an amplified remote-control car — was the only sound the engine produced; it refused to turn over.

"No, no, no, no! Damnit!" Zoey smacked the steering wheel. Frustration filled her eyes with tears as she dropped her forehead to the wheel in defeat.

"Zoey?" Rendash asked gently from behind her.

"The car's broken," she said. "Now we're stuck in the middle of nowhere."

"We can walk to the next settlement," he suggested. His practicality almost made her want to scream.

Zoey lifted her head and looked around the car; they were in a snow-dusted desert with barely enough light to see by.

"We're *maybe* halfway to the next town. That'd leave us with fifty miles to walk. Even if I was in the best shape of my life, that'd take me…I don't know, twelve or thirteen *hours*. And this is my *car*! Even if I had my phone to call for a tow, I can't afford to repair it. I have nothing!" She let her head fall back against the seat. "*Nothing.*"

Was this rock bottom, so quick to introduce itself after she'd been having a decent day? It sure felt like it. Funny how rock bottom seemed to get a little lower every time she thought she'd finally hit it.

Can't even win at losing.

"We cannot simply give up and sit here," Rendash said. "This is a complication. A setback. But it is not the end, Zoey."

She closed her eyes. "I know. Just give me a few minutes to wallow in self-pity."

The car rocked gently as Rendash moved. He settled his fingers on her left cheek, and she opened her eyes as he guided her to face him. His features were largely cast in shadow, but his eyes gleamed with faint, reflected light.

"You will not *wallow in self-pity*," he said firmly. "We will take action, no matter how small. While we still breathe, we will carry on. Do you understand?"

"Yes," Zoey sighed. "Okay, okay. No more self-pity."

One day at a time, Zoey. One day at a time.

Though reluctant to break contact with him, Zoey sat up. She pulled the keys out of the ignition, popped the trunk, picked up her purse, and climbed out of the car. The cold sucker-punched her.

"So not dressed for this," she muttered, rubbing her arms through her long sleeves.

The back door opened and closed as she went to the trunk. Ren stood beside her while she rummaged through her suitcases, stuffing as much of her clothing into the larger of the two as she could. She made sure her photo album was in there, too, before she zipped it up.

Setting the bulging suitcase on the ground, she wrapped her blanket around her shoulders and closed the trunk. As much as it hurt to ditch her belongings, Ren's statement after he'd smashed her phone had been true — *stuff* could be replaced. Their lives, not so much.

"Bet you're glad I got you those clothes and boots now, huh?" she asked, looking at Ren.

He glanced down at himself. Even though she'd bought clothes from a big and tall store, they'd had to tear the sides of his shirt and hoodie to allow his lower arms to fit, and his long overcoat hung in a way that made him look too wide. He was also ridiculously tall.

Zoey cracked up laughing when the image of Ren's coat opening to reveal he'd been three waist-high aliens standing on each other's shoulders slipped into her mind.

"Should I be wary of the sudden shift in your demeanor, human?" Ren asked as he took the suitcase from her.

"No wallowing, right?"

"Right," he agreed. He shifted his attention to their surroundings. "Shall we begin?"

Zoey stared at her car. It wasn't new, luxurious, or even *nice*, but it had been the first major purchase of her life, bought with money she'd earned, and it had seen her through a lot over the years. This second cross-country trip had simply proven too much for it.

She closed her eyes and exhaled softly.

One day at a time.

A few cars drove by on either side as they walked — none of which slowed down even slightly — but the road was otherwise deserted. Thanks to the darkness, Ren wasn't likely to be recognized as anything *other*, not that anyone would be encouraged to stop and help when they noticed an obscenely large man walking beside Zoey.

"So, I guess this means you'll need to find someone else to help you?" she asked after a while, keeping her eyes on the ground.

Anxiety soured her stomach. She didn't want Ren to leave her. Even though they'd just met the night before, she liked being around him. Her laughter had come naturally and been more genuine than it had in years. He made her feel...good.

There you go being desperate again, Zoey.

Maybe she *was* desperate for companionship, but this felt different. Was it wrong to like the way Rendash made her feel?

"We will simply need to obtain another means of transportation," he said.

"You say that like it's an easy thing."

Well, maybe it was for him. He just needed to go *poof!* and slip into someone's car.

"Whether it is easy or not, Zoey, it is necessary. We must find a way."

Another car drove by. She watched its taillights vanish around a bend.

"Maybe if you make yourself invisible, I might be able to grab us a ride," Zoey said. "With all the scary stuff on the news nowadays, people aren't likely to stop for hitchhikers, but maybe if they just saw me they'd be more willing to take a chance."

He walked a few more steps, boots crunching over dirt and snow, before responding. "Why are people more willing to assist females on this world?"

"Because we're basically labeled as the weaker sex." She raised a hand and jabbed her finger at him. "Don't you *dare* say anything. I didn't say we *are* weaker — I mean, physically, we usually are, but that's not the point. Anyway, you've made it clear what you think about humans to begin with."

"My species has been physically enhanced over many generations," Rendash said, placing a hand over her jutting finger and gently guiding it back down. "To compare aligarii to humans would be unfair. But I see great strength in you, Zoey."

"Well, I haven't broken yet. I guess that's something." She held out her hand. "Give that here."

He handed her the suitcase with his brow knitted in confusion.

"Do your disappearing act," she said, "and I'll see if I can get us a ride. If it's a truck, you can just climb in the back while I distract them. If it's a car…I don't know, I can ask to put my suitcase in the back seat, and you can climb in as carefully as you can. We'll play it by ear."

"I…am not sure how long I can maintain the cloaking field. I will wait for a vehicle to approach before I activate it," he replied.

"As long as they don't see you."

They continued walking. Zoey's suitcase bumped over rocks, snow, and uneven ground; it definitely wasn't an off-road model. The cold nipped at her cheeks and nose. "Was it something your captors did? To make your cloaking not work right?"

"My control of my *nyros* was disrupted during the crash due to my injuries. That disruption was exacerbated by my captors. They injected me with chemicals regularly, and repeated experimentation and beatings ensured that my body was in a continual state of healing. It left little energy for anything else.

"The connection to my *nyros* only rekindled when they were relocating me. They skipped the injections, and my body had adapted just enough to take advantage, but the chemicals haven't yet left my system entirely. They no longer block my *nyros*, but it takes an immense amount of effort to utilize it."

Zoey frowned. She couldn't imagine all they'd put him through. "I'll do whatever I can, Ren, to stop them from capturing you again."

He met her gaze, and his smile was visible even in the darkness. "I do not doubt your fierceness for a moment, little human."

She snorted. "That's just a nice way of saying you believe I'll try my best, but you doubt my ability." Zoey glanced at him. "That's also the second time you've called me little. There's not much *little* about me."

"By your own standards."

Before she could respond, a flash of light caught in the corner of her eye and she turned to look behind them. "Car!"

But Rendash had already vanished. Zoey turned and walked backward, raising her arm with her thumb out. "Come on, come on." The vehicle drove by without slowing, blasting her with chilled wind. "Damn."

"There will be others," Ren said.

A few more cars passed as time went by, but none of them stopped.

When another vehicle approached, Zoey turned again, only to realize at the last moment how close the car was driving to the shoulder. She jumped back with a shriek. The car sped by less than a foot from where she'd been standing as she stumbled and fell on her backside in the snow.

"Assholes!" she yelled.

Ren materialized and darted forward; somehow, she understood what he meant to do and caught the tail of his coat before he was beyond her reach. His momentum dragged her forward, her butt skidding over dirt and snow.

"Ren, stop!" she shouted, losing her grip on his coat.

He came to a staggering halt and twisted to look back at her. For several moments, he said nothing, and then he seemed to shake whatever mood had overcome him. He kneeled. She reached toward him to accept the hand she expected him to offer, but instead he slipped his upper arms beneath her armpits and lifted her off the ground, depositing her on her feet.

He'd picked her up as though she were as light as a feather. A *feather*!

"Are you all right, Zoey?"

Cheeks heating, Zoey brushed the snow from her chilled backside. "My ass is soaked, but yeah…I'm fine." She eyed him. "No more chasing after cars."

"They nearly struck you!"

"But they didn't, and you shouldn't reveal yourself, remember?"

He scowled, and Zoey had a feeling that there wouldn't have been anyone left to report the sighting if he'd caught the car. It was an unsettling thought.

But if the bastards had hit me, maybe they deserved it.

Ugh, begone dark thoughts!

She bent down and righted her suitcase, which had fallen over. When they continued walking, Rendash positioned himself between Zoey and the highway.

It was a small gesture, but she'd be lying to herself if she didn't admit it warmed her heart.

Headlights from behind had Zoey turning again. She stuck her thumb out, and the vehicle — a big, red pickup truck — slowed as it passed them.

"Yes!" she exclaimed as the truck pulled over on the shoulder ahead. "Remember, climb into the back of the truck as carefully as you can."

The only signs of Rendash's presence were the ghostlike boot prints that appeared in the snow beside her as she hurried toward the waiting truck.

The window rolled down when Zoey approached the passenger-side door.

"Need a lift?" a man asked from inside.

Zoey looked into the dark cab. The faint light from the dashboard bathed the man's face in a soft green glow. Though it was difficult to tell because of his facial hair, he looked to be in his late thirties. He had short-cropped blonde hair and a neatly trimmed beard. Heat pulsed from inside, which explained why he wore a t-shirt, one muscled arm draped over a fold-down armrest beside him. His jacket lay on the passenger seat.

"If you don't mind," she replied. "I have a suitcase."

"Toss it in back and hop in." He smiled, flashing straight teeth.

Zoey moved to the back of the truck. "He's going to give us a ride," she whispered. "Climb in as I toss my bag in."

She lifted her bag over the edge of the bed and dropped it in. The rear end of the truck rocked slightly, and she heard the gentle scrape of cloth as Rendash settled himself in.

"Be safe, little human," he whispered.

Zoey untied the blanket from her shoulders and dropped it into the back of the truck. "I will be. It shouldn't take more than an hour to reach the next town. We'll find a room there, okay?"

The blanket moved and then faded away, like it had been erased from existence. "An acceptable plan. I will await our arrival in the next town."

"You need help back there?" the man called.

Zoey hurried back to the cab, opened the door, and lifted herself in. He'd removed his jacket from the seat. "Thank you for this."

"No problem," he replied. "Heading the same way, right? Toward Green River?"

"Yeah," Zoey said, holding her hands up to the sweet, hot air blowing from the vents. The window beside her rolled up.

"What's your name?" the man asked as he eased back onto the highway.

"Zoey. Yours?"

He turned his head and smiled at her. "Matt." He slouched slightly, leaning on the armrest with his right arm while he kept his left hand draped over the top of the wheel. "Green River your final stop?"

"Just passing through," Zoey replied. She glanced in the side mirror, knowing the angle would be all wrong but longing for a glimpse of Ren anyway.

"Was that your car back there on the side of the road?"

"Yeah. All the power just suddenly cut out, and it wouldn't start."

"Sounds like it might be a timing belt."

Zoey arched a brow. "You a mechanic?"

"Nah. I know just enough to get me in trouble."

Zoey chuckled. "Trouble? Sounds more like you'd be useful in that kind of situation."

"Knowing what's broken isn't the same as knowing how to fix it." His smile hadn't faded, hadn't changed at all.

They drove in silence for a time before his hand moved to the radio on the dash. "Music?"

"Sure."

"What do you like?"

"I'm good with anything."

He nodded, pressed a button, and the radio lit up. He flipped through the stations, stopping on the *Golden Oldies*. The same kind of music Bud played in his diner to *set the atmosphere*.

"This good?" he asked.

Zoey smiled. "Yeah."

He could've put anything on without objection from her; she

was just grateful to be out of the cold and moving forward. They'd be in Green River soon, and from there… Well, they'd figure something out. Rendash had made no indication that he intended to leave her, but that didn't mean he wouldn't. She couldn't blame him if he moved on alone.

Matt tapped his fingers on the steering wheel as he sang along with the music under his breath, casting occasional smiles in Zoey's direction. She offered one more smile of her own before turning her head to look out the window and watch the dark landscape pass.

The road was fairly smooth, so at least Rendash wouldn't get tossed around, but it was likely freezing back there. She wished they'd had some other choice.

"So where did you say you were going?" Matt asked.

"Green River," Zoey replied.

"I mean after that."

Zoey looked at him. "Des Moines."

"Long way. What's in Des Moines?"

"A friend. She invited me to live with her as her roommate."

"Does she know about your car?"

Zoey frowned. That was a strange question. "Yeah. I let her know my trip would be a little delayed. I already have a rental car set up in Green River."

"Really?" His tone implied surprise. "I've been through Green River a lot. Never saw any rental places."

"They were…offering a pickup service because of the circumstances."

"Tow truck driver probably would've given you a ride into town. Decided not to wait?"

"It's late," she said, "so I figured I'd get a room for the night and deal with it tomorrow. The car is likely totaled if you're right about the timing belt. Wouldn't be worth fixing."

"Most likely not." He cleared his throat. "Anyone else waiting for you in Des Moines? Parents? Siblings?" He glanced at her. "A boyfriend?"

"My husband. He just got out of the military."

"So why are you moving in with your roommate?"

Ah, fuck, I'm so bad at this.

Zoey rubbed her palms against her thighs. "He's moving in with us, too. Just until we get settled and find a place of our own."

"He didn't get you a ring?"

"What?"

Matt gestured toward her hand.

"Oh." She pulled her left hand back and covered it with the other. "I lost it."

"That sucks," he said with an oddly flat tone.

His questions stopped there.

Maybe it was just her imagination causing the strange, tight feeling in her chest. Matt was probably just trying to be friendly; picking up a hitchhiker under any circumstances had to be awkward, right? Still, if not for Ren, Zoey would've asked to be let out right here. The red flags were steadily mounting in her mind, and Green River couldn't be much farther.

But they needed to keep moving. She could suffer through some probing, uncomfortable conversation for Rendash's sake.

The truck slowed, and Matt turned off the highway. The headlights shone on an overgrown dirt path.

Heat tingled over Zoey's skin. Her back stiffened, and she twisted to look back at the interstate. "What are you doing?"

"I need to take a piss. How about you?"

Something about the way he'd asked that made her stomach twist into a knot. "Um, no. I'm good."

Matt kept driving, bouncing along the dirt road through scrubby vegetation until it finally dipped behind a small rise. When Zoey looked back again, the interstate was out of sight.

"Why are we so far off the road?" she asked, dropping her gaze to search for Ren in the pickup's bed. Knowing he was there, even if she couldn't see him, calmed her a bit, but her heart pounded with unease.

"Relax." Matt unbuckled his seatbelt and turned his body toward her. "Just want some privacy."

Zoey released her seatbelt and placed her hand on the door handle. "Okay. I'll stretch my legs while you…do your business." When she tugged on it, the door didn't open. With her other hand, she pulled the lock up, but the door still didn't budge. "It's stuck."

"I know."

She faced him again.

He grinned and slowly lifted the center armrest, sliding over the seat toward her. "It's nothing personal, okay? I just couldn't pass up the opportunity."

"W-What opportunity?" Her breath was suddenly ragged, struggling through a constricted throat.

"A young woman, all by herself, out here?" He chuckled and settled his hand on her knee, slowly moving it up her thigh.

Zoey smacked it away. "Don't touch me."

"You know you want me, too. Why else would a woman be out here by herself? You hoping to fulfill some fantasy? I can help with that." He sat back and dropped both hands to his pants, opening the fly and pulling out his junk. His dick was an angry red, already fully erect. He gave it a stroke before reaching for her again.

Zoey swung to bat his hand aside, but he was fast, grabbing hold of her wrist and tugging her closer. She slapped at him and lifted her leg to kick him, pressing her foot into his gut and pushing. He was nothing if not strong.

"I said don't touch me!" she yelled.

Balling her fist, she punched him in the temple.

Matt winced and snapped back, shaking his head. Within seconds, he shook off the blow, glaring at her. "I was going to take it easy on you, but I guess you want it rough. Fine. I can play rough."

He backhanded her.

The impact knocked her backward, disorienting her just long enough for him to shove her down onto the seat. He settled his weight atop her. She struggled as he attempted to grab her wrists.

"Hold still, damnit!" Matt snapped.

"Ren!" Zoey screamed.

Before the sound had fully left her mouth, the sliding panels on the back window exploded inward, knocked off their tracks by an immense force. Matt shouted in shock, but his voice was cut off when a huge arm snaked around his throat.

Zoey threw up her arms to shield herself from Matt's flailing limbs as Ren pulled him backward. The man's grunts and heavy, stilted breathing only grew in desperation as his shoulders caught on the window. Zoey scrambled aside, bracing her back against the door, and slammed her foot into Matt's abdomen, chest, and groin.

Once Ren forced Matt's shoulders through the opening in the back window, the struggle was over. The man's legs swung as he was dragged into the bed of the pickup, forcing Zoey to duck for cover. The truck rocked wildly with a series of bangs and bumps. Matt's cries were renewed, but they faded — as though with increasing distance — once the rocking ceased. Soon, the only sound in the cab was the crooning voice of Dean Martin.

She sat up and twisted to see Rendash on the ground outside the passenger door, hauling a still-struggling Matt toward the brush. Their forms vanished as they left the glow of the head-lights. A shiver crept up Zoey's spine; she told herself it was just the cold air coming in through the gap in the back window.

A short series of agonized, terrified screams rose over the music, and then fell silent.

Zoey pressed her trembling hands onto her thighs as minutes crept by.

Unable to wait any longer, she crawled over the seat and opened the driver-side door. She climbed out of the cab and steadied herself with a hand on the hood as she walked around to the front, the headlights making her shadow impossibly long. She barely registered the cold as she scanned the darkness.

"Ren?" she called.

Only the wailing of distant wind answered her. She folded her arms across her chest, tucking her hands beneath them, and strained to see anything outside the beams of the headlights.

The faint crunching of footsteps in the snow called her attention to the right. A large, shadowy figure came into view, cast in a soft-but-menacing glow at the farthest edge of the light. Zoey took a step backward.

The figure raised two hands — both on the right side of its body. "It's me."

"Rendash!" Relief washed through Zoey. Her legs wobbled, threatening to give out, but she remained upright. "Is he…?"

"I left his remains farther out in the wasteland, hidden in the vegetation. It should be some time before he is discovered."

Remains. She knew the word was basically interchangeable with *body* or *corpse*, but it made it sound like there were only pieces left of the man. Zoey's gut churned. The bastard had deserved it, but that didn't mean she wanted to imagine what Ren had done to him.

Rendash moved closer, entering the light fully. All four of his gleaming eyes focused on her as he angled his head down. "Are you all right, Zoey?"

"Yeah. No. I…" She shuddered. "I'll be fine."

Frowning, Ren placed a hand on her shoulder. "He cannot harm you now."

Zoey raised a hand and curled her fingers around his forearm. "Thank you."

A faint trembling ran through his arm, and she heard it echoed in his exhalations. She was more inclined to think of it as fury rather than nerves.

"We have a vehicle, now," he said after a while, voice strained. "We should make use of it before it gets much later."

She nodded and glanced toward the truck. It'd be best if she didn't reflect upon the circumstances that had brought it into their possession. God, she'd been stupid for so long. And tonight…

Zoey had been well aware of the dangers of hitchhiking, the dangers of being a woman alone after dark, and *of course* those dangers would coalesce into reality the one damned time she was in such a situation.

You keep swinging, life, and you're banging me up pretty good. But you know what? I'm still on my damn feet.

"Let's go," she said.

Ren's hand didn't fall away when she moved to walk around the truck. She glanced at him, and he guided her to turn toward him again. Taking gentle hold of her wrists, he spread her arms to either side. His eyes — and his lower hands — ran over her carefully. His touch sent a thrill along her limbs that shot straight to her core. It was the most inappropriate time to feel aroused — she'd been assaulted, and a man had been killed! — but she had no control of her body's reaction. She was aware of every point of contact between them.

"What are you doing?" she asked breathlessly.

"Making sure you are unharmed." That tremor remained in his voice, faint but audible.

He frowned as one of his fingers brushed over the spot on her cheek where she'd been struck.

"I'm fine. Really. I hit him more than he hit me."

His hands didn't still as he turned her around to continue his examination from behind. He moved close to her, so close that she felt the warmth of his breath on her hair as he slid his palms down to her hips.

Her breath quickened. "Ren?"

His only acknowledgement that she'd spoken was a soft, questioning grunt. His upper hands slid to her ribs, fingers curled just beneath her breasts, while his lower hands dipped to her outer thighs.

Zoey had a powerful urge to press herself against his hard body. Her sex clenched, and heat pooled between her thighs. "Ren…we…we should get going."

Finally, his hands stilled, though they lingered on her. "Yes. We should. It…is cold out here." His arms fell away, and he stepped back. Zoey shivered with the loss of his warmth.

The passenger door opened without issue from the outside,

and the truck dipped to one side as Ren entered. Zoey walked around to the driver's seat and climbed in; it was a small wonder she was able to, considering her limbs felt like jelly.

Helping Ren force the window panels back into place to block the cold offered her a few minutes of distraction, but reality soon reasserted itself.

Dean Martin had given way to Buddy Holly. Zoey turned off the radio; her appetite for music had fled.

Her appetite for Ren, however, still raged through her blood.

Chapter Nine

Zoey stepped into the motel room, leaving the door open for Rendash, who was still cloaked, to enter behind her. He brushed a finger over her arm as he passed to signal that he'd come in. Her lips parted with a soft inhalation before she shut the door, locked it, and drew the curtains closed to block the window that looked out over the vehicle storage lot.

Rendash released his cloaking field gratefully. Despite his recent experiences, he hadn't realized how difficult the field would be to maintain. His nyros were behaving like a muscle that had atrophied after a long period of disuse. It seemed to be improving with time, but at much too slow a rate. Without desperation to fuel him, his nyros was unreliable at best.

He lifted Zoey's suitcase onto the bed and turned to face her.

"Thank you," she murmured, stepping close and resting her hand atop it.

Rendash frowned; her behavior was strange, but his experience with humans was too narrow to tell whether this was normal or not. "I'm going to clean up, Zoey. I will be out shortly."

She nodded without looking at him.

After lingering near her briefly, Rendash walked into the bathroom, closed the door, and leaned over the sink to scrub the makeup off his scales with one of the folded cloths hanging nearby. The substance hadn't been comfortable from the beginning, but it had grown increasingly itchy and dry as the day wore on. He understood the necessity and would do his best to avoid complaint when she inevitably wanted to apply more makeup on him the next day, but he couldn't get it off quickly enough now.

Once his face was clean, he divested himself of his human garb and entered the shower, making the water as hot as it would go. After washing, drying, and relieving himself, he wrapped a large cloth — a *towel*, as Zoey had called it — around his waist and exited the bathroom.

He frowned. Zoey was sitting on the inside edge of the farthest bed, staring blankly at the floor.

Rendash crossed the distance between them and sat across from her on the other bed. "You've barely said a word since we entered the truck, Zoey. Speak to me now."

She looked up at him and attempted a smile. Her blue-gray eyes shimmered, standing out in sharp contrast to her dark brown hair. "Guess my mind has been preoccupied."

"With what?"

Her jaw muscles ticked. "I've made a lot of stupid choices in life, but tonight… I think that was the dumbest yet. I should have just listened to you. We could have walked."

"No one could have guessed what he was going to attempt."

"I should have known. I did know!" Zoey hung her head,

closed her eyes, and pressed the heels of her hands to her eyelids. "I just keep thinking about what would have happened if you hadn't been there."

Detachment.

But that wouldn't work now, would it? He'd been unable to detach himself from the details of the situation, had been unable to focus on the simple task at hand: *protect Zoey.* All that should have entailed was the assessment and elimination of threats.

Killing the male human should've been quick and efficient, should've been clean.

The truck's unexpected stop had confused Rendash. He'd guessed by the roughness of the ride that they'd left the main road, but there was so much unknown to him about humans and their planet that he couldn't risk alerting the driver by moving. The human voices had been muffled by the enclosed cab of the vehicle, and the music had been just loud enough to distort their words.

Even now, Rendash cursed himself for taking so long to respond.

By the time he'd dragged the struggling male into the brush, rage had overpowered all the tenets of his training but one — *instinct.* Rendash's instinct had been to tear the human apart for daring to lay hands on *his* Zoey. His nyros had responded to that rage by pouring excess strength into his limbs. Even after the kill had been made, Rendash had continued his assault with two thrumming vrahsks.

Though it had been far from painless, the human's death had been too swift for Rendash's liking. Zoey's fearful scream had repeated in Rendash's head over and over — it continued even now, when he stilled his mind and pushed aside his other thoughts.

He leaned forward and clasped her wrists in his lower hands, guiding her arms down before cupping her cheeks with his free hands.

"All that we have is what *did* happen, Zoey. Difficult as it may be, we must detach ourselves from what might have been and accept what is. Whatever dark thoughts you might have are a product only of your imaginings and not reality. You are safe."

When she raised her arms, he released his hold. She covered his upper hands with her own, pressing them against her warm cheeks. Then she slid her palms slowly along his arms, over his shoulders, and up his neck to cradle his face. She locked her eyes with his. "Thank you, Ren."

Rendash explored the depths of her alluring, alien eyes. He longed to feel her soft hands elsewhere on his body. Longed to touch *her* elsewhere, without the barrier of her clothing to separate them.

She lowered her hands and stood, stepping out of his reach. "I'm going to take a shower."

After gathering clothes from the open suitcase on her bed, she walked to the TV, grabbed the remote, and tossed it to him. "I'll order us some food when I get out. The lady at the front desk said there are a few pizza places nearby that deliver."

"I do not know what that is, but I trust it will be adequate."

Zoey shook her head, offering a fleeting glimpse of her smile in profile as she stepped into the bathroom. The door closed, and soon after, the shower came on.

Rendash picked up the remote. He pressed the red button at the top — the only one he knew, after his experience at the last place they'd slept — to turn the TV on, but that exhausted the full extent of his knowledge. All the symbols on the remote were alien to him. Stantz's scientists had taught Rendash to speak their language, not to read it.

He was greeted by a blank blue screen. Where were the moving images? The TV at their prior shelter had operated like a primitive holographic projector, displaying moving images of humans, strange animals, and clusters of symbols.

He pressed a finger down on one of the buttons at random. A line divided up into little bars appeared at the bottom of the screen. When he pressed the button down again, several of the bars disappeared. He pushed another button, and the screen displayed four human symbols accompanied by a triangle pointing to the right.

Two humans appeared on the TV, a male and a female. The female was seated on a chair covered in a pale brown fabric. The male was standing nearby, facing away from her, dressed in some sort of uniform vaguely reminiscent of Stantz's soldiers. Perhaps he was merely a differently specialized warrior?

"I am trying to investigate these crimes, Misses Haversnatch," the male said with an oddly stilted cadence. "If you don't cooperate, I'll have to book you for obstruction."

The female stood and approached the man with an exaggerated sway in her hips, grasping her shirt. "Does this look like obstruction to you, Officer Cumswell?"

Just as Rendash was looking for another button to press, the woman ripped open her shirt, and her large breasts sprang free. Rendash perked, back straightening and eyes widening. He'd never seen anything like them before. Was that what Zoey looked like beneath *her* shirt?

The male, Officer Cumswell, seemed to debate with himself.

"I can't have intimate relations with a person of interest in my investigation."

The woman dropped to her knees in front of the male. "Maybe I can change your mind." She tore open the male's pants as easily as she had her shirt. His erection jutted toward her. "Looks like your interest is more than professional."

Officer Cumswell moaned as the woman gripped his cock and took it into her mouth.

Rendash moved to the front edge of the bed and leaned forward to watch the bizarre mating ritual, resting his hands on his knees. The image zoomed in on the woman's mouth as she slid her lips back and forth along the male's shaft.

Their mating progressed rapidly through various positions and phases until they were both naked, slamming their bodies together with flesh slapping. Though the sounds they made seemed pained at times, neither of them slowed. They appeared to be enjoying themselves. Rendash was particularly interested in the male using his mouth on the female's genitals, which were so open and welcoming compared to those of female aligarii. The man's attentions seemed to drive her mad; her face contorted with overwhelming pleasure.

Immediately, Zoey's face came to mind. What did her body look like without coverings? What sounds would she make if it was Rendash's mouth between her thighs? What expression would she wear if she were filled with such passion and lust?

His cock stiffened with want at the mere thought of her in such positions. He dropped a hand to grasp his erection through the towel, hoping to alleviate some of the desirous ache. His own touch only strengthened his need.

He closed his eyes and stroked his shaft. Pleasure coursed through him, forcing him to grit his teeth and tighten his hold.

Control.

His gaze drifted toward the bathroom. If he couldn't detach himself from his rapidly growing feelings for Zoey, how could he expect to control his want for her?

He looked at the screen again. The couple had changed positions; the woman was on her hands and knees with the male thrusting into her from behind.

Human fornication was simultaneously confusing and fascinating. He was unfamiliar with their reproductive process, but surely it didn't take *this* long for them to complete their coupling. This mating... This looked as though it were purely for enjoyment.

The concept was foreign to Rendash. He was unsure about greater aligarii society, but amongst the Khorzar, sex served only two purposes — a quick means of release for those in the field or a fulfillment of reproductive duty for those who had been cleared to mate. Female aligarii could not reach their peak until the male had blossomed, meaning it was best for those involved to reach the point of mutual fulfillment as fast as possible.

What pleasure was involved was brief and never served as the primary focus. For those who were not mated, it was only a release of built-up desires to allow a clearer path to control.

And they certainly didn't use their mouths — at least not in his experience.

The bathroom door opened, and Zoey stepped out.

"I hope you like pepperoni be...cause..." Her wide eyes fell upon him, shifted to the hand grasping his cock, and then swung to the TV. "What the hell!"

"What is wrong?" Rendash stood and turned to face her. The towel around his hips fell to the floor.

Zoey stared at him — or, more specifically, his groin — with lips parted and cheeks reddening.

Rendash imagined his cock slipping past those lips and groaned.

"Oh, my God." Zoey's pupils dilated, and her breath quickened. "You…you're sitting here, doing this, while I was…" She looked at the TV again, silently watching. Finally, she snatched up the remote and turned off the screen.

"I only turned it on. I did not know how to change the image," he said, dipping into a crouch only long enough to snatch up his fallen towel and replace it. Though he felt no shame, he'd clearly made her uncomfortable. "I am sorry if I have violated your human customs again."

She walked to the TV and pressed a button on the small device beneath it. A tray slid out of its front with a faint mechanical whine. Zoey plucked out a round, thin disc from within. "Guess someone forgot to take their porn with them," she muttered, dropping the disc into a plastic bin on the floor nearby.

As she moved past him to sit on the other bed, he couldn't help but look at her differently; he couldn't ignore the curves he'd felt beneath his palms when he'd touched her earlier, couldn't forget how it had felt to hold her the night before. The hunger that had already been growing in him was intensified now; he *wanted* her.

"Are you all right, Zoey?"

"I'm fine." Leaning over the small table between the beds, she picked up a device attached to a spiral cord and held it to her ear.

"Remember, you are a poor liar," he said.

"I just really don't want to talk about catching you jerking off to porn, okay?"

He turned his head to glance at the plastic bin in which she'd deposited the disc. "I...don't understand what you mean."

Zoey looked at him with her eyebrows low. "Porn! The people having sex on the TV!" She pressed her lips together and turned her face away, glaring at the device in her hand. "A lot of men like to get off on it."

The displeasure in her voice was underscored by traces of anger, but he got the sense that there was more she wasn't saying. "I was not...getting off on it."

"I'm sorry, okay?" she said quickly. "I shouldn't have acted that way, much less make you feel...ashamed about it."

"I do not feel shame over it. Only confusion." He moved to sit on the bed opposite her. "You seem to have taken personal issue over the matter."

Anger flashed in her eyes when she looked at him, but it quickly died. She sighed. "I used to catch Joshua watching it. A lot."

Rendash leaned forward, resting his lower elbows on his thighs. "Help me understand why that is a problem. I have encountered nothing like this in my time."

Zoey lowered the device to its cradle and ran a hand through her hair. The action sent a burst of fragrance toward him, which he greedily inhaled.

"Humans...really enjoy sex. The gratification of it. That's what porn thrives on, giving people something to get excited about to help them to that point of climax. It's meant to arouse. And human men are very visual. Let's just say...I discovered just how important that was."

He frowned. "You seem hesitant to continue, but you've left me only with more questions."

"It's because I'm fat!" she snapped. "I'm not appealing. Josh watched porn because he was dissatisfied by my appearance. *Those* were the women he wanted. Not me. He turned it on every time we were…intimate. He said it was to *set the mood*. I was just too dumb, or too desperate, to acknowledge what he really meant." Her bottom lip trembled.

Rendash reached forward, and, before she could react, gathered her in his arms and pulled her into his lap.

"W-what are you doing?" she asked, body stiffening.

He brushed some of her still-damp hair out of her face. "This Josh must be a blind fool to want other females over you."

She tilted her head back and looked up at him. "What?"

"Josh is a blind fool." He turned his hand and trailed his knuckles over the soft skin of her cheek. She shivered. "If he could not see your appeal, he does not deserve to have you as a mate."

Zoey's breath hitched as she stared up at him. There was another scent coming from her. He'd smelled it before on a couple other occasions, but holding her in his arms now, so close to him, it was strengthened, heightening his awareness of her. It engaged those instincts — the deep, primal ones — over which he had little control.

He was hyperaware of every spot where their bodies were touching — her shoulder pressed against his chest, his hands on her ribcage just beneath her full breast, on her waist, and on her upper thigh. Most of all, her rounded backside upon his hardened cock.

"I…should call the pizza place before it gets too late," Zoey said. "A lot of, uh… A lot of places close early. In small towns… like this one."

Despite her words, she was subtly leaning closer to him, her pink lips parted. Rendash's heart pounded.

Control. Detachment.

He clenched his jaw and drew in a deep breath, filling his lungs until it hurt. He released the air slowly, closing his eyes. He'd never felt the need to possess anything like he longed to possess Zoey now.

"Warm food would be welcome," he finally said, gently sliding her off his lap and depositing her on her feet. It took an extra surge of willpower to remove his hands from her. "The sooner we eat and rest, the sooner we can continue on our way."

"Right." Zoey remained in place, staring at him; he didn't know if it was a trick of his mind, but she seemed to sway toward him infinitesimally before stepping back.

She picked up the corded handset again and pressed a series of buttons on its cradle. He distantly heard another voice coming through the device before Zoey responded.

Rendash tensed, barely stopping himself from snatching the device out of her hand.

Ordering food wouldn't reveal to anyone that Rendash was with Zoey.

She replaced the device on the cradle after a brief conversation and smiled at him. "Food should be here soon. Let's see if there's anything decent to watch while we wait." Retrieving the remote from where she'd dropped it, she jumped onto the bed and bunched up the pillows against the wall, sitting with her back against them. She looked at Rendash expectantly and patted the spot next to her.

The bed wobbled, creaked, and groaned as he joined her.

Zoey manipulated the remote, switching through various image feeds on the screen.

"Oh, I love this movie!" She grinned up at him. "You don't know what funny is until you've watched *Ace Ventura: When Nature Calls.*"

Intrigued by her excitement, Rendash shifted his attention to the TV. He couldn't pretend to understand what was going on, couldn't tell whether the humans on the screen were real or somehow exaggerated, and didn't understand what Zoey was laughing at much of the time, but her laughter was infectious. After a short while, he realized that it couldn't be real — the entertainment seemed to be in the absurdity of the characters and situations.

There was a knock on the door. Rendash sat up, fully alert, and prepared to summon an energy blade. He was swinging his legs out of bed when Zoey settled a hand on his shoulder, halting him.

"It's the pizza. Just cloak yourself for a minute," she said, slipping off the bed. "Just a sec!" she called to the person on the other side of the door as she dug some of her *money* out of her purse.

Rendash stood and pressed himself to the wall beside the window. His cloaking field sputtered into place, producing undulating waves of heat in his chest which rose to near-painful levels before dropping again. He gritted his teeth against the discomfort and turned his head to watch Zoey open the door.

"Hello," she said, smiling. The person on the other side muttered something, and she nodded, offering the money in her hand. "Here you go. I don't need change."

The unseen human took the money, and Zoey accepted a wide, flat box in exchange. She stepped back and closed the door, clicking the locks into place. Placing the box on the bed, she leaned over it and opened the lid. Rendash released the cloaking field — experiencing no small degree of relief — and walked over to inspect the source of the strange smell that was fast spreading through the air.

Inside the box lay a circular food. It was brown around its outside, pale orange on top, and had reddish circles all over it.

Zoey lifted a wedge-shaped piece and held it up to him. "Here. Taste this."

He accepted it skeptically. The orange part of the pizza was gooey and stringy, and he couldn't understand why anyone would consider it appetizing.

"Don't you curl your lip like that," Zoey laughed. "Just try it!"

Frowning, he lifted the food to his mouth and took a small bite. The orange topping stretched as he pulled the piece away, and only broke when he extended his arm. He drew the dangling strings into his mouth with his tongue and dropped his gaze as he carefully chewed.

"What is this part called?" he asked, poking one of the orange tendrils with a finger.

"Cheese." She tilted her head and continued to watch him. "Do you like it?"

He took another bite, much larger than his first. The red circles — some sort of meat, he guessed — added a kick of savory spice. "It's good." He bit off another piece before finishing his current mouthful.

Zoey chuckled and took a piece of her own from the box. "Mission complete. Now come sit down so we can finish the movie."

Rendash settled down beside her, eating more pizza as they

watched the movie. His laughter came more easily now; even when he didn't understand the humor, her reactions provided him enjoyment.

As time passed, he found himself reflecting upon the strangeness of their time together. The bonds an aekhora formed with his Umen'rak were supposed to be the deepest an aligarii could form. Even the mating bond he'd earned the right to forge once his duty was complete couldn't compare. The members of an Umen'rak were brothers and sisters, comrades, tied together on a level that superseded friendship and family.

But after only a few days, he felt a bond growing between himself and Zoey — similar in its strength, but quite different in its nature and boundless in its potential depth. Rendash had relied upon his Umen'rak to support him through moments of pain and weakness, though he'd always done his best to avoid such moments. To avoid burdening the individuals who relied upon him with his own inadequacy.

With Zoey, he didn't feel the need to hide.

After the pizza was gone — Zoey had insisted she was done after two pieces, leaving the rest to Rendash — she scooted closer and laid her head on his shoulder. He slipped his arms around her and held her. It was a simple form of contact, but it was powerful; they were here, *together*. Two individuals united in a common purpose: escape. It didn't matter what they were escaping from, only that they could rely on each other on the journey.

Rendash would never have guessed they'd grow so at ease with one another, so dependent upon one another, especially in so short a time. But they had, and he accepted it gladly.

When the movie was over, Zoey turned off the TV and pulled away from him. She closed the pizza box and placed it on the floor beside the plastic waste bin before walking to the bathroom, where she paused in the doorway and looked back at him.

"Come here, Ren."

Unable to ignore the fluttering, foolish sense of anticipation that sparked in his chest, he stood up and went to join her inside the bathroom.

She opened a small bag on the sink and produced two small brushes with long handles from within. "I brought my spare toothbrush just in case. Guess it'll come in handy. Hold this."

After handing him one of the brushes, she withdrew a small tube from the bag, removed the cap, and held the opening over bristles of his brush. A white substance oozed out when she squeezed, and she left a bit of it on each brush.

He raised the brush and sniffed at the pasty goo. "What is this for?"

"For cleaning your teeth."

"I see. We perform similar activities on my planet."

"To clean teeth!" she said, raising her brush high before slipping it into her mouth. She grinned at him as she scrubbed.

Rendash couldn't help but smile back at her as he cleaned his teeth.

Though it was unlike anything he'd ever encountered — or, perhaps, *because* it was unlike anything he'd ever encountered — he found her lively spirit endearing. He'd meant what he said; Josh was a blind fool. Zoey was more than any one man deserved.

But Rendash was no man. He was an aekhora who'd earned the right to choose a mate.

I want Zoey.

The thought was startling, despite how fast his feelings for her had been evolving. It didn't seem like the sort of choice that could be made in so short a time, but it was the truth of his heart. He wanted her.

He told himself it was merely lust. His attraction to her was an attraction to the exotic, no more than an overextension of his curiosity. He'd seen only humans during his long captivity, and it was natural that he'd developed a fascination with them, regardless of how he'd been treated.

Perhaps I am not any better at lying than Zoey is.

When they finished brushing their teeth, they returned to the main room. Zoey moved to the bed farthest from the window, pulled back the covers, and climbed in. Rendash swallowed his desire and stopped at the empty bed. There was no excuse to sleep with her tonight, and he wasn't sure if he could trust himself this time.

He eased down and covered himself with the bedding. Zoey reached for the light on the stand between the two beds and clicked it off, plunging the room into darkness.

"Goodnight, Ren," she said.

"Goodnight, Zoey."

Rendash shifted, causing the bed's supports to creak as he sought a more comfortable position. Time passed, and he moved again and again; no matter how he lay, something seemed to be missing.

In the back of his mind, he knew Zoey was the missing piece. His dependence upon her had grown dangerous in their short time together. When he'd slept with her in his arms the night before, he'd rested more fully than he had since crashing on this planet. She provided peace. Comfort. Security. All without conscious effort on her part.

"Ren?" Zoey called quietly.

His heart skipped a beat. "Yes?"

"Could I…sleep with you?"

Ren opened his mouth to reply, but she continued before he found any words.

"I know there are two beds, but I just really don't want to be alone. Not like we *are* alone and all, but I mean… What I want is… I want to…to…"

"Come, Zoey. Come lie with me."

There was a rustle of covers, a squeak from her bed, and then she was there. She lifted the blankets and hesitated briefly before sliding in and laying on her side, facing him.

"Thank you," She said, scooting close.

Her scent filled his nose, and warmth radiated from her body. Rendash tensed; the urge to draw her closer, to strip her of her clothing and feel her bare softness beneath him, was powerful. His cock throbbed. It was torture; it was divine.

Control.

"Goodnight, Zoey."

"Goodnight, Ren."

Chapter Ten

Zoey was surprisingly refreshed when she woke curled up against Rendash. They brushed their teeth and got dressed, and he offered no complaint — unless she counted his sneer — when she smeared foundation on his face.

After she checked out and they climbed into the truck, she checked the road atlas. If she was finger-measuring the distance correctly, she guessed they could make it through Colorado and well into Kansas within ten hours. That'd be the farthest she'd traveled in a day since leaving Santa Barbara. It would feel good to put real distance between them and the people hunting for Ren.

They pulled onto the interstate under an overcast sky, but the weather held until they were winding through the mountains of Colorado several hours later. She saw a single, fat snowflake tumble into the windshield, and then the snowfall began in earnest.

Their pace slowed to a crawl as snow accumulated on the road and greatly reduced visibility. Before long, traffic came to a near-stop. For a while, it felt like they'd be better off measuring their speed in inches per hour rather than miles.

She turned on the satellite radio and searched through the channels until she found a weather station. The droning meteorologist reported that the snowfall was the leading edge of a massive storm system expected to intensify over the next few days. If she'd had her phone or had turned on the local news in the hotel room before they left, she might've seen some warning, but what good would it have done?

Somehow, she hadn't put together the obvious pieces — December plus the Rocky Mountains meant winter weather.

Maybe we can drive through it. If we get past this traffic and make some distance, get out of the mountains…

Finally, they rounded a bend and discovered the reason for the long delay. The flashing lights of emergency vehicles illuminated the surrounding landscape. Police officers in heavy coats with reflective strips were directing traffic around an overturned SUV while a tow truck with a winch slowly hauled a second vehicle up a drop-off at the side of the road.

She caught herself holding her breath as they neared the police, forcing herself to keep her eyes ahead. Not only was she traveling with an illegal alien from outer space, but she was in a stolen car that belonged to a man who'd been murdered the night before. Her tension didn't ease until the flashing lights had vanished behind them as they rounded the next bend.

Zoey had made more than her share of dumb decisions during her life, but this was the first time she was a criminal because of them. How was she only now recognizing the potential consequences of her choices over the last two days? Accessory to murder was just one on a growing list of crimes.

And yet, if offered the chance, she wouldn't change any of

it. She was doing the right thing. Helping Ren escape from unjust imprisonment — from torture and eventual death — was what any kindhearted person would do, regardless of what the law or the government said. Whether or not Ren was human, their treatment of him was *wrong*.

The eight-hour mark since their departure from Green River came and went, and though the traffic was moving steadily, it was still slow going. The heavy snow continued after the sun went down, and darkness descended over the interstate. A sign appeared out of the gloom declaring they could find food, gas, and lodging at the next exit — Vail.

"I think we should stop and find a room in this next town," Zoey said, glancing at Rendash.

"I will welcome the chance to stretch my legs, though you do not sound happy about it."

She sighed, and — not for the first time — attempted to turn the already frantic windshield wipers to a higher speed. "Because…we might need to stay longer than one night."

His lips fell in a troubled frown. "The weather they spoke of on the radio is that severe?"

Zoey would have given him a droll look if she didn't have to keep her eyes on the road. Instead, she lifted a hand, palm up, to indicate the conditions in front of them. "I can barely see where we're going as it is, Ren, and this is supposed to get worse."

"We still have a long distance to travel." Ren pointed in a direction she thought was northeast. "That way. Farther still than we have already come."

"Ren, we can't travel in these conditions. It's dangerous."

He half-grunted, half-snorted. "I will trust your judgment. If you say we must stop, then we will stop."

Zoey was surprised he didn't put up more of a fight.

She pulled off the interstate when the exit came up and stopped at the first hotel they came across. It had no vacancy, and neither did the second; they informed her that I-70 was being closed east of Vail due to the hazardous conditions, causing an influx of guests. At the third hotel, Zoey stood with her mouth gaping at the desk clerk, stunned to temporary silence by her disbelief.

He had a room available with a single queen bed for *only* three hundred dollars.

"That's insane!" she yelled.

The clerk gave her Zoey a look that made her feel like a piece of trash that had blown in through the lobby doors. "Between ski season and the blizzard, ma'am, you're not likely to find accommodations in town for anything less."

"Aren't there any places around here with rooms for like… sixty bucks a night?" she asked hopefully.

The man tilted his head back and laughed. "Are you serious?"

Zoey scowled. "Why wouldn't I be? What you are asking is robbery!"

"Under the circumstance, it's *quite* reasonable. If you prefer inferior accommodations, that's your business, and you are free to look elsewhere."

She pressed her lips together and glared at the man. Of course she didn't *prefer* inferior accommodations, she just couldn't *afford* nice places. Three hundred bucks a night would wipe out everything she had if they needed to stay multiple nights.

Zoey smiled sweetly. "You know what? You can take that that three-hundred-dollar room and shove it up your ass." She turned, keeping her back straight, and walked to the doors.

Snow and wind blasted her as she stepped outside, and she nearly slipped twice on her way back to the truck. If circumstances were different, she might've welcomed a good fall, just to have a reason to sue the stuck-up bastards in the hotel.

When she reached the truck, she yanked the door open, climbed in, and slammed it closed. Snow fell from her hair and shoulders to melt on the seat around her. She was freezing; her fingers were stiff and numb, and her clothing was soaked. Though her time outside had been limited to trips to and from hotel lobbies, the effects of the weather had cumulated into this misery.

"They have rooms, but they are asking too much for them," Zoey said, stretching and bending her fingers to coax some feeling back into them.

Rendash frowned. He cranked up the heater before closing the vents on his side, increasing the airflow to her. The gesture was a small one, but it was so thoughtful and heartfelt that it eased away most of her annoyance.

"So what options are left to us?" he asked.

She gratefully held her hands up to the warm air. "I don't know. This is a resort town. Everything is outrageously overpriced, and they're only making it worse because of the storm. The interstate is getting shut down because it's unsafe, and people have nowhere else to go right now."

"Can we stay in the truck tonight?" he asked.

"We could. But we'd need to keep it idling all night so we don't freeze, and if a cop decides we're mucking up the scenery... The last thing we need is for me to have to lie to a cop about borrowing the truck from a relative or something like that."

"Is there anywhere in the mountains?" Ren gestured beyond

the hotel, where the dark form of a large hill was barely visible through the snow and gloom.

"There are probably a bunch of cabins up there. Vacation homes and places to rent. But if I can't afford a couple nights in a hotel, I *definitely* can't afford to rent one of those places."

"And if we can find one where no one is staying?"

Zoey tilted her head and arched a brow. "Ren, what are you thinking?"

"Sometimes, survival must be placed before honor."

"What does that mean?"

"Stay here, Zoey." He pressed the button to lower the passenger window, letting in a blast of cold air and stinging flakes. "I will scout the area and return as soon as I am able."

"But it's freezing out there!"

"I know. You will have to make it up to me when we find a warm place to shelter." He reached out the window and opened the door using the outside handle before pulling himself out of the cab. His eyes met hers as he closed the window. "Be safe. I will return soon."

He shut the door and vanished. She stared out the window, unsure if the faint disturbance she saw in the flow of snowflakes was a trick of the wind, a trick of her eyes, or Ren moving while cloaked.

You will have to make it up to me when we find a warm place to shelter.

Had he realized what his words implied? There was no way he could've known…

But what if he had?

Zoey shoved those thoughts away and locked the doors. Now was not the time to think of the way he'd held her, touched her, and looked at her.

She kept her hands in front of the heater as she scanned her surroundings. The glow from the hotel and the nearby light posts was swallowed up by the storm before it reached the boundaries of the parking lot, leaving the area beyond shrouded in darkness.

Time crawled. Zoey glanced at the clock often, counting the minutes since his departure. She turned on the radio to distract herself, but nothing held her interest — not even songs she normally sang along to could break her thoughts away from Rendash. Was he okay? Had he been spotted?

Would he come back?

If he didn't, wouldn't that be easier for her? She could continue to Des Moines, move into Melissa's apartment, and start over like none of this had ever happened.

Except I abandoned my car in Utah, and a man is dead and I'm driving the dead man's truck, and how am I going to explain any of that away when it catches up with me?

Zoey dropped her gaze to the instruments on the dashboard.

I don't want Ren to leave me.

It wasn't because of his promise to protect her, even though she *did* feel safe with him around. She *liked* him. A lot. He made her laugh, listened to what she had to say, made her feel like she mattered.

He made her feel good. Desirable, even. She hadn't felt that way in…well, she'd *never* felt that way. When he looked at her, she felt like she was enough, like she was *more* than enough. Like she was *everything*.

But Rendash *was* leaving. As soon as they reached his ship, he would fly away from here — and out of her life — for good. There was no sense in getting attached or hoping for anything more. He had a home somewhere out there, and she wasn't part of it.

Over an hour had gone by when a large, dark figure approached the truck from the passenger side. Zoey's eyes widened, and her heart skipped a beat. The figure stopped beside the passenger window, raised an arm, and pressed a now familiar four-fingered hand against the glass. Zoey immediately unlocked the doors.

Ren tugged the door open and climbed into the truck. Even with the cab being so high off the ground, he still had to fold himself to get in. She shivered against the cold air that followed him in, but he quickly pulled the door shut.

"Where have you been?" Zoey demanded, at once angry and relieved. He'd been gone far too long. She reached across him to open the passenger-side vents. "It's an ice storm out there!"

"I'm aware," he replied, brushing crusted snow off the shoulders of his coat.

She grabbed one of his upper hands. It was freezing.

"Jesus," she said, snagging hold of the other. Without thought, she shoved them up her shirt, placing them high against her sides. His fingers brushed the bottom of her bra. She clenched her jaw to hold in her cry of shock at the chill of his palms against her bare flesh and caught his other hands, placing them below the first pair. When they were in place, she tugged her shirt down to lock in what body heat she could offer.

"What are you doing, Zoey?" he asked, voice tight as he pulled back. She had a sense that the slight trembling in his hands wasn't because of the cold.

She grasped the wrists of his upper arms and held them in place. "Warming your hands."

He frowned, but his fingers clutched her a little tighter. "They will warm easily enough on their own. You've only managed to make yourself cold."

"This is faster," she said, trying to ignore the way her body was reacting to his touch. A combination of cold and desirous anticipation made her nipples tighten. "Everyone knows that body heat works best."

He watched her skeptically with all four eyes but didn't withdraw. After a short while, his hands slid a little higher, the slight roughness of his scales grazing her sides. Zoey's breath quickened as her skin heated.

Rendash released a heavy breath. His hands stilled before he abruptly pulled them away. "We should go," he said hurriedly. "I found a place for us to stay."

Zoey stared at him. He'd curled his hands into fists and dropped them onto his thighs as though that were the only way to maintain control of them. No one had ever acted that way with her before, no one had ever struggled *not* to touch her. But she *wanted* his hands on her. She'd been so close to lifting her bra and leaning forward to press her breasts into his hands.

But he was right; this was not the place, not the time, and she obviously wasn't thinking clearly.

It's been way too long…

Skin pulsing with the lingering effects of his touch, Zoey took hold of the steering wheel and backed out of their spot. Rendash directed her out of the parking lot and onto the main road. After a few minutes, they turned onto a side road that led higher into the hills. Between the thick snow, the trees on either side, and the darkness, she was lost after a few more turns.

"How did you get this far?" she asked. "You were on foot."

"I was sped on by my *nyros*. Fortunately, my control held long enough for me to find a place and return."

Though there was snow on the roads, they had clearly been plowed recently — one thing to be grateful for, at least. Even the single-lane road he told her to turn onto looked to have been well-maintained, though it couldn't have been more than a long driveway.

They turned off that path and onto another, passing through a thick copse of fir trees. Zoey's jaw dropped as the headlights finally hit the building at the end.

"This place?" she asked, unable to look away.

The cabin before them was something out of the movies — specifically, movies about rich families that went to their fancy getaway homes in the mountains to ski and wear matching sweaters by the fire. It was two stories tall, with vertical wood siding on the top that only *appeared* weatherworn and old, and gorgeous stonework on the lower floor. The windows were wide and generous, without a curtain in sight, but who would look in? The place was surrounded by trees, a private little slice of the Rockies.

"It appeared to be unoccupied," he said, "and there is some sort of computer system handling its security. I was able to interface with the system and deactivate it."

Zoey tore her gaze away from the cabin to look at Ren. "You did what? How?"

"My *nyros* holds a great deal of information within it to aid me on alien worlds, which happens frequently. Its energy can be used to interface with various systems and disrupt their operations in a variety of ways. The technology on this planet is relatively simple compared to what it must usually interface with, so it was not difficult to override the security."

"You can *do* that? Like, with your mind?"

He nodded, an amused smile on his face.

"And we're just going to walk in there? Just like that? How do you know it's unoccupied? What if the owners come back?"

Any more questions, and even I'm going to be tired of them.

"None of the lights are on, inside or outside, but the system was set to activate the lights in ten days."

Zoey looked back at the building. "So, they'll be here in ten days. Hopefully not sooner, though the weather should probably prevent that. We should be long gone before then anyway."

Rendash settled a comforting hand on her thigh. "We are doing what we must." His gaze shifted to the cabin. "And I would guess the owners of this building have plenty of your *money* to spare, to have a place such as this."

"Just because they have money to spare, doesn't mean they'd part with it willingly, or that this is right." She inhaled deeply. What other choice did they have right now? "Okay, let's get inside."

Despite her misgivings, she thrummed with excitement.

They climbed out of the truck together. Rendash retrieved her suitcase from inside the tool bin in back, and Zoey followed him to the front door. There were no visible key holes on the handle, only some sort of touch-screen on the right side of the door frame.

Before she could ask how they were going to get in, he touched a finger to the pad. The screen lit up and flashed wildly in different colors. There was a click, and Rendash took hold of the handle and swung the door open.

"That's some high-tech shit," Zoey muttered. "I thought hacking was only that easy in the movies."

"Most of it is automated." He stood aside to allow her entry. "I simply provide commands, and my *nyros* do the rest."

No wonder the government was so driven to get Rendash back. They'd be desperate to replicate his capabilities. He was a tool, a weapon to be reverse-engineered, and if what she'd seen was only a taste of what he could do, they'd stop at nothing to obtain him.

Rendash closed the door and walked further into the dark foyer. Another touchpad came to life, and lights flared on overhead.

She'd never been in a smart home before, and her first thought was an odd one: *what the hell do people have against light switches these days?*

The foyer had a lovely area rug draped over the stone floor, and a wooden bench to one side where guests could remove their boots. Zoey hurriedly kicked off her shoes and entered the room ahead.

"Oh my God. This is gorgeous!" she cried as she entered the open living room. The wood of the walls gleamed in the golden light, and the stonework on the lower portion ringed the room to meet on the far wall in a huge fireplace.

A long, brown sectional sat in a semicircle in the center of the room, facing the fire. The polished coffee table in front of the couch looked like it was cut out of a large tree, granted additional beauty and uniqueness by its asymmetrical shape. The wood-framed chairs arranged near the floor-to-ceiling window to the right were all draped with cozy-looking throw blankets. Large snowflakes fell in a constant stream beyond the glass.

Moving closer to the fireplace, she swept her gaze over the obligatory flat screen TV hung over the mantle before following the naked wooden beams up to the ceiling. She turned to see a second-floor walkway over the foyer side of the room.

She continued farther into the house, entering the kitchen, which was just as open and spacious as the living room. Wide windows with a pair of glass doors lined one wall with open wooden shelves mounted beside them. The counters and island were topped with black, sparkling granite. A bottle of wine stood on the island.

Zoey picked up the bottle, and her eyes nearly popped out of their sockets when she saw the label. "This stuff has got to be at least two-hundred dollars a bottle!"

She had a sudden urge to open the wine and was soon wrestling with herself on whether to pop the cork. This wasn't her home, these weren't her belongings. She'd already added trespassing to her list of crimes by being in here. Did she want to push that into burglary, too?

Biting her lip, she looked at Ren, who'd entered the kitchen behind her. Her suitcase stood beside him.

He offered her an exaggerated shrug. "I do not know what that bottle contains or what two hundred dollars is. We are here. There is no reason not to enjoy it."

"You know, you sound like criminal activity is a regular thing for you."

"The humans hunting me aren't going to let me go either way. I wish the owners of this building no ill will, but if they are likely able to easily replace food and drink...why should we worry about it?"

Zoey chuckled. "Okay, let's just go with your logic."

She opened and closed drawers one at a time, working her way around the kitchen, until she found a corkscrew. After some wiggling, the cork came free with a loud *pop*. Zoey raised the bottle to her nose and inhaled.

Her eyes nearly rolled back into her head. "It's been so long since I had good wine…not that I've ever had *anything* like this."

She brought the rim to her mouth, tilted her head back, and drank straight from the fucking bottle. The thought of how hard wine connoisseurs would've lost their shit if they saw her now only urged her on.

Rendash searched the kitchen while she enjoyed a prolonged sample of the wine, checking every drawer and cabinet, seeming to take stock of everything inside each of them even though she was pretty sure he couldn't read the writing on anything. He stopped longest at the refrigerator.

"There are many provisions in this place," he said, lifting three packaged ham steaks from the freezer.

Zoey set the wine bottle down and joined Ren. There were plenty of items inside that wouldn't go bad over a short amount of time — mostly condiments in the fridge, but meat and vegetables in the freezer. No milk or fresh produce, but that was expected for a vacation house. The pantry was a bit more lucrative, brimming with canned, powdered, and dried goods. She took out a couple cans of green beans and a bag of biscuit mix, placing them on the counter.

"Let's get cooking," she said, taking the ham from Ren.

He scrubbed the foundation off his face at the sink while Zoey prepared the ham, green beans, and biscuits. Her search for plates turned up wine glasses in one of the cabinets, so she decided to show the wine a little respect by using one.

"You want any?" she asked Rendash.

He took a tentative sniff from the bottle, seemed to consider it for a few moments, and declined. She shrugged; that meant more for her. The alcohol was already warming her from the inside out. Tomorrow was uncertain, but tonight, they'd live in luxury.

When the food was done, they stood at the island counter and ate together. By the time Zoey finished her first plate, Rendash had almost demolished all the rest of the food; he scarfed down helping after helping like he hadn't eaten for weeks.

Zoey smiled and gathered up the empty plates, taking them to the sink to rinse off. It required a surprising amount of concentration to hold the plates steady while she washed them.

"Hungry, I take it?" she asked over her shoulder.

"Yes," he said around the biscuit in his mouth — not a *bite* of biscuit, but an *entire* biscuit. "Certain functions of my *nyros* burn excess energy, and I have yet to fully recover from my captivity." He paused to swallow and run his tongue over his teeth. "Also, this is *good*."

"They say the way to a man's heart is through his stomach, but the way to a girl's is to compliment her cooking."

"This is *very* good," he said with a grin.

Zoey laughed. "Wait till I make you an omelet in the morning. For now—" she drained her fourth glass of wine and returned to the island counter to collect the nearly empty bottle, bracing herself with one hand on the granite "—I'm going to go explore upstairs. You look around down here."

He covered her free hand with one of his own, stopping her before she walked away. "Are you sure we should separate?"

Zoey threw her arm wide, swaying against his anchoring hold. Why did the bottle feel heavier even though the wine was mostly gone? It didn't matter; *she* felt great. "We have this whole place to ourselves. Lock the doors, and we'll be fine. Besides, upstairs isn't *that* far away."

He looked her over, his expression oddly drawn with apprehension even though there was the hint of a wicked gleam in his eyes. "But you seem a bit…off balance. Are you sure you don't want me to stay near?"

She set the bottle on the counter — ignoring the fact that she missed it by almost a foot on her first attempt — and stepped closer to him, pressing her chest against his abdomen. Smiling, she toyed with the lapels of his overcoat with her fingers as she looked into his eyes. She wanted him to remove it. "How about you look around down here and join me upstairs in about thirty minutes?"

"I'm not very accustomed to your reckoning of time," he replied, voice lower, raspier. One of his hands settled on the underside of her arm, just above her elbow.

"Hmm…then just come up after you lock the doors." She rubbed a finger at the base of his throat. He had a sexy neck; thick, corded, strong. Who cared if it had scales? Scales were sexy, too. "I'll check upstairs for a place we can *sleep*."

His nostrils flared with a heavy inhalation, and his hand trailed farther up her arm. He nodded. "Yes. Good. I will see you soon." But he made no move to pull away; instead, his head tipped toward her.

Zoey's lifted her lashes and settled her gaze on his mouth. It should've been illegal for a man to have such defined lips. They were sinful, offering teasing flashes of his fangs.

She lifted her hand and trailed a finger over his bottom lip; his lips were firm, but softer than they appeared. What would they taste like?

What would they feel like against her own?

. . .

Rendash stared down at Zoey, unable to break away as he'd meant to. He'd seen that light in her eyes before, but never so strongly, so openly. Her gaze blazed like fire, spreading heat through his veins. His lips tingled beneath her bold but gentle touch. She'd leaned her body against his, and it seemed only natural to place his lower hands on her waist and draw her a little closer.

"I want to kiss you," she murmured.

Though the light in her eyes didn't explain what she meant, it was enough to make his cock ache with want for her.

"What does *kiss* mean?" he asked.

Her brows furrowed. "Kiss?" She laughed. "Did I say that out loud?"

He raised his only free hand and pressed it to her flushed cheek. "Are you sure you—"

Zoey slipped a hand behind his neck, wrapped her fingers around one of his crest locks, and rose up on her toes as she yanked his head down. She pressed her mouth against his.

Rendash's eyes widened. He was rarely surprised, but her action caught him completely off-guard; it was overwhelming, foreign, and incredibly intimate. Her lips moved over his with unexpected pliability; their touch began light and soothing but grew increasingly bolder and insistent. He groaned as he slipped his lower arms around the small of her back and embraced her fully.

Zoey moaned. The sound vibrated into him and rippled through his body. Her mouth opened, and her tongue flicked against his lips. It sent a bolt of pleasure straight to his cock, causing his hips to jerk forward.

"You taste so good," Zoey rasped, then moved her mouth from his to brush her lips along his chin and jaw and down his neck. When his coat stopped her downward progress, she growled. Rendash's fingers flexed.

Deep within his mind — a mind hazy with desire and need — those old lessons struggled to reassert themselves.

Control.

He dropped his lower hands to Zoey's rounded backside, cupping her soft flesh, and lifted her off her feet. She yelped and threw her arms around his neck. Turning, he set her down on the edge of the freestanding counter and guided her legs around his sides. With one hand flat on the counter to brace himself, he leaned forward, shifting another arm up along Zoey's spine to support her and twine his fingers in her hair.

"Ren," she breathed, squeezing her legs around him. She crossed her ankles behind his back and pulled him closer to her core.

Tantalizing heat radiated from between her thighs. He inhaled deeply. It was that same smell he'd picked up before, the same fragrance, even more enticing now. Every time they'd gotten close, every time lust had lit her eyes, she produced that scent.

And it was for *him.*

Instinct.

Rendash lowered his mouth and kissed her neck, sampling the taste of her skin with flicks of his tongue. She released a heavy sigh. He brushed his lips over the base of her throat and up, along her jaw, and finally back to her mouth. She responded ravenously, her tongue slipping past his lips to stroke his. It was a new, erotic experience, and it elicited the most exquisite sensations.

Now that he knew what a *kiss* was, he would master it.

Having learned the motions of the sensual dance between their tongues, he took the lead, grasping her hair and angling her mouth to delve deeper.

Her hands slid from his shoulder to fight with his clothing, shoving his coat down his arms until it caught on his elbows before yanking his shirt up. She pressed her palms to his abdomen and trailed them upward until her arms caught on his clothing.

"Take them off," Zoey begged, kissing the side of his mouth and nipping his lower lip.

She propped herself on her elbows as Rendash straightened. He shrugged off the coat, thrusting it behind him, and grabbed the bottoms of his hoodie and shirt to peel them up over his head simultaneously. While his vision was obscured by the cloth, he felt Zoey sit up. He tugged the clothing off to see her remove her own shirt and cast it aside. Her dark hair cascaded around her shoulders.

He trailed his hungry gaze over her bared torso.

Her flesh was pale with a soft pink undertone, and there was nothing to hide the enticing flare of her hips. Her lush breasts were contained only by a small, lacy, purple harness, wholly unlike any clothing he'd ever seen — the only functions he could imagine for such a thing were to tease and arouse.

Zoey reached for him, cupped his face, and kissed him again. He wrapped his lower arms around her, palms flattened against the scalding skin of her back.

Her hands fell away to smooth down his abdomen and chest, fingers tracing the contours of his muscles. His scales tingled in the wake of her touch. When she trailed her fingertips over the sensitive scales of his lower stomach, the sensation was too much. His hips bucked, and his straining cock — confined painfully within his pants — pressed between her legs.

Zoey gasped against his mouth and undulated her pelvis, creating such exquisite friction that tremors coursed through his body.

She tore her lips away; they were pink, swollen, and utterly enticing. "Touch me, Ren." She ran a single finger down the center of his chest, pulled back, and looked up at him. "Where do you want to touch me first?"

"Everywhere," he rasped, sliding his palms up her back.

His instincts were nearly too much to ignore. He needed to have her *now*, to taste her fully, to claim her, but another part of him wanted to savor their coupling — to prolong it and allow them both time to reach new heights of pleasure. Heights he hadn't known existed until recently.

His gaze fell on her chest.

Zoey chuckled. "Everywhere, but you're staring at my breasts."

She sat up straighter and reached behind her. The action thrust her chest toward him, forcing the mounds to strain against the fabric of her harness. Rendash's mouth watered. He suddenly understood why the man in the *porn* had put his mouth on the female's body.

Rendash wanted to put his mouth on Zoey, and he knew exactly where he wanted to taste her the most. His gaze dipped to the spot between her legs, the source of that enticing scent.

She loosened her harness, slipped it off, and flung it away. Grinning, she leaned back and braced herself with her hands flat on the counter behind her.

Rendash gripped the edge of the counter as his desire grew as hot as a supernova. His self-control, which had been tenuous at best, threatened to shatter. Her breasts were large and soft, tipped with pink nipples. He didn't await further invitation. Rendash leaned over her and placed a hand on each of her breasts, palming their yielding flesh. Apart from her hardened nipples, they were the softest things he'd ever touched.

Zoey moaned, dropping her head back.

His eyes shifted to her bared throat. Lowering his head, he brushed his lips over the sensitive skin there, grazing it lightly with his teeth. She cried out and grabbed a fistful of his crest. Her pelvis rocked, sliding over his erection through their clothes.

"Zoey," he growled against her flesh as a shudder rippled through him. The aligarii females he'd been with had never acted this way, had never pushed him to the point of such overwhelming need that he could scarce control his impulses before their bodies were even connected.

She lay back and raised her knees higher. "More, Ren. Please. Please touch me more."

Selflessness.

This was not about his pleasure, it was about Zoey. About *her* needs. She'd done so much for him, risked so much, and he'd given so little in return. He knew this wasn't true selflessness — her pleasure was a joy to him, and he would take from it greedily — but it was the best he could do to control himself.

He trailed kisses down her throat, along her shoulder, and finally to her breast. Moving his hand to cradle the soft mound from beneath, he took the nub of her nipple in his mouth and flicked his tongue over it.

Zoey moaned, her fingers tightening around his locks. Ren glanced up. Her lower lip was caught between her teeth, and her eyes were closed. He sucked on the little bud, and she sighed her pleasure.

He watched her reactions, listened to her breathy sounds, and focused on every little movement of her body, learning everything he could about what she enjoyed. Learning how to please her.

Rendash moved to her other breast and closed his eyes as he lavished the same attention upon it as he had the first.

Finally, he could no longer resist the lure of her scent. He trailed his lips between her breasts and lower, toward the hem of her pants. Zoey's hand fell from the locks of his crest to rest upon the counter, and her legs sagged. As he moved his fingers to her belt, he realized her sounds had stopped.

"Zoey?"

He looked up to see her head turned to the side. Rising over her, Rendash frowned; her eyes were closed, her breathing deep. He gently grasped her wrist and lifted her arm off the counter. When he released it, it dropped limply to rest over her stomach.

His eyes shifted to the bottle from which she'd been drinking. It was nearly empty. Had the liquid had some effect on her, or was it simply the culmination of stress over the last few days?

He shook his head and smiled ruefully; he was sure that she'd appreciate the humor of the situation, but the ache in his groin was not amusing. His blood was hot, and his limbs trembled as he pushed himself up.

Control. Detachment.

Rendash closed his eyes and forced his breathing to slow. It didn't help that her scent clung to him, that her arousal perfumed the air.

It is for the best, he told himself. *She was not of her right mind because of that drink.*

He looked at her again. She was naked from the waist up, nipples hard, skin pinkened from his ravenous kisses, her hair a tousled, chaotic mess around her. She was the most beautiful thing he'd ever seen.

I was so close to tasting her.

His cock twitched. Rendash gritted his teeth.

"Ah, Zoey," he said quietly before gathering her carefully in his arms. She inhaled deeply and nuzzled her face against his bare chest. "What am I to do with you?"

There were several rooms beyond the kitchen; fortunately, one of them contained a bed and an adjoining bathroom. Holding her with three arms, he pulled back the bedding. She stirred again when he laid her down but didn't wake.

He stared at her leg coverings. He found such pants — jeans, she'd called them — uncomfortable, and doubted she would want to sleep in them. After a brief debate, he unbuckled her belt, opened her pants, and slid them off her legs, leaving only the little bit of cloth she wore around her pelvis and back-side. It was the same color as her breast harness.

And it was damp with her slick.

Rendash clenched his fists as the heavy scent of her arousal washed over him again, stronger than before. His body stiffened, primed and ready to mate, and his throbbing cock ached for release. All that stood between him and taking his woman was an insignificant shred of cloth. He could tear it off effortlessly with his teeth and run his tongue over her sex to taste her. The sensation would undoubtedly wake her up, and then they could connect their bodies and fulfill their desires.

A low growl emanated from his chest as he strained against the temptation, against *instinct*, against everything he'd come to want so desperately.

Finally, he turned his head away and drew the blankets over her body. For several moments, all he could do was sit on the edge of the bed with his eyes closed. To do anything more now — no matter how willing she'd been after their meal — was wrong.

"Would that I could bring you with me when I go," he said softly. Opening his eyes, he looked at her and brushed a lock of hair from her face.

Humans had been so strange when he'd first encountered them. So soft and weak, seemingly incomplete for their lack of limbs and eyes. He would never have believed that a human would become the most beautiful thing in his universe.

Rendash stood up and walked out of the room, not allowing himself to look at her as he paused to turn off the light. She needed rest, and he needed distance, if only to master his desires.

Chapter Eleven

Zoey moaned. It sounded different to her ears than it had in her dreams; this wasn't a sound of ecstasy, it was one of agony. But then, her dreams usually weren't accompanied by an intense throbbing in her skull, either.

"Zoey?" Ren's voice, though soft, rolled through her head like a peal of thunder.

The mattress dipped, and her body slid toward the newly opened valley to stop against Ren. His hand settled on her side. Strange, but it felt as though his palm was touching her bare skin. Her nightshirt must have ridden up in her sleep. Right now, she couldn't bring herself to care.

She brought her hands to her head and clenched her temples. It would be less painful if her head were cracked open — at least that would stand a chance of releasing some of the pressure.

"I'm dying, Ren," she rasped. Each word was a unique pain in her throat, scraping like sandpaper on the way out, and her mouth was so dry that she wouldn't have been surprised to see dust billowing from her lips as she spoke.

He sat up abruptly, making the mattress bounce. Zoey's stomach lurched.

"What can I do to help?" he asked hurriedly.

Zoey cringed. "You can lower your voice, for starters."

"I do not see how the volume of my voice has any effect on your condition," he whispered.

"Because my head is going to explode if you don't." She moaned again, rolling onto her back.

His silence told her he'd taken her words literally.

Zoey cracked open her eyes and winced, shutting them again. Part of her brain understood that the room wasn't brightly lit by any standards, but the glow from outside pierced her brain like a shard of glass.

"I need water," she said. "And aspirin. An entire bottle of aspirin."

"I will get you water," he said gently, "but I do not know *aspirin.*"

The bed creaked and wobbled again as he got up.

"Hold up," she said, opening her eyes and scrambling off the bed. She clamped a hand over her mouth to contain the bile climbing her throat and stumbled across the floor until her vision adjusted to the light enough to identify the nearby bathroom. She was vaguely aware of Ren calling her name as she raced through the doorway and dropped to her knees in front of the toilet.

This was a new kind of hell. She gripped the edges of the bowl and retched, emptying her stomach of everything she'd eaten the night before. Agony clawed through her with each gag. Stars burst across her vision, blinding her with flashes of light that were blurred by the tears in her eyes, and her head really felt as though it would explode.

She became suddenly aware of Ren's presence. Somehow, he folded himself into the small space without crowding her, pulled back her hair, and placed a comforting hand on her back. At that moment, it was the sweetest thing anyone had ever done for her. She was utterly embarrassed to be in such a state around him.

"I want to die," Zoey cried.

"You are not allowed to," he said firmly.

"You can't stop me."

"Watch me."

Zoey heaved. It strained every muscle in her chest, neck, and face, and burned, and suffocated, and she hated it and really did want to die.

"Don't argue with me when I'm sick," she muttered weakly after it passed.

"Don't argue with *me* when you're sick," he replied. He turned on the sink and handed her a little paper cup of water a moment later.

She used it to rinse her mouth. She was thirsty enough that she considered swallowing, but the thought made her shudder and threatened another bout of puking. Her mouth absorbed some moisture from it, at least.

Ren took the cup back and refilled it. "You need to drink, Zoey."

"I don't know if I can."

"You need to try."

"I don't wanna."

"Doesn't matter." He held the water under her face. "Just drink."

Pouting, she accepted the cup. She took a tiny sip.

Ugh.

"Good. Now drink some more, human."

"You're extra bossy this morning." She took another drink. A shiver ran through her. The water was foul, tainted by the taste in her mouth.

"I told you, you're not allowed to die." Rendash placed a finger beneath the cup and tipped it to her lips. "Keep going. A little at a time."

She drank small sips until the cup was empty. When she was done, she rested her head on her arm and closed her eyes.

Ren remained in place beside her, slowly stroking her back.

Which was still bare.

Zoey's brows furrowed. She lowered her other arm and touched her chest. Her *bare* chest. Shifting her arm aside, she looked down at herself.

Had she been embarrassed before? She was fucking *mortified* now! Here she was draped over the toilet, puking her guts out, dressed in nothing but a pair of purple panties with her boobs and every roll on display!

She crossed her arms over her chest. "Ren, why am I naked?"

At the corner of her vision, he tilted his head in apparent confusion. "You removed your shirt and harness before I brought you to bed."

"My shirt and my *what*?" She winced as a bolt of pain split through her skull.

"Your...*harness*," he said, holding up two of his hands and cupping them in front of his chest as though cradling a pair of objects in his palms.

"My...*bra*? Are you saying I took off my shirt and bra? No, no way. I wouldn't…"

He frowned. The hurt in his eyes was strong enough to clear her head a little. "You don't remember what happened last night?"

"Y-you mean… That we… Oh God, it wasn't a dream was it?" she asked, staring at him. Her gaze dipped briefly, and sure enough, his junk was just *there*, dangling between his legs. "Did we…?"

"We kissed. I touched you. And then you fell asleep."

Please let me be struck with lightning now. Like right *now.*

All at once, she remembered kissing him, running her hands over his chest, feeling his hands on her…

It wasn't a dream. It had really happened.

And she'd fallen *asleep*!

"I'm sorry," she said. "It wasn't… I didn't…"

Ren moved a hand to her cheek and guided her eyes to his. "It was good, Zoey. More than good. I cannot blame you for having been exhausted."

Her cheeks flamed; despite the combined effects of her hangover and her embarrassment, warmth spread through her at his words. Had he really liked it? Liked *her*? Kissing her, touching her, and…seeing her?

"It wasn't exhaustion, Ren," she said quietly. Damn her headache. Damn the fucking hangover. If she didn't feel like keeling over, and if her mouth didn't taste like vomit and ass, she would have kissed him. "It was the wine. I drank too much."

"It was the drink?" he asked, blinking his outside and inside eyes slightly out of sync. "Is…is that also why you are sick today?"

"Yeah. Wine is an alcoholic beverage. It's basically a drug that helps humans forget their inhibitions. Helps us relax and loosen up. Sometimes, a little too much. It's been a long time since I drank, and I guess I forgot to limit myself."

"You drank nearly the entire bottle."

She winced. "Uh, yeah… Like I said, I forgot to limit myself."

"There is a substance on my planet called *tsirisk*," he said as he took the cup from her hand, refilled it, and passed it back to her. "It is something that has been known to my people for thousands of generations, made from a plant that grows deep in the jungle. The lesser of the *Khorzar*, those who do not have *nyros*, sometimes consume *tsirisk* before battle. It imbues them with great strength and speed.

"But when it has run its course, their bodies are left in weakened states, and the more they use it, the more dependent they grow upon it. *Tsirisk* is not the same as your *alcohol*, but what you said reminds me of it. And because of that, I will allow you no further *alcohol* while you are in my company."

Zoey groaned and laid her head back down, keeping one arm across her breasts for modesty's sake — though she was sure all her modesty had been murdered and buried in the back yard by now. "Not even a little?"

"No."

"A smidge?"

"*Human…*"

Zoey smiled despite her discomfort. "At this point, I don't want any more either." Just the thought of more alcohol made her nauseous.

Rendash looked her over and released a sigh. "I dislike seeing you suffer like this."

"Believe me, I don't like it either."

"Do you feel well enough to move back to the bed?"

"Just…give me a little while longer."

Ren continued to rub her back, trailing his hand up and down along the line of her spine, then back and forth across her shoulders. The fingers still holding her hair up lightly massaged her scalp. Before long, Zoey's eyes drifted closed.

"I think I can go back to bed now," she mumbled.

Slowly, and with impossible gentleness, Rendash gathered Zoey into his arms. Her eyes flashed open and she tensed, trying to sit up. *Big* mistake. She groaned with pain and sagged into his hold.

"I'm too heavy for this," she complained, crossing her arms over her chest. "I can walk."

"You are a fool," he replied affectionately. He stood up, all four of his arms supporting her weight evenly so there wasn't painful pressure concentrated on any single spot. Moving with care, he turned and carried her through the doorway — somehow managing not to bump any part of her on the door-frame — and to the bed.

For the first time in her adult life, Zoey felt dainty. She couldn't articulate the thought, not in a way he'd understand, so she simply curled against him until he sat her down on the bed.

Once she was in place, he stepped away to retrieve her shirt from atop the nearby dresser. She took it from him and pulled it on over her head.

"Thank you," she said.

"Do you want your pants? The soft ones?"

Zoey stared at her bare legs for a moment before shaking her head. She lay down, reached for the covers, and pulled them up to her chin.

"I'm going to find a more suitable container for water," he said.

Zoey reached out and caught one of his wrists before he could step away. "Stay."

"I won't be gone long."

She frowned. "Promise?"

"Yes."

"Okay."

Zoey watched him leave the room, unable to help but stare at his ass and the way it flexed as he walked.

Why do I keep telling him to cover up?

She distantly heard him rummaging through the kitchen. Her body eased, and her eyelids slid shut. Sleep had nearly overtaken her when a soft sound nearby caught her attention.

Ren had returned. He stood beside the bed, one hand lingering on the cup he'd placed on the nearby nightstand. The cup itself seemed surreal, something from a distant memory — it was one of those oversized plastic mugs with a lid and a fat bendy straw. The kind the nurses had given her father while he was in the hospital.

Her eyes stung with a sudden welling of tears, making her headache all the fiercer, and she squeezed them shut.

A gust of cool air flowed beneath the blanket. The bed creaked, and the mattress dipped. Two of Ren's arms slipped beneath Zoey, drawing her against his hard, warm body.

Zoey turned to face him. She met his gaze as she snuggled close, one of her legs draped over his thighs and her body tucked against his side. Reaching up, she cupped his jaw, brushing her thumb over his lower lip.

"I remember last night," she said, and kissed his shoulder before resting her head upon it, lowering her hand to his chest.

"I will remember it forever," he replied softly as she drifted to sleep.

Chapter Twelve

Zoey felt much better when she woke up later that day. Her stomach had settled, and her minor, lingering headache would likely go away once she got some food and water in her system. And best of all?

She was cocooned in Ren's arms. All four of them.

He lay with her back flush against his chest, and she was thankful to be facing away — he didn't need to catch a whiff of her rank breath after her pukefest. If she weren't so cozy and warm in his arms, she would've jumped out of bed to brush her teeth immediately.

The security of his embrace and the heat of his body weren't all she was aware of, however; there was also a *log* nestled against her ass cheeks. A day ago, that would've sent her running for the hills, but now?

She'd used up all her embarrassment that morning, so rather than feeling ashamed, she reveled in the feel of him. Ren was attracted to her. He'd been *aroused* by her. She knew morning wood was just something that happened to men —

human men, anyway — while they slept, but God, feeling his cock against her backside turned her on. Her nipples hardened and pussy clenched, hollow and achy, and if not for an exceedingly full bladder, she might've been so bold as to wiggle her bottom against him and finish what they'd started the night before.

That was one way to make up for passing out in the heat of the moment thanks to her stupid overindulgence.

Hell, just lounging in bed with him sounded divine. She was warm, safe, and comfortable, without a care in the world.

Well, except that insistent urge to pee.

Way to ruin the moment, bladder.

Zoey placed her hand on one of Rendash's wrists and carefully lifted it. His arms tightened around her in response, holding her that much closer.

"How do you feel?" he murmured huskily.

Oh my God! Can a man's voice be any sexier?

"Better." She turned her head to look at him. "How long have you been awake?"

"Long enough." There was a hint of mischief in his voice, adding a layer to it she'd not heard before — it was seductive as hell.

Her arousal grew.

Damn you, bladder!

"I, uh, need to pee," she said, cheeks ablaze.

"You need to pee?"

"Yeah. Like, *right now.*"

Ren withdrew his arms, but not without a hint of reluctance — his fingertips lingered on her bicep and hip for just a bit longer than seemed necessary.

As soon as she was free, Zoey leapt out of bed and ran to the bathroom, closing the door behind her. Sweet relief swept in to fill the growing space as her bladder emptied.

While she was washing her hands, she realized that the small toiletry bag on the counter was hers. With a silent thanks to Ren, she took out her toothbrush and scrubbed her teeth and tongue like they'd never been cleaned before.

Despite her thoroughness, she still ached with desire when she was done, and decided to hop into the shower to avoid returning to the bedroom — to temptation.

It was amazing how much better the hot water made her feel, and the tub had ample space to move around in, meaning she didn't even have to deal with the shower curtain blowing in and slapping her leg with a jolt of cold. The showerhead was big enough that she felt more like she was standing in a rainstorm than in a bathroom.

When she finished, she returned to the bedroom with her breath smelling of mint, her hair wet, and nothing covering her body but a towel. Ren was sitting on the edge of the bed with his pants on. Her suitcase was set beside him, open to display her clothes.

His eyes swept over her hungrily. She could almost *feel* him looking through the towel, and that ignited her blood all over again. She bit her lip approached the bed.

"Thanks," she said, picking out a pair of leggings and a tunic. She blushed anew as she withdrew a pair of red panties.

Awesome. My face is going to match my underwear.

Ren reached into her suitcase, plucked up her red bra, and — dangling it from a single finger — held it out to her. "Your harness."

"You're horrible," she laughed. Snatching the bra from him, she hightailed it back into the bathroom — back to safety.

I must really *be desperate for physical contact.*

Okay, so not just physical contact, but *sex.* She'd only had two partners in her life — the first a one-night stand that popped her cherry when she was nineteen, and then Joshua seven years later. Sex had never been a huge part of her life. She'd gotten herself off far more times by her own efforts than with men, but that didn't mean she didn't want it. Didn't *crave* it.

And *boy* did she want it with Rendash. With an *alien.*

So why not just do it? Why not get her freak on with this sexy, four-armed hunk of muscle?

Because it's…because…

It's wrong?

She knew that wasn't the truth. A few days ago, yeah, it certainly would've been, but she'd spent time with him, had come to know him. He was still *other*, but she'd seen human qualities in him.

And yet, Zoey couldn't be anything more than a curiosity to him. She didn't want to be someone's…curiosity fuck. She didn't want to be used again. She deserved better, deserved more.

She *wanted* more.

It didn't matter how much she longed for *more* with Rendash; he'd leave soon, and she'd never see him again. She couldn't stand the thought of that loss as it was, so why get more involved with him and increase the hurt when that moment came?

But if we both want it, why not take it, even if it's only one time? Why not be selfish for a change?

Because I want more than a one-night stand, damnit.

She wanted stability. She wanted love. She wanted it all.

And she needed to be stronger to obtain it.

Mind made up, Zoey hurriedly pulled on her clothes. She would have to keep some distance between them. Set some boundaries.

Once she was dressed, she stepped back into the bedroom.

"Are you ready for those omelets I promised?"

He straightened and offered her a smile, flashing his fangs. Zoey's entire body reacted to it.

Damnit. Boundaries, woman, boundaries!

"I would ask what that is," he said as he stood up, "but I doubt I would understand your explanation."

"No need for explanation. Just enjoy it."

Zoey ended up making Ren four omelets with powdered eggs and a little cheddar cheese that, despite the expiration date being two days earlier, appeared to be totally fine. When she joked that it was one for each arm, he laughed, and there was something endearing about his appreciation of her humor even at its corniest. More serious was his ability to throw down food; she was grateful the pantry was well-stocked.

Ren excused himself to take a shower after he helped clean up. Zoey stared out the kitchen window for a few minutes, listening to the wind wail over the roof. The snow hadn't slowed, and the drifts beside the house had already piled up over the base of the first-floor windows.

They were going to be here for a while.

She set to exploring the cabin while he finished. The place was, by far, the nicest she'd ever been in. Everything was so elegant, but it was somehow made accessible by the little, down-to-earth, rustic touches throughout. There were two bedrooms, a media room — complete with a stupid-big television and leather recliners — and a sun room on the lower floor. The garage looked large enough to house an RV, a boat, and three cars all at once.

Upstairs, she found two more guest bedrooms. Each of the guest rooms had a different color scheme, but all were decorated tastefully and coherently. She had no doubt that some of the old objects used as décor in the rooms hadn't been purchased at thrift stores, like the stuff in her apartment, but in *antique shops*. She was thoroughly impressed.

She took a moment to breathe as she looked down over the living room from the second-floor walkway. Then she discovered the master bedroom at the end of the walkway and went from impressed to stunned.

The woodwork on the floors, walls, and ceilings here was taken to a new level of simplistic grace, paired with intricate stonework that culminated in a large fireplace directly ahead of the massive bed. A wide bay window stretched across the far wall with a cushioned bench running its length, granting full view of fat snowflakes in their chaotic dances outside.

A pair of leather armchairs with sculpted-wood frames were positioned in front of the fireplace. A cozy oval rug was positioned beneath them. She turned to see a dual vanity sink near the corner, with a stone countertop and gleaming, old-fashioned copper fixtures. Nearby sat a huge, jetted bathtub. It was built into its own nook, surrounded by stonework that would've been at home on a New England farm, with wide steps leading up to it.

The bathtub had its own glass-enclosed fireplace and a window looking out toward the snow-laden fir trees that surrounded the cabin. On the opposite side of the tub's fireplace wall — and with a shared view of the fire — stood a large shower stall with stone on three sides and glass on the fourth. It looked like it had one of those state-of-the-art, multi-headed, multidirectional shower systems.

"If I had a dream home, this would be it," Zoey said, running her fingers over the rough stone on the wall. She stared at the bathtub. "I am so using this before we leave."

She turned away and moved to the dresser, pulling open the drawers one by one. There was an even split between men's and women's clothing inside. The walk-in closet, on the other hand, was dominated by women's clothing and shoes. To Zoey's surprise and excitement, the footwear *and* the clothing fit her.

Stealing wasn't right, but she hadn't exactly had an abundance of winter clothes to bring with her from Santa Barbara, and Ren had even said this was *survival*. From all she'd seen in this house, she doubted the owners would have a problem replacing a pair of boots, a sweater, and a coat — if they even noticed they were missing to begin with.

I already drank their two-hundred-dollar bottle of wine. Why not add more to the list?

What was that old saying? *In for a penny, in for a pound.*

Zoey had just stepped out of the bedroom when Rendash emerged from the staircase onto the second-floor walkway.

"Did you finally get your exploring in?" he asked.

"Yes! This place is a-*mazing!*" She looked over the railing toward the bottom floor. "I've never been in a place so beautiful before."

"I suppose the bad weather has given us something to be thankful for, after all." That gleam had returned to his eyes, though it was subtler now; she didn't think he was talking about the cabin.

Zoey cleared her throat. "I know you want to get to your ship, and this is a delay, but it'll give you time to rest and regain your strength." Despite her best efforts, she couldn't quite stop her gaze from roaming over his bare chest. He'd donned a towel instead of pants, but the towel couldn't cover her clear mental image of his cock. "You, uh, should get some pants on. With it being cold and all."

"I have already adjusted the temperature inside this building to a comfortable level. Do you need me to increase it?"

"No, I'm good. But you should *really* put some pants on."

Please, for the sake of my lady-bits, put on some pants…

…or take off the towel.

He frowned, and she wasn't sure if the knowing look in his eyes was real or a product of her imagination. "They are restrictive. I prefer not to wear them without need."

"Do you walk around naked back home?"

"No. But aligarii clothing favors simplicity and comfort. It is also tailored to the…proper proportions."

Unable to resist, she dropped her eyes to his groin again. Not surprisingly, he was tenting.

"Okay! Well, um…" She looked anywhere but at him. *Boundaries.* "Oh! You should see the home theater here." She squeezed by him, sucking it in to avoid any inadvertent brushes with a certain part of his anatomy, and made her way downstairs. "We can watch a movie!"

The steps creaked as he followed her down. "Is it going to be the same as the other movie? The…*Ace Ventures?*"

"*Ace Ventura.* And no. We'll have to check out their collection, and you can pick this time."

They entered the media room. The TV mounted on the wall had to be eighty-plus inches, the biggest she'd ever seen, and there were surround-sound speakers set into little alcoves all around the room. There were no wires to be seen anywhere — and no DVD player, cable box, or anything of the sort.

She found a remote control, set in its own charging dock, on a stand beside one of the eight leather recliners. It was the most complicated remote she'd ever seen, complete with its own display screen.

At the back of the room, she discovered a small, black handle on the wall. When she tugged on it, a door — which had blended seamless with the paneling — swung open. She stepped through the doorway to find what could pass for a small bedroom in most of the houses she'd been in. Here it was probably just referred to as the *media closet* or something like that.

Shelves upon shelves stuffed with DVDs and Blu-rays lined the walls. There had to be more than five hundred titles. The missing electronics were set on a shelf near the door; a Blu-ray player, a gaming console, a satellite receiver, and the surround sound unit. The neatly-bundled cords for each device ran into the wall.

"This is so neat." Zoey looked at Ren and grinned. "Pick a movie that looks interesting while I try to figure out how to get all this going."

Rendash joined her in the closet; they were able to both fit inside without bumping into one another. His eyes widened. "All of those are movies?"

"Yep. And that's not even close to how many movies are out there."

Tentatively, he reached forward and removed a DVD from the nearest shelf, turning the case in his hand to look at the front. "And you mean for me to choose based on the picture?"

"A lot of people find movies that way." She pressed the power button on the Blu-ray player, and there was a soft chiming sound from the main room. She poked her head out of the closet to see the TV turning on before returning her attention to Ren. "If the cover looks interesting, we can check the back to see what it's about."

He flipped the case to glance at the back and frowned. "I still cannot read human writing."

"I can read it to you, or we can leave it as a surprise." She stepped closer to him. "If you want a certain genre, I can point out a few to you."

Moving back, he swept his gaze over the collection. She could understand how it would be overwhelming; she could read, and had at least heard of most of the movies, but Zoey doubted even she could make a choice in any reasonable amount of time given so many options.

She watched while he slid movies out for closer inspection, unable to tell if he was choosing randomly or based on whichever spine-logos were most appealing to him. In most cases, he only asked for the title, if for anything, but he had her read the back descriptions on a few.

When he made his choice, she wasn't sure if she should've been surprised or not; he selected *Galaxy Quest*. She took the case from him, opened it, set the disc in the tray and pressed the button to close it.

"Come on," she said, grabbing one of his hands and pulling him into the main room. He closed the door as he passed through.

Zoey released his hand when they reached the chairs, plopping onto one of the center seats. He settled into the chair beside hers, a comical look of worry on his face as the leather squeaked and creaked.

"Is that normal?" he asked, holding all four of his arms up as though afraid to lower them onto the chair.

Zoey laughed. "Yes, it is. I guess we'll find out if leather sticks to scales like it does to bare skin before too long."

Rendash lowered his arms slowly, settling the lower pair on the armrests with the upper pair atop them. He nearly leapt out of the seat when his leg bumped the recliner button and the whole chair tilted back.

Giggling, Zoey placed a hand on his shoulder. "It's fine. Lay back and relax."

Leaning back, he shifted a hand to the recliner controls and tipped the seat backwards. Once he settled, he clasped the fingers on both sets of hands, resting them atop his bare abdomen.

From the moment the movie began, Zoey found her attention on Ren nearly as often as it was on the TV. His comments, often muttered absently, added a new layer of comedy to the film that she hadn't guessed was possible. Whether he was questioning the existence of the alien species depicted on screen or debunking Hollywood physics, his earnestness was endearing and entertaining at once.

Toward the end, Zoey found herself watching Rendash rather than the movie, taking note of every shift in his expression — each curl or twist of his lip, the subtle twitches of his brow, and the intense look that often came to his eyes. It wasn't exactly conscious. She just…

She was going to miss him when he left.

Rendash had quickly become an important part of her life, and despite the circumstances, these last few days with him were some of the best she'd ever had. She felt closer to him than any person should to another in so short a time. It didn't make sense. She just…didn't want him to go.

One of his side eyes flicked toward her. He lifted his head and turned it to face her, all four of his eyes focusing on her. "Shouldn't you be enjoying the movie, Zoey?"

Zoey smiled. "I am. I'm also enjoying the company."

"I cannot see how watching me is more engaging than watching that." He gestured to the TV. "Though it is rife with inaccuracy, it is, at least, entertaining. You humans have quaint notions of space and the intergalactic community."

"Hmm." She continued watching him.

He arched his brow and held her gaze, though she caught one of his side eyes straying toward the TV.

Zoey burst out laughing. "Having so many eyes is not fair!"

"I cannot be held responsible for the shortcomings of your species."

"Shortcomings?" Zoey gaped at him. "You can make your own dinner next time." She crossed her arms over her chest and faced the screen.

From the corner of her eye, she saw him lean toward her and reach an arm out. He brushed his fingers along the side of her neck. "Just because you have freakishly few eyes and limbs doesn't mean I think less of you."

"Freakishly few?" Zoey looked at him and raised her brows. "Maybe *you* have freakishly too many."

"Perhaps. By your own standards," he replied with a grin.

"Humph." She lifted her chin haughtily. "Well then, based on those standards, maybe I prefer a male with two arms and two eyes."

"Oh?" Ren pushed himself out of the chair to loom over

her, features cast in shadow as he blocked the screen. "Explain, human."

He slipped one hand up from her neck to cup the back of her head, twining his fingers in her hair, while his other hands moved to different parts of her body — her side, just beneath her breasts; her hip; her upper thigh.

"Explain why you do not prefer this," he rasped.

Zoey's breath quickened, and her heart raced. She stared into his eyes. "I-I don't...don't have to explain myself to you, alien."

He stared right back at her, and damnit if he wasn't giving her his *full* attention, if he wasn't seeing *all* of her and making her feel it. His lips parted in a smile, offering another glimpse of his fangs. His hands moved slowly, sensually, blazing hot despite the protection of her clothing. "Your reactions explain enough, I think...as does your scent."

"My scent?"

He leaned forward, his face so close to hers that their lips would touch if she tilted her chin up. He lowered his head past her neck and breasts, past her stomach, lower and lower until it hovered over her thighs.

Rendash's lower hands grasped her knees and spread them before he dropped his head between her legs inhaled deeply. "The scent of your desire."

Zoey gasped. She pushed her hands against his forehead and squeezed her legs, but he kept himself in place. "Oh my God. That's so—" *sexy* "—dirty!"

"What do you mean, it is *dirty?*" he asked, lifting his gaze but not his head.

Zoey burned inside and out. It was arousing as hell having

him positioned between her legs like that, but she couldn't let go of her self-consciousness. "It's…naughty."

"So is it *dirty* or *naughty*? Those words have different meanings, don't they?"

Oh, God. She could feel the heat of his breath through her leggings. Her pussy clenched and liquid fire flooded her. She didn't have wine to bolster her courage this time. "Both!"

"This scent is natural. It is a part of you." His upper hands smoothed down her neck and shoulders and slid over her sides, brushing her breasts on their way. Zoey shivered. "All of this is part of you, and there is nothing but beauty to behold."

How did he always say the perfect things to make her heart go pitter-patter? His words filled her with confidence and desire, something that Joshua had never bothered to attempt.

Boundaries, Zoey! Don't let yourself be a doormat!

Not that she believed Rendash would treat her like one, but he was still going to leave. Whether he intended to or not, he was still going to walk on her heart before the end.

Then shouldn't I want something more to remember him by?

No. This was about that soon-to-be-trampled heart, not the sex. Ren had come to mean more to her in a few days than Joshua had in a year. Josh's betrayal had hurt, but she'd known she would recover with a little time. Rendash's departure, on the other hand, was going to *devastate* her. That was the truth deep in her heart.

Everyone she'd cared about abandoned her eventually, one way or another — her mother, her father, her grandmother, her foster parents, Joshua.

Rendash would, too.

If she got intimate with him, it would open her up for a whole new kind of pain. There was no way she could have sex with Ren and not grow even more attached than she already was.

"Ren," Zoey said, exerting gentle pressure to push his face away, "we need to stop."

He furrowed his brows and finally lifted his head. "Why do we need to stop?"

"Because I—"

Just lie!

"—don't want this."

Bullshit. You're so revved up that if he so much as stuck out the tip of his tongue you'd jump his bones and screw his brains out. He can smell you, remember?

"I just got out of a relationship, and we're...we're two different species," she said.

"Different species, yes, but both thinking, *feeling* beings with many similarities." The confusion on his face only deepened. "And your reactions—"

"Are natural, as you said. But they're not voluntary." Zoey cringed. That hadn't come out right.

God, I hate myself right now.

Rendash clenched his jaw and averted his gaze for several seconds. His breathing was slow, deliberate, as though damming some immense reservoir of emotion. Finally, he pushed up off her chair, breaking all contact with her, and returned to his own seat.

She felt like a complete ass. She hadn't meant for the words to come out like that, hadn't meant to hurt him.

"I'll let you finish the movie while I fix us some dinner," Zoey said, standing.

"You said I had to make my own next time," he replied.

There was no hurt in his voice, but there was no joy, either. Was he truly unaffected? Had she…made the right choice?

Without another word, she left him, softly closing the media door behind her. It was too late to put distance between them to protect herself from hurt. Stinging tears brimmed in her eyes as she walked to the kitchen, and her legs were so wobbly that she had to lean on the island counter until she regained her composure.

She'd already let him get too close.

Shortly after she finished making dinner — elk steaks, canned corn, instant mashed potatoes, and more of the biscuits he liked — Ren emerged from the media room. Zoey set a large plate on the counter in front of him, offering a smile.

"Hungry?" she asked, hoping to diffuse the tension in the air.

"Yes." He set into the food slower than normal, as though his usual appetite was diminished.

Zoey picked at her own meal.

They ate in silence. Zoey missed the sound of his voice, missed their playful banter.

Isn't this what you wanted? Distance?

Appetite having fled, she scraped her leftovers into the trash and cleaned her plate.

Time to put that final nail in the coffin.

"I'm going to sleep in the master bedroom upstairs," she said. "You can stay in the room down here, if you want, or pick one of the others."

His hand stilled midway between his plate and his mouth, a skewered piece of elk steak quivering on his fork. "Why?"

"Why not? There are so many beds here, and so much space. Might as well put it to use while we're safe."

Rendash's jaw muscles bulged, and his nostrils flared. A hard light entered his eyes — hard, but somehow vulnerable. When he lowered his fork, he did it with enough force to clank on the plate, and she jumped. He flattened his other hands on the counter and pushed himself to his feet.

"Even when we had two beds, you wanted to sleep with me. Why do you want space now? Why are you pushing me away? Explain it, human, in a way I can understand, because it makes no sense to me!"

"Because you're leaving, and after you're gone, I'll still be here!" she yelled without meaning to. Her eyes widened, and she took a step back. "You're leaving," she repeated softly.

"Yes, I'm leaving. What is there for me on this planet but captivity?"

Zoey stared at him silently for a time before nodding. "You're right." Painful tightness seized her chest. "Nothing. Which means I made the right decision. Goodnight, Ren."

She turned her back on him, but not before catching a look of shocked realization in his eyes. He was silent as she walked away. She didn't look back.

Entering the room they'd shared, she stuffed her toiletry bag into her suitcase and hauled her meager belongings — this was *everything* she had, now — upstairs and into the master bedroom. She slammed the door closed behind her. Only when that solid barrier was between them did she allow herself to slide to the floor and cry.

Chapter Thirteen

Zoey woke with a headache for the second morning in a row. Though this one wasn't nearly as intense or painful as her hangover headache, it was in some ways worse — this time, her heart ached, too, enough so to prevent her from falling back to sleep. Her eyes were swollen from crying the night before, and she was miserable.

You made your bed, now lie in it.

Oh, she'd lain in it, alright. Alone and filled with regret.

After tossing and turning for a long while, she finally glanced at the clock. The glowing green numbers taunted her — *4:45, and you sure as hell aren't getting any more sleep.*

Giving in to her frustration, she tossed the blankets off and slipped out of bed. She brushed her teeth, took a shower — acknowledging in some part of her mind that the fancy system of hidden showerheads provided an *amazing* experience, though she was unable to enjoy it in her current state — and got dressed. With nothing else to do, she tip-toed downstairs to the kitchen to occupy herself.

Twenty minutes later, a second-floor door opened. The stairs groaned to announce their displeasure at supporting Rendash's weight. He entered the kitchen and stopped just inside the doorway.

Zoey slowed the whisk and looked up from the large bowl of powdered eggs tucked in her arm. She made eye contact with Ren, but his expression was unreadable. He sighed softly and walked to the table, seating himself in a chair that faced the glass doors, giving her his back. The snow was three-fourths of the way to the top of the doors today.

At least he put on some pants this morning.

Way to look on the bright side, Zoey.

She frowned and looked down at the bowl, resuming her whisking. "I couldn't sleep. Figured I'd come down and start breakfast."

"I heard you pass in the hallway," he said.

"Sorry if I woke you."

"You didn't."

She pressed her lips together. What a mess. How could sex complicate things so much when they hadn't even *had* it?

He turned his head slightly, his leftmost eye shifting toward her. "Whatever you are cooking, it smells good."

She placed the whisk in the sink. The aroma from the oven had spread sweetly through the kitchen. "It's a surprise."

Rendash twisted in the chair, looking at her over his shoulder. "A surprise?"

"Yep." Turning her back to him, she poured most of the egg into the waiting skillet and picked up the spatula.

"Even if you tell me what it is called, the word will be meaningless to me. You can give me that much, at least."

"Doesn't matter. It's a surprise, which means you're going to have to wait to find out."

"Zoey…"

"Don't you growl at me."

The wood of his chair creaked, conveying his impatience even before he spoke. "Well how long do I have to wait?"

Zoey glanced at the oven. "Ten minutes. But then it will need a little time to cool."

"What should I do until then? I…I do not wish to be of no use."

"You…could tell me about yourself. Or about your planet, or how you got here."

She peeked at him as she moved the clumping eggs with the spatula. He turned back toward the windows, leaning forward with all four elbows on the table. His silence stretched, leaving only the sound of the wind over the roof and the gentle sizzle from the skillet.

"You don't have to. It was only a suggestion," Zoey said.

"My *Umen'rak* was traveling through this system because it was the shortest route home," he said after a few more seconds. "We had completed our *Nes'rak* and struck a *korvaxx* staging point elsewhere in this galaxy."

"What do *nezrack* and *korvaxx* mean?" she asked.

"*Nes'rak* is…duty. I think the word *mission* is the closest in your language. A task of great importance that is given to an *Umen'rak* to complete. And the korvaxx are an alien species we have warred with for a long while. After raiding an outpost on a world in the korvaxx's control, we obtained intelligence on their war effort, and had learned of many more worlds they meant to conquer and enslave. That is what the korvaxx do; take and take until nothing is left. But with that information, we would've had the chance to stop many of their assaults before they were underway."

She looked at him again; his posture was hunched, his head bowed.

"While we were on the enemy world, our ship must've been…sabotaged, or something of the sort," he continued. "I was jolted from stasis by an explosion that destroyed a large portion of our ship. Our pods were automatically jettisoned to this planet, and the command module was separated from the wreckage. That module can function as a ship of its own, though its defenses and weaponry are somewhat lacking. That is what I'm trying to reach. I don't know if it landed safely or if it crashed, but it is my only chance to get off this planet."

"Was your *Umen'rak* captured with you?" she asked, frowning.

"Many died in the explosion or did not survive the fall to the surface because their pods were too damaged. But yes…some of them were captured with me."

Zoey stilled the spatula, keeping her eyes fixed on him. "What happened to them?"

"I…" He lifted his head for a moment before sagging down again like a great weight was pressing down on him; she understood why. "I do not know. Not with any certainty. A couple were likely too wounded to have survived long, even with their *nyros*. The rest…the *scientists* were eager to learn our anatomy and had no qualms about inflicting harm upon us. Some of what I'd heard indicated that at least one of my companions was cut open while still living. The leader of the operation implied that the rest were killed due to similar experiments, but I was never offered any solid information."

Annnnnd you *just made him relive all that. Way to go, Zo. You're really crushing it lately.*

Without paying much attention to what she was doing, she removed the skillet from the stove and scooped a pile of scrambled eggs onto one of the plates she'd set out.

Zoey didn't want to imagine what he'd been through while he was in captivity. She didn't need to. As big and strong as Ren was, the horror and trauma he'd experienced was evident in his voice, in his body language, in the thickness of the air around him. She was glad that he'd confided in her, but seeing him like this made her chest hurt and her stomach flutter anxiously.

She carried the plate of eggs and a fork over to the table, setting them in front of him. He made no move to eat.

"What will you do if the command module doesn't work?" she asked.

"Attempt to get the communications into working order to call for rescue."

Zoey nodded and returned to the stove to cook the remaining eggs.

"Thank you for the food," he said after a long silence.

"You're welcome."

A few minutes later, the oven timer beeped. Turning it off, she grabbed a pot holder, opened the oven, and removed the pan of blueberry muffins from within.

She wasn't sure if she should be impressed or concerned when Ren didn't turn to look at what she was doing. He sat hunched forward, lower elbows on the table, eating his eggs with slow, stiff movements. His fork occasionally clinked or lightly scraped against the plate, but he was otherwise quiet.

Zoey plucked two muffins from the pan, hissing at the heat on her palm, and dropped them on a small plate to top each with a bit of butter. She brought the muffins and her plate of eggs to the table, sitting across from him. She placed the muffins on his side.

"Surprise," she said half-heartedly, forcing a smile as she pushed the muffin plate a little closer to him. Her smile quickly faded. "I don't want us to fight."

Ren reached forward with one of his lower hands and picked up a muffin, drawing it closer for inspection. He gently poked it with a finger. "I don't want to fight, either," he said softly, meeting her gaze. "It's all I've done for my whole life, and I am tired of it. Even when it does not involve bloodshed."

Zoey bit the inside of her bottom lip. "Forgive me?"

"Yes. So long as you forgive me. I did not mean it the way I said it."

"I didn't mean it the way I said it, either."

"I suppose we are a pair of fools, you and I. But…" He extended an upper arm and placed his hand over hers. "I have greatly enjoyed your company, despite the unpleasant circumstances that brought us together."

She stared at their hands and brushed her thumb against his. "Me too."

Using his lower hands, he tore off a chunk of the muffin and slipped it into his mouth. A smile, small but genuine, crept across his lips as he chewed. "Somehow, it tastes even better than it smells."

Zoey grinned. "They say the way to a man's heart is through his stomach."

"And this does taste *very* good," he replied, smile widening.

She placed a hand over her chest. "Aww."

Despite her overacting, the fire inside her had rekindled. She'd tried to force distance between them, had tried to tell herself there was nothing to pursue here, that there was no future for them. That it would only end in heartbreak.

But she couldn't stay away from him.

Maybe…she didn't have to.

The day was a good one, and they passed it as though the night before never happened. They talked in the kitchen as the sun rose, which, thanks to the continuing storm, only meant a shift from black to gray outside. Afterward, they watched a couple more movies. Zoey found popcorn in the pantry, and Rendash partook eagerly until the skins started getting stuck in his teeth. He scowled so darkly at the bag that she thought he was going to murder it.

When the end credits started rolling on the second movie, Zoey stood. Rendash moved to join her, but she stilled him with an extended hand. "Stay here, Ren. I'll be right back."

She hurried upstairs to the master bedroom. Kneeling on the floor beside her suitcase, she opened it and dug through her clothing until she found her little photo album. It was her most treasured possession. Her fingertips trailed over its worn, familiar front cover, and she felt a single moment of doubt. She hadn't even shown Joshua these pictures, even after almost a year. Would Rendash care? Her father meant nothing to him, and his relationship with his parents hadn't exactly been close.

But it will mean that dad's memory, at least in part, is with one other person in this universe.

Zoey returned to the media room with the album clutched to her chest and smiled at Ren.

"What is that, Zoey?" he asked.

She sat next to him and lowered her arms, holding the album on her palms. Taking a deep breath, she cast aside her lingering anxiety.

"This," she said as she opened the cover, "is my dad."

The first picture was her father fresh out of high school — a young man, hair cropped short, face as bare as a baby's ass. He wore a huge, proud, goofy grin.

"And this," she pointed to the newborn baby in his arms, "is me."

Ren leaned down to study the picture more closely before pulling back to glance at her again. "That was really you?" he asked. "You were so tiny. And wrinkly."

She chuckled, eyes on the picture. "Yeah, that was me."

Rendash tilted his head. "Ah, but there you are. Your eyes were just as beautiful then as they are now."

Zoey looked up to find Ren staring at her. Her heart did a little flip, and she blushed. She'd received so few compliments since her father passed that she couldn't accept them easily, but his conviction made it impossible to reject his words.

Though her eyes blurred with tears, Zoey smiled as she turned the pages, sharing each photo with Ren. Her as a baby; posing with her dad on her first day of kindergarten; her and her dad eating ice cream at the zoo; the two of them dressed as Sailor Moon and Tuxedo Mask in hand-made costumes on Halloween when she was nine. With each picture, she shared a little bit of herself with Ren, shared a little bit of her father. He hadn't been a perfect man, and even as a child she'd understood they had struggled financially, but they'd been *happy*.

Her tears didn't spill until she reached the final photograph.

She gently brushed her finger over the plastic sleeve holding the picture. "It was his birthday and he was stuck in the hospital, so my grandma helped me bring him balloons and a cake. One of the nurses took this picture for us because grandma couldn't figure out how to use the camera."

Little Zoey had climbed onto the bed behind him, smiling over his shoulder. Her father — emaciated and with a sickly pallor — had smiled just as wide, eyes sparkling with happiness despite his pain.

"This was last picture we took together. He, uh—" she hurriedly wiped the moisture from her cheeks to keep it from dripping on the page and sniffled. "He died a few days later."

When she blinked away her tears, she realized Rendash was staring at her again.

He lifted his hands and covered her cheeks, stroking them gently with his thumbs. "It seems to me that he had the heart of a warrior," he said, "just like his daughter. He deserves every honor you give him. Thank you for sharing this with me."

Fresh tears flooded her eyes as she felt that pain, that loss, all over again. She knew it would never go away...but that was okay, wasn't it? That was part of loving someone.

Zoey slipped her arms around Ren and silently cried. He embraced her, sliding one hand up and down her back soothingly, and said nothing.

"Thank you, Ren," she whispered when her tears slowed. She turned her face toward him and rested her head on his shoulder, inhaling deeply. His scent reminded her of sandalwood, with a rich, earthy undertone. "Thank you for listening. For caring."

Without thinking, she pressed a kiss to the side of his neck.

His hand stilled, and his muscles tensed, but his only move was to lay his cheek on her hair. "Thank you for trusting me enough to share him."

They remained like that for a while, and she let herself melt into his embrace, relishing the comfort he provided. He didn't push her away, didn't take anything for himself.

Finally, she placed her hands on his shoulders and drew back with a soft smile. "I'm going to go wash up, and then we can make some dinner."

"King me!" Zoey plopped her piece down on a black square at Rendash's edge of the board.

He frowned, staring down for several seconds before finally picking up one of the discarded red checkers and crowning her new king. "How do you consistently penetrate my defenses?"

"Guess I just have that effect on you."

After they'd eaten and cleaned up, their exploration had led Zoey to a stash of board and card games in one of the closets. Her excited shout had brought Rendash running. She hadn't played such games since she was a little girl.

Because Ren couldn't read English, their choices had been limited, but they enjoyed the simple games as much as they would have anything else — it had taken several hands of poker before he was able to remember which card combinations were the most valuable, but he'd understood dominoes and checkers almost immediately.

This was their fifth round of checkers. Zoey had won the first four, and each time she'd jumped his final piece, Rendash demanded a rematch.

"The game is so simple, and yet I am unable to overcome you."

"I'm just that good." Zoey grinned. "Maybe you need the right incentive."

He lifted his gaze to meet hers and tilted his head. "What do you mean?"

Zoey toyed with the small stack of checker chips she'd captured from Ren, lips pursed. "What if...every time you capture one of my pieces, you can ask me a question, and I'll answer truthfully. If you get kinged, you can ask me to do something. Anything."

A mischievous gleam sparked in his eyes. "*Anything?*"

"Anything at all." She leaned forward. "But the same applies to you."

He rested his upper arms on the table and grasped the edge with his lower hands. As he held her gaze, a faint smile touched his lips. "Very well, little human."

Zoey shifted in her seat, a bit unnerved by his sudden confidence. But there was no way he was going to beat her. She'd already won four times, and she was well on her way to another victory. "Let's do this, then."

There was a new intensity in the air as he made his move, and excitement danced low in Zoey's belly. She couldn't have realized that upping the stakes could turn the game into something so much more exciting.

They each took another turn before Zoey jumped one of his chips. "Ha!" She added the checker to her pile and looked at Ren. "How many relationships have you been in?"

"Based on my understanding of the term, according to humans, none."

Zoey furrowed her brow. "None?"

"None." Without breaking eye contact with her, he settled a finger on one of his pieces and slid it forward.

She mulled over his answer as they played. How had he never been in a relationship? She knew he'd been raised as a warrior, but shouldn't he have had *something* along the way? Did his answer mean he'd had sexual relations without emotional attachment?

Two more turns passed before he jumped one of her chips. He claimed the red checker slowly, staring down at it as though in deep consideration. "How many males have you had sex with?"

Zoey blushed. That was what she should've asked him — *how many females have you had sex with?* "You go right for the throat, don't you? Two."

Palm up, he gestured to the board.

Zoey moved her piece, not realizing until she'd already lifted her finger that it was a mistake. "Shit."

Rendash took his checker between two long fingers. It came down once, twice, each drop a rumble of thunder. One of his lower arms stretched forward to pluck two of her chips off the board.

"King me," he said.

Reluctantly, Zoey set one of the captured black pieces atop his newly anointed king.

"That's two questions and an action, correct?" he asked.

"Yes," Zoey replied, bracing herself.

"Are you attracted to me, Zoey?"

She lifted her gaze. Her eyes roamed over his body of their own accord. She took in his broad shoulders, his strong arms, the rippling muscle of his bare chest and abdomen, and his hands. Zoey remembered *exactly* what those hands felt like upon her body.

Arousal ignited deep within, flooding her core with sudden heat.

She looked into his eyes. "Yes."

The corners of his mouth lifted in a small, satisfied smile. He spread his arms a little wider and leaned back in his chair. "What do you want, Zoey? What do you *really* want, to make you happy?"

Zoey swallowed, her heart skipping.

I want someone to look at me like you are right now for every day of the rest of my life.

She dropped her attention to the table, absently tracing the tiny, raised crown on the top face of Ren's king.

"I want stability. I want…a home." she answered.

"Explain, human."

"You're out of questions."

"I wasn't asking."

Zoey glared at him but couldn't hold back a smile. "Bossy alien." She sighed and shrugged as the seriousness of the explanation settled over her. "After my dad died, I never had a real home. I went to live with my grandmother for a little while, but she passed away the next year. After that…I had no one. I was put in foster homes with strangers, moved around from place to place — some good, some not so good. That was my life until I was eighteen. Then I got a job and saved up to get my own place.

"My friend Melissa, the one who I was driving to meet, was in the last foster home I lived in. We became friends and shared an apartment for a little while but I…I wanted to see things." *More like I wanted to run away before everything fell apart, because why wouldn't it have?* "So, I hit the road and left Des Moines behind. I always wanted to see the ocean, and when I ended up in Santa

Barbara, California, I just kind of…stuck around. I didn't mean to stay, but traveling was expensive, so I got a job.

"And then I met Joshua." She frowned, sitting back in her chair and settling her hands atop the table. "I thought I had a future with him. We both had jobs, we found an apartment for a decent price, and I thought… He lost his job not long after we moved in together. We weren't doing great, but we were making it, so I told myself it was okay. We'd make it work. One day at a time." Zoey scowled. "But I found out the truth, *eventually*."

"And then I forced my way into your life, at that lowest point," he said softly.

Zoey smiled at him. "My time with you has been the highest point in my life since my dad passed."

"I am glad to give you something in return for what you've done for me. Though now I feel the mood may be too serious for what I was going to ask you to do."

Zoey had completely forgotten about that part of their deal; she owed him an action.

"Well, a deal is a deal," she said. "Lay it on me."

He stared at her for a few moments, lightly tapping three of his fingers on the table, as though hesitant to tell her. "You're sure?"

"Would you back out of our deal it was me asking?"

One corner of his mouth rose in a half-smile, displaying his right pair of fangs. "No. I wouldn't." Keeping his upper arms on the table, he settled his lower hands over his abdomen, twining their fingers together. "I want you to remove your harness — your *bra* — and hand it to me. You don't have to take off your top covering."

Zoey stared at him blankly. "You want my bra?"

"I'll return it later."

Laughing, she shook her head. "Okay. You sure I can't just go and grab one out of my suitcase?"

"Only if you wish to incur my wrath, human."

"Of course not." Zoey stood up and turned her back to Ren. She pulled her arms into her sweater, reached behind her back, and unhooked her bra. After sliding the *harness* off, she passed it between her hands as she slipped her arms back into her sleeves.

She turned to face Ren and held her bra out to him. "Your prize."

Ren leaned forward and plucked it from her grasp. He raised the bra to his face, inhaled deeply, and smiled. Zoey's jaw dropped. That small action, combined with the smoldering intensity in his eyes, made her body react instantly. A flush spread throughout her body, and her breasts, now free of restriction, felt heavy and full. Her nipples tightened as they brushed against her sweater.

He draped her bra over the empty chair beside him. "Your move, Zoey."

"You'd better hope I don't get another king," she said, sitting down.

"Part of me hopes you do."

They played a few more turns, and it felt like a cat and mouse game — she'd move her king up, then he'd crowd her and force her back. Her brow fell as she studied the board. His moves grew bolder with each passing turn; he had her on the defensive, and he knew it.

He slid another piece into a square at her end of the board. "King me."

She stacked one of his fallen checkers onto the new king and met his gaze expectantly.

"Let your hair down," he said.

Zoey released a slow breath and did as he instructed. Not so bad. On her turn, she jumped one of his few remaining pieces.

"What are you going to do when you get home?" she asked.

"I will honor my fallen *Umen'rak* as my final duty, and then I will have earned the right to claim a mate and live out the remainder of my life in peace."

"Oh."

Claim a mate — those few, simple words were like a punch to her gut. But what had she thought was going to happen? He was going home to live his life on another planet. If it included a…a mate, and a family, that was his business. Just like she'd be moving on with her life when he was gone…

The thought of him having that life proved a powerful distraction; two turns later, he jumped another of her checkers and landed on her end of the board. He demanded she king him again.

Maybe she shouldn't have given him an incentive to play better.

"You are troubled," he said. "What are you thinking about?"

"You."

"Me? What specifically?"

"I answered you honestly. You only won a single question."

Mischief lit in his gaze again. "Is that how we're going to play, then?"

"Haven't we already been playing it that way?" she asked, arching a brow as she glanced at her bra.

He placed all four of his hands on the edge of the table, lifted himself slightly, and scooted his chair back. When he eased down again, he spread his arms to the sides. "Come and sit."

"What?"

Rendash patted his thigh with one hand and smiled. "Come sit with me, Zoey."

"Like, on your lap?"

"Yes."

"No way!"

His smile fell. "But you said *anything*. Are you breaking your word to me?"

"Oh, you are so...so..." Zoey pushed her chair back and rounded the table, stopping next to Ren. He had his head turned to watch her and wore such a smug smile on his face that she wondered if he'd been playing her all along.

"Well? Sit, human. The game will not complete itself."

Zoey glared at him — she felt like she'd be a pro at that, before long — and turned. She eased her bottom onto his thigh, leaning most of her weight on her feet.

Rendash encircled her with his arms, brushing the underside of her breast with a forearm. She yelped as he pulled her fully onto his lap with her legs hanging to the side. He settled his left arms over her lap and placed a hand on the outside of her thigh.

"I believe it's your turn," he said.

Zoey went still. She'd always been self-conscious about her weight. Girls like her didn't get to sit on men's laps. It didn't matter how big Ren was, she was too heavy to sit on him.

He slipped a hand between her thighs, jarring her from her thoughts. "Ren!"

"You haven't lost. Yet. Make your move."

She looked back at the board. Despite the relatively small number of chips remaining for either of them, it was difficult to concentrate. All she could focus on was the heat radiating from his body, the hand between her thighs, fiery as a brand, and the prominent erection beneath her backside.

As she leaned forward to reach for a checker, her nipple scraped against Ren's arm, and the material of her sweater only enhanced the friction to send a thrill through her. She inhaled sharply.

"Something wrong?" he asked. His nose brushed against the side of her neck, and his breath was warm against her skin.

"You are *not* playing fair," Zoey said, making her move in a hurry.

"I am simply making use of the tools you provided to me." He extended his arm and slid one of his pieces. Zoey scanned the board. His checkers were closing in on hers like a net; one of his kings had two of hers blocked in. "What do I get when I win?"

"I don't know." She took her turn. "What do you want?"

Rendash moved another king into place. She'd lose a piece after her next turn, no matter what she did. She was running out of moves.

"A kiss," he said.

"Okay," she replied; a peck on his cheek would be quick, simple, and at least somewhat innocent, and it'd be his fault for not being more specific.

"Like the one we shared the night before last."

Suddenly, her heart was pounding.

He made another casual move, and the circle grew tighter.

They continued their turns; one by one, Zoey's final pieces were jumped or trapped against the edges of the board. Ren didn't bother with questions, saying he was more interested in the prize at the end.

Zoey stared woefully at her final checker. It was over, but

Rendash hadn't claimed his victory. She knew he wanted her to make her move, as futile as it would be; he had a piece waiting to pounce no matter which direction she chose.

With a sigh, she placed her finger on the piece and slid it up to meet its doom.

Rendash moved with nonchalance, taking one of his kings between two fingers and a thumb and lifting it in a little arc over her last piece. It came down like a meteor in slow motion to smash her winning streak to pieces.

"This battle has its victor," he said.

"So it does. I guess that means game over!" She leaned forward to slip off his lap.

He held her firmly in place; his grip wasn't painful, by any means, but it was clear she'd never break it on her own.

"I believe there is the matter of my prize to be settled, little human."

Well damnit, if I'm going to kiss him, I'm going to give him a kiss to remember me by.

Zoey turned her torso toward him and placed her hands on his shoulders. His grip yielded as she shifted her legs, swinging one to the other side of his lap to straddle him. It placed her sex right up against his hard, constrained cock.

Ren's smug grin vanished, his expression becoming something she could only describe as a lustful smolder. His eyes burned with desire, with intent, with promise. He slid his lower hands to her outer thighs while he moved his upper hands over her ribs to brush the undersides of her breasts with his thumbs.

Just one kiss. One incredible, unforgettable kiss.

But could she stop herself there?

Zoey reached up and cupped his face. "You wanted a kiss? I'll give you a kiss."

She parted her lips, pulled his head down, and claimed his mouth with hers. Electric jolts coursed through her as their connection sealed. His hands tightened on her, urging her on, but she didn't need any encouragement to give more, to *take* more.

She flicked her tongue against his lips and he opened to her, but this time she did not allow him to take control; she set the pace, and she explored him firmly, boldly, and at her leisure.

Of their own accord, her hips undulated against him. His hard shaft stroked her clit through her pants, and she moaned as a bolt of pleasure pierced her core. Moisture flooded her. She knew her panties would be soaked by the time the kiss ended.

His nostrils flared as he inhaled. Body tensing, he groaned against her mouth and raised his hips to meet her gyrations.

Zoey gasped. She was wracked by a shudder, and dropped her hands to his shoulders, digging her fingernails into his scales. She was so close, just a few strokes away from coming.

But this needs to stop.

Grasping for the willpower that she knew was buried somewhere deep within, Zoey pulled away from him, catching his lower lip between her teeth as she broke the kiss.

Rendash growled, head falling back and chest swelling with a deep breath.

"You got your prize," she said.

He didn't release her when she tried to climb down.

"Why stop there?" he asked huskily.

"A kiss, Ren. That was the deal."

With a frustrated sigh, he released her, curling his hands into fists and letting his arms dangle at his sides.

Zoey slid off his lap, making sure to brush his cock with her leg in the process. He shivered and groaned.

"You are not playing fair," he said.

"Here's another Earth saying for you — all's fair in love and war." She grinned and stepped away from him. He wasn't the only one suffering. She was paying for her teasing, too, but hell if she was going to let him see it.

"Where are you going, Zoey?"

"It's late, and kicking your ass five times in a row wore me out. I'm going to bed."

"Five times in a row? I won the last match."

She glanced at him over her shoulder, dropping her gaze quite deliberately to his groin. "Oh, did you? Goodnight, Ren. See you in the morning."

Slowly — as though it pained him — he leaned forward and rested his arms on the table. "In the morning? You're making me sleep in a separate room again?"

"It's for the best." She settled her hand on the banister. "Sleep well."

"Maybe my understanding of the word *best* is incorrect," she heard him mutter before she climbed the steps.

Once in the safety of the master bedroom, Zoey closed the door and sighed. Her skin was flushed, and she ached between her legs. Torturing Ren had turned out to be self-inflicted punishment.

A cold shower will help.

But even after standing under icy water for several minutes, she discovered that the moment she thought of Ren — which was essentially *every* moment — her desire flared back to life.

She wanted him. Needed him. It didn't matter how many times her brain said no, her pussy was screaming *yes!*

"Traitor," Zoey muttered, looking down.

There was only one thing she could do. It wouldn't be the

same, wouldn't be remotely close, but at least it would take the edge off.

She dried off, turned out the lights, and crawled naked into the bed. Blanketed by a soft, warm comforter, she gave her body one more chance to settle, but it was no use. She sighed.

Closing her eyes, she imagined Ren. She pictured his tall, broad body and his lickable abs, recalled the texture of his scales against her skin, the feel of his strong hands brushing over her.

She kicked off the bedding.

Zoey cupped her breasts and tweaked her nipples. It wasn't his fingers, nor his mouth. It wasn't the same and never would be. She bit her lip and pressed her imagination harder. She trailed a hand down her body, over her stomach and toward her pelvis. Parting her thighs, she ran her fingers through the short hair of her sex, hesitating only a moment before sliding her fingers into the folds of her pussy to find her clit.

"Ren," she whispered in time with her first stroke.

Chapter Fourteen

Rendash was dying.

He knew, through tattered remnants of his rationality, that he wasn't *truly* dying, but that didn't change how he felt.

The room was dark, the air a comfortable temperature, if a bit too dry, and the only sounds were the muted wailing of the wind — hardly enough to keep him awake — and the creaking of the bed as he shifted restlessly in his search for a position that would allow sleep to finally overtake him.

Believing that he could find the right position was his first mistake. The bed should have been comfortable; though his feet hung off the end, the mattress had a good balance between softness and support. Yet no matter how he lay, comfort remained elusive.

The largest portion of blame fell upon his own arousal; his cock ached, and he'd grasped it through his pants several times in fruitless attempts to alleviate the pressure. He'd left the restraining garment on, fearful of what his instincts would demand if he released his throbbing shaft from its confines. It was nearly impossible to sleep while his blood was ablaze, while his lips tingled with the remembrance of Zoey's kiss, while her scent lingered upon him.

During the final game of checkers, he'd managed to swing the battle in his favor on multiple fronts. Despite her insistence on putting space between them, despite her deciding not to mate with him, he knew Zoey desired him, and he'd turned her desire into a weapon. He'd won the battle, but her final effort...

She'd won the war. He'd maintained a tenuous control throughout, even with her sitting on his lap and her bottom pressed over his cock, but that *kiss*!

Control. Detachment. Control. Detachment.

The words repeated in his mind until they lost all meaning. Neither were currently attainable to him; why should they hold any significance?

The rest of his discomfort couldn't be attributed to anything physical; it was the same as it had been the night before, when he'd tossed and turned, his fitful sleep ending well before dawn light stained the sky beyond the window.

The reason for his broken sleep had been simple, and even though it affected him now, his pride demanded he not admit it. Better to cast truth aside and carry on without giving it acknowledgment.

Rendash — Aekhora, Blade of the Aligarii, forged by a lifetime of war — had become dependent on a human. A little female human who had become the most important thing in his life, who was perhaps the only reason he hadn't been recaptured. A human who'd fought him to a stalemate. They warred with desire for each other, but she refused to succumb, and he wouldn't force her into something against her will no matter how much she seemed to want it.

As foolish and unlikely as it might sound if spoken aloud, he *needed* her near to sleep soundly. Zoey's presence seemed to keep his mind at ease, somehow holding back thoughts — some of them memories, some imaginings — of his captivity and the many battles he'd waged. She'd provided his only comfort on this world, his only companionship, his only *hope*. With her, he could be Rendash — or simply *Ren*, as she affectionately called him. He could be who he was, or who he *wanted* to be: an aligarii who'd done his duty. An aligarii who could know peace.

Without her, he was simply a fugitive on an alien planet, desperate and alone.

No more of this. No more of this separation, no more of this loneliness.

Even if they didn't mate, he needed to be with her. He needed to hold her in his arms and have that little taste of hope.

He thrust the blankets aside, sat up, and left the bed. A long stride brought him to the door, and then he stalked down the walkway to the room Zoey had claimed. She was likely asleep by now. He'd slip into bed beside her, gently take her into his arms, and find his comfort. Any issues she had when she woke could be dealt with in the morning. Until then, she'd never know. She was a heavy sleeper.

Ren opened the door silently and entered the chamber. A powerful scent — familiar and tantalizing — struck him immediately.

The fragrance of her arousal.

Though the sun had set long before, and snow continued to fall outside, enough light streamed in through the windows to grant Rendash visibility without engaging his *nyros*. Still, it took him a moment to realize what he was seeing on the large bed as he crept toward it. Instinct — that old, bone-deep instinct that superseded all his training — roared to the forefront.

Zoey lay naked in the center of the bed. Her head was turned to one side, hair spread out around her. One of her hands clutched her breast. The other was between her legs, stroking her sex. She bit her lip and moaned, tilting her head back.

Rendash narrowed his eyes to sharpen his vision. He inhaled deeply, taking in her scent. His chest heaved with his quickening breath, and he bared his teeth, clenching his fists at his sides. His erection strained against his pants.

A low growl clawed its way up from his chest.

Zoey screamed, eyes snapping open, and hurled a pillow at him. It struck him in the face with a soft *whump*.

She scrambled away as he tossed the pillow aside. Rendash threw himself atop the bed, catching her with his upper hands before she could dive to the floor.

"Zoey," he rasped as he pulled her close, catching her flailing arms at the wrists and straddling her thighs to protect himself from her wild kicks.

Her struggles ceased, and she stared up at him with wide eyes. "Ren?"

"Who else would it be?"

"I don't know! It's dark and you...you... Oh God. You *saw* me." She tried to yank her arms away.

Something glistened on her fingers in the faint light. He slowly drew her hand close to his face. That *scent*, that intoxicating scent, drifted from her hand. He closed his eyes and growled again, painfully aware of her body pinned beneath his.

"I saw you," he said, "and I want you." He dipped his head, took her fingers into his mouth, and sucked. Her flavor burst across his tongue, unlike anything he'd tasted. Unlike anything he'd imagined.

Zoey's breath hitched. "I can't...I can't believe you just did that."

Ren slid her fingers out of his mouth, running his lips and tongue over their length to catch any remnants of her taste. "I will have more of this. Directly from the source."

"What?"

He pressed her arms onto the bed as he slid his lower palms down her sides. His mouth settled on the hollow at the base of her throat before traversing the valley between her breasts, slowly moving lower and lower as he crawled backward.

"Ren?" Zoey asked breathlessly. "What are you doing?"

"Tell me, Zoey." He reached her abdomen, brushing hungry kisses over her soft flesh. Her stomach quivered. "Tell me you want this. You want *me*."

"We shouldn't..."

"No more games." Another kiss, another small taste. "No more denial. What we want," his lower arms reached her legs, and he grasped her thighs, forcing them wider apart, "we *take*. Tell me you *want*, like I do." He kissed just above the thatch of hair on her pelvis.

Zoey shivered, and her fragrance strengthened. Ren's mouth watered.

"Yes," she breathed, clutching fistfuls of bedding. "Yes, I want you." She raised her head. "But what are you—"

Zoey gasped, hips jerking when his mouth came down on her open sex. She attempted to close her legs, but Ren held them firmly in place.

"Oh my God, don't...don't... *Oh*, don't stop!" She fell back with a throaty moan.

Her scent and taste dominated his senses. He'd wanted to do this to her from the moment he'd seen it on the TV, had imagined it, but his imagination could do no justice to how incredible the reality was — not merely her taste, but her reactions, the way her entire body responded to the motions of his lips and tongue. Zoey exhibited none of the hollow reactions he'd seen from the male and female on the TV; she came to life with his touch.

He explored her with his tongue, greedily lapping her nectar as he lavished her soft, slick flesh with his attention.

"Ren!" Zoey cried and bucked her hips when his tongue flicked the top of her sex.

He paused, looking up along her body to watch her face, and flicked his tongue again. She twitched and released a muffled moan. He hummed his pleasure.

Releasing her wrists, he slid his upper hands to her breasts, stroking her nipples with his thumbs. She covered his hands with hers and arched her back. Her hips undulated, demanding more — more pressure, more of his mouth, more of *him*. He didn't keep her waiting. He latched onto the tiny bud that gave her so much pleasure and sucked.

Zoey's body went taut, and then she writhed beneath him. Her cries of pleasure filled the room as she gyrated against his mouth. She moved her hands to his head, clutching his crest and bringing a sharp sting to his scalp, but he didn't care; the hint of pain drove him on. He licked, nipped, and sucked, unwilling to waste a drop of her sweetness as she came.

The abandon with which she'd so completely lost herself was unlike anything Ren had ever experienced. Aligarii, male and female alike, were far more reserved, and females only received stimulation through intercourse. This — like everything else on this world — was alien to him, but delightfully so. Zoey was adrift on an ocean of pleasure before he'd even entered her.

That was arousing to him beyond description, beyond understanding.

Rendash continued to lap at her sex as she descended from her climax. He watched her the entire time. She buried her fingers in her hair, swept it out of her face, and sighed in contentment. Finally, she lifted her head and met his gaze.

Rendash reluctantly removed his mouth from her sex and licked his lips. He withdrew his upper hands from her breasts and flattened them on the bed, pushing himself up to lean over her as he planted his feet on the floor.

"No one's ever done that to me," Zoey said. There was a shyness in her voice that Rendash hadn't heard before. That shyness made her words genuine to him; otherwise, how could he believe any male would be stupid enough to forgo an experience like this?

Her scent was still driving him wild, and her taste had only strengthened his hunger. His erection pulsed inside his pants, reminding him of its deep, desperate ache.

"I need more of you, Zoey," he rasped. "Do you want more of me?"

Zoey sat up, wrapped an arm around his neck, and pressed her hand to his cheek. He knew she had difficulty seeing in the dark, but she looked directly into his center eyes. "I do. I need you, too, Ren."

He dipped his head forward and kissed her, closing his eyes. She returned the kiss with equal fervor. He dropped his lower hands to his pants and unfastened them, shoving them down his hips before lifting one leg at a time to divest himself of the restrictive clothing. Freeing his cock was a relief, but only a minor one. His aches required a different sort of release.

TIFFANY ROBERTS

Zoey's hand fell away, and her right arm joined her left around his neck to pull him deeper into the kiss.

He slipped his arms around her and lifted her off the bed. Her hot, slick sex pressed to his abdomen as he turned around.

Zoey inhaled sharply, pulling her head back. She wrapped her legs around his middle and tightened her hold on him. "What are you doing?"

"I want to see you." He grasped his shaft with one of his lower hands and guided its tip to her sex. "I want to watch your face as we join."

Her eyes widened, and her hips undulated as though seeking more of him.

"What about…protection?" she asked.

"Protection from what, Zoey?"

She bit her lip and looked away, fingers idly toying with the locks of his crest. "Protection from pregnancy, diseases — not that I'm saying either of us have any, but you know, stuff like that?" She glanced at him. "Could we…even have a baby?"

He couldn't help but smile as he touched a finger to her cheek and guided her to face him again. "My *nyros* destroys diseases, even those alien to me. As for offspring… We are a different species. We cannot procreate, Zoey."

"Oh." She frowned.

"That saddens you?"

Though it was difficult to make out the subtle change in the low light, her cheeks darkened. "No. I guess that's a good thing right now, huh?"

The lie was an obvious one, and her sorrow produced a series of questions he'd not considered. How would Zoey look with her belly round with child? How tender and gentle a mother would she be, how much love would she shower upon her babe? What amount of pride would swell his chest if her child were his? Her sorrow, in that moment, became Rendash's, and it only heightened his desire for her.

He had no answers. All he knew with any certainty was that his need was raging, scalding his insides like fire. He *needed* release, and his instinct demanded he claim her, demanded he plant his seed deep inside her in defiance of their biology, in defiance of fate.

She kissed his jaw below his ear. "Just make love to me, Ren. I want to really experience it at least once in my life."

He didn't fully understand *make love*; it was likely one of those human phrases that altered the meanings of the words it contained. It had to mean *sex*, but he knew that wasn't entirely right. She was asking for something more.

Ren looked into her eyes. They were deeper and more intense than ever, even if their color was muted by shadow; the strangest, most beautiful eyes he'd ever beheld. This was the female who'd stood beside him at great danger to herself, who'd proven worthy of his trust time and again, though she had no stake in his plight. The woman who shared with him freely, who laughed with him, who confided in him and listened without judgment when he opened himself to her.

He slipped a hand into her hair, cupping the back of her head, and kissed her lips. At the same time, he lowered her onto his waiting shaft. Incredible warmth enveloped him as he slid into her sex. Her slick nectar eased his passage, and her inner walls gripped him, tightening as they accepted more of him.

Zoey's breath quickened. He shifted his lower hands to her backside and wrapped an upper arm around her waist, releasing a slow, shaky exhalation as overwhelming pleasure rippled through his body.

"Ren," she rasped against his mouth, pressing her breasts to his chest.

"Zoey," he growled as he sat down on the edge of the bed, and the change of position forced his cock deeper inside her. "I *need* you. Need to take you."

She tugged on his crest and kissed him. "Yes. Now. *Please.*"

Instinct collided with his conscious thought, threatening to take control, but he didn't allow it to yet. He wasn't sure what she could endure; humans were smaller and weaker than aligarii. It stood to reason that they were also more delicate. If he hurt her, he'd never forgive himself.

Zoey shifted, lifting her hips, and her sex caressed his aching shaft with delicious, maddening insistence.

Rendash's control shattered. He grasped her hips and slammed her down onto him. Her sex suddenly clamped around him, fluttering, and coated him with liquid heat.

Zoey cried out, gasping against his shoulder, and shuddered in his embrace.

Pressing his fingers into her yielding flesh, Rendash finally gave over to instinct.

Mind-numbing bliss filled Zoey as a second orgasm roared through her, triggered and prolonged by Ren's thrusting cock. It filled her, stretched her to the brink and beyond, sank deeper and deeper each time they moved. And she took him, all of him. The scales and ridges on the top of his shaft rubbed every spot inside and out to make her reel with pleasure.

She lifted her head and forced her eyes open. Rendash met her gaze fully, his slit pupils contracting and dilating, lips pulled back to bare his fangs. He was so alien, so *other*, but she didn't care. This was Ren, *her* Ren. And right now, he was a beast, pounding into her without relent, releasing feral, guttural sounds that made her wetter.

He left no room for self-consciousness, no place for her to worry about how she looked, if she was jiggling too much, or if she was too loud. All he allowed was for a massive wave of passion to sweep her away; she let go of everything else.

Ren growled a warning when she pulled back, but she wasn't going anywhere. She moved her hands to his shoulders, digging her nails into his scales, and let him use her as he willed. He lifted and slammed her back down on his rock-hard cock. The sounds of flesh meeting flesh and their heavy breathing mingled with their grunts and cries of pleasure.

Her head fell back, and her lashes fluttered closed. Her inner thighs scraped against his sides; in her lust, her skin's sensitivity was heightened, and the brush of his scales was a thrill all its own.

He cupped her breast and pinched her nipple between his fingers. Another bolt of sensation flashed through her, triggering another release, another cry. Zoey was awash in pleasure, paralyzed but for the ravenous pulsing of her sex as waves of ecstasy crashed through her.

Rendash growled. He tightened the grip of his lower hands and slammed her down upon his cock, holding her there firmly. His upper arms encircled her, cocooning her in his strength, and his muscles tensed.

He released a roar that reverberated to Zoey's core, an animalistic declaration that he'd reached his peak. She felt his shaft grow impossibly larger, then strangely unfurl as something pressed even deeper inside her. She gasped and clutched him as a spike of pleasure-pain pierced her. A gush of heat followed.

Ren grasped a fistful of her hair and stared at her; his eyes seemed more reflective, almost supernatural in the gloom. He took her in a claiming kiss, nipping her lip with his fangs, while his cock pulsed inside her, flooding her with more of that heat. He ground his hips, stroking her clit, but kept her pinned in place.

His movements, combined with the fire he'd set inside her, pushed Zoey into another frenzy. She bit and clawed at him and writhed on his lap, unable to move from where he held her. She craved more, needed more, but it was too much, too powerful, not enough. She screamed, throwing her head back in bliss as her sex clenched around his cock, but it felt different than before. Something inside her...*fluttered*.

Body trembling, Zoey went limp, sagging against Ren as she floated down from the heights to which he'd carried her. He remained upright but his muscles eased, his broad chest heaving with ragged breaths. He ran one hand down her spine to possessively cup her ass cheek.

"Tell me again why I waited to do this?" Zoey mumbled against his chest.

"Because you are stubborn to the point of foolishness, *kun'ia*."

Zoey chuckled. He hadn't released her, and she still felt that strange fluttering inside her. She attempted to rise, but his fingers flexed on her hip, and he held her in place.

"No," he said. "Not yet."

Zoey tilted her head back to look up at him questioningly.

"I need...time to relax," he said. "Let me hold you for a while longer."

She turned her head to rest her cheek on his shoulder and smiled. Running a hand over his chest, she marveled at the feel of his scales as she traced their tiny seams with the tip of her finger, wishing there were enough light to see their color.

The quivering continued inside her, accompanied by that faint pinch of pleasure-pain. Zoey furrowed her brow and swiveled her hips. The sensation intensified. Though it didn't hurt, the feeling was strange. She moved to rise, but the pinch sharpened into something more pain than pleasure.

Ren hissed and tightened his grip on her, pressing her sex back down upon him. "Be still, Zoey."

She stilled, but now her previously languid body thrummed with tension. "Ren... What is going on?"

"I imagine we discovered another difference in the reproductive anatomy of our species. Aligarii males...latch on. Inside."

"Latch on? You mean your...your...your penis is *attached* to me?" Her voice steadily rose with her fear.

"Not *attached*," he replied, smoothing a hand over her tousled hair and down her back. "It is temporary, Zoey. Aligarii females cannot reach their..." He raised a hand and wagged it in a small circle, as though searching for a word.

"Climax?"

"Yes. That is a good word. They cannot reach their climax before that point."

She struggled for calm; she trusted that Rendash wouldn't hurt her, and that this would turn out fine, but a little forewarning might've been nice.

Oh, by the way, Zoey, my penis is going to open up and latch onto your cervix. No big deal, we'll just be stuck together for a while. And if you move it'll hurt. Well, let's get to it!

And if I'd known and turned it down, I wouldn't have experienced those mind-blowing orgasms.

Perhaps it was best that she'd been kept ignorant.

"But why…latch?" she asked.

"To maximize the chances of conception," he said.

"But you said we couldn't have kids."

"We can't," he assured her, sliding his hand to her cheek and holding her gaze. "This is just the natural process for my kind."

Zoey relaxed a little. It was strange to know that part of him was physically connected to her, but it didn't hurt as long as she didn't attempt to pull away from him. As she stilled and focused on the sensation, the lingering pain faded, and she discovered it was pleasurable — *very* pleasurable. She soon found it difficult to keep from moving.

"Um, Ren?" she asked, voice breathy. Her skin tingled with spreading warmth.

His tongue — barely visible in the shadows — slipped out of his mouth and ran over his upper lip, reminding Zoey of what he'd done to her with it. The memory made her pussy clench.

"Yes, Zoey?" By the huskiness of his voice, he already knew what was happening.

"I don't know if I'll be able to sit still much longer." A tremor swept through her. She caught her lip between her teeth and leaned against him, gasping.

"Then don't," Ren replied. His hands guided her hips through slow gyrations without lifting her pelvis. The movement stroked her clit and increased the pressure in all the right places.

The steady, deliberate rhythm built her gradually to a climax, urged on by his touch and their increasingly ragged breathing. When it hit, it was no less powerful than the last. Ren growled along with her cries, filling her with a burst of new heat.

Shortly after they'd both settled, he lay back on the bed,

drawing her along with him, and his cock released its inner hold. Liquid gushed from her, trailing down her thighs.

Zoey rolled out of his embrace and got to her knees, reaching to switch on the lamp on the nightstand. She immediately turned back to Ren and dropped her gaze to his cock.

If she hadn't felt him inside her, if he hadn't explained what had happened, she might have freaked the fuck out. Even having experienced it, she had a hard time believing that his cock had been inside her like *that*.

Did I let myself forget that he's an alien? Of course *sex would remind me of that.*

His cock lay against his inner thigh, but it didn't look anything like it normally did; her closest comparison was a stargazer lily. The head of his shaft had unfurled like the petals of a flower, revealing unscaled, pink skin inside. At the center was a smooth, pink, tube-like *thing*, a cross between a penis and a chameleon tongue. Before her eyes, the central *thing* withdrew, and the petals closed, their seams vanishing a little at a time.

"Holy shit," Zoey said, unable to look away even after it was sealed. Because of the overlapping scales, she couldn't even see the seams where it had split open.

"Your parts aren't exactly normal-looking to me, either," he said defensively. He'd propped himself on his elbows to meet her gaze.

Zoey looked down at her thighs, fearful she'd find green goo oozing out of her like in one of the sci-fi romances books she'd read. There was an awful lot of seed running down her legs, but thankfully it looked like it could have come from any human male; no stringy, neon green globs to be seen.

"How do your females look?" she asked, only barely stopping her imagination from picturing some kind of Venus flytrap vagina opening wide for his lily-cock.

"More...discreet."

She lifted her eyes to meet his gaze, her eyebrows falling low. "What does *that* mean?"

His brow furrowed with a blend of confusion and mild alarm; even though he was a different species, it seemed he, too, was hardwired to recognize the danger when a woman used that tone.

"Female aligarii have a slit. It is in the same place, but it is essentially hidden. Obviously, for your kind, things are a bit more...exposed."

Zoey pressed her thighs together and crossed her arms over her chest, suddenly very self-conscious.

"No," he said firmly as he sat up, making no effort to mask his nudity. His upper hands pulled her arms away from her breasts, and his lower hands slid between her thighs, forcing them apart. He cupped her pelvis, sliding a finger into her sex.

Zoey gasped, abandoning her brief struggle. She grasped his upper biceps to steady herself.

"This is beautiful to me," he said. One of his hands closed over her breast. "This is beautiful." He touched her hips, her stomach, her legs; her hair, neck and face. "All of this is beautiful, Zoey. In part *because* it is different. Because it is *you*."

Her eyes strung with tears. Her first instinct was to mistrust his words, but she knew he was being honest. She *felt* his sincerity. There was no disgust in his eyes, no regret. He was touching her and seeing her. In the light.

"You see me," she said quietly.

"I have since that first night." He removed his hand from between her thighs — not without reluctance — and slid both of his lower hands around her, cupping her backside to pull her close. "I will always see you, *kun'ia*."

Zoey searched his eyes, all of them. When she blinked, her tears spilled, trailing down her cheeks, but she smiled despite them. "You called me that before. What does that word mean?"

He gently brushed way her tears with his thumb. "It is just something to call a person you care about."

Zoey reached up and placed her hands on his jaw. "Then I also see you, *kun'ia*."

Ren returned the smile, and the reflection in his eyes took on a more tender, sentimental cast. He closed them as he dipped his head down, pressing his forehead to hers. "It is late. We should rest, little human."

"Considering this little human just had four orgasms, I think so." Zoey grinned.

"*Orgasm*... Is that another word for climax?"

"Yes."

"And you only had four?"

Zoey tilted her head back and narrowed her eyes in response to the mischievous tone in his voice.

"Surely we can do better," he suggested.

"Um..."

Holy hell, what had she gotten herself into? From virtually no sex to being sexed to death.

Heh. What a way to go.

She raked her gaze over Rendash again, appreciating him in the lamplight. All things considered, she couldn't let a small chance of death-by-sex deter her from having more of him — lily penis and all.

"Could I...be on top?" she asked. She trailed a finger down his torso, following the valleys between his ridges of muscle, and traced a circle around the tip of his erection with her fingertip. It jerked.

Grasping her hips, he lay back and drew her atop him. Zoey released a startled cry and laughed. Her laughter swiftly became a moan of pleasure as he simultaneously thrust upward and pulled her down onto his cock.

"For as long as you want, *kun'ia*," he said.

Rendash watched Zoey sleep, much as he had during their first night together. So much had changed since then, though only four days had passed. She'd kept her back to him and had lain as far away from him as possible without tumbling out of the bed that first night, whereas now she lay facing him, wrapped in his arms by her own choice. Much more than their sleeping positions had changed, though, and those changes had come long before they'd finally succumbed to mutual desire.

She seemed so at peace now, so happy, without worry or conflict on her face. Her breathing was easy, her body relaxed.

This was how he wanted to remember her — content and beautiful, alien but familiar. Everything he'd never known he wanted. *His*, if only for a short while.

He gently brushed rogue locks of hair from her face. He'd grown accustomed to the oddly full, relatively soft facial features of humans during his captivity, but Zoey's was the first and only such face in which he saw beauty — beauty as deep in her as his *nyros* were in him, beauty that permeated all of her, inside and out.

Why should he only have her for a brief time? Why should

he leave her behind to become little more than a bright, fleeting highlight in an otherwise troubled life?

As far as Ren was concerned, he'd already earned his peace, had already earned his choice. All that remained was the formality of returning to Algar to declare his intent. Tradition did not dictate that he was required to take a mate. Nor did it dictate that his mate had to be aligarii. The only thing stopping him from bringing Zoey along was his adherence to the nature of the traditions, his devotion to the unspoken duty that lay beneath them — to carry on the aligarii race, to continue to keep the Khorzar strong with his bloodline.

What did all that matter now? His Umen'rak was gone, his life was in danger, and he'd made a connection with another being beyond anything he could've imagined possible. His relationship with Zoey was precious. Too precious to throw away if there were any chance to maintain it — or even better, any chance to let it grow.

I can take her with me.

The thought crackled through him like a bolt of lightning, arcing across his every cell. He'd dismissed the notion when it had presented itself before, had been unable to view it beyond the lens of his experience and the culture that had raised him.

It was a thing that had not been done. But that didn't mean it *could not* be done.

So few aekhora survived to the point of earning their freedom; would the Halvari truly deny him, when he wouldn't, in truth, be violating the traditions?

He could take her with him, and thus bring his happiness home rather than return alone and seek happiness blindly, knowing that any life he might make on Algar without Zoey would never compare to what he shared with her now. He could take her with him and hold on to this contentment. He could take her with him and grow *more* content.

Ren trailed the pads of his fingers over her cheek. Zoey smiled and nuzzled her face against his hand.

Would she *want* to go? Would she want to leave her world, leave her people, leave everything she knew behind?

He understood how it felt to be on an alien world. Understood the sense of loss, loneliness, *wrongness*. Even with all his training and experience, it affected him. How would she cope? Ren's presence had already disrupted so much of her life, but she'd told him she had nothing left, no *one* left. Did she have any reason to remain on Earth?

"When the time comes, *kun'ia*, I hope you choose to accompany me," he whispered.

Until that time, he would not trouble her with worrying over it, would not burden her with the weight of the unknown. Zoey deserved nothing but happiness. He hoped that, one day soon, he'd be able to make that happiness something lasting. He hoped he could grant her the comfort, stability, and love for which she'd always longed.

Wasn't that what she'd truly meant when she spoke of wanting a home?

Drawing in another deep breath to appreciate their mingled scents, Ren finally closed his eyes and allowed sleep to claim him, keeping his kun'ia — his *mate* — secure in his arms.

Chapter Fifteen

Stantz stepped out of the SUV and straightened his coat. He walked directly to his agents, not bothering to glance at the state troopers gathered fifty feet away around their white vehicles. He'd seen the displeasure and confusion on their faces as he pulled up. He felt their glares on his back even now. During his career, he'd dealt with their type often enough to know what they were thinking — *fuck these feds for coming onto our turf, for taking over our investigation, for forcing us out.*

National Security was a great catchall justification for seizing investigations, but it never set anyone at ease.

Stantz didn't have time to set anyone at ease.

The agent in charge of the scene, Calder, led Stantz along a well-trodden path through snow and scrub to the taped-off area with the body.

Crouching, Stantz examined the remains. His stomach clenched and churned.

"Wounds are consistent with those inflicted on our agents during the incident," Calder said. "All cauterized."

Stantz rose. His hands were already cold, and it felt like his dry skin would split along his knuckles any second, but he didn't slip them into his pockets or reach for his gloves. The discomfort gave him a good reason to focus on the task at hand. On the mutilated corpse.

"What about the other injuries?"

"Animals. Been out here for a few days, at least."

This was what Stantz had unleashed upon an unsuspecting world. This savagery, this hatred, this…*splendor*.

Only the narrow-minded and shortsighted would view the Fox's escape as a setback. Stantz understood what the director could not — this wasn't a failure, but an unexpected, unprecedented opportunity. Specimen Ten had finally shown them its capabilities. Now they knew those tiny machines could do so much more than accelerate healing.

Now they knew the alien's nanotechnology could be used as a weapon.

"You've already begun the cleanup?" Stantz asked.

"Yes, sir. The coroner's report will detail a mundane stabbing."

"Good. Keep in close contact."

Stantz walked back toward his vehicle. The cluster of state troopers in their brown coats frowned at him. Offering no response, he climbed into the backseat of the SUV and opened his computer. He touched the button on his ear piece.

"MCC, this is the Huntsman," he said, pouring half a roll of antacids into his mouth.

Damn the director and his foolish protocols.

"Hawk acknowledges, Huntsman," Fairborough replied through the comms.

"Mark my location. Find a spot nearby to move the MCC. The Fox is heading east."

"Copy that." Fairborough hesitated. "Sir, we may have found something relevant to the hunt."

Stantz shifted the remaining chunks of chalky antacid to one side of his mouth. "Go."

"One of the women Branson stopped on the night of the incident was reported missing. Zoey Weston."

The woman's file appeared on Stantz's screen; she was the curvy girl Branson had been hostile with.

"And?"

"Her car was found abandoned on I-70 Tuesday morning, about ten miles west of your current location."

Stantz ground his teeth together. "We might have another body out here."

"Maybe, sir. But look at these records."

The computer screen flashed as a list appeared. It took Stantz a moment to realize he was looking at a bank statement.

"One hundred and twelve dollars in a big-and-tall store in Vegas on Monday." Stantz's heart rate increased. "Strange for a girl listed as five-foot-seven on her license. And she rented a room in Green River on Monday night."

He dumped a few more antacid tablets into his hand and slammed them into his open mouth before pulling up the satellite map.

"Start driving for Green River," he said to the driver. "Hawk, I need you to get the story out about Weston. We need people to be aware she's missing. Would be a shame if she doesn't turn up."

"Copy that, Huntsman."

"Get her picture out to all field agents and send the description of our murder victim's registered vehicle along with it. Matthew Johnson, independent contractor out of Elko, Nevada. We're shifting our search area into eastern Utah and western Colorado. We'll find this woman, and then we'll bag our Fox."

Chapter Sixteen

Movement disturbed Rendash's slumber. Beside him, Zoey delicately shifted his arms off her, removing herself from his hold. He listened as the bedding whispered over her bare skin but didn't lift his head and open his eyes until she was padding across the floor.

He watched the sway of her backside appreciatively as she walked to the corner bathroom, allowing his gaze to roam from the top of her dark hair all the way down to her feet, admiring every curve along the way.

Over the last two days, he'd thoroughly studied her body, had learned how to provide her with as much pleasure as possible. She'd done the same for him. His cock hardened with the memory of her *explorations*; her tongue had slid down his abdomen, trailing lower and lower until it finally flowed over the ridges of his shaft. The sight of her pink lips wrapped around him as she sucked had combined with the feel of her wicked tongue to create the most exquisite torture of his life.

She switched on the corner light and manipulated the

controls outside the shower stall. The water came on, falling like a gentle waterfall from overhead. She delayed, likely allowing the water time to heat. Her body's angle offered him a profile view of her breast and its pink nipple.

Ren licked his lips. Rather than satisfy his hunger, their initial joining had only confirmed that his desire for Zoey was insatiable.

She pulled open the stall door and slipped into the shower. The condensation clinging to the glass obscured his view of her, leaving only a shadowy figure; somehow, that only increased his excitement.

The faint, grayish light of early dawn filled the room, not bright enough to dispel the shadows but enough to see by. Ren slid out of bed, stretched his limbs, and approached the large windows running across the wall. The snowfall had finally ceased the night before. Everything outside was blanketed in unbroken white, but there was no more falling from the sky.

He couldn't know if the break would last, couldn't know if they'd be able to leave or not, but it was the first time the weather had relented since they'd entered what Zoey called the *Rocky Mountains* — which seemed to him a redundant name, as most mountains were, by default, made of rock. Such specifications only needed to be made when an object deviated from the normal composition.

He shook off the tangential thought, recognizing it as a subconscious attempt to stray from the truth of the situation — they'd have to resume their journey to his ship.

That was a bittersweet realization. Getting back on the road just meant they'd be a little closer to his ship, to him escaping from a planet that caused him so much loss and pain. It also meant they'd be a little closer to her potentially choosing to stay on Earth. She was the only good part of his time here and had become the *best* part of his entire life.

Was it wrong for him to want more time without having to face that looming uncertainty? This had been a long delay, but it had been worth the time.

Rendash swung his gaze toward the shower. While it lasted, he intended to use this time to the fullest. He strode to the shower, tugged the door open, and ducked inside.

The hot water and steamy air was comforting, far closer to the climate of his youth than anything he'd encountered on Earth thus far. He hoped to return to that climate, to those humid jungles, with the female standing before him.

He watched water stream over her skin, followed its path down her back, over the curve of her ass, and along her thighs. She stood beneath the falling water, hands over her face, and gave no indication that she knew he'd joined her.

For several moments, he contented himself with admiring her. That she didn't know her own beauty seemed a crime to him. That she hadn't been told of it by her prior mates every day only attested to the dishonor and blindness of the men she'd known.

Ren stepped up behind her. He settled his lower hands on her hips and moved his upper hands around her to cup her breasts.

She started, bumping into him with a sharp intake of breath.

"I didn't know you were in here," she said, tipping her head back onto his shoulder to look up at him.

"I'm not disturbing you, am I?" he asked, taking each of her nipples between a finger and thumb.

"No." Zoey closed her eyes and leaned against him, pressing

her breasts into his hands. "Not at all," she continued breathlessly.

Slowly, he slid one of his lower hands around the front of her hip, fingertips brushing over the patch of hair at her pelvis. "You've woken early today."

"I couldn't fall back to sleep."

Ren dipped his head, touching his lips to her ear as he lowered his voice. "A failure on my part. If you are restless, I must remedy the situation and assure your relaxation."

She released a low moan as he slid his fingers into her welcoming heat and stroked her *clit*. She lifted an arm, slipping it around his head to clutch at his crest, and undulated her hips against his hand.

"Does this feel good, *kun'ia?*" he asked.

"Yes," she rasped. "Don't stop."

Zoey didn't need to beg; he'd come to crave her reactions so much that he wouldn't stop until she was done — if he stopped at all. He drew her backside against him, pressing his throbbing cock along her spine, and continued to caress her. The gyration of her hips created sweet pressure along his shaft. Soon, his own breath was ragged.

She moaned and arched against him. Her thighs quivered against his hand, a telling sign that she was close.

"Ren, I need you. I want to feel you in me. Now. *Please.*"

He hummed deep in his chest; he ached with need of his own and would gladly give her what she wanted…but anticipation often heightened the sensations when release was finally granted.

"Soon," he said, increasing the pressure of his fingers. "You are not ready, little human, and I want to *hear* your pleasure, first."

Her moans filled the shower, and her body moved desperately against his hand. When she came, her mouth opened in a silent cry, and only her strengthening tremors forced a scream of pleasure from her throat. She clutched at him as her sex coated his hand with her nectar, which immediately mingled with the running water. Her knees buckled, but he supported her on his thigh and continued to stroke until her cries subsided.

Zoey took in a deep breath, limbs faintly trembling.

Turning her around, Ren picked her up off her feet, pressed her against the wall with legs spread, and thrust into her, his cock sinking deep into her welcoming heat. She gasped, meeting his gaze with half-lidded eyes. He braced his upper forearms against the wall and clenched her backside with his lower hands. Her thighs squeezed his waist.

"Fuck me," Zoey begged. "Fuck me hard. I want everything you have to give." She nipped at his lips. "Don't hold back with me. I won't break, Ren."

Her words burst inside him like a bomb, blasting apart the final barrier between control and instinct. He pounded into her again and again, reveled in her heat, her tightness, in the building pleasure and pressure within him. It was an indulgence of the primal, a part of Ren that could never be eliminated no matter how advanced his people became, a part that would always reside within the hearts of all aligarii.

He hissed and growled in response to the sensations; his sounds mingled with her cries, which punctuated each of his savage upward thrusts. Her nails clawed at him, too blunt to break his scales but strongly enough to inflict pricks of pain that heightened his need for her.

Zoey's body stiffened, and she screamed, pouring heat over him as she came.

"You are *mine*," he snarled against her neck, bucking his hips one last time before he forced her down firmly upon his cock. Her sex tightened around him, her inner walls contracting to draw him deeper. Her juices flowed around his shaft and trickled down his thighs.

In that moment, Ren roared his own climax. The built-up pressure exploded, rocking him, and triggered a now-familiar surge in his nyros that sent fire through his entire body. His cock opened, and his stem thrust forward to latch onto her and pump his seed into her womb. The sensitive, unscaled skin of his stem brushed her inner walls, pushing his pleasure to new heights.

He rested his forehead against hers, teeth bared in a growl as he ground his hips against her. Each of her movements, no matter how small, produced a new wave of ecstasy.

Zoey's arms loosened around his neck. She ran her palms down his back and up to his shoulders soothingly, humming in contentment.

"I think I am properly relaxed," she said, smiling.

"Are you?" He kissed her cheek, her jaw, and finally her lips.

"Mhmm." Zoey raised her head and looked at him. Her eyes were bright, pupils large. She cupped his jaw and brushed her thumb over his bottom lip. "I love it when you let go."

With the tips of his fingers, he swept strands of wet hair out of her face, tucking them behind her rounded ear. "Only for you, *kun'ia*. Anything for you."

Zoey brought her mouth to his in a tender kiss. "*Kun'ia.*" When she drew back, her playfulness had faded, leaving something softer, deeper, more powerful in her eyes, something he couldn't place.

His chest swelled with emotion — adoration, desire, contentment, possessiveness, need. He couldn't bear the thought of leaving her behind anymore, couldn't allow himself to even entertain the possibility.

Zoey was *his*, and he would never let her go.

Zoey lounged on the sectional in the living room, flipping through the channels on the TV, too preoccupied with her thoughts to pay much attention to what was on.

The last few days had been the best of her life. For the first time since her father's passing, she felt connected to someone, more connected than she'd ever believed possible. Ren made her happy, *deliriously* happy. And the sex? She thought that kind of sex only happened in romance novels. It was absolutely mind blowing.

She squeezed her thighs together. It was as though she could still feel him inside her, the lingering sensation serving as a reminder that he was the master of her body. She was deliciously sore in all the right places.

But their time here was nearing its end. The owners would arrive in a few days' time to find their food eaten and their house lived in — *especially* the beds. Rendash was outside now, scouting the area, checking if the roads were clear. The snow had stopped, and they'd be on the road again soon. Heading toward his ship, toward his final destination.

Toward the moment when he'd leave her.

It was far too late to pretend she didn't care about him. Her pathetic attempts at distance had failed, and she was glad for it; those attempts had only made them miserable. Other people would call her insane or depraved, but her heart had decided, and it was all-in when it came to Rendash. It leapt at the sight of him, warmed when he smiled, and thumped excitedly at his smallest touch.

And it was breaking at the mere thought of having to say goodbye.

Something on TV caught her eye, but her finger automatically pressed the channel up button several times before her brain relayed the command to stop. Frowning, she flipped back. She stared at the screen in disbelief, hand dropping to her lap.

Zoey's picture was being displayed one the news for the world to see. Her first thought — undoubtedly enabled by her shock — was that it wasn't even a *flattering* picture. Then her rational mind kicked in, and she turned up the volume.

"—vehicle was discovered abandoned on I-70 in Utah between Salina and Green River on Tuesday. According to a friend, Weston was traveling from Santa Barbara, California to Des Moines, Iowa, but has reportedly been out of contact since early Monday morning. Her boyfriend, Joshua Martins, is the last known person to speak with her.

"Martins stated that there was another man in the background during his conversation with Weston, which was ended abruptly. Since that conversation, her phone has been unreachable. Utah State Troopers have requested assistance from the FBI, as they suspect potential foul play in her disappearance and the trail may span several states. Bank activity shows Miss Weston's debit card last being used in Green River, Utah, on Tuesday morning.

"If you have any information on the whereabouts of Zoey Weston, please contact the Utah Highway Patrol..."

"Oh shit," Zoey said.

She didn't know what to do. Should she call them and say she was fine? How would that conversation go?

Yeah, yeah, no problems here. I just took a dead man's truck — yes, I'm probably an accomplice to his murder — and broke into a luxury cabin to relax while a blizzard passed. Oh, I'm also hiding an alien from the government, if you really wanted to know.

What kind of life would she have after Ren was gone? At best, she'd have a lot of clever explaining to do and a hefty impound fee for her car, and even if she could pay that fee she couldn't afford repairs on the damned thing.

The only way to be safe was to remain hidden, but how was she supposed to do that? She was a waitress, not a criminal mastermind, and she'd left a trail behind her the entire way. Hell, her DNA was all over this place.

Especially the bed. *Definitely* the bed.

I really should wash the bed linen before we leave…

Zoey paced the living room, anxious for Ren's return. When she heard the front door open, she rushed into the foyer and threw her arms around him. A blast of cold from the open door seeped in and made her shiver.

He put three of his arms around her and reached back with the fourth to shut the door. "I haven't been gone for *that* long," he said, and she could hear the smile in his voice.

"I missed you, anyway," she replied, hugging him tighter, "and I just found out that I'm all over the news. They're looking for me now, too."

"Who is looking for you? The same ones looking for me?"

Zoey drew back and looked up at him. "No, not the government. The police. I'm officially a missing person. But you can be sure the government will know if the police find me with you."

Ren shifted that fourth arm to press his palm to her cheek. "Good thing I found you first, *kun'ia.*"

Her heart did a happy little flip at his words, warming her

TIFFANY ROBERTS

from within. She grinned, pretty sure it was the biggest, goofiest grin of her life, but she didn't give a damn. She gripped the collar of his coat and tugged him down. He offered no resistance.

"Me too," she said before pressing her lips to his.

He returned the kiss with familiarity and ease, relishing in the contact and prolonging it while giving her, subtly, everything of himself. Her lips iced over with the absence of his when he finally pulled away.

"The main road is clear, and the clouds are moving away," he said.

"I guess that means it's time to move on," she said regretfully, brushing a finger over the pointed tip of his ear then down the scales of his neck. "I wish we could stay here forever."

He combed his fingers through her hair, gently sweeping it back. "The time to move on was always going to come, Zoey. But we aren't parting yet. And I don't know if I could stay *here* forever. The cold would eventually drive me mad."

"Wishful thinking on my part. And you know I'd keep you warm." The corner of her mouth tilted up.

Ren's smile broadened into a grin, displaying his fangs. "You always do." She didn't miss his reluctance as he broke their embrace. "We should prepare. We have a long journey ahead of us, despite how far we've come, and we'll have to proceed with greater caution now that we are both hunted."

Zoey nodded. "I'll get my suitcase packed up and brought downstairs." She turned to walk away, but halted abruptly, looking back at Ren. "Um, actually, I think we'll need to delay leaving just for a bit. I'm going to wash the bedding. It's the *least* we can do."

"Is it important?"

"I guess it's not really *important*, but… It's the…honorable thing to do."

He regarded her in silence before finally nodding. "Very well. See to it, and I will find a means to extract our vehicle from the snow."

"I saw some snow shovels in the garage. When you're done with that," Zoey brushed a finger over her bottom lip, "maybe you could join me in the kitchen? If you're *hungry*, that is. I might have something on the menu you'll enjoy."

Zoey couldn't believe she was saying these things. She never dreamed she'd tease a man like this, much less possess any degree of confidence in herself. She'd never been outspoken when it came to sex, and the deed had always been done with the lights off. But with Ren, she wanted to explore *all* the possibilities. He made her feel sexy.

No, it was more than that. She *was* sexy. She wouldn't shy away from the pleasures of the flesh when it came to Ren…and that included asking him to eat her out on a stranger's island counter.

His brows rose, and his pupils narrowed to slits. "I'm *very* hungry, little human. I'll have to hurry, won't I?"

"You better, or I might start without you."

Ren smirked and locked his eyes with hers. "That might be more interesting to walk in on. Perhaps I'll have a taste now—" He stepped forward, took her hand, and brought it to his mouth to slip her index finger between his lips. His tongue swirled around her finger as he slowly pulled it back out. "—and more after my work."

Zoey's breath quickened, and her pussy tightened in sudden need.

Oh God, that's some sexy shit.

"What do you have in mind?" she asked, staring at his mouth.

His gaze slid down her body, gleaming with hunger. Without a word, Ren darted forward, startling a gasp from her. He lifted her and had her leggings off before her feet completely left the floor. He swept her legs over his shoulders and pressed her back against the wall, and then his hands spread her thighs wide and his mouth was *there*. Zoey's lips parted in a silent cry as her fingers tangled in his crest locks.

Her last conscious thought — before she was carried away on a tidal wave of pleasure — was that maybe he wasn't quite as eager to leave as he'd made it seem.

Chapter Seventeen

Following the signs for I-70, Zoey drove west along South Frontage Road. She was decked out in her freshly stolen winter attire — a cozy coat, woolen leggings, and comfortable, plush snow boots. She *might* have taken a few extras for just-in-cases, but she'd made sure the cabin was tidied and the bedding washed before they departed.

If it weren't for Rendash, she would've left a combination thank you and apology note on the island. He nixed the idea, pointing out that even though they'd left evidence of their presence, the security system wouldn't offer any indication that they'd ever been there. He'd argued there was no reason to give any sign of their presence freely now that she was being searched for.

She'd fought a little, but she knew he was right, and ultimately gave in.

It's the thought that counts, right?

It was midafternoon by the time they'd left. Laundry hadn't been their only delay, or even their primary one. Neither of

253

them could get enough of the other. She'd secretly hoped to stay another day, but they were already pushing their luck. What if the owners arrived earlier than expected?

What if they woke to the sound of low-flying helicopters in the middle of the night?

Zoey hated leaving. She hadn't lied to Ren when she said she wished they could stay forever. The cabin had been a dream, made more wonderful because she'd shared it with him.

Her chest constricted.

No. I won't think of him leaving right now. We still have time together.

She glanced at him. Even though the truck was bigger than her car, he still looked awkwardly large inside, with his knees up against the dash. He wore his oversized coat with the torn clothing beneath. A pair of dark sunglasses aided his raised hood in obscuring his makeup-caked face from would-be onlookers. The disguise seemed flimsy to her now, having seen his natural face for such a long stretch, especially with the bright sunshine reflecting off the snow and wet roads to light everything from all angles.

She hoped the glare on the windshield would be enough to prevent anyone from noticing him, because more than a passing glance would reveal his inhumanity to anyone with half a brain.

"My ship is that way," he said, pointing over his right shoulder.

"Yeah, I know. You told me."

"Why aren't we going in that direction?"

"Because, like I've explained to you, that's not how these roads work. Sometimes you have to go the wrong direction to go in the right one."

Thanks to his impatience, she'd decided it best not to tell him that the interstate had been directly to their left, running parallel to them, ever since they pulled onto South Frontage; she was afraid he might've simply jerked the wheel aside and forced them over the grassy median and onto the freeway.

He frowned deeply. "Is that another one of those human sayings?"

"It doesn't matter if it's a saying or not, because it's true. We have a stop to make real quick before we head out of town, anyway."

Zoey drove on, squinting against the snow glare as she searched for a gas station. She was beginning to lose hope when the gentle curve of the road revealed a sign up ahead that had been hidden by trees — a big, bright red gas station sign.

She turned into the gas station lot with a muttered *thank you*. She pulled up to a pump, killed the engine, and climbed out. Despite the clear blue sky and bright sunlight, the air was cold. Once the truck was filled, she leaned into the cab.

"I'm going to run inside," she said.

Ren nodded, but his frown firmly in place. "Quickly. The longer we wait, the more likely I am to be noticed."

"I'll hurry. Just keep your head down. Maybe pretend to be asleep, or something."

"Quickly, little human."

"Okay, okay," she said, closing the door.

She rounded the truck and looked both ways before crossing the parking lot and entering the convenience store. She responded to the clerk's greeting with a smile and wave before she found the ATM near the entrance. Pulling her debit card out of her wallet, she inserted it into the machine and entered her PIN.

Within a few minutes, she'd withdrawn eight hundred and twenty dollars from her account, leaving the last three dollars and thirty-seven cents as a loss. She put everything in her wallet but two twenties and grabbed some snacks — including a few Twix bars, which had become Ren's favorite — and a pair of sunglasses for herself. She stuffed her change, bills and coins, into her coat pocket.

She tossed her debit card into the trash outside the door on her way out, and her heart stopped when she looked up. A police car was parked not ten feet away.

It's okay. Cops like gas station snacks too, right? It's got nothing to do with me.

As she hurried back to the truck, she glanced back at the parked police cruiser. A uniformed police officer emerged from the store a second later.

How had she not noticed him walking in?

Zoey yanked the truck door open, climbed in, and started the engine. She dropped the bag of snacks onto the seat between herself and Ren.

"What's wrong?" he asked.

"Probably nothing." She pulled away from the pump and stopped at the road, waiting for an opening to turn out of the lot. When she checked the rearview mirror, her breath hitched. The cop car was right behind them.

The onramp for Interstate 70 was just down the road. Just two more turns, a left and a right, and they'd be free and clear. Local police didn't have any jurisdiction on the interstate…did they?

She turned left onto South Frontage at the first opportunity. Her heart pounded, and her eyes darted repeatedly to the mirrors. The cop pulled out behind her, moving in the same direction, and steadily closed the gap between their vehicles.

"Zoey?" Ren's voice was firmer.

"Trying not to panic," she replied, hands tightening on the wheel.

Her gaze swung forward. The onramp was only a couple hundred feet away.

The cop threw on his lights. Scalding heat and icy cold flowed through her veins simultaneously.

"Oh God. No, no, no no no. This can't be happening right now," she said quickly, breaths short.

The cop remained behind her, rolling along steadily to match her pace. Her knuckles went white, and the anxious blend of fire and ice spread out from her veins to encompass her entire body, making her skin itch beneath the heavy clothing even as she shivered.

"Control, Zoey," Ren said. "Can we outrun him?"

"What?" She gave him a brief, incredulous glance. "No! That'll make things worse." Refocusing on the road, she shifted her eyes continuously to the mirror and back again. "I don't know what to do! I-I have to pull over."

"Then do what is expected of you in this situation," he said, words calm and measured. She didn't know if he simply didn't understand why freaking out was the reasonable response right now or if he just couldn't feel fear, but he betrayed not an ounce of worry.

"Okay. Okay, I can do that. I can do this."

She took a deep breath and checked the speedometer to make sure she wasn't speeding in her panic. The upcoming turn lane had eliminated the shoulder on her side of the road, so she proceeded straight into the roundabout, following it around until it opened into a hotel parking lot.

Forcing herself to continue breathing steadily, she parked in the first open spot — which faced a steep hill — lowered her window, and turned off the engine. The cop pulled up behind her, trapping them between a mound of snow in front and his vehicle behind.

"Is there anything I need to do?" Ren asked.

"Just…just keep your head down and your hands up on the dash." Zoey watched the cop in the rearview mirror; it looked like he was doing something on the computer mounted in his cab. "Oh, this is *so* not good."

"Zoey?" The question in Rendash's voice drew her attention to him. He held up one of his hands; its green scales and lacking finger were difficult to miss in broad daylight.

"So, you just… I don't know, Ren! Just go invisible."

"I'm fairly certain that he's already seen me, Zoey."

She glanced in the mirror again. The cop had opened his door and was climbing out. "He's not looking right now, though. Just do it!"

Ren obeyed, but not before giving her an exaggerated frown.

The cop walked around his car, dropping one hand to his belt — close to his gun. Zoey moved her hands to the top of the steering wheel to keep them visible.

"Afternoon, ma'am," the cop said as he walked up to her car. "I—" Brow furrowed, he lowered his sunglasses and looked past her into the cab. "Where is your passenger?"

"Passenger?" Zoey laughed nervously. "It's just me."

"There was a man in the passenger seat, a very large man, right before I walked over."

"I-I don't know what to say, officer. It's just me in this truck. Maybe it was just a…a reflection on the back window?"

He backed away, settling his hand on the grip of his pistol as he searched the immediate area. Allowing the truck wide berth, he walked around to the passenger side. Zoey watched in the mirrors as he dipped, probably checking underneath the truck, and popped back up.

Her mouth was terribly dry.

The cop's eyebrows were low when he returned to her window, but his eyes were wide and troubled. He stammered and stuttered a few times before he regained his composure, and his demeanor made a subtle shift from confused to annoyed.

"License and registration, ma'am."

"My license is in my purse, and I'll have to get the registration out of the glove compartment. Is that okay?"

"Not a problem."

Moving as slowly and non-threateningly as possible, she unbuckled her seatbelt and turned to her purse, removing her license from her wallet. She leaned over the passenger seat, placing a hand down to hold herself up.

But her hand didn't land on the seat.

Rendash released a muffled grunt.

Zoey cringed. She knew exactly where she'd set her hand by the feel of it. "Sorry," she whispered.

"Everything all right, ma'am?" the cop asked.

"Yeah, one sec." She opened the glove box and rummaged through the contents. She froze when she discovered a black revolver with a short barrel tucked between various papers and the owner's manual.

It probably would've been the last thing she saw that night in Utah if Ren hadn't intervened.

The chill creeping along her spine had nothing to do with the cold air flowing in through the open window. There was a *gun* in the truck, and there was a cop behind her!

"Control," Ren whispered, barely loud enough to hear.

Easier said than done, big guy.

Zoey rounded her lips and exhaled slowly. She plucked the registration out and closed the glove compartment. Sitting back in her seat, she extended her arm through the window to hand the cop her license and the registration.

He seemed to only give the license a cursory glance. "California, huh? Bet this weather's a big change for you. Do you know why I pulled you over today, ma'am?"

"I don't." She returned her hands to the steering wheel. It took *a lot* of willpower to keep her fingers from fidgeting nervously.

"The tags on this vehicle's license plates are two months expired."

"Really? I didn't think to check when—" she swallowed, giving her a moment to recall her would-be murderer's name "—when Matt leant me the truck. I'm so sorry."

"It happens. But it's something that really needs to be corrected, miss—" the cop lifted the license closer "—Weston." The cop tilted his head.

A two-ton ball of dread sank in her stomach.

"Zoey Weston?" He shifted his hold on her license and pulled his sunglasses down again, leaning closer. "Would you mind removing your sunglasses, ma'am?"

Oh, shit. Shit shit shit.

"Sure," she replied in a small voice, raising a hand to comply.

His eyes rounded. "You're the woman whose car they found on I-70 in Utah, aren't you?

"Um, yeah. Car broke down on the interstate, which is why I'm borrowing the truck."

"I'm going to need you to come with me, Miss Weston," the cop said, taking a step back. Zoey noticed that his right hand had settled on his gun again. "I'm sure we'll be able to get all of this sorted out."

"Am...am I being arrested?" she asked, the weight of her dread growing.

"I'm sure we'd both rather it not come to that."

"What do you mean?"

"Please step out of the vehicle, ma'am."

"If I haven't committed a crime, I'd like to leave. I'll take a ticket for the expired tags."

"I won't ask again," he said firmly.

"I haven't done anything!" Well, she had, but he didn't know that! Her hands shook despite her crushing grip on the wheel.

The cop took another step back and thumbed the radio on his shoulder, dipping his chin down and to the side to speak into it. He requested backup.

"We need to leave," Ren whispered from beside her.

"I know that!" she snapped at him, and immediately felt sorry for doing so. It wasn't Ren's fault.

"*Now.*"

"We're kinda stuck, don't you think?"

She didn't realize until it was too late that it must've looked to the cop like she was having an argument with her invisible friend in the passenger seat.

The cop drew his gun. Though he didn't point it directly at her, Zoey's heart stuttered before pounding so hard and fast that there might as well have been a herd of wild horses galloping through her chest. She lifted her hands, struggling to breathe, but her tight chest and constricted throat made it hard.

"Step out of the vehicle. Now." If there'd been any friendliness or civility in the cop's voice earlier, it was gone now, replaced by a hard edge.

Fear soured her stomach as she lowered a hand to the handle and opened her door. Once it was opened wide, she lifted her hand again and slid down until her feet touched the ground. It was only then she noticed the small crowd that had gathered fifty or so feet away, most of them bundled in winter gear with bright hats and scarves.

"Move to the front of the vehicle and place your hands on the hood," the cop commanded.

She obeyed, wishing that she'd put on the pair of gloves she'd taken from the cabin. Her breath came out in puffy clouds as the sound of boots on pavement signaled the cop's cautious approach.

This was it. She'd hoped for more time with Ren before they separated, but at least they'd come to know each other in what little time they'd shared. Tears brimmed in her eyes, blurring her vision.

The truck rocked as though a great weight were moving inside. The cop muttered something in confusion as the shocks squeaked.

A startled gasp erupted from the onlookers.

"What the fuck?" the cop said in awe.

Zoey turned her head to see Rendash, fully visible, standing just outside the truck. He reached up and pulled off the sunglasses, opening all his eyes and directing them at the cop. She'd never seen so much fury in his expression.

"On the ground!" The cop shouted.

Zoey shifted to see the cop's gun aimed at Ren. Something cold wrapped around her heart and squeezed.

Why didn't he just go? Why is he risking himself now?

"No!" she shouted, stepping toward Rendash.

The cop swung his arms, directing his pistol at her.

. . .

Control, Rendash reminded himself.

Fuck control! That human threatened my kun'ia.

Ren slammed the door shut and thrust an arm to the side, catching Zoey and forcing her behind him.

The human in front of him was some sort of soldier — a peacekeeper, perhaps, or an enforcer. Ren was unfamiliar with their designations for such positions. It didn't matter, either way. Fear had settled into the man and made him weak, and that weakness made him dangerous.

Rage burned through Rendash's body like a ravenous wildfire; this enforcer had drawn a weapon and aimed it at Zoey. *His* Zoey.

That was unacceptable.

"On the ground, now!" the enforcer shouted, backing away while adjusting his hold on his weapon.

Removed from the confrontation by scant distance, a small crowd of humans watched with expressions of shock and horror. Rendash didn't care; Zoey's safety was more important than being exposed. He couldn't allow her to be harmed or taken. He couldn't continue without her.

"Put your weapon down," Ren growled at the enforcer.

"Requesting immediate backup," the man said into the device on his shoulder. "Repeat, request—"

"I will not tolerate you directing your weapon at an innocent," Rendash said.

"Down on the fucking ground, hands behind your head!"

A strange wailing sound carried to Rendash on the wind, slowly growing stronger, as though something were approaching. Was it more enforcers? Were they so foolish — or so arrogant — as to announce their approach?

"You cannot have this female. She is *mine*. Return to your

vehicle."

"Ren," Zoey pleaded, placing a hand on his back, "just go. This is going to get bad unless I do what he says, do you understand? You need to just leave! Don't let them get you!"

"They will have neither of us, *kun'ia*," he said gently, turning his head to see her from his outer eye. She stared up at him with fear and concern straining her face. He shifted aside the hanging fabric of his coat and reached back to her with his lower arms, hoping to offer her some comfort.

"Holy shit," the enforcer said.

"We are leaving now," Rendash declared. The threat of violence from the enforcer could easily have been answered with violence, and Ren was prepared to act — his nyros were functioning far better than they had since his arrival on Earth — but Zoey's safety was tantamount. Battle, however brief or limited in scale, often took unforeseen tolls, especially when innocent non-combatants were near.

"Just…just get the fuck down!" the enforcer shouted.

Rendash took a step to the side, guiding Zoey to stay behind him with his lower hands.

He saw it in the male human's eyes — a flare of terror, a gut reaction that any aligarii child in the Khorzar would have been conditioned to avoid — and projected a shield a fraction of an instant before the man's finger squeezed the trigger of his blaster.

A chaotic eruption of sound dominated those drawn-out moments; five booms in quick succession, the hiss of the shield — flashing purple with each impact — destroying the projectiles, screaming from Zoey and the human onlookers, the intensified wailing and roaring engines of more enforcer vehicles as they raced along the nearby road.

Instinct.

Rendash darted forward, keeping the shield in front of him. The enforcer stumbled backward, firing several more shots. The shield pulsed but held firm.

The enforcer's path was blocked by a vehicle; he nearly fell over when he struck it, and fear twisted his features into something primal. Such fear was not uncommon on a battlefield, but it served as a reminder to Rendash that these people were not nearly as advanced as his own.

The technology that aligarii took for granted was awe-inspiring and potentially terrifying for humans.

Somehow, it was enough to convince Rendash to be merciful.

He grabbed the man's extended hand, and bones crunched as he wrenched the small, black weapon from the human's hold. The enforcer screamed. Rendash threw the weapon into the snow before grasping fistfuls of the man's clothing, lifting him overhead, and hurling him into the nearest pile of white. The human vanished in the deep snow.

Rendash surveyed his surroundings. Several of the human onlookers had fled, but several more remained in place, holding up small, rectangular devices — phones, similar to the one Zoey had possessed.

The other enforcer vehicles screeched around the turn and came to abrupt halts nearby; Ren counted four, with at least six more enforcers.

Their truck was blocked in, and he had no desire to battle more humans. The risk to Zoey would be too great. Ren alone couldn't protect her from all angles.

"Ren!" Zoey yelled. "Oh my God, Ren, are you okay?"

He turned to see her hurrying toward him. She stopped,

eyes roving over him, likely searching for wounds, but there was no time for that. Due to her limited field of vision, he doubted she could see the other vehicles while her eyes were focused on him.

The door of one of the newly arrived vehicles swung open, and another uniformed enforcer climbed out with blaster in hand.

Ren wrapped his arms around Zoey and poured as much strength into his legs as was possible, filling them with searing heat. Her startled cry — along with the shouts of the other humans — was lost in a rush of wind when he leapt high into the air, directing them toward the snowy hill behind the black stone lot. Zoey clung to him with startling strength.

The impact of his landing jolted his legs, but it wasn't nearly as jarring as it had been the night he escaped. He leapt over tall trees and landed on more black stone at the end of a road lined with dwellings. Zoey began to speak, but her words were cut off when he jumped again, and again, and again, putting increasing distance between them and the enforcers.

When they reached the cover of the thicker trees in the hills behind the clustered human dwellings, Ren decided it was better to remain on the ground. Holding Zoey firmly against his chest, he ran between the trunks, crunching snow beneath his boots and forging a wide, deep trail in the unbroken white.

He wasn't sure how much time had passed when he finally slowed, only that his instinct shifted his priorities to the conservation of energy and allowing Zoey to catch her breath. Down the hill, barely visible through the trees, lay more human dwellings, but he was confident that they had adequate cover to avoid detection — at least for now.

The trail he'd left behind was obvious, and it wouldn't take the enforcers long to locate it.

"Are you all right, Zoey?" he asked as he set her on her feet. The snow came up to her thighs. Her legs gave out, and she grasped his arms to remain upright. He accepted her weight easily. "Just breathe, *kun'ia*."

Panting, Zoey looked up at him with wide, terrified eyes. Her entire body shivered, and she clutched at him with desperation-fueled strength. "W-what are we going to do?"

"We need to get as far away from here as we can, as quickly as we can," he said, smoothing a hand over her hair.

Her eyes locked with his. "Why didn't you go? Why didn't you leave me? You could've gotten away!"

"Every time you had a chance to betray me, to leave me, you chose to stay with me. How could I abandon you, after everything?"

"Because the worst they'd do to me is toss me in jail! They weren't going to hurt me. But you? They would've *killed* you!" She twisted to look behind her. "God, he was shooting at you! And all those people, Ren… They had their phones, recording the whole thing."

Ren cupped her cheek and guided her to face him. Despite the danger to herself, her only concern was for him. The way that made him feel was indescribable; how could he ever have considered leaving Earth without her at his side?

Tears ran down her cheeks, which were red from the cold. "They'll know you're here. They'll find you. You *have* to leave me."

"It is not for you to decide what I must or must not do, little human," he replied gently. "This journey is *ours* to make, together. I cannot proceed without you, and I gave you my word to keep you safe. The price paid is more than worth it, knowing that you are here now, that you are safe and in my arms."

Zoey sniffled and threw her arms around him, holding him close. "I thought they shot you."

"My connection to my *nyros* has recovered. They'll have to do far better than that, if they mean to kill me." He turned his head and glanced down the hill, toward the human dwellings in the distance. "Come. We need to obtain a new vehicle."

"Oh, no," Zoey cried quietly, drawing her head back. "My purse, my clothes, everything! Everything is gone. Now they know who I am, that I'm with you. Even if we get another car, how are we supposed to keep it running? I have no money!"

Her face suddenly fell, and her cheeks drained of color. "My photo album. My photo album is in that truck, and that's all I have of my father. That's all I had left from him, and now it's gone, too. I lost him again. He's gone."

Eyes glistening with another wave of tears, she pulled away from Rendash. She turned and stumbled in the direction from which they'd come. The snow was too deep; Zoey fell forward, catching herself on her hands, and clawed at the snow to drag herself forward. "I have to get it. I have to get him. Ren, please, it's all I have of him!"

His heart ached as he stepped to her. He bent down, slipping his arms around her middle to pull her out of the snow. She strained against his hold, moving her legs in a futile attempt to continue forward.

"Be still, *kun'ia*," he whispered.

"I need to go back," she rasped. Her struggles ceased abruptly, and she sagged in his arms. Her body shook with heart-wrenching sobs. "I need to go back…"

Rendash turned her to face him, supporting her with his

hands, and kneeled to put himself at eye level with her. The whites of her eyes were pink from crying, moisture coated her blotchy cheeks, and the skin beneath her eyelids was puffy; she was still beautiful to him, more so now, seeing the depths of her caring.

"Your father is with you forever," he said, touching the tip of a finger to her temple, "here. And because you shared him with me, he is here, as well." He touched his own temple. "We will carry him, together."

She nodded, sniffled, and closed her eyes, forcing out the last of her tears. "What are we going to do, Ren? No money, no car, the cops after us, you're going to be all over the internet. What do we do?"

He stood up and dipped his head to place a soft kiss atop Zoey's hair. "Do not worry, *kun'ia*. We will solve all those problems, one at a time."

"Okay." Zoey sniffled again, and her trembling lips shifted into a small smile. "That sounds like something my dad would say. *One day at a time.*"

"Let us honor him by pressing on. We'll see to the vehicle first."

Based on her coloring — where her skin wasn't an irritated red, it was paler than ever, taking on a faint blue undertone — and her shivering, she was suffering from the cold. Trudging through the snow wasn't likely to help with that. With his nyros functional, Ren's body adjusted its temperature to counteract the conditions, but the chill in the air was still uncomfortable to him despite his adaptations.

He picked her up and carried her down the hill, only setting her on her feet when they reached the road below — which, like the other roads in town, had been cleared of snow. All was quiet save for the gentle wind rustling the boughs of the nearby trees.

Zoey leaned against his side, wrapped in his long coat, as they walked. He swung his gaze between the many vehicles parked in front of the dwellings along the road.

The distant wail of enforcer vehicles carried faintly over the treetops. How long would it be before Stantz's soldiers arrived in their helicopters?

"How are we going to get a car?" Zoey asked.

"We must focus on finding a suitable vehicle first," he replied, "and then we'll figure out how to take it."

"That one, the SUV." Zoey pointed at a large vehicle with black windows. "It's got tinted windows, so we won't have to worry about people seeing you from outside, and the interior should be big enough for you to have some leg space."

The *SUV* vaguely reminded Ren of the truck they'd left behind; it had a similar, somewhat blocky front end and was of comparable length. However, this vehicle had four doors rather than two, and its back end was closed in. Its exterior was black, and reflective silver metal gleamed on its wheels.

They approached the SUV cautiously. The windows in the dwelling behind it were covered and there were no lights on, and a quick check of the area revealed no nearby humans.

Ren shifted his primary attention to the vehicle, though he continued to watch their surroundings with his side-eyes.

He opened his nyros, allowing it to enter an automatic scanner mode for only the second time since he'd crashed on Earth. He didn't understand *how* it worked — the technology was so intricate and advanced that it was beyond his compre-hension — only that it *did* work. Here, in a more densely popu-lated area, his nyros detected countless signals being broadcast, many of them easily accessible with limited security. Some came from devices inside the dwellings, some were transmitted in the air from far-away sources, and some came from the vehicles.

Like the black SUV.

His nyros interfaced with the vehicle through its over-air signal, breaking through its simple security system and delving directly into its core controls. His nyros had already encountered human language and coding, thanks to what he'd done at the cabin, and the process was even faster now.

Ren's interaction with it occurred on an instinctual level. The characters flitting through his mind's eye were unfamiliar to him, but his nyros knew them, and it granted him an intuitive understanding of the systems. He instructed it to deactivate the security and tracking and block any further interfacing with over-air signals.

He touched the handle, engaging a direct, physical connection with the internal computer, and the locks disengaged with a popping sound. He pulled it open for Zoey and stepped aside to allow her entry.

She climbed in, and Ren's gaze locked on her backside; it was absolutely not the right time or place, but he couldn't pass up the opportunity. His cock didn't care whether it was appropriate. He barely withheld a groan. She deposited that luscious ass in the seat and adjusted its position. With her body in profile, he took a moment to follow the curve of her legs. He frowned when he noticed how wet her pants were; that couldn't be helping her stay warm.

"Are you…going to get in?" she asked, staring at him.

"Yes." He tore his gaze away from her legs, closed her door, and walked around the vehicle. With a final glance at the surrounding area, he tugged open the passenger door, slid the seat back as far as it could go, and pulled himself in.

Zoey rubbed her hands together before lifting them to blow into her cupped palms. "So…now what?"

Ren took her hands between two of his and gradually increased the temperature of his skin. He placed another hand on the SUV's control panel, which was currently dark.

A connection crackled through his fingertips like a spark, producing a faint, fleeting tingling in his fingertips. He held it for only a fraction of a second; just long enough to start the vehicle's engine. The instruments came to life, lighting up across the console, and cold air blew through the vents.

"How are you doing all this?" Zoey asked, wide eyes flicking between Ren and the console.

"It is my *nyros*," he said. "My understanding of how it works is little better than yours. I know how to wield it as a tool…the same way you know how to operate one of these vehicles, but not how to fix it."

"So, you did the same to the car as you did to the security system at the cabin?"

"Yes. And, like the system at the cabin, I disabled its ability to communicate with any external systems."

"Good idea. I think most of these new cars — especially higher-end ones like this — can be tracked by GPS, or whatever."

"How do your hands feel, Zoey?"

She looked down, and a small smile appeared on her lips. "Better. Thank you."

He released her hands, telling himself that it was necessary — she needed them free to drive, and they *had* to move. To ease the sudden feeling of emptiness, he dropped a hand to her thigh, raising the temperature of his palm further to warm the cold flesh beneath her wet legging.

She covered his hand with one of hers briefly, brushing her fingertips over his scales, before taking hold of the wheel.

"I...I think we'll need to backtrack. That cop probably realized we were going to get on I-70 before he pulled us over, and they saw us run in this direction."

Rendash nodded, smiling pridefully. "And the last thing they would expect is for us to move directly toward their search."

"Right. We're supposed to be running *away*." She inhaled deeply, moved the stick on the wheel column, and backed the vehicle out onto the road. "You wouldn't happen to be able to access any kind of maps with this thing, can you?"

Ren was silent for a moment as he interfaced with the vehicle's internal systems. "No. Not without enabling functions that would allow us to be tracked."

"Okay. Well, we have almost a full tank of gas, so we have room for a couple wrong turns." Shifting the wheel-stick again, she drove the vehicle forward, her gaze restlessly scanning the area. Her muscles were tight beneath his hand, and she kept adjusting her grip on the wheel as though her fingers were stiff. She was frightened, and he couldn't blame her.

She guided the vehicle slowly down narrow roads lined by large dwellings and tall trees on both sides. The snow piled along the edges of the road was black and gray rather than the pristine white he'd grown used to over the last several days.

Gradually, the air blowing from the vents warmed.

"Maybe it'd be better if you go invisible," she said after a little while. Up ahead, the road descended into a place where the buildings were positioned closer together and the roads were wider. Numerous vehicles were moving through the area.

He obeyed without question. Though they were both being hunted, the enforcers were likely more interested in locating Rendash. Having a completely different vehicle with darkened windows would help, but she stood the best chance if she appeared to be alone.

The cloaking field was easy to maintain now, completely unlike it had been when he first encountered her. He'd considered it before, but he couldn't stop the thought from reemerging — so much had changed since that night.

He turned his head to watch her. She kept her face surprisingly neutral, but he could see in her eyes that she was still shaken up. He gave her thigh a gentle squeeze. Zoey offered a soft, brief smile in reply.

Rendash had told himself — had told her — that he'd stayed to ensure her safety.

Selflessness.

That was one of the core tenets of the aekhora, and he'd neglected it so thoroughly that he should have been ashamed of himself. There was little selflessness in him protecting Zoey — she deserved comfort, security, and happiness, that could not be denied, but he was not doing it simply because it was right.

He was doing it because his want for her, his *need* for her, had grown to become a driving force in his mind. If he truly wanted her safe beyond all else, he would have left her behind days ago. Before he'd destroyed her life. Before he'd taken away her future on this planet.

It wasn't so much that he wanted her safe as that he wanted her safe *with him*.

After some aimless wandering, Zoey found the road she

called the *Interstate* and directed their SUV onto it. The insistent call of his ship, clear but still distant, screamed that he was going the wrong way. Even knowing that they were deliberately back-tracking, it was a struggle to prevent himself from correcting her course.

With the weather having cleared, there were far more cars on the road than he'd seen so far, and he was glad that she'd told him to cloak himself. They saw several enforcer vehicles driving on the sideroads just off the interstate as the town passed around them, but no such vehicles crossed their path.

"Okay," she said as they approached a fork in the road, "I think this is our exit coming up. One-seventy-one. I've never been great with maps, but I think I remember this cutting south...and then bringing us somewhere east where we can get back onto seventy?" She sighed heavily and shook her head. "How the hell did people do this before GPS?"

"What is GPS?" Ren asked.

"I think it stands for Global Positioning System, or something like that. It uses satellites to pinpoint your location, and then translates that onto a map. You basically tell it where you want to go, and it figures out the best route for you to take based on where you are."

She took the right fork, following it around a sharp loop and onto a narrower road, which only had one lane going in each direction. A river flowed to their left, and the road seemed to more-or-less follow its course as it wound through the hills and mountains.

Before long, Zoey leaned forward, her gaze flicking upward. The sky in the distance had an ugly gray cast to it, as though there'd be more bad weather soon, but that wasn't what she was focused on.

"That's not a coincidence, right?" she asked.

Ren's gaze followed hers. Far-off — but approaching rapidly — were three black, familiar shapes.

Helicopters.

It seemed as though he and Zoey both held their breath as the helicopters passed overhead, the chopping whir of their blades audible even with the windows closed and the rush of wind that enveloped their vehicle. Rendash shifted to look in the side mirror and watch the aircraft speeding toward Vail.

Zoey released a shaky breath. "I think we're safe. For now."

Ren stared at the darkening sky reflected in the mirror. When the helicopters didn't reappear, he nodded and squeezed her thigh again. "Yes. We're safe."

Chapter Eighteen

"I'm working on containing—"

"Damnit, Charlie, I might as well have a red-assed baboon running that operation at this point," the director shouted. Stantz gritted his teeth and moved the phone away from his ear. "Your fucking dog is all over the web, and it's only been a few hours! Explain to me how the fuck you're going to contain that? You shit the bed, Charlie."

"Because of this, sir, we've discovered entirely new applications for—"

"I got Homeland Security and the Pentagon ringing my damned phone right off the hook, Charlie. You think they're going to just shrug and leave us to it if I tell them we might be able to make them magical force fields in twenty years if they'd just please leave us alone?"

Pressing his lips together, Stantz squeezed his phone. The edges bit painfully into his fingers.

"One more chance, Charlie. You know I don't like to retire assets, but when an asset becomes a liability… Fix this."

The call ended with a double beep that felt far too final.

Stantz growled and threw the phone against the wall; the plaster, to his annoyance, took all the damage. He made himself pick the phone up and return it to the case on his belt before he stormed out of the hotel room.

The command trailer was at the rear of the parking lot, which was slick from the snowfall that had begun shortly after the incident in town. Stantz walked to the trailer, welcoming the cold blast of wind through his button-down shirt; it was a good distraction from his sour gut and boiling blood.

He found Fairborough inside the trailer. The man was sickly pale and had dark circles under his eyes. He looked like he hadn't shaved in days. Stantz frowned; Fairborough oversaw a team within Stantz's unit. It would befit him to present a more respectable countenance as an example to his men.

"Nothing," Fairborough said, dragging a handkerchief over his glistening forehead. "Alpha Team found a trail over the hills, but it went dead at a residential road."

"I need your people to get this video corrected, Fairborough. We need a clean version. Something to make the real thing look like it was tampered with."

"We can do it, but it's going to take a few days."

"We don't have that kind of time."

"Sir, it's very detailed work, and—"

"I need it done, Fairborough, and I need it done *now*. The director's breathing down the back of my neck, ready to throw everything I've worked for away because of this. Because he's too stupid to see the endgame. We need that video discredited, and we need those two found."

"They have to be somewhere in town. They have no vehicle,

and her money, identification, and clothing were left behind. They couldn't have made it far."

Stantz shook his head and faced one of the monitor-lined walls. An overwhelming amount of information flitted across the screens — camera feeds, transcriptions of text and phone conversations, personal files, satellite feeds. None of it adequate enough to hunt down a green, seven-foot-tall alien and a waitress from California by way of Iowa.

"He can. Have the choppers expand their search eastward."

"We already have roadblocks in place that way, and with this weather—"

Stantz silenced Fairborough with a hard look. Fairborough held his; gaze for several seconds before looking down.

"It is *imperative* that we locate my specimen," Stantz said in a low voice. "We must be willing to risk everything for it. That specimen is the key to the future of our species. I don't care if the weather is dangerous, I don't care if everyone is tired. Give the message to the pilots and keep those ground crews moving."

Fairborough nodded and pulled up his headset. Stantz listened as his orders were relayed over the comm system. When it was done, Fairborough gave him a final, troubled look and walked away.

Stantz turned back to the screens. He moved his gaze over them slowly, searching for the next clue that would lead him toward his Fox.

Chapter Nineteen

Zoey stopped beside the outermost gas pump, threw the SUV into park, and had Ren kill the engine. When she climbed out, she made sure to leave the door wide open for him. Her breath fogged around her as she stood aside. Country music twanged on the overhead speakers, and the lights were almost unbearably bright after the impenetrable darkness that had assailed them through the mountains. She loosely balled her fists and rubbed her tired eyes.

The SUV swayed as Ren — still invisible after remaining cloaked for the entire ride — climbed out.

Zoey looked around the parking lot nervously. Fortunately, there weren't many people present — it was after eight o'clock in the middle of December, and the light snowfall was enough to keep most sensible people indoors.

She wished, not for the first time, that they'd stayed in the cabin, where they'd been warm, happy, and comfortable. Instead they were on the run, strapped for money and lacking so much as an extra set of clothes. Just to make the situation even *better*, the contrast between the heated cab of the SUV and the icy winter air outside had her instantly shivering.

"Are you sure this will work?" Zoey asked. "That we won't… get caught?"

"I don't know if it will work," Ren said from somewhere beside her. One of his hands settled on her hip, and its welcome warmth seeped through her clothing. "But regardless, we will not be captured."

"Okay. Let's get this over with." She battled the urge to look for cameras; the feeling of being watched made her skin crawl, but looking up would only offer a clear view of her face. She'd seen enough TV to fear the government had facial-recognition technology that would allow a computer in some secret base to pick her out of a million simultaneous video feeds if it got a direct image to work with.

She stepped close to the pump and raised her hand as though she were going to insert her debit card.

Ren's hand remained on her hip, her only source of comfort. The display on the pump flashed, the numbers changing wildly — displaying all eights, flickering out, switching to strange, distorted characters — before the screen prompted her to select her grade of fuel.

"It worked," Zoey whispered. Her relief was short-lived; she wouldn't be able to relax until they were back on the road, away from prying eyes…and even then, her relaxation would be minimal.

She hurriedly opened the SUV's fuel cover and removed the cap. After selecting unleaded fuel, the display changed to *BEGIN FUELING*. She lifted the nozzle, inserted it into the tank, and pulled the trigger. It began to pump.

Releasing a shaky sigh, she leaned against Ren and watched

the numbers run steadily higher. The sound of flowing gasoline and the faint ticking of the pump seemed oddly in-time with the current country song. The more she focused on it, the more soothing it became.

Zoey's eyelids drifted shut.

Her knees buckled, and her head dipped back, jarring her to sudden alertness.

You're about to eat pavement, kid.

She threw her arms back to catch herself reflexively, but it was Ren's unseen hands that prevented her fall.

"Are you all right, Zoey?" he asked, voice thick with concern.

"Yeah. Just tired. Really, really tired." She smiled slightly, staring at the place she believed his eyes to be as she righted herself and all but one of his hands moved away. "Woke up pretty early this morning, remember?"

And since then, she'd been pleasured well beyond what she'd thought possible, cleaned a house and done two loads of laundry, helped Ren clear snow from around the buried truck, been pulled over and shot at by a cop, been carried through the woods by an alien, stolen a car, and driven for five-and-a-half hours along dark, winding, icy roads.

She didn't regret the first thing on that list, but she could've done without all the rest.

"Then you need to sleep," he said.

"We can't stop now, Ren. Not when they got so close. Plus, I don't have enough money for a room, and I doubt I'd be able to find one that didn't want an ID and a credit card."

"Such obstacles have not stopped us before, and they will not stop us now." His light touch on her cheek gently guided her attention to the convenience store. "They have food and drink in that building, correct?"

Zoey leaned her face into his warm palm and nodded. "Yeah."

"Do you have enough money to obtain some for us?"

"Some." She was thankful she'd been in so much of a hurry leaving the last convenience store that she'd stuffed some cash into her coat. It wasn't much, but it was a hell of a lot better than nothing.

"Go use the restroom. Purchase food and drink for us. When you come back, I will drive."

"What?" Zoey straightened, her eyes widening. She suddenly felt *quite* awake. "You don't know how."

"I've had plenty of time to observe you. It's not that complicated, human."

Zoey snorted, rolling her eyes. "Back to just *human*, huh?"

The automatic shutoff ended the flow of gasoline with a *pop*, signaling a full tank.

"I tend to be terse when I desperately need to relieve myself," he replied.

She snickered, removing the gas nozzle and hanging it on the pump. "Okay, okay. I'll hold the door, if you want to slip inside around me."

He patted her shoulder. "No need to trouble yourself. I think, this time, I will try it in the snow."

"Men," Zoey muttered as she screwed on the fuel cap.

"It was on TV," he said, tone slightly defensive. "Male humans seem fond of doing it."

"You shouldn't do everything you see on TV, Ren."

His hand slipped between her legs. She gasped, and heat immediately flooded her.

"I've done many things I saw on TV, without you complaining before now."

"I'm not complaining," she said breathlessly.

"Good. Now cease your argument," he commanded, and his hands moved away. "Go see to yourself, *kun'ia*, so we may be on our way."

Zoey walked away with a big, stupid grin on her face, and it took a surprising effort to wipe it away before she entered the convenience store.

The clerk, a young man with long, dark hair, looked up from his magazine and raised a hand in greeting. "Hey."

"Hi. I just need to use the restroom, and I'll be right back."

"Sure thing. It's in the hall at the back of the store."

"Thanks."

In the restroom, she moaned as she emptied her bladder; she hadn't realized how badly she had to go before sitting down. They hadn't stopped since leaving Vail. It didn't help that Ren usually pumped her full of enough seed to start a damned farm.

She chuckled to herself.

After washing her hands, she exited the bathroom and strolled through the aisles. She grabbed two large bottles of water from the fridge and, though she cringed at their prices, selected two sandwiches from the deli area. At the register, the gold-and-red wrapper of a Twix bar caught her eye. They were Ren's favorite.

She added it to the pile and paid.

"Ren?" she asked quietly when she returned to the car.

"Here," he answered softly from nearby.

She opened the passenger door and leaned in to deposit the drinks and snacks in the center console. She stepped back when she was done, allowing him a few moments to climb in before she closed the door again. Rounding the car, she slid into the driver's seat, closed the door, and buckled up.

The engine started as she picked up one of the sandwiches.

"Here," she said, handing it to him.

"Thank you," he replied. The moment it left her hand, the sandwich vanished. The only evidence that it had existed was the soft sound of the wrapper being opened.

Zoey tilted her head. "Why don't I vanish when you touch me?"

"I have to extend the cloaking field to encompass other objects or individuals."

"Does it...feel strange, when you're invisible?"

As she stared at the seemingly empty space where he sat, she caught sight, for an instant, of falling crumbs. They disappeared before she could tell if they were real or not.

"No," he said with his mouth full. "But I was trained to use it for a long while and have employed it frequently during my service. It is natural to me."

Maybe it was because she was tired, but a naughty thought slipped into her mind, making her grin.

"What does that look mean, Zoey?"

"Oh, nothing," she replied, grin widening as she shifted the SUV into drive and pulled back onto the highway.

Once they were beyond the lights of the gas station, Ren's form materialized beside her. He held the sandwich — missing a huge chunk — in one hand, seemingly forgotten.

"I know there's something," he said.

"Hmm?" She arched a brow.

"You had a thought, and whatever it was, it made you grin like you do when we're about to mate. What was the thought?"

"It was such a dirty thought, too." She glanced at him. "So, you're saying I have a certain grin for that?"

"I will not allow you to shift the subject." He frowned, all four eyes intent upon her, and folded the wrapper over his sandwich before setting it down. "What was the thought? Surely your people have some sort of saying about teasing like this, and how it is dangerous and discourteous."

"We do have a lot of sayings. I'll have to think about it for a bit."

"Zoey. Do not play these games with me."

"But it's so fun!" She laughed; behind her laughter, weariness crept around the edges of her consciousness, as though seeking a crack through which to invade her mind. Teasing Ren helped keep her awake, but it would only be a matter of time before the urge to sleep struck again.

"If you had some specific thought, perhaps we could work together to make it a reality?" He settled his lower left hand on her thigh. *High* on her thigh.

Her sex clenched, and liquid heat pooled between her legs. It seriously didn't take much to get her going, apparently, when it came to him. She bit her lip.

"I was thinking...it might be naughty if we were to...if we were to have sex while you're invisible. It'd be like having sex with a ghost, or being blindfolded, but not. I'd never know what you intended to do to me next."

A slow grin spread across his lips, revealing his fangs a little at a time — it was wicked, and promising, and only turned her on more.

"Whenever you'd like, *kun'ia*," he said.

Right now. I can pull over right now...

Zoey blushed as she peeked at him from the corner of her

eye. He stared at her intently, hand inching a little higher, his thumb massaging her leg. Cruise control could take care of the speed, but would she be able to keep the car straight if she had him pleasure her while driving?

"Oh, fuck it," she said. There were no lights, traffic was nearly nonexistent, and she was horny as hell. She pulled onto the shoulder and threw the car into park. Ripping off her seatbelt, she turned to Ren. The devilish gleam in his eyes told her he knew *exactly* what she wanted.

She shimmed out of her coat and shoved her leggings and panties down as she climbed across the central console to position herself on Ren's lap. Her hands fell to the top button of his pants, desperately seeking to free his cock.

And Ren disappeared. She felt him beneath her, though part of her mind dismissed it as an impossibility; all that remained in the car were shadows, and shadow could not have solid form.

Three of his hands settled on her bare skin, hot as branding irons. The seat tipped back suddenly. He caught her upper arms, holding her steady, allowing her to fumble with his buttons. Then that fourth hand made itself known, sliding between her legs. One of his thick fingers slid into her folds and stroked her clit.

"Ah, Zoey. So wet and needy for me." His gravelly voice rumbled through her, felt as much as heard.

"Yes," Zoey whispered as pleasure pulsed outward from her core.

She moaned, grinding against his finger. Two of his hands dropped to her hips, encouraging her undulations, pushing her harder but allowing her no more speed. His remaining hand slipped under her shirt. It trailed fire over her belly before lifting the cup of her bra to caress her hard, sensitive nipple.

Zoey released the final button. His erection sprang free, radiating heat as it brushed against her hands. She wrapped her fingers around it. Ren growled and lifted his hips. His shaft was hot steel in her palm, throbbing with need.

Biting her lip, she guided the tip of his cock to her entrance. In the faint light from the dashboard, she could see the depressions on her hips where his fingers pressed into her skin, but there was nothing beneath her, nothing in her hand — only darkness. Wicked, tempting, delectable darkness.

Ren's strong hands lifted her and impaled her on his thrusting length.

Zoey's mouth opened in a silent cry as she fell forward, flattening her palms on the hard scales of his broad chest. He filled her, stretched her, claimed every bit of her. They connected in a way that was beyond the physical; she felt him in her heart, in her soul, like he'd become part of her.

Guided by his hands, she raised and lowered her hips, relishing each slow, deliberate, maddening stroke of his cock. His other hands glided over her skin, their touch equal parts fire and honey; the delicate brush of his fingertips raised goosebumps on her arms, the scalding press of his palms over her breasts fanned the flames of her lust, the firm grasp of his hands on her thighs and calves made her sex clench with want, the scrape of his blunt nails on her lower back made her moan in delight.

The rasp of his scales over her skin amplified every sensation, pushing her body to the limits of pleasure and beyond. Shivers coursed through her, made stronger by the ridges on his shaft sliding over her clit.

"Give me more, *kun'ia*," Ren growled. One of his hands followed her spine from her ass to her neck, its touch so delicate it might have been imagined until it grabbed a fistful of her hair and forced her down into a searing kiss. "Give me *all*."

Instinct overtook her as she closed her eyes. Her hips quickened, and she became a wild thing, desperately seeking that final piece, that release that would fully tie their bodies together as they tumbled down from the heights of their passion.

Her ragged breaths mingled with his grunts to fill the cab, their combined scents permeating the air to further increase her arousal. The SUV rocked; anyone driving by would have no doubt of what was happening inside. Zoey didn't care.

She opened her eyes to find Rendash staring up at her, his eyes four glowing orbs, his face defined only by the greenish highlights cast on the sharp edges of his features by the dashboard lights. It hit her in that moment, like the striking of a match sparking an explosion.

Ecstasy blazed through her, ravenously devouring her entire being, flaring hotter and hotter as Ren continued his thrusts. She sealed her mouth to his, muffling her cries as she wrapped her arms around his neck.

Ren's roar rumbled from his chest and into Zoey. His already viselike grip tightened, anchoring her body to his as he burst and flooded her with his white-hot seed. She felt that connection the instant it was made and ground her sex against him as the aftershocks of her climax resonated through her.

Finally, she collapsed atop him, panting, and rested her head on his chest. She idly stroked her thumb along his jaw. Exhaustion swept in on the tails of her euphoria, demanding she close her eyes.

Neither of them spoke; their actions had been enough. But one thought echoed her mind, solidifying with each repetition.

I don't want him to leave me.

He released a long, slow breath, and combed his fingertips through her tousled hair. She lay in his embrace, unsure of how much time had passed. At least three vehicles drove by, their headlights casting fleeting, magical lights and shadows across his features.

"We should continue on," he finally said. She felt his words rolling in his chest.

"Mmm." Zoey sighed, closing her eyes. "I like where we are."

"So do I, but we've far to go, and our pursuers are too close behind."

"I don't want to leave you," Zoey mumbled. She moved a hand to his shoulder, giving the hard, ridged scales there a weak squeeze. She was distantly aware of his light touch on her cheek before she drifted to sleep.

Rendash lay still as Zoey's breathing evened out and her weight settled atop him fully. Her exhaustion had been evident for a long while, and she'd fought it admirably. They needed to keep moving, needed to stay ahead of their pursuers, but it wouldn't do either of them any good for her to push herself so hard.

He couldn't help feeling a touch of guilt. She was doing it for *him*. She was sacrificing the life she'd known for *him*.

I don't want to leave you.

Had she meant now or when the time came for him to leave Earth? He couldn't be certain, and he wasn't going to wake her just to ask, but her words had made his heart flutter and his blood heat — it was *hope* again, that wonderful, dangerous emotion.

My ability to detach myself from this — from her — has long since died.

What remained, then, but to look toward the future? To embrace a little of that hope?

The true problem lay in the contrast between desire and reality. He'd been taught, beyond those basic lessons, to antici-pate as many potential outcomes as possible. Military action rarely went according to plan, and responding to complications grew easier when one had taken time to consider a multitude of complications beforehand.

The practice was far from perfect, but it encouraged focus, critical thinking, and improvisation under stressful circumstances.

There were enough ways for this to go wrong — enough ways for Zoey to get hurt — to make Ren's gut churn.

He pulled the lever on the side of the chair and sat up to return the seat to its upright position, holding Zoey against him to disturb her as little as possible. His shaft had released her some time ago, but he'd been unable to bring himself to pull away. He wanted nothing but moments like this. Nothing but this easy, passionate closeness, nothing but the feeling that they were the only two beings in existence and everything would be fine.

He opened the door, wincing at the gust of cold air that flowed into the vehicle. Zoey stirred, curling against him. As carefully as he could, he slipped from beneath her and out of the SUV, leaning down to pull her leggings back up and shift her into what he hoped was a more comfortable position.

A shiver crept up his spine; it was cold despite his nyros adjusting his body temperature. He reached down, regretfully stuffed his cock back into his restrictive pants, and fastened the buttons. After clicking her seatbelt into place, he found Zoey's coat on the floor and draped it over her. Before he closed the door, he used the lever to ease the seat back down.

The road was deserted as he walked to the driver's side. All the better; he *might* have exaggerated his confidence in being able to drive the human transport, and from what he understood, there were protocols specific to their operation that were expected to be obeyed. The fewer the potential witnesses, the better.

Rendash pulled the door open and crouched to adjust the seat. The control on this side was automatic and moved the seat in a variety of directions. He shifted it as low and far back as it could go. When he entered the vehicle, his knees bumped the steering wheel at its sides.

Frowning, he tugged the door closed, hissing in pain as his knee was caught between the wheel and the door.

The vehicle shook as he fought to tear his leg out of the tight space. Once it was free, he bent his leg at a more acute angle to keep it clear of the wheel. His gaze flicked to Zoey; fortunately, she slept soundly, undisturbed by the closing door and his car-shaking reaction to his pain.

Control, Aekhora. This is no difficult task.

He closed two hands around the wheel and tested its responsiveness and range of motion — the latter of which was somewhat restricted by the position of his right knee.

It would've been simple enough, in theory, to wake Zoey and ask her to explain some of the functions, but he couldn't bring himself to disturb her slumber. Besides, he was Blade of the Aligarii; he would not be bested by this primitive technology.

Eventually, he figured out how to operate the mechanism to

adjust the angle of the steering wheel and shifted it into a more comfortable position.

"Much better," he muttered as he turned the wheel from side to side again, checking the resistance from the otherwise motionless tires. It felt strange, but he supposed vehicles limited to moving only on the ground were strange to him to begin with.

Tilting his head down until his chin was against his chest, he studied the pedals on the floor in front of him. He'd not lied — he *had* observed her frequently while she drove, and he knew the narrow right pedal was to accelerate while the other, wider pedal was to decelerate.

Simple. Easy. No challenge for a being trained to operate interstellar ships and sophisticated machines of war.

He pressed his foot on the accelerator. The engine revved with a guttural growl, but the vehicle didn't move. Frowning, he pressed harder. The engine roared, and the movement of hidden machinery in the vehicle's front end was strong enough to make it vibrate.

Lifting his foot, he mumbled a few of the inappropriate words he'd learned from Zoey.

What am I missing?

He glanced at her again while, in his mind, he sorted through days' worth of memories of her driving.

Ren almost slapped himself when he realized what he'd done wrong. The vehicle had several different modes, one of which was its currently stationary state. He pressed a foot down on the wide pedal, as he'd seen Zoey do so many times, and moved the stick on the right side of the wheel down until the display showed a crescent closed by vertical line — a human symbol for *forward*, or *go*, or something along those lines.

As he eased off the decelerator, the vehicle slowly rolled forward.

Ren moved his foot to the other pedal and pressed it down. The vehicle lurched ahead, the burst of speed forcing him back against the chair. He turned the wheel, and his stomach lurched as the transport darted onto the main road. Lights illuminated the interior from behind.

A high, droning sound, reminiscent of battle horns from the aligarii historical annals, preceded a car approaching rapidly from behind; the other vehicle sped past, a hand's breadth from a collision.

Startled, Ren wrenched the wheel to the right to avoid the other vehicle, slamming down the decelerator. The tires screeched. His vehicle turned wildly, and he felt it trying to pitch over as its momentum dragged against its high center of gravity. He threw his weight against the spin's force, clutching the wheel desperately as his insides seemed to mash together. The world rotated wildly around him.

Finally, the spinning ceased, and the vehicle rocked for a moment before halting completely. Ren blinked and reluctantly released his crushing hold on the steering wheel.

They were facing in the direction they'd been heading. The vehicle that had nearly collided with them was fading in the distance, little more than a pair of red lights in the darkness, like the eyes of a smug, playful predator.

Rendash looked at Zoey, ready for her to declare she was taking over and that he was never allowed to drive again.

She had turned her head toward him, features strained and brow drawn, but her eyes were still closed. "Make sure…you drive…" She yawned widely and nuzzled her face against the seat. "…the speed limit."

Wide-eyed, he watched as she sank back into sleep. After what felt like an eternity, he released the breath he'd been holding.

Zoey slept like the dead; in most situations, that wasn't a good thing, but he found himself grateful for it now.

His hands ached, likely due to how tightly he'd clutched the wheel, as he figured out how to adjust the mirrors so he could see behind the SUV.

Now that he had a better feel for the transport's handling, his second attempt to get on the road was far smoother.

As he drove, something dinged at him inside the vehicle. The sound repeated a few times and ceased. After several moments, it returned, slightly faster. Keeping part of his attention on the road, he searched for the source of the sound, but it seemed to come from all directions at once.

It faded again, but when it returned for the third time, it was with an incessant insistence that almost made his skin crawl. The sound grated on his nerves; the closest thing he'd ever heard to it were impact alarms — either warning of an imminent crash, or of some sort of weapon about to strike.

Yet the road was once again empty and dark; he saw no sign of other vehicles about to hit his, no sign of weapons being discharged, and the SUV seemed to be suffering no performance issues, as far as he could tell.

"Ren," Zoey groaned, covering her ear with one hand, "put on your seatbelt."

Annoyed and confused, he reached over his shoulder and grabbed the latch. "I will slice you in half, vehicle, if you do not cease this noise," he grumbled.

The seatbelt locked twice as he attempted to pull it across his torso. All the while, the sound continued, each repeated note more piercing than the last.

Heat blossomed along one of his forearms; it took him a moment to realize he was about to form a vrahsk to cut the cursed seatbelt off.

Control!

He redirected the gathering energy, allowing it to disperse throughout his body, and drew in several deep, steadying breaths. The seatbelt finally clicked into the buckle. The chiming sound ceased abruptly.

"I have never hated a machine, but you are pushing me to reconsider," he said through clenched teeth.

Before long, he passed one of the white signs Zoey had told him about while they traveled away from Vail — a *Speed Limit* sign. He adjusted his pressure on the accelerator to match the number on the vehicle's internal display to the number on the sign. The pedal seemed a bit overly sensitive, making it a challenge to maintain the right number, but he figured it was close enough.

Though it was dark and overcast, Ren could make out enough of the surrounding landscape to tell that it was unlike anywhere he'd been on Earth so far. They'd descended from the mountains onto a vast, flat plain that had begun so abruptly its existence seemed impossible, contrasting far too heavily with the rocky peaks they'd left behind.

It didn't take him long to feel exposed; there was nowhere to hide out here.

Without a map to guide him — and unable to read anything but the numbers, which he'd only learned by playing *Cards* with Zoey — he followed the road's course without deviation. If nothing else, it was leading in roughly the right direction to bring them to his ship, though he sensed the distance was still great. Their direction changed when the road merged onto a larger pathway — the *Interstate*, perhaps? — but he didn't panic. They were moving closer to the ship, and that was all that mattered.

He reached into the bag between him and Zoey with one of his lower hands, feeling around for one of the water bottles she'd purchased, when his fingers brushed over something familiar — a smooth wrapper with two solid, stick-like objects inside. He withdrew the item. Its wrapper gleamed in the glow of the vehicle's control panel.

Twix.

Even when she'd been rundown, exhausted, and pushed beyond her limits, Zoey had still taken a moment to think of Ren and obtain something he enjoyed. A small gesture, but so full of kindness and consideration.

Ren looked at her again; she was fast asleep, her tousled hair partially obscuring her face.

After all he'd been through in his life, all the battles, all the blood he'd given toward fulfilling his duty, he wasn't sure that he deserved her.

But he sure as hell wasn't going to give her up for *anything*.

"A little longer, *kun'ia*. Then we can find peace together."

Chapter Twenty

"If I were piloting my ship, I would blast you off the road!" Rendash growled.

Zoey's eyes fluttered open. The sky was dark, and the only illumination was provided by the glow of the dash and the headlights of the other cars on the road. She looked at the clock; 4:17. She'd slept that long? With Ren driving that *whole* time?

"Yes, you pass me, too!" he said. "You are without honor!"

Zoey settled her gaze on Ren. He was scrunched up in the driver's seat, knees so high that they were mere inches from bumping his hands on the wheel. His jaw muscles ticked in frustration, and his brows were low.

She giggled.

He glanced at her, and the hard light in his eyes softened. "You are awake," he said, with a touch of guilt. "I'm sorry."

"Don't be," she replied, reaching down to pull the seat lever and return her seat to its upright position. She groaned, closing her eyes as she rubbed the side of her neck. She hated sleeping in cars. "I didn't mean to sleep for so long. Honestly, I'm surprised I woke up at all. I kind of expected you to crash a long time ago."

Ren frowned deeply. "If there have been issues, it is only because your fellow humans are too stupid to obey the very laws they have put in place."

"What do you mean, Ren?"

"You told me to follow the speed limit. I have been doing so, but *no one else* on this entire road has done the same!"

As far as she recalled, she hadn't given him *any* driving pointers, which — now that she was rested and alert — made her wonder if she had some subconscious death wish. "Um, right." She beamed at him. "You're doing great!"

Though he'd returned his primary attention to the road, she couldn't help but notice his rightmost eye watching her. "So… you don't recall any…disturbances during the trip?"

Nope. You shagged me into a coma.

Shagged? He's an alien, not Austin Powers!

"Yeah, baby, yeah!" she said in a terrible accent, grinning to herself. Boy, she was going absolutely nuts.

"What, Zoey?"

She cleared her throat. "Nothing." Her grin abruptly faded when she realized what his original question had been. "Wait. *Disturbances?* What did I miss?"

"Nothing," Rendash replied hurriedly, gaze reverting to the road ahead. "Nothing has happened. It's been quiet, apart from all the humans breaking the law."

Zoey eyed him. "Mhmm."

He rummaged through the plastic bag in the center console. After a moment, he produced the Twix bar she'd bought for him. The package was torn open. "I saved one for you."

"Awww." Zoey accepted the candy bar. "I totally know what you're doing, but that was super sweet of you."

"I am not sure what you're talking about. I just wanted to ensure you had something to enjoy when you woke."

She smiled, leaned toward him, and kissed his cheek.

He returned the smile and focused on driving.

She looked out the window as she ate. The chocolate and caramel were a little much, right after waking up, but she didn't want to reject his kind gesture. Besides, sugar overload was secondary to the true problem — she *really* had to pee.

Granted focus by her discomfort, she watched with the eyes of a hawk for a rest stop sign, jabbing her finger toward the first one that appeared on the roadside. "Let's stop there. We can take a bathroom break, and I'll take over driving again."

"All right. It will feel nice to stretch my legs."

Zoey looked at him again. Even with the seat all the way back, his legs were folded up so much that he'd knee himself in the face if he braked suddenly. She couldn't help but chuckle.

Ren's application of the brakes was somewhat uneven as they pulled into the rest area. Zoey braced herself with a hand on the dashboard, using her other hand to cover her mouth, smothering her laughter. Somehow, he managed to pull into one of the spots on the edge of the lot without smashing his chin into his knee.

There were only a few other vehicles at the rest stop, all parked closer to the building and its bright spotlights.

"Well, you're crooked as hell, but at least you're in the lines," Zoey said, sitting up to check in the side mirror.

"I told you it's not that complicated."

"I'm sure you didn't run into any *disturbances*."

He offered her an exaggerated frown. "Don't you have to

pee, human?"

"There you go, changing the subject again." Zoey laughed as she opened her door and climbed out.

Ren emerged from the driver's side, pulling his hood up. He glanced toward the lights. "We've made it this far without incident, as far as you're aware. What reason is there to worry over what might've happened?"

"You're right. Thank you for driving, Ren."

He dipped his head in a half-nod, half-bow as they walked toward the restrooms. "As long as it gave you a chance to rest and recover, it was worth all the disturbances that certainly did *not* occur."

Zoey laughed. "I'm so glad I was asleep for everything that *didn't* happen."

They split when they reached the building. Zoey pushed open the door to the ladies' restroom and entered. Two women stood in front of the mirror, voices echoing as they chatted while washing their hands. They both looked up at Zoey in the mirror as she passed.

"Oh, my God," one of them said, eyes widening.

Zoey's brows lowered in confusion. The women looked at her…with fear.

Without another word, the women hurried out the door, leaving Zoey alone. They didn't even pause to dry their hands.

"Um, okay. That was…weird." She stared at the closed door. A strange feeling filled her, but she couldn't quite place it. Paranoia? Dread? The incident, however brief, seemed too surreal to fully acknowledge.

She stepped into a stall and relieved herself. Her lips twitched into a smirk as she realized the main reason why she had to go so badly.

When she was finished, she washed her hands and exited the restroom. The women were standing next to their cars with two men, speaking rapidly to one another. One of the men held up a hand to silence them. He had a phone to his ear.

Both women pointed at Zoey when they realized she'd come out. "That's her! That one from the video with the *alien*," one of them said.

"Yeah, we're sure it's her," the man said into the phone.

The other man stared at Zoey. "Shit, I think you're right. Get in the car. She's wanted for—"

The man's eye rounded, and looks of horror contorted the faces of his companions. Zoey knew without a doubt that Ren was next to her, and he wasn't trying to hide.

"We should probably go, Ren," she said, words scratching out of a suddenly dry throat.

"Yes! Hurry!" the man yelled into the phone as he tore open the driver door of his car. The other three were hurrying to their own doors, a man and woman to each car.

The other man paused, lifting his own phone to snap a few pictures.

Oh, shit.

Rendash shoved an armful of snacks and sodas at Zoey. She accepted them numbly, and only registered that Ren meant to charge at them when he lunged toward the vehicles.

The women screamed and scrambled into their cars.

Before he was out of her reach, Zoey thrust an arm forward and caught the back of Ren's coat. Some of the snacks and bottles fell from her hold, but that was totally unimportant.

Ren halted and looked at her over his shoulder. "Shouldn't I do something about them?"

"Like what, *kill* them?" she asked incredulously.

"No. There's no honor in that. I could smash their phones, though. I have some experience with it."

The engines of both cars roared to life, and the frantic drivers peeled out of the parking lot with screeching tires, leaving a lovely, burnt-rubber aroma in their wake.

Zoey scrunched her nose at the stink. "What's done is done. We're already plastered all over the internet, and they already talked to the police by the sound of it. We better go."

"I should have cloaked. I shouldn't have taken the chance."

"No, Ren. This one's on me. I should've guessed people would know about it, after that scene back in Vail." She released her hold on him and rubbed her hand over her face. "God, my life is officially over. They recognized me the moment I stepped into that restroom."

"We aren't dead yet, Zoey." Ren crouched briefly to gather the fallen goods and walked toward the car in long, easy strides; she had to jog to keep up with him.

They climbed into the SUV and deposited Ren's bounty into the plastic bag in the central console. Ren placed his hand on the dash and started the engine. Zoey felt like a child; her feet could barely reach the pedals, and she had to extend her arms fully to touch the wheel. After hurriedly adjusting the seat, steering wheel, and mirrors, she shifted into reverse, looking down at the instrument panel before backing out.

"How are we at three quarters of a tank?" she asked.

"I stopped for fuel while you were sleeping."

She frowned as she guided the car toward the interstate. "Was that one of those *disturbances*?"

"No. *That* was rather quiet."

The next sign declared they were approaching Kansas City. Zoey glanced at the rearview mirror every few seconds, expecting to see flashing lights behind them, or a helicopter hovering just over the road with a glaring searchlight. Her heart pounded the entire way. Despite sleeping for eight hours, she'd likely be well on her way to exhaustion before the sun came up.

They weren't dead yet, but there certainly was no future for her after this.

Zoey stopped in Kansas City. Though it was still mostly dark, the first hints of dawn had touched the eastern sky with a gentle glow. Ren slunk off, using the lingering shadows to procure another vehicle, leaving Zoey to wait alone. She constantly checked her surroundings, scared out of her wits. If the cops found her while Ren was gone…

At the first opportunity, she'd have to do something to ensure she wasn't so easily recognizable.

"Most people get to *enjoy* their fifteen minutes of fame," she muttered, holding her hands up to the heater.

She nearly pissed herself when a big, white SUV pulled up beside her, fully expecting to see *POLICE* printed on the side in large, bold letters. When Ren walked around the front and waved at her, she collapsed back in her seat and let out the biggest sigh of relief in her life.

Ren killed the engine in the black SUV and grabbed the bag of drinks and snacks as Zoey climbed into the driver's seat of her *new* stolen vehicle. He joined her a few moments later, sliding the passenger seat back while she moved the driver's seat forward.

"While I was looking for a suitable vehicle, I saw someone use a machine," Ren said after they were back on the road. She glanced at him as he reached into an inside pocket of his coat and withdrew a wad of cash. "Apparently, it gives money."

Zoey's eyes widened. "Did you just rob an ATM?"

"Isn't that money free to take?"

"No, not even a little bit. It belongs to other people, and to the bank... Didn't I explain how money was earned?" She let out a long sigh that became a chuckle. "What does it matter? We've broken so many laws already. This is our third stolen car."

"We are surviving," he said.

"I know, Ren." She looked at the money again. There was a lot. "Did you...happen to notice a camera?"

"I was cloaked. If there was surveillance, it likely couldn't detect me."

"Okay, good. We *do* need to be more careful going forward."

They found a baseball hat and a pair of big sunglasses inside the SUV, and Zoey put them on when the sun came up, tucking her hair under the cap. Ren placed a hand on her thigh, absently brushing his thumb over the fabric of her pants. That simple touch kept her grounded.

They left Kansas City, continuing east. Ren kept her posted on the relative direction of his ship as the miles rolled by. Though it was probably more dangerous, she kept to the major roadways. It would be too difficult to navigate the smaller highways crisscrossing the country without a map.

As they passed through Missouri, Zoey noted at least three groups of black SUVs driving in the opposite direction. She told herself it was nothing more than a coincidence, or her imagination playing tricks on her, but she knew better by now, didn't she? She was in a stolen car with an alien, and the government was hunting him. This wasn't a conspiracy theory or paranoia. It was *fact*.

She held her calm. Their progress slowed as they passed through St. Louis, but her inner tourist was allowed to thrive for a few minutes — as they crossed the Mississippi River, she happened to glance out the passenger window and caught a glimpse of the St. Louis Arch.

It was a silly thing to get excited over, but it was normal, and a little bit of normal went a long way these days.

They continued through Illinois, Indiana, and into Ohio, stopping only for food, gas, and restroom breaks — bundling all three together as often as possible.

The sun had long since set by the time they passed through Columbus, and Zoey decided it was time for them to stop for the night. Ren insisted he could take over, but she refused, countering his insistence with her own — he needed to sleep, also.

She made a quick stop at a department store for a few necessities, leaving a grumpy Ren in the SUV to wait. If anyone recognized her, they made no indication; hopefully the cap and sunglasses had made enough difference, though she felt like a jerk wearing sunglasses after dark *inside* a store.

Finding a place to stay was a little more difficult. Without ID or credit cards, they were stuck with only the seediest motels. Lacking a phone to search for those places didn't help. They drove around for another hour before she finally spotted a place with a sign that looked like it hadn't been updated or repaired since the 60's.

The man at the desk didn't ask any questions. He took her cash — twenty-five bucks for the night — and handed her a key.

Zoey hesitated after pulling into a parking spot close to their room, afraid of what she'd find inside. Her fears were realized when they entered — there were stains on the ceiling, the carpet, and the peeling wallpaper. There was one bed, covered with a scratchy-looking brown blanket pocked with cigarette burns. The smell — mildew and stale puke — was thankfully faint.

She reluctantly placed the shopping bags on the bed as Ren closed the door.

Ren walked to the bed and picked up the bags. "I think we should sleep in our vehicle."

"We'll be fine," Zoey replied. She checked through the bags, found the one she wanted, and slipped it out of his hold. "I've slept in worse places."

Not that I liked it.

"So have I," he said, "but I'd rather you not sleep here."

Zoey smiled, rose on her tip-toes, and pulled him down into a kiss. When she broke the contact between their lips, she rested her forehead against his. "We'll be fine. We both need some sleep."

He frowned but offered no further argument.

"Just try to relax for a little bit. I've got something to do, and it might take a little while," Zoey said.

"What do you have to do? I can't let you go out on your own."

She walked toward the bathroom, glancing at him over her shoulder. "I'll be right in here. Eat. I grabbed some more sandwiches while I was in the store. And a Twix."

"Why won't you tell me what you're going to do in there, Zoey?"

"You'll see when I'm done."

Zoey closed and locked the door before he could say anything else. The bathroom lived up to the promise made by the rest of the room, with exposed, rusted pipes, chipped porcelain, and broken tiles, but it was surprisingly clean.

She set the bag on the edge of the sink and removed the small boxes and pair of scissors from within. Watching herself in the mirror, she removed the baseball cap and set it aside, letting her hair fall around her shoulders. She picked up the scissors in one hand and lifted a thick hank of hair in the other.

Tears blurred her eyes. She'd always loved her hair — it was one of the only things she'd been happy with when it came to her appearance. But it was just hair. It would grow back in time.

So why am I crying over it?

Because this is me.

No, that wasn't it. There was a deeper truth, and all she needed to do was admit it to herself.

It's because when Ren is gone I'll have nothing and no one.

"I can do this," Zoey whispered. She took a deep breath and made her first snip. The flow of tears began as the lock of hair fell to the floor.

Ren sighed and turned away from the bathroom door. He trusted her, but her refusal to answer him was troubling.

He swept his gaze over the rest of the room. He'd endured objectively worse accommodations many times during his life, but he wanted better for Zoey. She deserved better. That their circumstances — circumstances caused by Ren — had brought them to this was regrettable. But they were together, and they were safe. That meant something.

That meant *everything*.

He switched on the TV to pass the time. He'd learned that all remote controls had similar functions for their buttons, even though their layouts varied; unfortunately, all but three channels displayed only a snowy picture.

He left it on the *news*. Though much of what the man and woman on the screen spoke about was meaningless to him, one thing carried through — violence. Most of their stories seemed to touch upon it in some way. If not a violent event, it was the threat of one. Even having been raised in the Khorzar, bred and conditioned for war, Ren was surprised at the prevalence of such savagery among the humans.

Warriors were supposed to battle to protect civilians from acts like this. To provide their people peace.

Though their society was not free of crime, the aligarii and the other species who lived with them enjoyed safe, happy lives, without the fear of being harmed by one another.

Did the humans need guidance? Their technology, though primitive, had the potential to grow and eventually bring their species beyond the bounds of their home planet. Would they join the intergalactic community as friends and allies, or as would-be conquerors? Should they be considered a future threat or an opportunity to enrich intergalactic society?

Was Zoey an exception to their seemingly cruel, violent nature, or was she the truth of who the humans were as a people? The truth of who they *could* be?

His thoughts were broken when the TV displayed an oddly familiar scene in a still image — a snowy parking lot, a red truck, and an enforcer aiming his weapon at a large individual in a long coat and a hood.

"New information on the viral video that's taken the world by storm over the last twenty-four hours," the woman's voice said.

Ren watched as the enforcer fired his weapon, watched the shield flash as it absorbed the projectiles, watched the camera shake as the figure on the screen charged the enforcer. Ren hadn't hidden his arms or his eyes. He'd been too angry to care.

"Though many are calling the footage an expertly executed hoax, it seems the woman in the footage, who has been identified as Zoey Weston of Santa Barbara, California, is currently on the FBI's Most Wanted List."

The moving image froze and zoomed in, offering a grainy view of Zoey's face, and then split to display a clear image of her beside it. Most of her body was blocked by the enforcer and Rendash due to the angle of the recording. Despite the poor quality of the image, Ren recognized the fear on her face.

"We go now to an excerpt of the press conference held this evening in Vail, Colorado."

The screen changed to a man standing in front of a crowd, leaning over a podium and speaking. Several uniformed enforcers stood behind and around him. "Though we cannot currently share the details," the man said, "Zoey Weston is wanted for the murder of Matthew Johnson in Utah last week. We consider Weston and her unidentified companion armed and extremely dangerous. Any information on their where-abouts should be reported directly to your local law enforce-ment. We have reason to believe they are moving eastbound through the Midwestern states."

The crowd began speaking all at once, their voices too jumbled to make out, until the man at the podium acknowl-edged one of the audience members.

"Can you comment on the alien that was clearly displayed in the footage?" came the muted question.

"We have no comment on the authenticity of that footage at this time. The events surrounding this traffic stop are currently under investigation, and the police officer involved is recovering from his injuries. What is important is that Zoey Weston and her companion are dangerous, and they need to be caught so they can face justice for their crimes — *before* they do any more damage."

The screen returned to the male and female who were presenting the news, both sitting at a wide desk. In the corner, a small image depicted Ren in the moment of his attack on the enforcer.

"The FBI says that they have information stating Weston and her companion may have been spotted outside of Kansas City early this morning," the male said. A picture of Zoey with Ren behind her, arms full of vending machine food and drink, appeared on screen. The restrooms they'd stopped at that morning were in the background.

"If you see Zoey Weston or her companion, authorities say you should not approach them under any circumstances," the female said. "Here are some local numbers for us around the Columbus area to call, if they happen to come through this way."

A series of symbols and numbers appeared on the screen, many of which were meaningless to Ren, but he understood the implication: Zoey's people were now against her.

The picture returned to the two humans at their desk. "What a wild story," the male said.

"Absolutely," the female replied. "And that video is amazing. Very well done. Always interesting when something on the internet turns out to have such significance. This may be the key in bringing a murderer to justice."

"Well, I don't—"

Ren turned off the TV. He stared at the black screen for a while before pulling himself out of his daze; it wouldn't do them any good to dwell on what had happened or to wish things had gone differently. This was their situation, and they would face it head-on.

He took one of the sandwiches out of the bag, paired it with a drink in a red can, and ate in silence. The sandwich was good. The drink, on the other hand, was overly sweet, and he cringed involuntarily after the first sip. He set it aside for Zoey and drank from one of the water bottles instead. It was a strange meal for him; eating had always been a matter of filling his body with as much fuel as possible in a short time to counteract the additional energy burned through use of his nyros.

This time, he made his food last, taking his time to enjoy the flavors and textures.

When the sandwich was gone, he took out the Twix she'd obtained at their last stop and placed it, unopened, on the bed. He found he enjoyed it more when he shared; Zoey's pleasure, no matter how small, immensely enhanced his own. He'd wait until she was ready and eat it with her.

The shower came on in the bathroom shortly after, preceded by a brief bout of squeaking — likely from Zoey turning the control knobs. Ren listened to the running water and forced his mind away from gloomy thoughts of how everything could all go wrong.

Eventually, the shower turned off, and Zoey emerged a little later, clad only in a towel. The cloth wasn't large enough to cover her completely, and the sides spread from where she held them together at her breasts, revealing her middle and the entirety of one pale, curvy leg.

Despite that enticing display, it wasn't her body that caught his attention.

Ren pushed himself to his feet, eyes wide. "What happened to your hair?"

She raised a hand and touch the short, damp, reddish-gold locks. Before she'd entered the bathroom, her dark hair had cascaded to a point midway down her back. He'd loved to see it draped over her shoulders and chest, to run his fingers through it.

Now her hair was many shades lighter, with that reddish tint, and barely hung past her jaw. Some of it was swept over her forehead, shorter than the rest, to brush her eyelashes.

"Does it look bad?" she asked with a timidity in her voice he'd never heard before.

He closed the distance between them. The scent of unknown chemicals wafted from the bathroom, and he picked up some of it from her. He reached forward and took a lock of her hair between his fingers. Even its texture had changed; the difference was subtle, but he *noticed* it.

"What did you do?" he asked softly.

"I changed it so people won't recognize me." She looked up to meet his gaze. The evidence of already shed tears was apparent in her reddened eyes and the lightly swollen flesh around them.

His chest felt suddenly hollow, and then seemed to collapse in on itself like a star imploding to leave a black hole behind. This was his fault. She'd had to change because of him, because of his interference in her life. Because he hadn't exercised more caution.

But it was more than just her hair; it had been so much more since the beginning. This was simply a visual, physical representation of all she'd given up for him so far. Zoey hadn't considered her life *good*, but it had been *hers*. She would've figured it out, would've found her way. He'd taken everything from her.

And even if it weren't too late to change course, Ren couldn't bring himself to let her go.

She'd worked her way into him, into his life, into his mind, into his deepest desires. She was as much a part of him as his arms and legs, his eyes, his heart, his *nyros*. She was *his*. Losing her…

He should've been prepared for it. Should've accepted the possibility days ago. Losing the people he was close to had been a constant threat throughout his life, and he'd always taken that risk as an unavoidable truth. There'd never been reason to rail against it, never been a reason to reject it, but even the slightest thought of losing Zoey was heavy enough to crush him.

"It's horrible, isn't it?" she asked, turning her face away.

"I see you." He cupped her cheek and guided her face back to his. "I will always see you, *kun'ia*. And you are beautiful."

Zoey's smile began as a sparkle in her eyes an instant before it slowly spread across her lips. She settled her palms on his shoulders, and Rendash lowered himself just enough to wrap his arms around her, lift her off the floor, and draw her against him.

Their mouths met in a sealing kiss, tender and raw all at once, filled with unspoken words. Her fingers delved into his crest, and she slipped her legs around his waist as he carried her to the bed. Once there, he laid her upon it and drew back. The towel fell to the sides, revealing her bountiful curves. She lay before him, a vision of all that was beautiful, of all he desired, and everything else faded from his awareness.

He worshipped her body from her toes to the top of her head, trailing his lips and fingertips over her soft, sensitive skin, lingering in every spot that elicited reactions from her. She accepted his attention without shame, without self-consciousness, and caressed his body with equal reverence. When he slid into her heat, she welcomed him.

As their pleasure built, he saw the entire universe reflected in her eyes — all the joy, all the potential, all that was good and hopeful and kind. He saw Zoey. His Zoey. His kun'ia.

When they climaxed together, it was the merging of two souls, of two beings who belonged to one another, who'd found each other despite the impossible distances between the stars and galaxies that had separated them.

They lay together afterward, with Zoey atop Ren, bodies still connected. He knew in that moment without any doubt that the place didn't matter. So long as he had her, he would be happy.

Zoey rested her head upon his shoulder as she idly traced his chest scales and scars with her fingertips. Her fingers slowed, and she flattened her palm over his heart.

"I didn't think it was possible in such a short time," she said softly, "but I love you. I wanted to tell you, wanted you to know, just in case…" She rubbed her cheek against him. "I wanted you to know before you left."

"I've heard you say *love* before. What does it mean?" he asked. She'd called sex *lovemaking*, and he'd not entirely understood it, then.

"Come on, Ren. You know what it means."

"I want to know what it means to *you, kun'ia*."

"It means…everything." Zoey raised her head and met his gaze. "It means I would go anywhere with you, do anything for you, make any sacrifice necessary to protect you because you mean *everything* to me."

He stared into her eyes and saw her words reflected, *magnified*, in their gray-blue depths. "I love you, also."

"You don't have to say it because I did. I'm not… I wouldn't hold it against you. I know you care about me, but—"

"I *love* you, Zoey." He combed his fingertips through her

short hair; though it was different, it was still *hers*, still beautiful.

"I claimed you as my own long ago. *Kun'ia* means *my mate*."

Her eyes widened. "That first time we...?"

"Yes. As you slept afterward, I decided that I would take you with me when I left, if you wanted to come. But the more time we spent together, the more determined I became to take you regardless. I vowed to protect you, and this planet ceased to be safe for you when I entered your vehicle that first night."

He cupped her cheek with his palm and smiled at her, brushing the pad of his thumb over her cheekbone to wipe away a freshly-spilled tear. "Did you really think I would abandon you after all this, little human?"

Her lower lip trembled, and she threw her arms around him, shoulders shaking with her sobs.

"I did," she mumbled against him. "I never thought..."

He wrapped his arms around her and held her tight, smoothing her hair with one hand. "I should have told you, Zoey. I didn't want to burden you with the choice, when we had so much farther to go."

She raised her head and smiled, bringing her lips to his. He tasted the salt of her tears, the sweetness of her skin, everything that was Zoey.

"You're really going to bring me with you?" she asked.

"Yes," he promised, and then hesitated. "As long as the ship actually works."

"We'll find a way, Ren. That's what we've been doing all along. One problem at a time, one day at a time."

He kissed her again. "Yes, my mate. We will find a way. One day at a time."

Chapter Twenty-One

Charles Stantz stood with his hands flat on the desk, leaning forward. The command trailer was quiet but for the hum of computer fans and the soft crackle of voices over the headset draped around his neck. He'd stopped paying attention to the comms more than an hour ago — not long after he'd sent everyone, Fairborough included, outside. They were only getting in his way. Fairborough's team could find the pieces, but they were no help in putting those pieces together to solve the puzzle.

Without taking his eyes off the monitors, he reached up, loosened his tie further, and plucked the cigarette out of the corner of his mouth. He flicked the ashes from its tip onto the floor and tucked the filter between his lips for another long drag. His lungs burned. A looming cough tickled his throat.

He hadn't smoked in ten years.

Blowing out a lungful of stinking smoke, he shifted his eyes between the screens. The nicotine dulled the edge on his nerves.

It had become increasingly troubling that Stantz's imminent success — the recapture of the Fox and the subsequent reverse engineering of its alien technology — would be credited to the director's leadership of the Organization.

Stantz left the cigarette to dangle between his lips and returned his hand to the desk.

The pieces: one escaped EBE — extraterrestrial biological entity — one twenty-seven-year-old Caucasian woman, five dead bodies, an injured police officer, and a growing trail of sightings. There was evidence in California, Nevada, Utah, Colorado, and Kansas, and rumors from at least six other states.

A picture of Weston and Specimen Ten outside a Kansas rest stop. A stolen car with Colorado plates, reported missing in Vail on the day of the infamous video, found on a Kansas City backstreet. A small string of electronic terminals hacked from Colorado Springs to Indianapolis — four gas pumps and an ATM, the latter of which was in Kansas City, not far from the stolen car.

He slid a mouse and keyboard closer and pinpointed the events and sightings on the map, from the Mojave to the Midwest. The Fox had slunk eastward since escaping. The trail seemed too perfect now, too obvious, for Stantz not to have guessed sooner. He'd have to commend the tech who'd discovered the small chain of hacked electronics, when this was all done.

Stantz's gaze flowed across the map. Ohio, next. They'd be in Ohio, and then…

The cigarette fell from his mouth as he grinned. He didn't notice the ash burning his hand. His phone rang, and he ignored it.

Within five minutes, Stantz got Fairborough and all the techs back into the trailer and at their posts. He looked them over;

they were a disheveled bunch, wearing their exhaustion openly, but they'd done decent work.

They listened as he gave them their orders, and they dutifully set to their tasks. Only Fairborough hesitated, wearing that damnably judgmental look.

"What about the woman?" Fairborough asked.

"The woman doesn't matter, beyond holding some kind of significance for my specimen," Stantz replied. "Her presence will slow him down, but we can't take special precautions for her sake, especially after she's betrayed her country and her species. If she dies, at least her life will have contributed to the realization of something meaningful. If she lives, that'll be one more subject to study."

"Sir, that's…"

"Necessary. A few deaths are meaningless compared to what we stand to gain from this." Stantz placed a hand on Fairborough's shoulder and squeezed. "Now do your job and round up those helicopters."

Fairborough's throat bobbed nervously, but he nodded and walked to his station.

The Fox was priority one, and Stantz knew where he was heading now. They'd get the specimen, shut the director up, and push forward on their research with renewed energy and inspiration.

Stantz glanced at Fairborough.

And then a few assets that were incapable of comprehending the grand vision could be retired.

Chapter Twenty-Two

Zoey woke with an excited flutter in her chest, a surprising but welcome change from the anxiety that had pervaded her since leaving the cabin. There was plenty of uncertainty ahead — they were going to leave Earth! She didn't know what awaited her in space, didn't know what awaited on his planet, didn't know if his people would accept her.

But she knew without a doubt that she could face anything with Rendash at her side.

They left before the sun had fully risen. The day was overcast and dreary, and the wet roads meant she had to use the windshield washer fluid constantly to wipe away the dirty mist kicked up by other cars. Zoey refused to let the weather bring her down.

Ren guided her northeast, following the inner sense that linked him to his ship; he thought they were close enough to arrive before nightfall, if they were lucky.

She enjoyed the conversation and the scenery. The country seemed increasingly forested the farther east they traveled, and it was unlike anywhere else she'd been. She'd spent most of her childhood in Midwestern farmland, where everything was green, brown, and gold, carefully ordered and cultivated. So much of this area seemed so wild, so primal.

Their route took them through northern Ohio, across the northwestern corner of Pennsylvania, and finally into New York. It was nothing like she'd imagined — any mention of New York usually conjured images of a city that made Los Angeles look tame in comparison, with towering concrete on all sides, millions of taxis, and people who'd sooner trample you than give you the time of day. She knew at heart those images were myths, at least to some degree, but it was so ingrained into American culture that it was hard to shake.

This part of New York state was dense forestland that appeared unbroken for huge expanses. She wondered what it looked like when everything was green and alive, bathed in the sunlight, or when the autumn chill turned the leaves orange, red, and yellow.

The drive was strangely relaxing, even if she kept checking the mirrors and oncoming traffic for signs of government agents in pursuit.

I-90 took them along Lake Erie — which, to her disappointment, she didn't get many good looks at along the way. They stopped for food somewhere south of Buffalo, and, despite the danger, she considered following the signs to Niagara Falls. It was an opportunity she'd never get again.

Instead, she picked up a New York State highway map and spread it across the middle of the dashboard so she and Ren could look it over together.

They used the SUV's onboard compass to determine what

direction they were facing, guessed at their current location, and tried to piece together some sort of plan.

"It is somewhere around here," Ren said, tapping his finger over a large, forested area on the map near the Adirondack Mountains.

"That's a pretty big search area. How do you know for sure it's there?"

He lifted another hand and waved to the northeast. "Because it is that way." Then he moved his finger to Buffalo and slid it northeast, ending up in roughly the same place he'd originally indicated. "As we get closer, I am better able to pinpoint its location."

"I believe you. It's just that, at least on this map, it doesn't look like there's much in the way of roads over there. Even if we get close to your ship, we may have to travel part of the way on foot, and that's going to slow us down."

"I will carry you if it comes to that." He smiled at her. "We are *close*, *kun'ia*. This long journey is nearly at its end."

"Yeah, it is," she said, returning the smile.

They continued their drive under a bleak gray sky, and Ren seemed to grow increasingly impatient as the miles passed. They saw another small convoy of black SUVs before they moved off the four-lane interstate, and not long after spied helicopters in the distance, neither of which eased their nerves. At various points on the two-lane highways, they were caught behind vehicles driving well under the speed limit, which almost pushed Rendash to fury.

"I can get out and *push* them faster than they are driving!" he growled.

"Control," Zoey whispered to him, unable to keep from smirking.

He snapped his head aside to look at her with low brows, but his expression crumbled after he opened his mouth and seemed to be unable to find any words. He shook his head and chuckled.

His frustration was compounded again when it seemed that none of the roads led the right way.

"We're so close!" He thumped his fist on the dashboard. "This road is going to take us too far in the wrong direction."

Zoey reached across the space separating them, caught his chin, and turned his face toward her. "We'll make it. Ren. *Patience*. You've been around humans too long." Despite her best efforts to hold it back, her smirk had returned.

"You're the only human who's influenced these changes in me, *kun'ia*," he replied. He smiled, but the expression was strained.

It was dark by the time they neared the small town of Lowville.

"Are you sure you don't want to stop for the night?" Zoey asked as she held the button to spray the windshield for the thousandth time. The wet roads were likely to freeze over as the temperature continued to drop. "We could wait until it's light out to search for the ship."

And I could have one more night with you before we leave for the unknown.

"We have to keep going," he said, turning his gleaming gaze toward her. "We're close, but so are *they*. Any delay gives them that much more time to find us."

"Okay…but we *do* need to stop for some gas. We're almost running on empty."

The tightness in his expression gave her the impression, for a moment, that he was going to refuse. Instead, his features softened. "Do you feel well enough to continue, Zoey? If you are tired, or need rest, we can stop for a while." He settled a hand on her thigh and squeezed gently.

Zoey placed her hand on top his. "I'm fine. I'll just grab some coffee while we fill up."

A few minutes later — and with Ren cloaked — they pulled into a gas station on the western edge of town, lured by the out-of-place lights at the end of a dark residential street.

Zoey opened her door and hesitated as she climbed out, frowning to herself. "Do you think they can track it when you hack the gas pumps?"

"I don't know," he replied. "They may be able to detect some anomaly in the computers."

Biting her lip, Zoey nodded. "I'm just going to prepay with cash this time. Just in case. We have the money, and it's not worth the risk after how far we've come. Do you need to get out to use the restroom or anything?"

"No. I'll be fine, Zoey."

"Okay. I'll be right back." She closed the door and crossed the parking lot toward the convenience store.

A bell over the door jingled as she entered the store. Music played overhead — Christmas music; how had she forgotten that was right around the corner? — but it was otherwise quiet inside. Zoey returned the cashier's friendly smile before walking to the coffee machines in the back of the store. She selected the largest available cup and filled it with the best-sounding flavor, closing her eyes for a moment to enjoy the rich aroma. The smell of brewing coffee behind the counter at Bud's Diner remained a pleasant memory, despite everything.

The bell jingled again, but she paid it no mind. Once her cup was three-fourths full, she added enough creamer and sugar that the mix couldn't legally be called coffee anymore, plucked a lid out of the dispenser, and pressed it on.

Did they have anything like coffee on Ren's planet?

She still couldn't believe this was happening. They would be *leaving* Earth. That was a slightly more significant move than Des Moines to California and back again.

Zoey turned, and her smile faded when she noticed a man standing nearby. Her coffee nearly slipped from her fingers. Not just a man, but a police officer, dressed in a heavy coat, staring at her through his sunglasses.

Who the hell wore sunglasses at night apart from fugitives?

Recognition hit her; she knew his face. Officer Asswipe. His uniform was different, but it was the same cop she'd spoken to the night she left Santa Barbara, the cop at the roadblock on the California-Nevada border. Why was he *here*?

He's not really a cop. He's one of them.

Ice filled Zoey's veins, but she somehow plastered a smile back on her face. "Evening, officer."

He nodded slightly. "Ma'am. Cold night tonight. Where are you headed?"

"Just visiting some family." She stepped past him and placed her coffee on the counter in front of the cashier. "Twenty on pump two, please."

She fished the money out of her coat pocket as the cashier rang it up. "Keep the change," she said. "Merry Christmas."

The cashier smiled widely. "Thank you. Merry Christmas to you, too."

Zoey grabbed her coffee and walked toward the door, fighting the instinct to run. No way he'd recognized her, right? There'd been hundreds of people going through the checkpoint that night. She'd been just one of many faces.

"Ma'am," Officer Asswipe called as her fingers touched the door handle. She froze, heart leaping into her throat, and turned to face him as his boots thumped over the tile floor.

"Yes, officer?" She stared up at his sunglasses and swore she saw a tiny flash of light behind them, gone as quickly as it had come.

"We've had reports of strange occurrences in the area tonight. Have you seen anything out of the ordinary?"

"Nope. I haven't seen anything. But I really am in a hurry. I hope you find what you're looking for." She pulled on the door.

He stuck an arm out and stopped the door from opening more than a few inches. The gust of cold air that flowed in was nothing compared to the ice in her veins in that moment.

Officer Asswipe leaned down, face close to hers. "I'm going to need you to come with me, Miss Weston."

Zoey's eyes widened, and her heart stopped. "I-I don't know who you've mistaken me for but—"

He turned his head slightly, as though looking at someone else. "We've got her. Gas station on State," he said.

She pulled on the door again. "Let me go."

The man closed his free hand around her wrist and tugged her away from the door. "This'll be much easier if you cooperate."

He bent her arm, causing intense pain through her elbow. She cried out and did the only thing she could think to do — she swung her coffee cup, squeezing the sides so the lid popped off, and splashed the scalding liquid in his face.

Officer Asswipe flinched back, releasing her as he shouted in pain. Zoey threw open the door and ran out.

"Ren!" she yelled.

He appeared in front of her an instant later and caught her

in his arms. She started, gaze darting up at him before sweeping around the parking lot. There, on the other side of the building, was one of the black SUVs. Its driver's door opened and a man in a black uniform climbed out.

"They're here," she rasped.

"I know," Ren replied, lifting her off her feet and running to their car. From somewhere in the distance — but not nearly far enough away — came the sound of screeching tires and revving engines.

Their vehicle shook as they both jumped inside. Ren sparked the engine to life and Zoey wasted no time throwing it into drive.

"How did they find us so fast?" she asked as the car bounced hard over the curb and back onto the road.

She screamed as several popping sounds went off behind them, accompanied by an equal number of objects hitting their car with metallic thumps.

"They're *shooting* at us?" she screamed.

"That way," Ren commanded.

Their tires wailed as she slowed to take the sharp turn. Fortunately, the road he'd directed her onto was fairly straight, and she floored the accelerator.

Ren twisted to look behind them. "I don't know how they found us. You may be correct about them tracking my interference with electronics. I think Stantz also knew my ship was somewhere in this area. He implied that they'd detected its impact but had been unable to locate it. He might not have known all along, but our path might have led him directly to it."

Headlights appeared in the rearview mirror. They grew from pinpricks of illumination to terrifying, unblinking eyes of fire in the darkness.

"Oh shit. They're coming, Ren."

"Drive faster, Zoey."

She squeezed the wheel as she lurched into the left lane to pass a slower vehicle. The headlights of an oncoming car glared at her, but she swerved back into the right lane before causing an accident.

She followed the road around a curve, pressing the pedal down once it straightened out again. Fear and adrenaline sped her pounding heart. The homes that lined either side of the road rapidly thinned, until Zoey and Ren were left on a pitch-black country highway, zipping past snowy fields and copses of leafless trees.

A huge pool of light swung out from one of the fields and came toward them. Zoey leaned forward and gazed up to see a low-flying helicopter silhouetted against the dark clouds.

"Oh, my God," Zoey said. She sat back and looked in the mirror. The vehicles behind them had fanned out to drive in both lanes, the SUV in front taking the center with two more flanking it. "Ren, what do we do?"

"We drive as far as we can, and when we stop, we go on foot."

"They have helicopters!"

"We'll figure it out, Zoey. Trust me."

"How can you be so calm about this?"

She chanced a glance at him. His eyes were on her, gleaming with a strange, deep sadness. "This is all I knew for my entire life. Before you."

"We're going to die, aren't we?"

She screamed as a burst of bullets hit the road in front of them, kicking up chunks of asphalt.

"We aren't going to die, *kun'ia*," Ren shouted over her

scream. "They want me alive. They won't risk it, especially if they think I'm leading them to—"

Another burst of gunfire struck the road, panged on the hood of their car, and punched through the roof. There was a loud *pop* as something heavy struck Zoey's thigh. She inhaled sharply, and warmth spread over her leg. The front end of the SUV bounced viciously.

They blew out a tire, and I've been shot, she thought dazedly. *Always figured it would hurt more...*

Then the SUV decided it had had enough of driving straight and swerved wildly to the side. The slick road offered no traction. She could almost hear its voice in her delirious mind — *guess you shouldn't've been driving so fast, huh?* — just before the SUV flipped.

"Zoey!" Ren shouted.

Zoey was weightless for a split second. Ren wrapped his arms around her, crushing her against him as the SUV landed on its roof and continued tumbling. Strangely, she felt no pain. Ren's body jolted with the impact, and her head struck something beside her — the window, or maybe the door. The sound was the worst part, all crunching steel and shattering glass and tons of machinery protesting at such harsh treatment.

The SUV came down on the driver's side. She felt a strange pinch in her arm, and then the rolling continued. When the world finally stilled, and the tension in Ren's body eased slightly, Zoey peeked past his arms to see that the vehicle had landed — rather lopsidedly — on its wheels.

Nailed it.

She might've laughed at any other time, but she couldn't catch her breath, couldn't fill her lungs.

Her ears rang, and her vision dimmed to black.

Zoey.

The voice in her head sounded a lot like Ren, if he were calling her underwater, or through a stack of pillows.

There was so much pain now, pain everywhere.

Zoey!

She struggled against the darkness. Ren needed her. He was calling her!

But she was tired. So, so tired. She just needed a little rest…

Chapter Twenty-Three

"Zoey!" Ren called again, shaking her gently.

Her head lolled, but she did not respond.

Fire burned in his veins as he checked her breathing — present, but shallow and weak. Despite his best efforts to shield her, she was banged up and splattered with blood, most of which seemed to be from wounds on her head and her thigh.

The helicopter's blades whirred overhead, creating a chilled breeze that blew into the broken SUV through the shattered windows. He heard vehicle doors opening outside. Human voices rose in shouts over the aircraft's din.

His ship was so close. So close, but they were surrounded, and Zoey was hurt...

She'd shown him a life he could never have imagined. Had woken within him feelings he'd never known could exist. Over a few days — so short a time, *too* short a time — she'd become everything to him. She'd become the future he wanted, she'd become his hope, his peace.

His love.

And now she was on the brink of being taken from him. He couldn't lose her. Couldn't bear it, couldn't survive it.

"Stay with me, Zoey," he commanded. "You may *not* give in."

"Out of the vehicle!" a human shouted as Ren tore the sleeve off his coat and hurriedly tied it around Zoey's leg, hoping to staunch the bleeding.

When he lifted his hands, they were stained crimson, glistening in the high-powered lights from the helicopter and nearby ground vehicles.

Zoey is hurt. My Zoey. My kun'ia.

He hadn't wanted conflict, hadn't wanted battle; he had resolved himself to simply return home, to put his time on this planet behind him, to fulfill his final duty. The lives he'd taken had been out of necessity and had not matched the aligarii lives claimed by these humans. He'd been willing to forgive them.

But they'd harmed Zoey. They'd declared war.

This is all I knew for my entire life.

And now, the humans would know the wrath of an aekhora.

Rendash twisted in the seat, bent his legs, and kicked the passenger door off the vehicle. It skidded away in the snow. He cast any lingering pretenses of detachment aside with it.

He latched onto the doorframe with all four hands, poured strength into his arms, and launched himself out of the vehicle. His cloaking field settled into place almost immediately.

The human soldiers — he counted twelve standing in the snowy field, with one more at each of the three black transports and at least two in the aircraft — shouted their surprise and confusion.

Rendash formed a vrahsk on each arm, causing his cloaking

field to falter just before he landed atop the nearest soldier, plunging two of the blades through the man's chest.

The impact kicked up loose powder. The hard packed snow beneath the human's body sizzled against the blades, evaporating to steam.

The other soldiers opened fire, launching dozens of projectiles into Ren's shield. He leapt into the humans clustered nearby, drawing their gunfire as far away from Zoey as possible. More snow flew into the air to sparkle in the artificial light like stars scattered across the night sky as Ren wove among the soldiers in a battle dance, his vrahsks singing.

Pained screams and gurgling cries mingled with bursts of gunfire and the beating of the helicopter's blades to create a bone-chilling dirge.

With each strike, Ren saw Zoey, pale and unconscious, in his mind, saw the blood — *her* blood — soaking her clothing, covering his hands. With each strike, he amplified his strength, his speed, his reflexes, producing scorching heat inside his body. He darted from soldier to soldier, offering no mercy to his enemies.

The helicopter banked around, and a soldier fired a large gun mounted at its side opening. Snow sprayed everywhere, and the projectiles slammed into Ren's shield in an unrelenting torrent. He staggered against the onslaught; the air around him lit up with purple flashes as his shield strained against the repeated impact.

She may die if I succeed.

She will *die if I fail.*

Releasing a roar, Rendash jumped out of the gunfire, hitting the cold snow in a roll, and snatched up an object from the ground as he faced the helicopter again — the detached door of the destroyed SUV. The helicopter's operator turned the aircraft around to grant the gunner a clear line of fire.

Grasping the door by its thin, bent upper frame, Ren spun to build momentum and hurled it at the helicopter.

The door struck at the base of the blades, smashing the machinery. The helicopter pitched wildly to the side. Screaming, the gunner tumbled out, dangling by a strap. Ren bolted clear as the blades bit into the ground. Snow, ice, and frozen dirt sprayed at him with enough force to trigger his shield. The Earth itself shook when the body of the helicopter whipped into the ground in a massive, deafening crash.

Ren didn't look back; he charged the remaining soldiers in the field, dodging through bursts of projectiles to attack with his blades.

One of the soldiers tugged a cylindrical object from his chest, pulled a small ring from its top, and threw it at Rendash.

Dismissing a vrahsk, Ren extended a hand, catching the cylinder on his palm. He lifted his arm and catapulted the object into the cluster of soldiers. Two of the humans were quick enough to dive onto the ground, throwing their arms over their heads.

The cylinder's explosion echoed through the night like rolling thunder. Its concussive force hurled a pair of humans through the air, their blood spraying like mist to paint the snow. Despite the ringing in his ears, Ren heard the pained screams of the survivors. He killed them swiftly and picked up two of their long guns.

A fire in the helicopter wreckage cast a flickering orange glow on the bloody snow, deepening the surrounding shadows and highlighting the lifeless corpses scattered nearby.

The sound of roaring engines came from somewhere down the road; more land vehicles were inbound.

Ren shouldered the human weapons, took aim at the men standing at the stationary SUVs, and squeezed the triggers. The weapons flashed as they sprayed projectiles with surprising accuracy. All three men crumpled, the doors of their vehicles offering inadequate cover; one lived long enough to cry out in pain as he hit the ground.

Lights at the edge of Ren's peripheral vision caught his attention. More black SUVs. Somehow, he knew Stantz was in one of them.

He shifted his gaze to the damaged vehicle that sheltered his mate.

How much time did she have?

They are too close for me to move her safely.

His insides twisted and clenched sickeningly; he wanted to go to her, *needed* to go to her, but he had to end this first. Had to commit fully to the part of himself he so desperately longed to leave behind. And he had to do so with haste, or he'd lose her forever.

His mate, his love, his everything.

Dismissing his remaining blades, he crouched over the nearest bodies and gathered two of the explosive cylinders. He engaged his cloaking field and sprinted through the snow along the side of the road, toward the oncoming vehicles.

Steeling himself, Rendash veered into the road. His cloaking field fell as he reinforced his shield and strengthened his leg muscles to the point of searing pain, and he slammed into the driver's side of the lead vehicle, smashing metal and shattering glass. His shield flared as it absorbed the impact with the SUV.

The vehicle bounced and stuttered over the road before tipping into the ditch on the far side.

The impact rattled Ren, but he didn't allow himself a moment's delay. He spun toward the second SUV as it swerved to avoid the first and emptied both long guns into the windshield. The vehicle lost control and went off the road, crashing into a wooden pole. The pole sagged toward the SUV as electricity crackled and buzzed overhead. The vehicle's front end was destroyed, wrapped around the base of the pole in a mangled mess of bent metal.

He tossed the firearms aside, bunched his legs, and leapt onto the final vehicle, extending his nails into sharpened claws through his nyros to latch onto the roof. The transport swayed as it sped along the road. Ren's lower half flailed from side to side.

Dragging himself forward, he hammered his fist into the windshield. Cracks blossomed across the glass. Another blow saw it buckle, opening along the top seam.

He pulled the ring out of one of the cylinders and dropped the explosive through the windshield gap.

Ren jumped off the vehicle, tumbling over a snow bank on the side of the road.

The passenger door swung open and a soldier inside desperately struggled to abandon the SUV. Red lights flared on the back of the vehicle, and its tires screeched as it was brought to a halt. A thumping explosion sounded within, breaking the windows and scattering glass in the road. The soldier on the passenger side was blasted out through the open door, hitting the ground in a heap. Smoke curled up from his shredded back.

He lay unmoving on the road.

The SUV rolled forward slowly, stopping only when it crashed into one of the parked vehicles.

Regaining his feet, Rendash ran to the lead vehicle, which lay on its side in the ditch. A bloodied soldier was attempting to climb out through the broken driver's window. Ren buried a vrahsk in the human's throat and tossed the remaining explosive into the open window. The screams from within were cut short by another thumping explosion.

"Nearly back, Zoey," he whispered as he approached the last vehicle at the damaged pole. Smoke billowed from its destroyed engine.

He tugged open the passenger door. The two humans in the front seats were dead, their bodies riddled with projectile wounds. The rear driver's side door was open, and a lone human was trudging through the snowy field beyond.

Ren pulled a small gun from the dead passenger's belt and fired three projectiles into the struggling human in the back seat. Tossing the weapon down, he vaulted over the vehicle to pursue the last survivor.

"Get those birds here *now!*" the man — *Stantz* — shouted.

As Ren closed the distance between them, he made no attempt to mask the crunch of snow beneath his feet.

Stantz spun to look at Ren, eyes wide and fearful, and stumbled, crashing to the ground. He turned onto his back and scrambled away in retreat as Ren leapt at him.

Ren landed with his legs on either side of Stantz's and loomed over the human.

"You're declaring war against the United States of America!" Stantz shouted desperately. "Think about it. Even you can't stand against this country!"

Grabbing a fistful of the man's coat, Ren lifted the man's

torso off the ground. Stantz drew a gun from a hip holster.
Before he could aim the weapon, Ren caught his wrist in a hand
and squeezed. Bone snapped under the aligarii's crushing grip.
The human screamed.

A distant whirring sound heralded the approach of more
helicopters.

"Mercy! Show mercy, and I'll make sure you and the woman
aren't killed!" Stantz pleaded.

Zoey.

Leaning down over the human, Ren bared his teeth. "You
may have doomed her already."

"W-w-we can get her m-medical attention," the human
stammered, "the b-best in the world!"

"You tortured and killed all that remained of my *Umen'rak*,"
Ren growled as he formed a blade on his lower right arm. "You
took my people from me, took my home from me, and now you
seek to take Zoey from me, as well? Now you face justice for
what you've done."

Stantz stared at the thrumming vrahsk, which cast a pink-
purple glow on his terrified face. "The woman can go. She
can—"

The human's words ended in a pained, startled grunt
when Ren thrust the blade into his gut, beneath his ribs, and
into his heart. Shock and confusion mingled on Stantz's
features.

"This is a better death than you deserve," Ren spat. He
dismissed the vrahsk and let the lifeless body collapse in the
snow.

Without wasting another breath, Ren raced back to Zoey.
The sound of helicopters was rapidly growing louder.

He leaned into the battered vehicle from the open passenger

side. She was pale, lips tinged blue, but turned her head toward him.

"Ren?" she asked weakly. One of her hands fell on his arm, her icy fingers closing in a weak grasp.

"I'm here," he replied. His internal temperature, already high from pushing his nyros, only increased as he examined Zoey. Her left forearm had an odd bend in its center, and the flesh around it was dark with bruising. Her skin was cold, her breathing labored, and though the flow from her leg wound had slowed, she'd lost a great deal of blood. Too much.

The steam rising from his body made the air inside the vehicle waver.

More. Need to force out a little more…

"We need to go, *kun'ia*," he said as he carefully gathered her in his arms, somehow managing to suppress the tremors threatening to course through his limbs.

"I'm s-s-so cold."

"I know, Zoey." He drew Zoey out of the vehicle, wrapped his arms around her, and held her to his chest. She cried out as he moved her. The sound pierced him, more painful than any wound he'd ever suffered.

"I l-love y-you, Ren," she said quietly against his shoulder, her body limp but shivering.

"And I love you."

Spotlights swept across the open field as the helicopters came over the trees. Gritting his teeth, Ren projected his cloaking field to encompass himself and Zoey together. "I'm sorry it hurts. We just have a little farther to go." He kissed the top of her head and held her tighter. "Stay with me, *kun'ia*. I can't lose you."

He ran through the snow and plunged into the woods,

leaving the blood and searchlights behind. The speed was jarring to her, but he couldn't move any slower. He didn't have to know much about human biology to guess that she was near the limits of what her body could endure.

She was dying, and Rendash didn't know how to save her.

The ship was his only hope. There were medical pods aboard; it didn't matter if there was a chance they weren't functioning, or if they were only attuned to his species. He'd find a way.

He *had* to find a way.

Soon, the only sounds were the icy top layer of snow breaking beneath his feet, his ragged breath, and the snapping of branches against his body. He shielded Zoey from the scratching limbs with his arms and shoulders. The heat within him steadily increased as he pushed his body beyond the limits of his nyros.

Finally, he reached a clearing deep within the woods. The unbroken snow bulged at the center in a shape familiar to him, mimicking the curves and planes of the command module. He reached out with his nyros to make a connection but couldn't initiate one beyond the basic tracking tether.

"*Fuck,*" he muttered.

Instinct. There was no time to overthink anything.

He carefully set Zoey down and hurriedly stripped off his clothing, laying it on the snow and moving her atop it to serve as a buffer between her and the cold. Then he rushed to the ship, using all four arms to claw through the snow, digging frantically toward the entry.

The snow was so cold compared to his skin that it burned, melting as he touched it. He didn't relent until he felt the hull — which had maintained its cloaking field — beneath his palms.

He held his hands to it and the connection crackled to life; nearly all the internal systems had been shut down to conserve power.

He forced his nyros to override the shutdown. Loose snow fell onto him from above, heavier than it had been during the blizzard in Vail, as the ship powered on. Ren stumbled back when the cloaking field switched off, and the craft rose slightly out of the snow, causing a small avalanche all around it. All the snow touching its hull quickly melted.

The entry slid open, extending a ramp to the ground and bathing it with gentle light.

Ren lifted Zoey, scooping up the clothing beneath her in the process. Her head lolled, and her limbs swayed limply; she was unconscious again.

He carried her onto the ship and rushed through the corridor into the main cabin, where all the command module's functional equipment was housed. As he moved, he prompted the ship to go through all the necessary functions to enter orbit. It shook slightly before the stabilization systems kicked in.

Crouching, he tore off Zoey's blood-soaked clothing and cast it aside. Her pale skin showed more signs of bruising. He carefully laid her in one of the medical pods and interfaced with the ship through his nyros. She looked so small inside, so fragile. The pod sealed with a hiss, pressurizing around her.

The medical systems scanned her but did not recognize her anatomy. Ren tried to force commands through, tried to force some sort of action, but the system rejected his attempts. All the while, her chest rose and fell with stilted, shallow breaths, each appearing weaker than the last. The scans had determined that she'd lost excessive blood, but the system did not have the resources to synthesize anything as a replacement.

He unleashed a torrent of human swears at the pod, his frustration overwhelming his clear thought. Drawing back an arm, he swung, and stopped himself only an instant before he would've plunged a vrahsk into the machine. Everything inside him stilled as he stared at the pulsating blade. He shifted his gaze to see Zoey's face bathed in the violet glow through the glass of the pod.

In that moment, he realized there was only one chance. Only one thing to try before it was too late.

He dismissed the blade, climbed into the secondary pod, and lay back, sealing himself inside.

It was against the traditions of his people, perhaps even against the laws, but he didn't care. He had to try for Zoey. Had to do all he could to avoid losing her.

The medical systems resisted his commands.

Control.

Fire blazed in his gut as he forced his nyros to override all the warnings and initiate the transfer. A blinding light filled the pod and forced him to squeeze his eyes shut. The pain was immense as the tiny machines — which had been part of him since he was young, bonded to the very molecules that comprised him — were torn from his body and transferred to Zoey's pod. All his muscles locked up at once, and his back arched off the padding.

As his nyros diminished, he felt the abuses his body had endured making themselves known, all the aches and old wounds reintroducing themselves. It was nothing compared to the agony of having part of himself ripped out, but he didn't voice his pain. It was for her.

A piece of his heart lay in that other pod already, and he'd give as much of himself as it took to keep it safe.

Something slipped in beneath the pain. It began subtly, but gradually strengthened as his nyros lessened.

Awareness.

He recognized the sensation — it was the bond shared by members of an Umen'rak, an invisible web binding their nyros together because of their common source. He *felt* Zoey; her body, her pain, her fear, her *love*. Her life, weak but not yet defeated. Shoving aside his own agony, he poured as much of his willpower through that bond as he could.

Live, kun'ia!

Finally, the light vanished, and he dropped onto the padding. He drew in several deep, burning breaths and turned his head to look at the other pod; Zoey was enveloped in the same light that had enveloped him a moment before.

His nyros stirred, as weak and unresponsive as it had been during his captivity. It would recover, in time, but he didn't care about that.

He could still feel her.

Zoey's scream was muffled as the light in her pod intensified.

Overriding the computer again, he forced his pod open and pulled himself out. His legs buckled under his weight. He caught himself against the wall before he fell and staggered to her side. His head spun, his stomach threatened upheaval, and every part of him was in agony, but it was nothing compared to what she was enduring.

Zoey's form, reduced to little more than a shadow in the intense glow, writhed as the nyros entered her body and bound themselves to her. He remembered that pain well from his own binding.

Ren braced his hands on the surface of the pod, curling his

fingers against it helplessly. He dropped his face onto it and forced air through his constricted throat.

This is the only way, he told himself. *The only chance.*

But his nyros were not made for her kind. His nyros were for the aekhora, and many aligarii perished during the pairing process. How would her fragile human body handle it? How could he have possibly thought it would work?

"Stay with me, *kun'ia*," he rasped.

Chapter Twenty-Four

Zoey woke to blinding light. She turned her face away, squinting against the glare. As her eyes adjusted, the light dimmed to something more tolerable. Confusion furrowed her brow.

She recalled the accident, the roar of twisting metal and shattering glass, and then explosions, gunfire, and screams. She remembered consuming pain and brutal cold.

Am I in a hospital?

She lifted an arm to touch her face, but it bumped into something above her. Frowning, she looked up to find herself beneath smooth, curved glass. Her breath quickened as she pressed her palms to the smooth surface.

Where the hell was she? Had...had the government caught them?

Ren! Oh, God, please don't let them have taken Ren!

Zoey smacked her hands against the glass. "Let me out!"

A strange, warm tingling blossomed inside her.

The glass slid up into a hidden recess with a hiss of air.

She hurriedly climbed out of the machine. Her knees

buckled as her feet touched the floor, and she crumpled. Absently, she covered her bare chest with an arm as she sat there panting; her nudity was the least of her problems. With wide eyes, she looked around her. There were two more of the bed-like things next to the one she'd been in, and those were the easiest part of her surroundings to wrap her mind around.

Zoey crawled backward until she bumped the wall.

The large room was sleek and polished, something right out of a sci-fi show, with strange controls, honest-to-God holograms, and pieces of equipment she couldn't identify along the walls. A circular platform stood at the front of the room, raised slightly off the floor, with several large chairs atop it. The chairs were surrounded by more controls. The lights overhead were soft and pure, neither too bright nor too dim.

This wasn't like any hospital room she'd ever seen.

"Zoey?"

One of the chairs on the platform turned, and Rendash rose out of it, all four of his eyes wide and staring at her in disbelief.

"Ren," she rasped.

He was here! He was safe!

By the time she pulled herself to her feet, he'd already crossed the distance between them. He gathered her into his arms for the most desperate, relieved hug she'd ever received, lifting her off the floor.

"You're awake," he said breathlessly. "You're *alive*. I was afraid you wouldn't…"

Zoey wrapped her arms around him, clutching at his back. "How? I thought I was…I was dying."

He gently lowered her, settling one pair of hands on her hips and the other on her shoulders. It was only then that she realized what he was wearing — a wide belt with intricate, alien patterns etched across it and a loose, layered cloth wrap around his waist, hanging to just above his knee. It was *almost* like a kilt, but the fabric and its bright colors didn't quite match that gruff Scottish look.

"You were," he said, calling her attention back to his face. He frowned deeply, a crease appearing between his center eyes. "A little longer, and you would've been gone. I transferred most of my *nyros* into you, hoping it would save your life. I had no other choice."

Zoey's eyes widened. "Your...*nyros?*" She focused on her body, searching for anything out of place, anything different, but she only felt *wonderful*. Whole. She felt...

Ren.

"I-I feel you." She placed a hand on her chest. "I feel you...*in* me."

She sensed him in her mind, her body, and in her heart. He was all around her, inside her; a steady, comforting presence. She smiled.

"And I feel you," he replied, settling a hand over hers. "I didn't know what else to do. Didn't know what it would do to you."

"You saved me," she said, leaning her head forward to press her lips against his bare chest. "Thank you."

"You saved me first." He kissed the top of her head. "I would not have made it far, were it not for you."

Zoey rested her cheek on his chest, relishing his closeness. They were alive.

After a while, she lifted her head and looked around again. "We're on your ship, aren't we? In space?"

Ren twisted, leaving his left hands in contact with her, and followed her gaze around the command module with his own. "Yes. We're currently on the fringes of your star system."

"And we're going to your home?"

Icy fear pricked in her gut. What would they think of her? She was an alien to his people, as foreign and strange as Ren had once been to her.

"We are. It is called Algar. But I have plotted a slow course. It will allow you time to learn of my language and culture *before* you are thrust into it…" He brushed the back of a finger along her jaw. "And it will be some time before I am ready to share your attention with anyone else."

Relief, warm and soothing, flowed into her to thaw her fear. Though she undoubtedly had a lot to learn, his consideration was touching.

"Thank you." She ran her hand down his chest and over his abdomen, smiling. "I'm not ready to share your attention either."

He grinned at her, granting her a wicked flash of his fangs. As always, his roguish smile flooded her with heat, but now it felt stronger, like her reactions to him had been enhanced.

"Do you feel as though you can handle my attentions, little human?" His gaze slid over her naked body, trailing fire across her skin.

"This little human has handled your attentions just fine." She dropped her gaze to his groin, where his erection was lifting the fabric of his wrap. "And I find myself craving *more*."

Zoey laughed when he closed the distance between them and lifted her body against his. She wrapped her arms behind his neck and her legs around his waist. A moment later, her back met the wall, leaving her no room for escape.

Why the hell would I want to escape?

Their lips met in a ravishing kiss, and he growled against her mouth. His lower hands slid between their bodies and unfastened his belt. It fell to the sides, the cloth falling with it.

"I need you in me, Ren," Zoey breathed, moaning as his scales grazed her nipples. "*Now.*"

"As you command, *kun'ia.*" Hands on her hips, he drew her down onto his cock, and her slick sex accepted it greedily.

She dropped her head back as he sank into her, stretching her, filling her. His hips pumped, setting a maddeningly steady rhythm that teased her with the slow glide of his shaft. He pushed deeper with every thrust, until finally the pleasure must have overpowered his control and his motions quickened.

She sensed him everywhere. Their coming together was the same as it had been before, but it was also *more*. It was galaxies crashing together, the cosmos swirling in a blinding display of a million impossible colors, and stars bursting to cast their brilliant dying light through space and time.

Lifting her head, she locked her gaze with his. The overhead light made his eyes sparkle like emeralds. He looked upon her with all the love in the universe, and Zoey knew that she had finally found her home.

"I love you," she whispered, pleasure spreading through her entire being as he thrust inside her one final time, fusing them together as close as any two bodies could be.

Rendash cupped her cheek and pressed his forehead to hers. "And I love you, *kun'ia.*"

Epilogue

Standing on the second-floor balcony, Zoey gazed out over the alien jungle she'd grown so fond of over the last several months. Towering trees with leaves in varying shades of green, purple, and pink stretched on as far as she could see, broken only by jutting, rocky peaks, the nearest of which hosted a waterfall that cooled the air with its mist. It was refreshing even if the heat didn't bother her like it used to. Back on Earth, temperatures like these would've been hell for her. But Ren's nyros had changed much of that for her.

It had forced her body to adapt, to compensate for heat and cold, for fluctuations in air pressure and oxygen levels, to heal rapidly from wounds — and that was only the start. Though it wasn't easy for her to harness yet, she could also tap into the nyros to perform feats of strength and speed like Ren could.

But it was the most unexpected change that had proven the most welcome.

Zoey smiled as she looked down, cradling her rounded stomach as her baby stirred inside.

It shouldn't have been possible. Ren had told her that they were two different species, that there could be no offspring between them, and he'd been right. But neither of them had ever imagined she'd be filled with nyros that would allow her body to adapt to almost anything — including, apparently, his seed.

Ren's reaction had been comically enthusiastic. In his shock and excitement, he'd managed to break the chair he'd been sitting in, but he had shrugged it off like it had never happened when he dropped to his knees and held her hips reverently between his hands, staring up her in wonder.

He came up behind her now, leaning down to rest his chin on her shoulder as he encircled her middle with all four arms.

"How are my *kun'ia* and child this morning?" he asked.

Zoey covered his lower hands with her own and turned her head to kiss him. "Good. He's very active this morning."

"Restless to be out in the world. The *Halvari* asked if we will offer him to be trained as a warrior in the Khorzar."

Zoey frowned. "Not even born yet and they're already asking me to give him up."

Ren soothed her with another kiss and smiled. "For those born into it, as I was — and my family for generations before me — it is tradition. Our child is of rare blood, to have two parents whose bodies accepted the *nyros*. But I already told them no."

Her eyes widened, and she turned to face him without breaking his embrace. "You did? Why?"

She'd gone before a huge crowd of aligarii when Ren had presented her to them as his mate; the Halvari had been at the forefront, and they'd been the ones who held the power to bless or deny his claim. To say they were an intimidating bunch would've been an understatement — they were all built like Ren, but their faces had held none of the softness he'd shown her. They were the leaders of their people, and they projected only strength and stoicism.

After they'd legitimized Ren's claims and welcomed him as a returned hero, they'd shown her great kindness and gratitude, praising her for her role in bringing him home, but she'd never forget how nervous she'd been when facing them that first time.

To know that Ren stood up to them and defied tradition a second time warmed her heart.

"Because our child will have strength of heart and spirit before he ever knows anything of war. If he chooses that path, let it be his choice when he is older. Those who choose the Khorzar of their own will are looked at with great honor for their selflessness. I will not send him down that road, and I will not have him taken from your arms."

Tears blurred her vision. "Do you have any idea how much I love you?"

"Hmm." He hooked her chin with a finger and turned her face slightly, studying her features. "I'm not sure. Perhaps you will have to show me, after we make our trip to the city."

"Or," Zoey said, placing her hands on his bare chest, "I could show you now. I'm feeling particularly *affectionate*, at the moment."

A slow grin spread across his lips, the one that always lit a fire low in her belly. "And...what of our appointment with the veringan clothiers?" he asked as he drew her body against his, voice growing husky.

"You know you're not supposed to deny a pregnant woman's desires." She slid her hands over his shoulders, lacing her fingers behind his neck and drawing his head down. "They can wait. Your *kun'ia* cannot."

Rendash groaned, his lower palms squeezing her backside. She felt his hardness against her abdomen.

"Perhaps I can fulfill your desire, little human, if you promise to let me select a few new articles of clothing for you to wear when we are home…"

"I promise," she said, smiling against his lips.

Zoey shrieked with laughter as he picked her up, strode back inside their room, and laid her down upon their bed.

"And *your kun'ia* desires a taste of your nectar," he declared, lifting her skirts and lowering his head between her thighs.

It wasn't long before her laughter gave way to pleasured moans.

Author's Note

It's crazy how a note at the end of the book can be just as difficult and intimidating as that blank page under *Chapter One*. So we'll begin with the easiest and most important part: Thank you. Thank you all so much for taking the time to read Claimed by an Alien Warrior! We hope you enjoyed Rendash and Zoey's little adventure. And if you reviewed it, thank you, thank you, thank you again! Your support means everything to us.

This book was such a blast to write. We probably laughed more writing this book than we have any other. We wanted to write something short and fun before we submersed ourselves in the Kraken Series again (oh, the puns!). It seems when it comes to our writing, though, *short* is a pretty difficult thing to achieve. Not that it's a bad thing! Ultimately, we met our goal for this project: we just wanted to have some fun, and that's exactly what we did.

If we may be so bold as to offer advice for any aspiring authors, it would be this: write what you're passionate about. Write what you love. We know our books vary in tone from series to series, and that's okay. Our goal is to tell the stories we want to tell in the ways they're meant to be told, and we hope that shines through in our work.

Claimed by an Alien Warrior came to be in a burst of inspiration while we were out on a morning walk. The issues Zoey faces are close to my (Tiffany's) heart. I struggle with my weight and a poor self-image every day, and I have for years. There are moments when I feel good about myself, but doubt and self-loathing always pull me back under. However, there is one person who sees me as Rendash sees Zoey: Robert. My best friend, my husband, and co-author. To him, I am beautiful no matter my age, my size, my shape, whether I'm having good days or bad days. He sees me.

Do you need a man to tell you you're beautiful? Of course not. I am so happy for everyone who feels comfortable in their own skin. But Robert always makes me feel good when I am down, when I doubt myself, or speak poorly about myself. He sees all of me, inside and out, and loves me.

So I want to shout out to all of you ladies who are reading this right now — You. Are. Beautiful. Never let anyone make you doubt that truth.

Also By Tiffany Roberts

THE SPIDER'S MATE TRILOGY

Ensnared

Enthralled

Bound

THE INFINITE CITY

Entwined Fates

Silent Lucidity

Shielded Heart

Untamed Hunger

Savage Desire

Tethered Souls (Coming 2022)

THE KRAKEN

Treasure of the Abyss

Jewel of the Sea

Hunter of the Tide

Heart of the Deep

Rising from the Depths

Fallen from the Stars

Lover from the Waves

ALIENS AMONG US

Taken by the Alien Next Door

Stalked by the Alien Assassin

Claimed by the Alien Bodyguard

STANDALONE TITLES

Claimed by an Alien Warrior

Dustwalker

Escaping Wonderland

His Darkest Craving

The Warlock's Kiss

Ice Bound: Short Story

ISLE OF THE FORGOTTEN

Make Me Burn

Make Me Hunger

Make Me Whole

Make Me Yours

VALOS OF SONHADRA COLLABORATION

Tiffany Roberts - Undying

Tiffany Roberts - Unleashed

VENYS NEEDS MEN COLLABORATION

Tiffany Roberts - To Tame a Dragon

Tiffany Roberts – To Love a Dragon

About the Author

Tiffany Roberts is the pseudonym for Tiffany and Robert Freund, a husband and wife writing duo. Tiffany was born and bred in Idaho, and Robert was a native of New York City before moving across the country to be with her. The two have always shared a passion for reading and writing, and it was their dream to combine their mighty powers to create the sorts of books they want to read. They write character driven sci-fi and fantasy romance, creating happily-ever-afters for the alien and unknown.

Connect with us:
Website:
https://authortiffanyroberts.wordpress.com
Facebook:
https://www.facebook.com/AuthorTiffanyRoberts
BookBub:
https://www.bookbub.com/authors/tiffany-roberts

Sign up for our Newsletter!

Made in the USA
Thornton, CO
08/12/23 17:58:32

06ddc671-62a6-4b66-891b-0187cd9261e8R02